THE ULTIMATUM: FIND THAT SHIP!

Don Gallardo tore off a sheet of note paper with the location of the missing freighter and handed it to Jorge. "We have an eighteen hour lead to locate our ship and retake control before the arrival of the Columbian Navy frigate. Our Command Center in Campanilla is waiting your instructions."

The icy look in Don Gallardo's eyes sent a chill through Jorge that seemed to still his blood. Jorge gulped down his cold coffee and stood up. "I've got some fires to put out."

"Get there and handle it. I want all our jet aircraft in the air immediately. When the precise location of the ship is determined, our helicopters will go in; the first wave will land security people aboard to secure the ship, the second will land a replacement crew to get the ship under way. I want you to board in the second wave and take personal charge of the shipment."

"What about the American destroyer?"

"A disabled destroyer won't pose any threat."

"And if the Americans are still aboard our freighter?"

Don Gallardo's eyes smiled. "You can preside over their burial at sea."

POINT OF HONOR

Maurice Medland

Pinnacle Books
Kensington Publishing Corp.
http://www.pinnaclebooks.com

PINNACLE BOOKS are published by

Kensington Publishing Corp.
850 Third Avenue
New York, NY 10022

Pinnacle and the P logo Reg. U.S. Pat. & TM Off.

First Kensington Hardcover Printing: September, 1997
First Pinnacle Printing: April, 1998
10 9 8 7 6 5 4 3 2 1

Printed in the United States of America

For Karen,
my wife, partner, and best friend,
whose love and encouragement made a dream come true.

ACKNOWLEDGMENTS

Grateful thanks are due to the following:

Melissa Cole, James Curtis, Jo-Ann Mapson, Gordon McAlpine, Raymond Obstfeld, and Maurice Ogden, for helpful comments and encouragement along the way.

Marta Robledo for some insightful Spanish translations.

My agent, Frank Weimann, and my editors, Sarah Gallick, and Karen Haas, for introducing me into the exciting world of publishing.

And a special thanks for comments and/or source material to Kings Pointers Heath Gehrke, Erik Palin, and my son, Lieutenant Steve Medland, USN, a Kings Pointer who proudly wears the gold dolphins of a nuclear submariner, and who exemplifies the versatility of Kings Pointers everywhere.

Acta non verba
—*Motto of the U.S. Merchant Marine Academy*
Kings Point, New York

Behind every great fortune is a crime.
—*Honoré de Balzac*

Chapter One

"Mr. Blake, sir. The cap'n wants you on the bridge." The voice behind the flashlight sounded deferential, but persistent.

Daniel Blake rolled over into the beam of light and squinted at his watch—0445. A long night was about to get longer. He swung out of his bunk and ground a pair of knuckles into his eyes.

"Evaporator unit again?"

"I don't know, sir." The captain's messenger, a seaman first named Durbin, had an accent that sounded like south Texas. "He just said, 'Get Mr. Blake up here on the double.'"

"I'm on my way," Blake said. The cool steel against his bare feet began to revive him. He ran a hand through his hair and reached for his khakis, still slung across the back of the chair where he'd thrown them.

Durbin peered into Blake's bloodshot eyes, which must have looked worse under the red lens of the flashlight, and winced. "You want some coffee or something, sir?"

"No, thanks," Blake said, rummaging in his wardrobe. "I'm still wired from that stuff they brew in the engine room."

"Yeah, I heard y'all pulled an all-nighter again. This old bucket's falling apart, ain't it, sir?"

Blake nodded. He'd spent most of the night making emergency repairs to the freshwater evaporator unit while the aging destroyer steamed through the perimeter of a tropical storm, and he was in no mood for conversation.

"Don't know how y'all stand it down there belowdecks all the time. Makes me glad I'm a deck-ape," Durbin said, disappearing through the curtain.

"You chose well," Blake said to the empty stateroom. He retrieved a seldom-used foul-weather jacket from his wardrobe. "Lt. (jg) Daniel F. Blake, USN" was stamped in gold letters above the pocket. Lieutenant junior grade. His first promotion had come through along with his billet as OIC of engineering. He should have been grateful—it was normally a job for a full lieutenant—but heading up the engineering department was exactly what he didn't want at this stage of his career.

He pulled on the new foul-weather jacket with a grimace, knowing he'd look out of place on the bridge. He hadn't yet qualified to stand deck watches on the destroyer, and it was a sore point. He liked engineering well enough, had majored in Marine Engineering Systems at Kings Point, but after sailing in the merchant fleet for two years after graduation, he'd come to realize what he really wanted. He wanted to command his own ship, a route that was closed to him in the merchant marine if he followed the career path of an engineer. He could be chief engineer someday, but never captain. The Navy was his only shot at command. Vicki had been shocked and a little angry when he gave up a high-paying job with APL and activated his reserve commission. But he'd found that the Navy didn't want to let him break out of the mold, either. His first two years of active duty had been spent patching up the aging machinery of an obsolete destroyer, and he was getting anxious. At twenty-eight, he couldn't afford to be stuck belowdecks much longer. Others were passing him by.

Blake made his way from his stateroom to the weather deck and climbed the starboard ladder to the bridge, grateful for the salt spray that stung his face. He felt a measure of pride in the steady hum of the main engines coming through the steel handrails, but nothing felt like being above deck on the old ship in the cool morning air. He pulled the clean air deep into his lungs and paused on the bridge wing, just to enjoy the sight and feel of her moving beneath his feet. His eyes took in every detail in the predawn glow: the undulating bow, the sweeping radar antenna, the stern light twinkling over the white wake which fanned out behind the destroyer, then dissipated into the sea.

A gallant old lady, Blake thought, glancing over the anti-quated ship, her once awesome technology now sadly outdated. Commissioned after World War II, and named for a Medal of Honor winner, the USS *Carlyle* was one of the last of her class of destroyers still on active duty. Scuttlebutt had it she'd been headed for the boneyard in Bremerton when the war on drugs heated up, amid much political posturing between the American and Colombian governments, giving her a new lease on life. The ship was into her third week of patrolling the Pacific Ocean waters off the coast of South America in this highly publicized joint venture, but not much was happening. Nothing like being on the fast track, Blake thought—stuck in the engine room of an obsolete destroyer assigned to fight a nonexistent drug war.

A light rain began to fall. Blake took a deep breath and stepped through the door leading to the bridge. Dawn was breaking as Captain Hammer and Lieutenant Commander May-field, the ship's executive officer, stared intently through the bridge windows with binoculars.

"Right standard rudder, all ahead one-third," Captain Hammer said.

"Right standard rudder, all ahead one-third, aye, sir," the helmsman echoed.

Blake heard the clang of the engine-order telegraph and felt the turbines begin their gradual decline. In his mind's eye, he could see Chief Kozlewski and his people scrambling into action in the engine room.

"Morning, Captain," Blake said.

"Well, at last, our resident expert on the merchant marine," Captain Hammer said without lowering his binoculars. "Mr. Harrington, let's get an expert opinion." He motioned with his head for the Officer of the Deck to hand his binoculars to Blake. "Take a look at that ship on the horizon, Mr. Blake, and tell me what you see."

Blake took the binoculars and tried to blink the fog out of his eyes. The sun was coming up behind the destroyer, and he could just make out the outline of the ship. "Looks like a breakbulk freighter, a 'stickship,'" he said, referring to the sticklike cargo booms emanating from deck. "I would say she's an older cargo vessel, possibly a C-2."

"And what else do you see, Mr. Blake?"

Blake stiffened at the captain's condescending tone. It had not gone unnoticed in the wardroom that Captain Hammer had singled out the junior officers who were Kings Point and Annapolis grads—Ringknockers, the captain called them—for this kind of patronizing treatment. For a while, he tried not wearing the heavy gold class ring that seemed to irritate the captain, but it didn't seem to help. He wore it openly now, a small fuck-you.

"She appears to be dead in the water, and I don't see any running lights, sir," Blake said, handing the binoculars back to the OOD.

"Well, Mr. Blake," the captain said, still staring through his binoculars, "we can't just let her drift in the middle of the sea-lanes without running lights, can we?"

"No, sir," Blake said, staring at the back of Captain Hammer's head. He glanced at the executive officer, then the OOD. Both looked away.

"Mr. Harrington, you have the conn," the captain said, returning control of the ship to the Officer of the Deck. He hung his binoculars on a hook and turned to Blake. "I want you to board that freighter and check it out. Take some of your engineering people, you may have to help get her under way. If she's been abandoned, you'll need to rig some power to the running lights. Take a corpsman and a supply of medication, there could be illness aboard. We can't rule out a drug connection, so you'd better draw side arms. Oh, and take that Colombian marine, Sergeant whatever-the-hell-his-name-is.'' The captain flashed a wry smile. "We want to be politically correct.''

Blake grimaced. *You wouldn't know the meaning of the word,* he thought. He'd caught only an occasional glimpse of the quiet marine who had reported aboard three weeks ago in Buenaventura, courtesy of the Colombian government. He'd been assigned to the ship as a result of the highly publicized, and highly political, joint venture between the two countries to bring the influx of drugs into North America under control. Blake could see that the enlisted troops were impressed with him, but the deployment of the lone sergeant from the tiny Colombian Marine Corps was seen in the wardroom as a joke, a token effort done more to ease political pressure from the Americans than any attempt to fight a drug war.

"Captain, may I have a word with you in private, sir?" Lieutenant Commander Mayfield said, turning his head to one side.

"Make it quick," the captain said, stepping a few paces away with the exec.

The wind buffeting the bridge whistled down to a low howl, and Blake could overhear the strained conversation. "Captain," he heard the exec say, "there's no telling what they could run into aboard that freighter. We haven't been able to raise anyone; could be she's been abandoned, or her crew's disabled. In either case, it's risky to put people aboard without knowing why—"

"Only way to find out why is to put people aboard, Commander."

"Yes, sir, but it's getting a bit rough to be launching small craft. The barometer's falling, and the wind's picking up. We can get a whaleboat over the side, but it might be tough to recover in a few hours—"

"Every situation has risks, Commander."

"I agree, Captain, but I think we're out of our league on

this one. I'd suggest we contact the Coast Guard station in Panama and ask them to send out a cutter with people trained to handle this. We can stand by until they get here.''

Blake saw a tinge of red creeping up the captain's neck, into his face.

''We're not standing by for anybody. That ship's a hazard to navigation. It would take two days to get a cutter out here, and we're not going to let her drift in the sea-lanes another night without running lights. What's the problem, Commander? Blake's a qualified engineer. All we're asking him to do is check it out. It's a simple assignment. No reason why he can't handle it.''

''I don't think it's quite that simple, sir—''

''And I don't like to give orders twice, Commander.''

Blake watched, mesmerized, as the executive officer coolly returned the captain's stare.

''Aye aye, Captain,'' the exec said finally.

''With the storm moving this way, time is of the essence,'' Captain Hammer said, turning back to Blake. ''Muster your party on the boat deck and be ready to shove off at 0600.''

Blake pitched forward, nearly colliding with the captain, as the forecastle of the destroyer was submerged under a huge wave that appeared out of nowhere. He struggled to regain his footing as the bow of the ship slowly broke through the surface, shedding tons of green water through the scuppers. The old destroyer resumed its familiar creaking roll as though nothing had happened. Blake glanced at the captain, then the exec, then out at the whitecaps being whipped around by the wind. He was grateful to Commander Mayfield for intervening, but the exec had struck out, and Blake knew it would be pointless to object. More to the point, he knew if he crossed the captain on this one, it would be the equivalent of career suicide. He would be stuck in the engine room for as long as Captain Hammer was in command of the *Carlyle,* and the die would be cast; he would never be seen as a line officer with the potential for command.

''Aye aye, Captain,'' he heard himself say.

Chapter Two

Jorge Cordoba awoke to the gentle snore of the two girls sleeping beside him. He stretched and yawned and blinked impassively at the crumpled forms, black hair askew on satin pillows. Another gift from Rafael Ayala. The director of security never missed an opportunity to ingratiate himself with Don Gallardo's godson.

Ayala had said the girls were twins, but Jorge doubted it, now that he saw them in the morning light. Sisters, perhaps, but not twins. It was hard to tell their ages—Indians tended to age quickly—but the older couldn't have been more than sixteen. He felt guilty, dallying with ones so young. Still, the thought pleased him. At twenty-eight, he could still exhaust two young wildcats such as these.

He rubbed his face in his hands. Enough self-indulgence. Today would be a busy day. He climbed over the one on his left—he thought her name was Margarita—and padded into the bathroom.

He stood naked on the cold tile and relieved himself, resisting the impulse to glance over his shoulder at his image in the mirror. Shaking himself off, he drew himself up straighter and turned sideways, increasing the tension in his stomach muscles. His olive skin took on a golden glow in the soft light. Tall and trim, with square, European features, he stood out from his Colombian associates. He knew what they called him behind his back. *El Bicho de Oro*. The Golden Cock. Let the jealous bastards talk. Soon they would have a new title to cluck about: *El Jefe de Finanzas*—what his classmates at Harvard would call Chief Financial Officer—of one of the richest and most powerful organizations on earth.

"*El Jefe de Finanzas,*" he said aloud, daubing shaving cream under his nose. He liked the way it sounded, echoing around the white marble of the bathroom. It was a goal he had pursued for the past eight years, and Don Gallardo had hinted that the announcement would be made at the next board meeting. It would come as no surprise. Everyone in the organization knew the prize would be his. And why should it not be? He had demonstrated his unique talents well enough. Under Jorge's management, hundreds of millions of dollars from the world's slums and barrios had been converted into legitimate investments which continued to grow each year at a prodigious rate.

The telephone in the bathroom chimed. He picked it up and cradled it against his cheek. "Yes?"

"Good morning, Señor Cordoba," the voice of his secretary purred. "I trust you slept well?"

"Yes, Elena."

"And your guests?"

Jorge pulled the razor down his cheek and smiled. "Still sleeping. They are quite exhausted."

"No doubt."

Jorge chuckled at the venom in Elena's voice. The tantrum of a jealous wife was not as interesting as the controlled restraint of a possessive secretary.

"Surely you have not called to inquire about my guests."

All business again, Elena said, "Señor Ayala called."

Jorge jerked and nicked his chin. "What does that *rana* want?"

Elena giggled. Jorge thought she took a perverse delight in

working for the only man in Don Gallardo's organization who would dare to call the director of security a frog.

"He won't say, just that it's urgent. He's been calling since I got here at five."

Jorge glowered at the tiny red dot welling up in the cleft of his chin. "Everything is urgent with him."

"He says he's coming over if you won't take his call."

"I have no time for that fool and his idiotic schemes." Jorge dabbed at the cut with a scrap of tissue paper. "We're closing the deal in Montevideo this morning. Call Rodriguez and remind him to be here for the conference call at six."

"As you wish, Señor."

Jorge replaced the phone in its wall mount and stepped into the shower, letting the steam take him. The stinging spray was like a baptism, washing the dried residue of the two girls down the drain, releasing him from his sins. He finger-combed his hair in the dripping silence and paused to examine the small bald spot forming on the back of his head. No bigger than a peso, it worried him constantly, though it didn't seem to be spreading. He fluffed his hair around it and stepped out into the apartment to towel off.

Jorge loved the solitude of the place, high above the city. He had managed to consolidate his financial operations by expropriating the entire top floor of the Augusto Gallardo Building, a circular tower of glass and steel rising phalliclike in the heart of the financial district. Unmarked, the financial nerve center of the organization was never acknowledged; the only clue to its existence was a key slot in a private elevator.

He stood at the foot of the bed, buffing his skin with the warm towel, and watched the sun begin its rise over the mountains. A lone hawk drifted by on air currents.

"Wake up, little birds. Time to fly away."

The girls began to stir. The one called Margarita stretched and spread her legs under the silk sheet, looking coy. "But the cock hasn't crowed yet. Is the golden one still asleep?"

"Out, my little chickens." Jorge whipped the sheet off, exposing the two girls. They lay open before him, gooseflesh rising on coffee-colored skin, little game hens waiting to be stuffed. He tightened his gut against the temptation. ''I have work to do.''

Jorge turned to walk away. The girls scrambled out of bed and tackled his legs, laughing and giggling like small children.

The door opened and Juan, his valet, entered, carrying a silver tray. In a world where silence and longevity went hand in hand, the sight of three naked people tussling in the center of the room drew not so much as a glance. Jorge stepped toward the bathroom and jerked a thumb toward the door. ''Get these *puta* out of here.'' He spoke English, the language of finance, most of the time, but preferred some Spanish words. Whore was too sharp for ones as lovely as these.

By the time he'd finished drying his hair, the girls were gone. The bed had been made up, and Juan had placed fresh flowers around the room, which now seemed unnaturally quiet and empty. Juan pressed a button on the wall, and the doors on a mirrored wardrobe drew back, exposing a row of dark suits.

Jorge looked over the array of garments, custom tailored on Fifth Avenue and Savile Row, while Juan laid out a selection of silk ties in muted shades of red and blue. Today would be the completion of a milestone event that could result in a congratulatory call from the Don himself, and Jorge wanted his appearance to reflect the moment. He selected a navy suit, with barely visible pinstripes, and a maroon foulard tie—the international uniform of corporate finance.

Dressing carefully, he stepped into the office adjacent to the bedroom and paused, as he did each morning, to admire his collection. The walls were lined with the paintings and drawings of Gregorio Vasquez de Arce y Ceballos, the most famous of Colombia's colonial artists. He studied his latest acquisition, a painting his agent had picked up last week at auction in Bogotá. He took a handkerchief from his pocket and gently wiped a speck of dust from the frame. He now owned twelve of the most sought-after pieces. Someday it would be known as the Jorge Cordoba Collection in one of the great museums of the world. He wouldn't die and be forgotten the way his parents had.

Glancing at his watch, he took his place behind the mahogany desk and buzzed for his secretary. The outer door to his office opened and Elena walked in. Two secretaries worked in shifts to accommodate Jorge's sixteen-hour-a-day schedule. Elena was his favorite. He watched the slight sway of her hips as she approached.

"*Buenos dí—*"

Jorge raised a finger.

Elena stopped, then smiled. "Good morning, Señor Cordoba."

"Good morning," Jorge said deliberately.

Elena placed the overnight mail on his desk and turned to pour his coffee. Jorge watched the long dark hair cascade down the back of her cotton blouse, just touching the waist of her skirt, wondering what charms were hidden beneath that plain skirt and white blouse. He shook off the thought; now that the confederation had been formed, discipline would be more important than ever.

"Did you call Rodriguez?"

"Yes, sir, he's on his way."

"I've scheduled a conference call at six with Señor Quintero and his staff in Montevideo. See that we're not disturbed."

"As you wish." Elena finished pouring the cup of *tinto,* and placed it on his desk.

Jorge watched her walk out, her perfume lingering behind. He picked up the tiny cup of mild black coffee and swiveled his chair around to face the window. Inhaling the vapors from the steaming brew, he took a sip, letting the bite of the coffee beans sit on his tongue while he watched the sun rise over the mountains. From the inside looking out, the windows surrounding the top floor gave a sweeping view of the fertile Valle del Cauca, nestled between the Western and Central Cordillera, two of the three massive Andes mountain ranges which divide Colombia from north to south. From the outside looking in, the windows were a dark mirror, impenetrable to machine-gun fire from a helicopter.

He leaned back in his chair, basking in the feeling of exuberance from the caffeine and the glorious sunrise. By the end of the day phase one of the plan would be fully in effect. Finally, he would show the arrogant *yanquis*. He was grateful to Don Gallardo for arranging his graduate studies in North America, but his stay there had left him with an intense hatred of all *Norte Americanos*. His classmates at Harvard had thought they were being clever with their knowing smirks and their snorting noises behind his back. That was humiliating enough, but the thing that galled him most was the implication that any fool could be successful as a financial executive with unlimited amounts of cash pouring in, an implication that negated his skills as a businessman. He would soon show them who was the businessman. In his fantasies, he could see them crawling to him, begging him for a job in his industries when the whole North American economy collapsed.

He turned back to his desk and leafed through his mail. An array of facsimile machines sat on his left, and a bank of video monitors blinked changing stock prices and foreign currency translations on his right. Before him sat a compact telephone console which kept him in daily contact with the investment banks and brokerage houses in New York, Montevideo, Paris, Rome and the City, London's main financial district, where Jorge transacted most of his business.

A white telephone handset with a single line stood prominently in the corner of the desk. The black console showed the wear of daily use, but the white telephone looked new. A direct line to the Don himself, it almost never rang. Jorge was proud of that; his operation was known for its efficiency.

He glanced at his watch for the third time in as many minutes, impatient for Rodriguez and the conference call. Uruguayans tended to work at a more leisurely pace than Jorge was accustomed to, but he enjoyed doing business there. Long known as South America's Switzerland, bank transactions were kept strictly secret. The stupid *yanquis* wondered how the organization disposed of such massive amounts of cash, but it was really quite simple. The friendly government of Uruguay had no awkward laws requiring banks—or those making deposits—to report large cash transactions. Not even the customs office required cash from foreign visitors to be declared. Tons of cash could be unloaded, like cargo, from ports in Montevideo and carted to banks for deposit into dollar-denominated accounts. From there, offshore banking services were available to transfer US dollars into, and out of, any bank in the world, leaving no trace of their origin. It was called *El Enjuague Uruguayo,* the Uruguayan Wash, and Jorge was grateful to the succession of military governments in Uruguay, all eager to attract foreign capital, that made it possible.

The intercom on the console buzzed. Jorge picked up the handset. ''Yes?''

''Señor Rodriguez is here for your conference call,'' Elena said.

''Send him in.''

The door opened, and Ernesto Rodriguez, Jorge's chief accountant, bustled into the room carrying a manila folder crammed with papers. Rodriguez pulled a chair out and sat down without being asked. He retrieved one of the pens arrayed across his plastic pocket protector and tapped it against the file folder.

''Ten days.''

''And a very good morning to you, Ernesto.'' The musky smell of overheated accountant drifted across Jorge's desk.

''I'm serious. We've got ten days.''

''Relax, Ernesto. It's on its way.''

''We're leveraged to the hilt. Do you realize what you've committed to?''

''Nothing we can't handle.''

The chief accountant opened a spreadsheet. ''On the seventh, 300 million, on the fifteenth, 400 million, on the twenty-third, 350 million. With what we're closing this morning, you've bought 1.3 billion dollars worth of gold bullion on a thirty-day contract with borrowed money. The first payment is due now in ten days. Three hundred fifty million. US.''

"I tell you it'll be there in plenty of time. Stop worrying. This is only the beginning.'' Jorge had purchased the bullion as the first step in the long-range plan he'd developed for Don Gallardo. The gold was of Brazilian origin, but he'd arranged for it to be purchased in Uruguay, which had no reporting and registration requirements on precious metals commerce. It was a plan that Jorge alone among the senior officers of the organization was privy to, but he suspected the canny chief accountant had an inkling of what they were doing.

"And look at this.'' Rodriguez spread out a chart showing gold exports by country. "You can't just keep buying gold at these levels in Montevideo. At this rate, it won't be long before Uruguay becomes the number one gold exporter in the world.''

Jorge yawned. "So what?''

"So what? The country itself has no gold reserves. How long do you think it'll take the *Norte Americanos* to figure out what you're doing?''

Jorge leveled his eyes at him. "And what are we doing?'' He liked the way it sounded. Polite, with just the right touch of menace.

Rodriguez retrieved a balled-up handkerchief and mopped at a thin film of perspiration on his forehead. "I don't know, and I don't want to know. It's my job to advise you, and I'm advising you.''

"You worry too much,'' Jorge said, leaning back. "No one will pay the slightest attention, least of all the *Norte Americanos*. The industrialized nations despise gold. It imposes too much discipline on their ability to print money. They all dropped the gold standard years ago. A 'barbarous relic,' they call it. No, my friend, they know what keeps them in power. Print money and spread it out among the people. A gold standard won't let them do that. They have no use for it and couldn't care less who buys it up.''

"Even if they don't, we're moving too fast, taking too big

a bite. If we stub our toe, we'll lose half our holdings in Argentina—''

"Nonsense," Jorge said. "You're a good man, Ernesto, but you lack vision. This is the beginning of a major event in history. Someday, you'll be able to tell your grandchildren you were there." He leaned farther back in his chair with his hands behind his head and flashed a self-satisfied smile. It was a global transaction worthy of a Harvard MBA, the largest of his career, and he had pulled it off without putting up a peso. The gold had been secured by the organization's massive real-estate and industrial holdings in Uruguay and Argentina, through a series of complex, short-term financings. Phase one had gone well. His promotion was assured. All that remained was the final confirmation from Montevideo, and for Jorge to deliver the cash.

The intercom on the console buzzed. He glanced at his watch, irritated. The conference call was due at any moment. He picked up the line. "Yes?"

"Señor Ayala is here," Elena said.

"I told you I can't see that fool. Tell him I'm busy."

"I did."

"What does he want?"

"He refuses to say, Señor Cordoba, and demands to see you at once."

Jorge glanced at his watch, then at the silent telephone console, and blew out a deep breath. "Tell him he's got two minutes."

The door clicked opened, and Rafael Ayala burst into the room. His eyes were bloodshot, his face was ashen. He looked over his shoulder, waiting for the door to close behind him.

Jorge remained seated, a calculated show of disrespect for this frog-faced, runt of a man who was more concerned with maintaining a full belly and an empty scrotum than taking care of business.

"And what brings our eminent director of security out at this hour of the morning?"

Rafael Ayala swallowed. "I need to see you alone."

"We're waiting for a call. You can speak in front of Ernesto."

"No." The chief accountant stood up. "I'll wait outside. Call me when you're ready."

Jorge smiled to himself, watching the bearlike Rodriguez walk out. The chief accountant never wanted to know more than he needed to. That made him smart. He waited for the door to click shut. "Now, what is so damned important?"

Rafael Ayala ran his tongue over dry lips. *"La Estrella Latina."* His voice was barely audible.

Jorge felt the blood drain from his face. He pushed himself up from the chair. "What did you say?"

"La Estrella Latina—"

"What about it? Speak English!"

"The *Latin Star*. It's missing."

Jorge stood, disbelieving, stomach churning, fighting for control, gazing at this Neanderthal whose stupidity was about to ruin him. *"Bastardo!* You did it, didn't you?"

"Now don't get excited. Just because we've lost radio contact, doesn't mean—"

The black telephone console began to ring. Jorge lunged across the desk, knocking over his coffee, and grabbed Ayala by the throat. *"¡Hijo de puta!* Son of a whore! I told you this would happen."

On the third ring, someone picked up the call. The intercom buzzed, and the light on the console flashed.

Jorge shoved the bug-eyed security director away. He could feel the blood raging in his eyes. He straightened his coat and picked up the phone. "Yes?"

"It's your conference call from Montevideo, Señor Cordoba," Elena said. "Señor Quintero on line one."

"Tell him I'm not in."

"But—"

"Are you deaf? Tell him I'm not in!" Jorge slammed down the receiver.

"I beg you, Señor Cordoba, don't jump to conclusions,"

Rafael Ayala said, rubbing his throat. "It could be anything, perhaps a faulty radio, or—"

"Shut up, you fool," Jorge said, staring at the white telephone now ringing in the corner of his desk. "We both know what it is."

Chapter Three

"You know how to use one of these, Lieutenant?" Chief Belsen squinted at Blake through the cage of the small-arms locker. "Snipes—I mean engineers don't usually—"

"I doubt if I'll need it, Gunny." Daniel Blake signed the receipt for the service pistol and handed the form back to the slightly obese chief gunner's mate wedged behind the screen.

"You better let me check you out, sir. Just in case."

"Sure," Blake said, glancing at his watch.

"Now this here is a Beretta nine millimeter, model 92F, also called the M9. Replaces the old Colt .45. Didn't nobody ask me, but myself, I like the Colt .45 better. Now that could stop a man."

"I'm in kind of a hurry, Gunny."

"Yes, sir. It's got a fifteen-round magazine. You just snap it in like this." The chief snicked the magazine in place with the heel of his hand. "Fifteen rounds because the nine-millimeter slug is smaller, lighter than a .45, but it's got a higher muzzle velocity, so they claim it's got a greater stopping power, but, myself, I don't believe—"

"I'm late, Gunny."

''Yes, sir. To cock it you just pull back on the slide and you got one in the chamber. Fifteen rounds as fast as you can pull the trigger. This here's the safety.''

''Thanks, Chief.'' Blake wrapped the webbed belt around his waist and felt the weight of the automatic settle on his hip.

He darted through the clatter of the mess deck, dodging startled mess boys, ignoring the sleepy-eyed stares. He couldn't blame them for wondering what the ship's engineering officer was doing wearing a combat helmet and side arm when he wasn't sure himself. He felt lean from missing dinner last night, but the institutional smell of creamed chipped beef on toast and boiled coffee made his stomach turn. He shrugged off his growling stomach, pushed the combat helmet down on his head and took the jingling ladder up to the weather deck, feeling a little like Wyatt Earp heading out for the OK Corral.

Emerging onto the weather deck, he blinked into the early-morning sun and glanced up at the bridge, knowing the exec would still be working on Captain Hammer, hoping the skipper would come to his senses and call this whole thing off. Suddenly he felt the ship begin to slow. The wail of the bosun's pipe crackled through the 1MC. ''Now the boarding party muster on the starboard boat deck,'' the boatswain's mate droned through the ship's loudspeaker system, ''now the boarding party . . .''

Blake felt his stomach tighten. He climbed the ladder to the boat deck and glanced around. The team he'd asked for had already begun to assemble. They were milling about, talking in clusters, helping each other buckle on life preservers, trying on unfamiliar combat helmets. Blake looked forward at the high rolling waves breaking over the forecastle. He shielded his eyes and looked out at sea. The wind was blowing harder now, kicking up six-foot waves and billowing clouds of spray. It was going to be a rough trip.

A team of young boatswain's mates struggled against the wind to get the starboard motor whaleboat into position for launching, under the direction of a sharp-eyed chief boatswain. The seamen all looked like kids to Blake, but the old chief played them like an instrument. Getting launched safely didn't worry him—it was the whaleboat itself. It looked like original equipment on the fifty-year-old destroyer, and the hull looked as dry as balsa wood.

"Lieutenant." Frank Kozlewski walked up with a clipboard under his arm, shivering in the wind like a mole above ground. He touched his helmet in what might pass for a salute.

"Chief." Blake returned the rare gesture—such formalities were usually dispensed with in the engine room—and smiled at the burly chief, trussed up in a life preserver with a combat helmet perched on the back of his head. The boiler tender wasn't the easiest man to get along with, but Blake had a soft spot for anyone who'd come up the hard way.

The chief looked out over the rolling sea and blew out a long breath. "Unbelievable," he said, shaking his head.

Blake nodded. "Bit rough out there."

"I'm not talking about the weather. I'm talking about the orders."

Blake threw him a cautionary glance. "Orders are orders. You don't get to pick the ones you like."

"You know what they're calling us? I just overheard some smart-ass deck-apes. Blake's raiders."

Blake felt a sardonic smile cross his face. At least somebody had a sense of humor around here. "Has a nice ring to it."

"I'll bet the exec didn't go along with this, did he?" The chief squinted at him.

Blake said nothing.

"I thought so," Kozlewski said, nodding. "He's the only son of a bitch on that bridge knows what he's doing." The chief stared off into the horizon, shaking his head. "Bunch of engineers going off to board a ship like that in weather like this. Crazy bastard's going to get us all killed."

"Knock it off," Blake said. "You're old enough to know better."

The chief eyed Blake. His watery eyes were still crinkled from looking out at sea. "Yes, sir, I reckon that's my problem. You don't question orders when you're young; you always figure the man on the bridge knows what he's doing. But you do when you start to get old. I got a fishing date with my grandson in a few months. Kind of like to be around to keep it."

"Hey, Chief," someone yelled from across the boat deck, "you going to shoot this thing and put it out of its misery?"

"Would if I thought I could hit it," the chief shouted back. He looked down at the automatic on his hip as though it were an appendage he'd just found growing there. "Last time I fired one of these was in boot camp, twenty-nine years ago."

"You'll be here for your gold watch," Blake said. The chief's upcoming retirement was an event welcomed by most of the officers on the *Carlyle* because of his outspokenness. Blake was used to it. He and the chief had had some spirited discussions when he'd reported aboard, imposing on what had been the chief's domain in the engine room, but an uneasy truce had gradually replaced the old rancor. "How's the plant?"

"Not bad, compared to the engine room of the *Arizona.*" The chief removed his helmet and ran a beefy hand through thinning gray hair. A gold wedding band was embedded in his fleshy finger.

Blake looked at the white strip on his finger where his own had been and felt something move in his stomach. He glanced out at the sea, thinking he'd made a bad bargain, losing Vicki for this.

"Try to be a little more specific, Chief."

"It's that number two boiler. Sounds like hell again. You need to tell that dumb son of a bitch he can't hot-rod this thing around like a sports car."

Blake shook his head. He'd tried before. "Skipper doesn't see it that way. He says it's up to us to deliver whatever he asks for."

"He'll get what he's asking for, all right. One of these days all hell's going to break loose in that engine room. I'm telling you, sir, it ain't safe down there no more. This ship's fifty years old. It needs to be retired, like me."

"Who's got the watch?"

"Chief McKinnon. Nervous as hell about you and me being gone at the same time. Thinks that boiler's just waiting for us to leave."

"If it goes, it won't matter who's aboard," Blake said.

"Well, if it goes, that freighter won't be the only ship dead in the water, that's for damn sure." The chief stared off at the dark outline on the horizon.

Blake looked at his watch. "Get everyone we asked for?"

"Pretty much."

"Let's have a look."

Kozlewski handed him the clipboard. Blake ran his eye down the list:

> USS *Carlyle* (DD949)—Boarding Party Roster
> 1. Blake, D.F., LTJG, OIC
> 2. Kozlewski, F.R., BTC
> 3. Sparks, J.L., EM1
> 4. Rivero, C., SSGT, CMI (TDA)
> 5. Robertson, J.P., BT2
> 6. Jones, M.D., HM2
> 7. Tobin, J.M., MM3
> 8. Kelly, D.L., RM3
> 9. Alvarez, L., SN, Coxswain

"Kelly?" Blake raised his eyebrows. "What happened to Williams?"

"Sick bay."

"Sorry to hear it." Blake's eyes swept the group and fell on a slender sailor with a radio backpack. "But I guess a radioman's a radioman."

"Sure, it is," Kozlewski said.

"What's that supposed to mean?"

The chief turned away so his voice wouldn't carry. "Now you tell me how a little girl like that is going to climb a twenty-foot Jacob's ladder with a twenty-five-pound radio on her back. I don't know what this goddamn Navy's coming to."

"It's coming to the twentieth century," Blake said. He

glanced at Kelly, struck by how different the shapeless dunga-rees looked on a female form. She stared back and made eye contact with Blake as if to say she knew they were talking about her. He turned away casually, and said to the chief, "In the first place, she's not a little girl, she's a young woman, and in the second place, she looks pretty healthy to me."

"You and the rest of the crew."

"I heard Gunderson bragging about her in the wardroom the other day. First in her class at 'A' school. Handpicked to be one of the first women to serve on a combat ship. I wouldn't sell her short."

"We'll see."

Blake glanced at the group of sailors forming up. "Where's Rivero?"

"Who? Oh, that spic marine. He'll be along," the chief said. "All them spics move kind of slow."

Blake stared at Kozlewski and shook his head. "You know, for a guy who's been on the receiving end of that kind of idiotic talk, you're pretty free at passing it out."

Kozlewski shrugged. "All I said was they was slow."

"Anyone who can make sergeant in the Colombian Marine Corps can't be too slow."

"We'll see."

Blake looked up as a tall figure in combat fatigues emerged onto the boat deck. He watched the Colombian marine approach with his catlike walk, and threw a satisfied glance at the chief. Rivero appeared to be about Blake's height, about six feet, with a heavily muscular frame to match. The sergeant was impressive by any standard, Blake thought. Pressed combat fatigues, boots polished to a dull sheen, well-worn but immaculate Colt M16A2 assault rifle on his shoulder, two thirty-round banana clips of 5.56mm NATO ammunition stuffed into his flak jacket. With a Ka-Bar marine combat knife strapped to his right ankle, he looked like a one-man army.

Rivero came to attention in front of Blake and snapped a smart salute. "Sir, Sergeant Rivero, CMI, reporting for duty, *sir.*"

Blake returned the salute casually. "Glad to have you along, Sergeant."

Frank Kozlewski peered at the tall marine suspiciously. "What the hell's 'CMI'?"

Sergeant Rivero stared impassively down on the chief. "Corps of Marine Infantry. Or if you prefer, CIM. *Cuerpo de Infanteria de Marina.*"

"No, I don't prefer," the chief said.

Blake threw a glance at Kozlewski that told him to knock it off. He could see the other members of the boarding party and the boatswain's mates working on deck stealing glances at the Colombian. He was quiet and kept to himself, which was grist enough for the rumor mill of a destroyer. Blake had heard all the scuttlebutt: He'd been trained in the martial arts and could kill a man using only his hands; his entire family had been wiped out by the drug lords; he had a personal vendetta against the Colombian drug cartels. Blake smiled to himself. The crew of a destroyer was nothing, if not imaginative.

"All right, listen up," Blake said after Sergeant Rivero took his place with the group. "As most of you know, our assignment is to board that freighter and determine why she's stopped in the sea-lanes. Our mission is to lend whatever assistance is necessary to get the ship under way, get some power to the running lights, or to help in any way we're needed. It's possible there could be illness aboard, so I've asked Doc Jones to join us." Blake nodded at a black hospital corpsman with a canvas medical bag on his shoulder.

"What did you bring in your black bag, Doc?" someone yelled over the wind.

"Enough antibiotics to cure all the clap in South America," the corpsman said, convulsing everyone except Sergeant Rivero, who stared stonily ahead. Blake tried not to smile but couldn't help himself. Like the rest of them, he'd heard the story that Jones had cured one of the *Carlyle*'s most chronic malingerers by brandishing a syringe he'd picked up at a veterinary supply house, muttering "about 500 cc in the groin should do it." There were some guys you had to like.

"We've spotted a Jacob's ladder hanging from the port quarter, near the stern of the ship," Blake said. "We'll circle once to do a hull inspection." He nodded to Seaman Luis Alvarez, the coxswain assigned to pilot the motor whaleboat. "If there's no visible damage, we'll tie up to the ladder and board that way. Once we get aboard, there's no telling what we'll find, so I want everyone to stick together in case we have to beat a hasty retreat. Any questions?"

John Sparks raised his hand. "Why the hell can't we get in closer, Lieutenant? That freighter must be two miles off."

Blake glanced at the chief, an acknowledgment that he'd been right. Frank Kozlewski had argued against taking the weasel-faced electrician because he had to hear his complaining all day.

"The skipper wouldn't be prudent to take the ship in closer without knowing more about it."

"You mean the son of a bitch might blow up or something?"

Blake tensed, beginning to regret his decision already. "I don't think there's much danger of that."

"Oh, well that's good," Sparks said. "Not much."

"Anything else?" Blake asked.

The group stood silent.

"Okay, let's load up." Blake held the boat for the others to board first, aware of the tradition that officers were last in, first out. Settling down in the bow of the whaleboat, he felt the USS *Carlyle* heave to a full stop. He gripped the monkey lines when he felt the whaleboat swing free from its davits and glanced at the seamen in life jackets struggling to keep their guy lines taut, waiting for the signal to release. All activity above decks had stopped while the crew of the destroyer leaned over lifelines to watch the dangerous maneuver.

Blake took one last look at the bridge, hoping the exec would appear and call it off. Captain Hammer stepped out on the bridge wing, shouted something unintelligible through a bullhorn, and dropped his arm. The starboard motor whaleboat, with its shoe-horned cargo of orange life jackets and combat helmets, glided out on steel cables, then plummeted down a gray cliff toward the surface of the ocean.

Blake glanced at the wall of steel rising up on the left, then down to the water rushing up to meet them. He felt a spine-twisting jolt as the whaleboat collided with the top of a swell, tossing it against the hull of the destroyer, then pulling it away.

Bow and stern sling lines were released as the diesel engine spun over with a gritty whine, belching black smoke. Alvarez leaned into the rudder and accelerated away, throwing up a rooster-tail of white spray. Blake glanced over his shoulder and watched the old gray lady receding into the background. He stared at the pudgy figure of Captain Hammer standing on the bridge wing watching him through binoculars, almost able to read his mind. If the mission was successful, Captain Hammer would take the credit. If it wasn't, Blake would take the heat. Even after he was out of sight, Blake could feel the captain's eyes on him through the binoculars, could feel the conflict in him, wanting him to succeed, yet wanting him to fail. He had no problem with the captain taking the credit if there was any, but he damned sure was not going to accommodate him by failing. He turned, finally, and squinted through the mist at the dark freighter riding low on the horizon, determined to show the bastard what ringknockers were made of.

Blake gripped the six-inch gunwales of the whaleboat and forced his stomach to stay down. The tiny craft bobbed up on the white crest of a wave, shuddered with its propeller out of the water, and crashed down into a foaming trough, drenching him with a vaporous cloud of spray. He glanced up at the slate-colored dome that covered them, overwhelmed with a feeling of insignificance. *Anyone who feels important,* he thought, *should spend some time in a twenty-foot whaleboat on the open sea.*

Gusts of wind whipped the boat, yawing it to starboard. Looking back, he saw Alvarez fighting the rudder over a mon-tage of grim faces. He pushed his helmet down and shielded his eyes, squinting through the mist at the freighter coming into view.

"This son of a bitch is filling up fast, sir." Frank Kozlewski clung to the seat next to him, peering down at the brown water bubbling up through the deck grids.

"We're almost there," Blake said, staring at the dark form.

"We better be."

"We'll be okay." Blake glanced down at the water washing over his shoes. He'd been watching the water level in the bilges since they'd passed the midway point. It was rising steadily now from the waves breaking over the gunwales, as well as from water seeping in through the seams of the dry hull.

"See anything yet?" the chief asked.

Blake shook his head. He cupped his hands around his eyes and scanned the weather deck and superstructure. The only movement on deck was a flag snapping briskly from the ensign staff. Red and blue stars. Panamanian registry. He motioned for Alvarez to cut his speed and circle the ship.

"What are you doing?" Chief Kozlewski said.

"I want to check the hull before we board," Blake said, squinting.

"I don't think that's a great idea—"

"Hey, Lieutenant," Alvarez shouted from the stern. "We're shipping a hell of a lot of water." The coxswain was standing up, pointing down to the bilges. "We better take her in, sir."

"He's right," the chief said. "We ain't got time for no hull inspection. Let's get aboard."

"That ship could be sinking for all we know," Blake said quietly to the chief. He glanced between the water in the bilges and the ship. It was a judgment call. He motioned again for Alvarez to circle the ship.

Alvarez throttled the whaleboat down and maneuvered along the port side of the freighter while Blake looked over the immense hull. She was a stately old ship, riding low in the water. Gashes of rust stains ran down the black hull, dusted pink from the early-morning sun fighting through gray clouds on the horizon. Large rolling waves broke against the hull, exposing flashes of copper-based red paint below the waterline.

Blake tingled with nostalgia, seeing the old freighter up close. He'd been a ship freak for as long as he could remember, spending hours after school sitting on the pier in San Diego, just watching the ships. He'd been fascinated with the Navy ships of the line, but it was the merchant ships from around the world that had captured his fancy. He loved to watch them coming in and going out, with their colorful flags and lyrical names, wondering where they were from, where they were bound, what kind of cargo they carried, what their crews were like. The old intrigue came flooding back.

"La Estrella Latina," Sergeant Rivero said behind him.

Blake glanced up at the bow curving over them and saw the name spelled out in block letters, welded just aft of the rust-stained anchor wells. The *Latin Star.* A bemused smile crossed his face. There was something about naming ships that brought out the poet in everyone.

Rounding the bow to the lee of the ship, the whaleboat stabilized, shielded from the wind. Blake squinted at the red Roman numerals of the waterline marker painted on the bow.

"Well, is she sinking? Can you tell?" Frank Kozlewski craned his neck to peer at the numbers.

"This just tells you how much hull is below the waterline," Blake said. "Looks like about thirty feet."

"Then how do you know if she's sinking?"

"The load line." Blake motioned Alvarez down the starboard side of the ship to a circle painted on the hull with a series of horizontal lines running through it, denoted with various letters. The water was roughly level with a line marked T.

"What's all that?" Frank Kozlewski said.

Blake glanced at the chief to see if he was serious and decided that he was. "The Plimsoll mark. Keeps ship owners from overloading. Named after Samuel Plimsoll, member of the British Parliament. Wrote the act that created it."

"What does it say?"

Blake looked at Kozlewski, resisting the impulse to shake

his head. Thirty years at sea and the chief couldn't read a load line. *That's what being stuck in the engine room will do for you,* he thought. It was a fate he was determined to avoid.

"See the line on top that says TF? Stands for tropical fresh. That means you could take her up a tropical river and load her up to that line in fresh water. When you take her back to sea, the density of the salt water would lift her up to the T line. That's as full as she can be loaded in a tropical ocean."

"So that means it ain't sinking?"

"Probably."

"Well, that's good, because this one is," Frank Kozlewski said, staring down. "Better kick this thing in the ass, Lieutenant."

Blake flinched at the water sloshing over the tops of his shoes. He'd been so fascinated with the old freighter, he hadn't noticed how much deeper it had gotten. He motioned for Alvarez to head for the Jacob's ladder.

Alvarez accelerated down the starboard side of the ship and maneuvered around the stern. Blake looked up at the fantail. The name of the ship was repeated in welded block letters just below the taffrail, with *Panama* in smaller letters on the line below.

Alvarez reversed the engine and coaxed the whaleboat toward the Jacob's ladder. Frank Kozlewski let out a gasp. "Mother of God, look at that."

Following Kozlewski's eyes, Blake looked off to port and saw a high rolling wave approaching like a mountain on wheels. It rolled toward them in slow motion and seemed to pause, looming over them like a cobra with its hood spread. Breaking against the stern of the freighter, it slammed down into the whaleboat, filling it with three feet of water. The boat listed to port, and water began sweeping over the gunwales.

"She's swamping!" Alvarez shoved the throttle forward, and the boat labored ahead a few feet before the engine clanked to a halt.

The turbulence of the water propelled the swamped boat toward the Jacob's ladder. Scooping up the boat hook, Blake lunged for the ladder and missed it by inches as the flurry of water sucked the boat away from the hull. The backlash of the wave pushed the boat back toward the ship, and Blake could tell by the declining momentum that this would be his last chance. Leaning over the bow of the boat, he stabbed the boat hook out as far as he could reach and caught the bottom rung of the ladder. Bracing himself, he pulled the boat in and secured the bowline. The boat was swamped, but still afloat. He looked back at the boarding party standing knee-deep in water.

"Let's go," he shouted, holding the ladder.

"Right behind you, sir," Chief Kozlewski said.

Blake scrambled up the swaying ladder and jumped over the weather rail, grateful for the firmness of the main deck under his feet. He glanced around and reached down to help the chief up, then extended a hand to Sergeant Rivero. As the Colombian marine turned and pulled Doc Jones over the weather rail, Blake reached down for Dana Kelly. "I can make it," Kelly said, refusing his hand. A gust of wind buffeted the Jacob's ladder, catching the radio backpack, pulling her backward. She looked up with a panicked expression as her grip on the wet rung loosened. Blake caught her by the wrist and helped her up.

"Losing our radio operator is not what we need right now," he said quietly, helping her over the weather rail. The clean scent of her hair displaced the organic smell of the sea for an instant.

"Sorry, sir," Kelly said, her face flushed.

"Get your radio set up," Blake said, reaching down for John Sparks. "I want to check in."

"Aye aye, sir." Kelly swung the SINCGARS radio down on deck and flipped open the canvas cover.

Blake and Sergeant Rivero helped Robertson, Tobin, and Alvarez over the weather rail. They stood dripping on the teak deck as Kelly telescoped the antenna.

"The old man's going to shit if we lose that boat," Alvarez said, shivering in the wind.

"Might be a sump pump in the engine room," the chief said.

"We better get it up here in a hurry," Alvarez said. "Another wave like that and she'll rip right off of that bowline."

"Nobody goes anywhere." Blake stood, shielding his eyes, staring at the superstructure.

"But Jesus Christ, sir, she's going to sink—"

"What would you plug a submersible pump into?" Blake said. "There's no power on this ship."

Alvarez went to the weather rail and peered down. "Maybe we can bail her out."

The others joined him at the rail and watched as the stern of the whaleboat settled down into the black water. Within seconds, only the bow was visible, still tied to the Jacob's ladder.

"She's gone," Blake said. "Go down and cut her loose."

"The old man's gonna shit," Alvarez said for the tenth time. He unsheathed his bosum's knife and eased over the weather rail. He paused and looked up hopefully. "This old tub's got booms, ain't it? Maybe we can rig up one of them—"

"Not without power," Blake said. "Cut it loose before it pulls the Jacob's ladder down with it."

Alvarez shinnied down the ladder and hung on with one hand as he sliced through the bowline. The whaleboat eased down beneath the waves, rolled over, and disappeared into the black depths, sending up a stream of bubbles. He watched until it was out of sight and scampered back up the ladder.

Blake turned back to the superstructure and squinted into the haze, bothered by something that he couldn't put his finger on. From the afterdeck, the ship appeared to be in good order— booms were properly secured to king posts, lines were coiled neatly on deck—but looking forward, something was missing. Suddenly he could see it: The lifeboats and life rafts were gone. All of them.

He cupped his hands and shouted a couple of "Ahoys" over the howl of the wind. The only other sounds were the whip and snap of the ensign flag and the bell-like clink of the cargo booms.

"Strange," Blake said, looking down at the deck.

"What is?" Chief Kozlewski asked, wiping salt water from his face.

"A helicopter landing pad on a merchant ship."

"What kind of ship is this, anyway?" Chief Kozlewski asked.

"A C-2," Blake said, glancing around. "A C2-S-AJ1, to be precise."

Kozlewski screwed his face up into an incredulous look. "Now, how in the world do you know that?"

Blake looked at Kozlewski, surprised at how little he knew outside the engine room. After a life at sea, the chief should have been able to recognize a C-2, though he understood that only a ship freak like himself would know which model it was.

"You can tell by the high, thin funnel," Blake said, pointing. "Quite a ship in her day. Five cargo holds and staterooms for twelve passengers."

"Humongous old bitch."

"Not really," Blake said. "Eight thousand tons gross, maybe five thousand net. Four hundred and fifty feet or so in length, displacing fourteen or fifteen thousand tons. Big compared to a destroyer, but pretty small for a merchant ship. Small by today's standards anyway. I didn't know any of these were still around."

"Looks like she's *been* around."

Blake nodded. "She's old, all right. I haven't seen one of these since I was a kid, and they were old then."

"Tobin," Blake shouted, "step over there and see if you can see any unreeled fire hoses on the starboard side."

"Aye aye, sir."

"Fire hoses?" the chief said. "What's that all about?"

"Pirates," Blake said, watching Tobin.

"You kidding, sir?"

"It's a big problem with merchant ships," Blake said. "They're basically unarmed except for a revolver the captain keeps locked in his safe. The only way to repel boarders is to break out the fire hoses."

Tobin came back shaking his head. "Nothing over there, sir."

"What do you think's happened?" the chief asked.

"Hard to say. The lifeboats and life rafts are all gone. My guess is she's been abandoned."

"Christ's sake, why would they do that?"

Blake shook his head. "I have no idea." He glanced at his watch. An hour had passed since they had cast off from the mother ship. "I guess we'd better call home. Skipper's not going to be too happy about losing a boat."

"Serves the bastard right."

Blake shot a disapproving look at the chief and looked past him at the *Carlyle* steaming on the horizon. The ship seemed a world away. Suddenly his mouth fell open.

"What is it—" the chief said, swiveling.

Blake stared at a ball of orange fire rising from the forward stack of the destroyer and flinched at the muffled sound of the blast that reached his ears a split second later. The others wheeled at the sound of the explosion and stared in silence at the cloud of black smoke that covered the center of the ship. A second, deadened explosion from the bowels of the ship was followed by a column of fire that shot out of the after stack. Through the dense black smoke, Blake could see flames lapping at the superstructure. There was total silence for ten seconds—seconds that seemed like minutes—before Blake heard the jarring sound of the klaxon horn and the call to general quarters.

Chapter Four

"No, goddammit, no!" Jorge Cordoba stepped into the Mercedes, jerked his tie loose, and sank back into the black leather seat.

Rafael Ayala elbowed the chauffeur out of the way and scampered into the limousine behind Jorge. He pulled the jump seat down and sat facing him.

"Just wait a minute, for God's sake."

Jorge stared at the rotund director of security. Perched on the jump seat before him, he looked like a frog on a lily pad, ready to spring.

"Take your own car. I need time to think."

"Please, we need to talk."

"Every time I talk to you it ends in disaster."

Ayala tugged the door inward.

The burly chauffeur, who was holding it effortlessly from outside, looked at Jorge. Jorge nodded and the door clicked shut.

The black Mercedes pulled away from the Augusto Gallardo Building into thin streams of sunlight breaking through the cluster of high-rises. Jorge opened the bar and poured himself a tumbler of Scotch.

Ayala took a deep breath. "Look, you've got to be the one to tell him."

Jorge grimaced at the taste of the whiskey. "You think he doesn't already know?" He stared out the window, watching the reflection of the limousine ripple across the forest of glass towers. He could see Ayala's limousine following behind, empty, in the nearly deserted streets.

Ayala blinked his thick eyelids. "How could he?"

"He knows, you idiot. You think this meeting is a coincidence?" Jorge could still hear the subdued voice over the white telephone droning in his ears. A meeting of the executive committee had been called for 6:45 A.M. It would be held in the boardroom of Don Gallardo's estate. The Don would dispatch his own car and driver. No agenda had been given.

Jorge Cordoba had no doubt about what was on the agenda. He tapped his foot and rubbed his temple. Ayala's cologne, mixed with the smell of wood, leather and carpet in the tightly sealed passenger compartment, made his head pound. "Do you have to douse yourself with that gasoline?" He lowered the window a crack and pulled the cool morning air into his lungs as the heavily armored limousine glided onto an expressway and headed east toward Palmira.

"If you talk to him, explain why we did it—"

"Why *we* did it? Let's get something straight right now. I was against it."

"But we talked. You said go ahead."

"I said nothing of the kind. What I said was, 'You're the director of security.'"

"Which I took to mean, 'Go ahead.'"

"How you took it is no affair of mine."

"Please. You've got to talk to him. You're his godson. He'll listen to you."

Jorge stared through the tinted window separating the passenger compartment at the thick neck and greasy black hair of Raul Francisco, Don Gallardo's personal bodyguard. His mind flashed on the silver Uzi he'd noticed under Raul's oversize suit jacket as he'd opened the door, bowing politely.

"I'm not so sure."

"Don't be ridiculous. He's been like a father to you since your parents were . . . Since the accident."

"I know." Jorge rubbed his eyes. *And this is how I repay him,* he thought. No man alive had done more for him than Don Augusto Gallardo. How could he explain this disaster to his mentor, his *padrino,* the man to whom he owed everything? He gazed distantly out the window as the limousine sped quietly by red-tiled plantations along the Cauca River. He normally enjoyed seeing these colonial relics, surrounded by green fields of softly rippling sugar cane, but today they were a blur in the distance.

"Please," Rafael Ayala said. "You've got to talk to him, or I'm a dead man."

"You made the decision on your own," Jorge said. "It will go better for you if you face up to it. Don Gallardo is a fair man."

Meaning, if you tell him the truth, he will kill you quickly; if you lie to him, he will kill you slowly, Jorge thought. He'd thought it through and knew now what his direction would be. He would distance himself from Rafael Ayala and deny any involvement in this harebrained scheme. No matter what Ayala said to implicate him, his godfather would give him the benefit of the doubt.

"What do I have to do? Beg you? All right. I'm begging you."

Jorge ignored him and looked out the window as the Mercedes slowed and turned off on the farm-to-market road that led to the estate. The limousine crunched on gravel for a short distance and pulled up to a heavy black iron gate mounted between stone columns.

The gate with no outward markings swung slowly inward, as though by some invisible hand. The limousine pulled forward, revealing a sanctuary that Jorge never tired of seeing. Of all the public gardens in the world, he thought, none could equal this, yet few people would ever see it. The grounds were a tropical paradise, a maze of manicured gardens which housed one of the largest private zoos in the world. Peacocks roamed the grounds at will, while African lions dozed in their compound.

Jorge stared out the window into the thick foliage. *To anyone caught out there, lions would be the least of their worries,* he thought. There was another kind of animal roaming the estate that was far more deadly. The casual observer wouldn't see them, wearing Czech-made, Russian AK-47 assault rifles on their shoulders, or their bosses, the security *patróns,* each assigned to a section of the estate, each wearing an Uzi machine pistol clipped to his belt. Nor would the casual observer hear the occasional crackle of two-way radios over the cacophony of bird and animal sounds. From inside the womb of the limousine's passenger compartment, Jorge could neither see nor hear them, but he knew they were there.

"I'm begging you," the director of security said. "One nod from the Don, and they'll hunt me down like an animal."

Jorge glanced at Ayala. He was staring out the opposite window into the dense vegetation, trembling.

"You've trained them well enough." Jorge hated the security measures—they were a constant reminder of the nature of the business he was in—but it would be a fitting end, he thought. It was this *rana*'s insistence on overzealous security measures that had gotten them into this mess in the first place. Let him stew in his own juice.

The gate swung inward again and two more limousines entered, following the pair of Mercedes up the winding drive, throwing up small dust clouds. At the end of a half-mile drive, the convoy came to a stop behind a string of identical vehicles parked in a courtyard surrounding a huge fifteenth-century fountain. The fountain, which had been imported stone by stone from Europe, was dwarfed by the structure it attempted to decorate.

Raul opened the rear door of the limousine, admitting a cloud of mist from the fountain, which helped clear Jorge's head. He stepped out into the morning sun and walked quickly away from Rafael Ayala.

The huge oak doors opened wide at his approach. Carlos, the horse-toothed butler who had been with the Gallardo family for decades, bowed as Jorge stepped into the reception area.

"Good morning, Dr. Cordoba." Carlos stood looking at him expectantly.

Jorge raised his arms, and Carlos ran his hands down his sides, legs, and crotch. Jorge flinched. It was ludicrous for Don Gallardo's godson to be patted down like a common thug, but after the last assassination attempt the Don had made it a hard-and-fast rule for everyone—no exceptions.

"Please go directly to the boardroom, Doctor."

Jorge smiled at the greeting. He'd always taken the title for granted—it was an honorary one customarily bestowed on all university graduates in Colombia—but his two-year stay with the *Norte Americanos,* who showed no respect for anyone, had finally made him appreciate it.

Jorge made his way down the long corridor to the boardroom, with Rafael Ayala panting behind.

"I have some girls that will make the twins look like hags." Ayala darted in front of Jorge and placed his arm across the door. "I'll send them over tonight."

Jorge looked down at Ayala's sweating face. "They weren't twins." He moved Ayala's arm away and opened the door. The security director scurried to the end of the table and took refuge with some cronies. Jorge went straight to Don Gallardo, who was standing near the head of the table.

"Buenos días, Padrino." Jorge nodded slightly and extended his hand, cursing his habit of lapsing into Spanish when he was nervous.

"Ah, Jorge." Don Gallardo gripped his hand and fixed him with a steady gaze. "It was good of you to come."

"An invitation to your home is always an honor." Jorge looked into the eyes of his mentor and tried to read what was there. The blue eyes, as dark as mountain lakes, were as impenetrable as ever.

"And how is your lovely wife?" Don Gallardo asked.

"Oh, you know Isabella. Healthy as a horse."

"How long has it been now? Three months?"

"Three wonderful months."

Don Gallardo put his hand on Jorge's arm. "It's good that you finally got married, Jorge. I want all my senior officers to be married to women from respectable families."

Jorge laughed. "A policy I don't mind complying with, where Isabella is concerned." He couldn't remember when he'd seen her last. At his godfather's urging, he had pursued and married the debutante but only saw her when he needed her for some social occasion.

"Would you like a cup of *tinto?*"

"*Café perico, por favor.*" Jorge could see the others out of the corner of his eye, standing around the long conference table, watching enviously as Don Gallardo poured his coffee and added a splash of milk.

"*Grac*— Thank you, Godfather." Jorge took the tiny cup and stood basking in the envy, forgetting for the moment why they were there.

Carlos entered the room and hovered over the side table, fussing with the food. Trays of *arepas* stood surrounded by sweating pitchers of orange juice, bowls of fruit, trays of eggs, butter, jam, and pastries. The *arepas* were a traditional favorite at meetings, little cakes made of ground corn, cheese, and eggs, and fried in fat. They looked and smelled fresh, but Jorge noticed none had been touched.

"Leave us," Don Gallardo said. Carlos turned and bowed his way out the door.

With an almost indiscernible gesture, Don Gallardo motioned for Jorge to be seated to his right at the table. It was the seat of honor, traditionally Jorge's at meetings, and the warm familiarity of it began to relax him. The door closed behind the retreating butler, and the room fell silent. The boardroom was windowless and completely soundproof; the family members of Don Gallardo were carefully insulated from the family business.

Jorge glanced at the imposing figure taking his seat at the head of the table. Middle-aged and substantial, Don Gallardo moved with the aid of a walking stick, a compensation for the slight limp he'd received in an earlier assassination attempt. The stick had been a gift from Jorge; a solid silver mallard head formed the handle. On some men, a limp would be a negative, but Don Gallardo's deft handling of the silver-headed walking stick only seemed to add to his mystique. With his silver hair, ruddy complexion, and dark business suit, Jorge thought he could pass for the chairman of a Fortune 100 corporation or the head of a Wall Street investment bank.

"Thank you for coming on short notice, gentlemen," Don Gallardo said. "Let us dispense with the usual formalities and get to the main purpose of this meeting. I have been informed that we have lost communication with our shipment to Montevideo."

A buzzing sound spun around the room. Don Gallardo lifted the fingers of his hand, and the room fell silent.

"Perhaps Señor Barranca will be good enough to give us an update."

"It would be my pleasure." The moon-faced director of logistics mopped his face with one hand and reached for the glass of mineral water before him with the other. He took a small sip and swallowed with a grating sound that was audible in the deathly quiet room. "The last communication we received was approximately forty-eight hours ago." Jorge detected a quaver in his voice.

"Forty-eight hours." Don Gallardo looked around the table. "And why were we not notified of this before now?"

"The Command Center failed to report it to me in a timely manner," Barranca said. A sheen of perspiration appeared on his forehead.

"Is that intended to be an excuse?"

"Those responsible have been dealt with," Barranca said, now sweating profusely. He dabbed at his face.

"I'm glad to see you bring up the subject of responsibility. Since you have, let us discuss yours." Don Gallardo's eyes narrowed. "It is your responsibility as chief transportation officer to ensure safe delivery of each shipment. It is your responsibility to maintain personal contact around the clock with a shipment of this magnitude. It is your responsibility to take care of business instead of cavorting with your *puta.*" He slammed his open hand down on the table.

Jorge flinched and shifted in his seat. Don Gallardo had begun his inquisition and he wouldn't rest until he had the truth. His probing demeanor was intimidating even to Jorge; he couldn't blame Gilberto Barranca for looking terrified.

"Yes, Don Gallardo." Barranca seemed to bow his head, accepting his fate.

Don Gallardo paused, and asked in a gentler tone, "And what is your expert opinion as to why communication has ceased?"

Barranca seemed to brighten. "I'm sure it's something simple. Perhaps a storm at sea preventing radio transmission, or perhaps the radio on the ship has failed."

Don Gallardo slammed his fist down on the table. "Enough of these guesses. What was the nature of the radio contact before communication ceased; what was the last message?"

"It was from the first mate," Barranca said. "Some problems they were having. Something about the security system."

Here it comes, Jorge thought.

"What kind of problems?"

"It wasn't clear, the transmission was breaking up, some kind of control problems. Yes, that's it," he said. "Something was out of control."

Jorge shuddered. He knew exactly what was out of control.

"And you chose not to share this information with us?"

"I did not think it important enough to bother the senior officers with," Barranca said, pausing for effect, "but I did report it to the director of security."

Jorge's stomach tightened. He squirmed in his seat as all eyes shifted to Rafael Ayala. Barranca sank back in his chair like a deflated balloon.

Jorge picked up a pencil and started tapping it against his

thumb, dancing his foot under the table, staring at Rafael Ayala. *If you so much as mention my name, you fat son of a whore . . .*

Don Gallardo gazed down the long table at Rafael Ayala and snorted. The director of security was seated facing him at the opposite end of the table, as far away from Don Gallardo as he could get. "So. Perhaps our chief security officer can explain this mysterious, final message."

Tell him what you've done and let's get on with it, Jorge thought. *Just leave me out of it.*

Rafael Ayala spread his hands and shrugged. "I am at a loss, Don Gallardo." His frog lips curled into a weak smile.

Jorge stiffened. The fool was going to try to bluff his way through.

"Are you?" Don Gallardo leaned back in his chair and rested his elbow on the table, cradling his chin with his thumb, tapping his cheek with his forefinger, staring across the table at the sweating security director. "Your security system is out of control, and you are at a loss to explain it." He studied Ayala's face for a long minute. "Well, then, perhaps we can assist you. Why don't you begin by enlightening us as to the security system you employed on this shipment?"

Rafael Ayala shrugged. "All the usual measures."

Don Gallardo smiled, tapping his cheek. "The usual measures?"

He knows, Jorge thought. *Tell him, you fool.*

"Plus one more . . . well . . . extra precaution because of the nature of the shipment." Beads of sweat standing on Ayala's forehead merged together and trickled down the side of his nose.

"Oh?"

"Yes, Don Gallardo." Ayala mopped at his forehead with a paper napkin. "I thought it advisable . . . that is, you, yourself, have said . . . a shipment of this magnitude required extraordinary security measures."

"And what were these extraordinary measures that you have taken upon yourself to use?"

Rafael Ayala swallowed hard. *"El Callado."* His voice cracked.

Augusto Gallardo brought his chair upright, staring across the table at Rafael Ayala. His eyes were the color of blue steel.

"So. 'The silent one.' And now the message becomes clear, does it not?"

"Please, I beg you, don't jump to conclusions. We don't know—"

"I think we know," Don Gallardo said, "that you have taken it upon yourself to make a unilateral decision that affects the entire organization and places it at risk."

"But this was not a unilateral decision. I discussed it with all the senior officers—"

"Did you? Then let us now hear from the senior officers." He glanced around the room, looking at everyone but Jorge.

Jorge Cordoba stared across the table at Rafael Ayala, sending a message with his eyes, holding his breath. No one spoke.

"Who agreed with this?"

Silence.

"Rodrigo, I discussed it with you," Rafael Ayala said.

Rodrigo Herrera, the director of communications, stared straight ahead.

"Enrique, we talked. You thought . . ."

The wall clock ticked loudly, as though timing Ayala's remaining minutes. The only other sound in the room was the rapid breathing of Rafael Ayala. His eyes darted around the room.

Jorge shifted in his seat. The son of a whore was staring at him.

"I discussed it with Señor Cordoba. Tell him." Ayala looked at Jorge, his eyes wide, pleading.

Jorge glared back, wanting to kill him.

Don Gallardo turned to Jorge. "You knew about this?"

"I advised against it."

"Then you knew," Don Gallardo said, turning away.

"But I didn't think—"

"No," Don Gallardo said, coming to his feet. "You didn't."

Jorge felt a red flush creep over him. "But I was opposed—"

"Success has many fathers," Don Gallardo said. He started around the table, leaning on his walking stick. "Failure is an orphan."

"But you don't understand . . ."

Jorge's voice fell away as he watched Don Gallardo walk slowly down the long table. His limp seemed more pronounced now, perhaps from sitting. He suddenly seemed old and tired.

"Let me see if I understand this," Don Gallardo said, almost talking to himself, leaning heavily on the silver mallard head, walking slowly. "After I ordered you to get rid of that monstrous pet of yours, you not only disobeyed me, but you placed it on the most important shipment in the history of this organization." He rounded the far end of the table and stood behind Rafael Ayala, leaning on his walking stick. "Is that correct?"

"It wasn't an order. You suggested—"

"And you think a suggestion from me is not an order?" Don Gallardo snorted with contempt. "You're even stupider than I thought."

Ayala's mouth hung open, his eyes wide, watery. He started to turn around.

"No one gave you permission to move."

Ayala's head snapped back around, jowls swinging.

Don Gallardo stood looking down on Ayala's bald head. "I asked you a question. Yes or no."

"Yes."

"I see."

Jorge saw his godfather's face transformed into a dark, seething mask, something out of a Kabuki play. Red beams of light seemed to shoot out of his eyes. Don Gallardo stepped back, raised his walking stick like a batter at the plate, and swung it sideways with a sharp whistling sound. The beak of the silver mallard head sank into Ayala's right temple with a crushing sound, like a pumpkin being smashed with a hammer.

Jorge jumped in his chair and gaped as Ayala slumped forward, pulling Don Gallardo with him by the walking stick embedded in his skull. Don Gallardo released the stick and stood leaning on the back of Ayala's chair, breathing hard, trying to recover his composure. His eyes darted to each of the sphinxlike faces around the table and came to rest on Jorge's stunned expression. He stared at Jorge for what seemed a full minute. His eyes had narrowed to cold red points of light. Gradually they softened. He straightened himself and managed a faint smile.

"Wait for me in my study, Jorge. Gentlemen, this meeting is adjourned."

Chapter Five

Blake stood on the fantail of the freighter, watching black smoke billow up from the *Carlyle* and fade into cloudy skies. Orange flames darted through the blanket of smoke, licking at the forward stack and superstructure. It was like watching his house burn.

He glanced at Dana Kelly, kneeling over the radio, frantically trying to get through to the ship.

"Anything yet?"

"I can't raise anyone, sir."

"The fire's probably close to the radio shack," Blake said.

Gusts of wind buffeted the ship, fanning the flames. Through the smoke, Blake thought he could see fire-fighting crews on deck, tiny specks moving in unison, advancing toward the flames behind thin streams of water, then retreating as the wind turned. Looking through the haze of mist and smoke, the scene was surreal, a grainy World War II newsreel come to life.

The flames surged higher, whipped by the wind. "If the magazine goes, it's all over," he said to Frank Kozlewski, who stood gripping the rail beside him.

"Mother of God," the chief said.

A deep sense of guilt pulled at him, watching safely from his vantage point a mile away while men were fighting for their lives. He wanted to be there, to be doing something. A drop of water slapped against his helmet. He looked up as huge raindrops spattered the deck.

"Thank you, sweet Jesus," he heard Tobin say behind him. A dense tropical rain began to fall. Blake held his hands and face up to the sky, and Chief Kozlewski made the sign of the cross. Heavy black clouds ruptured, and rain filled the air, blowing across the ocean in waves. They stood silently in the rain, watching spellbound as thick sheets of water swept over the destroyer, sending up black columns of smoke that faded to gray. From across the water, Blake thought he heard cheers rising from the deck of the *Carlyle*.

The flames began to subside and the tower of smoke dwindled to a wisp. Blake glanced over his shoulder at Kelly. She was still crouched over the radio, skipping through the frequencies in the VHS band, trying to get through to the ship.

"Thank God," Kelly said after a few minutes. "Am I glad to hear a friendly voice. What'd you guys do, take the day off? Yeah, I'd say you've been a little busy. Sure, we'll stand by." Kelly glanced up at Blake. "We're holding for the exec." After another minute, she said, "Yes, sir, here's Lieutenant Blake." She offered the handset up to Blake. "Commander Mayfield, sir."

Blake snugged the telephone-like handset up to his head and stuck his finger in his other ear. "Yes, sir?"

"Blake, can you hear me?" came the tinny voice of the executive officer through the earpiece.

"Yes, sir. Go ahead."

"I assume you saw the show?"

"Affirmative, sir. What happened?"

"We don't know. Damage-control reports still coming in. All we know for sure is it originated in the engine room. Took out both boilers. Heavy damage to the control-room console. Main distribution switchboard's down."

"Any casualties, sir?"

"Three dead and counting. Dozen injuries, some bad. Chief McKinnon's okay, but he's in over his head. Skipper's down there now. He wants you back aboard, pronto."

"Nothing I'd like better, Commander. But that's a problem. We lost the whaleboat."

There was a pause. "Any small craft on the freighter you can use?"

"Negative, sir. Lifeboats and rafts are gone. The ship appears to be abandoned. What about the port whaleboat?"

"Negative," the exec said. "We can't risk the last boat with the ship disabled. Listen, Dan. Even if we had a boat, it's too risky in this weather. Just stay aboard. The engine room looks like a junkyard. You couldn't do much here anyway. What have you found there?"

"Nothing yet, sir," Blake said. "We just got aboard when the show started."

"Any hull damage?"

"No, sir. The hull appears to be sound."

"Any other damage?"

"No, sir, nothing I can see from here."

"Anything toxic, any hazardous materials you can see?"

"Negative, sir. Nothing so far."

"Then just stay aboard and secure the ship. I'll fix it with the captain. We just got through to Colombian National Naval Headquarters in Bogotá. Closest ship is a Colombian frigate off Buenaventura. We've asked for a tow. We need to get the hell out of here while we're still afloat. Tropical cyclone moving this way. Picking up speed."

"When do you think it'll hit, sir?"

"Hard to say. Twenty-four, forty-eight hours. Keeps changing direction. Maybe we'll get lucky."

"Yes, sir." *We'd damn well better,* Blake thought. Ships the size of the *Carlyle* and the *Latin Star* wouldn't have a chance of surviving a full-blown tropical cyclone without some excellent ship handling and the ability to maneuver, and that required full power to the main engines. "What's the ETA on the frigate?"

"Forty-eight hours, hopefully sooner. If the storm hits before then, we'll just have to ride it out."

"That'll be one hell of a ride, Commander." Blake had to admire the exec's cool professionalism, but he was sure they both knew what the odds were of riding out a storm on a dead ship. Destroyers went down in typhoons, even with experienced captains and all the power that twin screws and thirty thousand horsepower could bring to bear. With her engines out of commission, the *Carlyle* wouldn't have a chance. And neither would the *Latin Star*.

After a pause, the executive officer said, "Listen, Dan. This is a long shot, but it's worth mentioning. I know you sailed in the merchant marine. Have you got enough bodies there to get that ship under way?"

"Negative, sir. These ships run lean, but a crew of nine's pretty light for a ship this size, even if we knew what we were doing. Only four of these guys are engineers. None of us has ever conned a ship before."

"You might want to start thinking about it. At least you'd have a chance if the storm hits before that frigate arrives."

"Thank you, sir. I'll take that under advisement." *Long shot is the understatement of the year,* Blake thought. With a single screw and the six thousand horsepower that a C-2 could muster, the aging freighter wouldn't have much chance of surviving a tropical cyclone, even if he could get her under way.

"That's the worst-case scenario," Commander Mayfield said. "Chances are it won't be necessary. Just something to think about. For now, just secure the ship. Rig some power to the running lights and maintain radio contact. When the frigate arrives, we'll send a boat for you and your crew."

"Aye aye, sir."

"Gotta go—"

"Commander?"

"Yes?"

Blake turned his face away from the others. "A boiler couldn't do that much damage. What happened?"

"I don't know, Dan," the exec said. "It's too soon to speculate."

Blake turned back to the group. His eyes swept the anxious faces, trying to assess how they were coping. Kelly, Tobin, Robertson, Rivero . . . He paused and stared at Sergeant Rivero. The Colombian marine was a wild card he'd been dealt, one he knew absolutely nothing about. The thought crossed his mind that Rivero had been the last man to muster on the boat deck. He stared at him. The Colombian returned the look with a level gaze. Blake told himself to get a grip. If anyone was getting edgy, he was. He tossed the handset back to Kelly. All eyes were focused on him. "All right, everybody, listen up. The ship has sustained considerable damage from an accident in the engine room. Both turbines are down. They've sent a request for a tow to the Colombian Navy, and help's on the way. Our orders are to remain aboard, secure the ship, rig some power to the running lights, and maintain radio contact."

"I don't believe this," John Sparks said. "How long're we gonna be stuck aboard this tub?"

Blake shot a hard look at the electrician. "A day or two."

"Jesus Christ, Lieutenant, this weather's going to hell. Blind man could see there's a storm coming. This piece of junk won't—"

"Think of it as a great adventure, Sparky," Blake said, cutting him off. He could see the fear in the faces of the crew and didn't want them any more frightened than they already were. "Let's get started. We'll split up into three teams. Chief, take Sparky, Tobin and Robertson and survey the engine room. Check out the propulsion system, fuel supply, and see what it'll take to get some electrical power to the running lights and living quarters. Sergeant Rivero, take Jones and Alvarez and do a check of the cargo holds. Doc, I want you to look for toxic or hazardous materials. I'll check out the bridge and pilothouse and try to locate the ship's log and manifest. Kelly, bring your radio and come with me."

* * *

Blake made his way forward to the superstructure, rising pagoda-like amidships, and climbed the ladder to the cabin deck. He wiped the water from his eyes and glanced down the narrow passageway at the louvered stateroom doors, four to starboard and four to port. Black-and-white linoleum tile curling with age ran down the passageway in a checkerboard pattern.

"Staterooms?" Kelly asked.

Blake nodded. "International maritime law allows cargo ships to carry up to a dozen passengers without having a doc on board. A lot of shipping companies do it for the added revenue."

"A dozen? I count eight."

"Four singles and four doubles. Adds up to twelve."

"Are they nice?"

"They probably were once upon a time, but this ship's pretty old. I doubt if they've been used in years."

Blake made a mental note to go through them later, and continued up the ladder to the bridge deck, then on up to the bridge wing. He paused on the bridge wing to get his bearings, and Kelly came up behind him, breathing hard.

A sudden feeling of unease came over him, and he froze at the entrance to the pilothouse, motioning for Kelly to stand fast. He stood quietly for a minute, listening to the wind whistling through the superstructure, glancing around at the green bulkheads dotted with blisters of peeling paint. It was nothing he could see or hear; it was a smell. Subtle at first, a gust of wind hit the pilothouse and he got the full effect. He stood motionless, apprehensive. Kelly wrinkled her nose and started to say something. Blake held up his hand and motioned for her to stand quietly.

Blake unbuckled his holster and withdrew the Beretta. He'd never fired one before—it was one subject they didn't teach at the Merchant Marine Academy—but the heft of the automatic in his hand reassured him. He pulled the slide back and felt the round slide into the chamber. Leading with the muzzle, he twisted the latch and nudged the door inward.

The dense odor in the pilothouse seemed to offer tangible resistance against the steel door. Blake stepped over the coaming and gasped. The smell of decaying flesh and human excrement flooded his mouth with an odor he could actually taste. He covered his mouth and nose with his left hand and looked around for what he knew had to be something dead.

He found it lying by the engine-order telegraph, which had been pulled to "All Stop." The body looked like a department-store mannequin twisted in a grotesque shape. The eyes stared vacantly from the head, resting on the steel deck at a ninety-degree angle from the trunk of the body. A river of clotted, black blood flowed from the corpse's mouth in a meandering tributary that had reached the bulkhead of the pilothouse before beginning to coagulate. Near the head, in a smaller pool of congealed blood, was a small, black object that reminded Blake of a dead toad he had come across in one of his boyhood adventures. He bent closer and saw that it was a human tongue, festering with minute life-forms.

"What *is* that," Kelly said. She stepped into the pilothouse and covered her mouth and nose with her hand. "Oh, my God."

Blake stood looking down on the body, stomach churning, not sure what to do next. He holstered the automatic and noticed the outline of a wallet in the corpse's right rear pocket. He rolled the body over a few inches. It moved in one piece, frozen. An eelskin wallet slid out into his hand. He flipped it open and laid out the contents on the chart table: a sheaf of paper currency—a mix of Colombian and Uruguayan pesos—pictures of a smiling family, credit cards, a Colombian driver's license and a pocket-sized first mate's license. He looked at the smiling face in the family portrait. No one would recognize it—or even the dark face in the driver's license mug shot—as the mutilated corpse on the deck before him. He stood there for a moment, not quite knowing what to do with the wallet, and finally laid it gently beside the body.

He glanced around. The deck was littered with what remained

of the ship's radio direction finder and chronometer, key pieces of navigation equipment. Whoever had done this didn't want them going anywhere.

He walked over to the small desk where the ship's log lay open and picked it up, relieved that it was neatly hand-lettered in English. His Spanish was weak to nonexistent. The last entry was dated June 12, 0830. Today was the fourteenth. Forty-eight hours. He read the final entry and felt something move in the pit of his stomach. Forcing himself not to react, he flipped back and read the previous week's entries, then casually closed the canvas-covered book.

"Shall we contact the ship, sir?" Kelly asked.

"No. They've got their hands full. We'll make a full report when we hear back from Kozlewski and Sergeant Rivero." Based on what he'd just read in the ship's log, his first instinct was to call them back and finish the search himself, but it was imperative to get a quick assessment of what they had, and he couldn't be everywhere at once. He told himself that they'd be okay; the skittish chief was always extra cautious, and Rivero could probably handle whatever came at him.

"I wonder what *they'll* find on the love boat?"

Blake glanced at Kelly. Her face was the color of parchment. He knew from what he'd just read in the log that they were in for much worse, but he saw no point in scaring her to death. He managed a faint smile. "How do you like sea duty so far?"

"I can't wait to see what happens next."

"You won't have long to wait." Blake tucked the ship's log under his arm. "Let's go."

"Where to?"

"The captain's quarters."

Frank Kozlewski descended the ladder into the machinery space, located directly below the superstructure. Beams from battery-powered emergency lanterns, which had come on automatically when the main power had gone off, cast a yellow glow over the compartment.

"From the look of those lights, I'd say the power's been off a while," John Sparks said from behind. His voice echoed in the eerie quiet.

"A day or two, I expect." Frank Kozlewski snapped on his flashlight and carefully followed the beam of light around the catwalk, pausing to look down into the lower level of the engine room. Darting among the bulbous shapes of machinery and equipment, the flashlight beam created looming shadows that rose and fell.

"Jesus, what's that smell, Chief?" Sparks's voice rang hollow.

Frank Kozlewski wrinkled his nose and sniffed. "Smells just like every engine room I've ever been in in my life: Bunker C fuel oil, diesel fuel, and sweat." He glanced at Sparks's worried face. "You're probably smelling your own BO blowing back in your face." Kozlewski peered down into the bowels of the machinery space. "Sparky, there's the main distribution switchboard, and it looks like an emergency diesel generator right behind it." He pointed with his flashlight. "Scoot down there and see what it'll take to get some power going."

"Dark down there. How am I gonna see anything?"

"Pull a battle lantern, for Christ's sake."

"I couldn't see to take a crap with one of these things." Sparks pulled one of the lanterns from its holder on the bulkhead above the catwalk. He clambered down the ladder, grumbling under his breath, and disappeared into the blackness.

"That guy'd bitch if they hung him with an old rope," Kozlewski said. He watched as Sparks and his bobbing yellow light were swallowed up by the darkness below. "Come on, lads. Let's check out the boilers." The chief motioned to Tobin and Robertson to follow him. They walked the twenty feet or so to the ladder leading down to the port side of the machinery space, their footsteps hollow thuds against the steel catwalk.

"*Holy shit!*" Sparks came bounding back up the ladder and stood panting, his eyes glazed.

Kozlewski wheeled around. "What's the matter with you?"

His flashlight splashed across Sparks's face. A look of sheer terror etched his eyes.

"Oh, Christ. Oh, Jesus Christ. I think I'm gonna be sick."

"What is it?"

"You ain't gonna believe what's down there."

"Oh, for Christ's sake, Sparky, what is it?" Kozlewski walked back toward him with a puzzled look.

Sparks stood gasping on the narrow catwalk, head down, clinging to the handrail, spittle dripping out of his mouth in a long string. As Kozlewski approached, Sparks looked up with haunted eyes and erupted over the rail, spewing vomit into the machinery space below.

"Jesus, Sparky." Kozlewski winced at the sour smell. "What the hell is it?"

Sparks stood retching, his forehead pressed against the coolness of the steel handrail, unable to answer.

Kozlewski thought he looked pathetic, like a sick dog he had once seen puking on the sidewalk in his old neighborhood in the south side of Chicago. "Well, get out of the way." He nudged Sparks to the side and started down the ladder, with Robertson and Tobin close behind.

Kozlewski descended the dozen steel steps of the ladder slowly, stopping every few steps, playing his flashlight around the machinery space. He noticed that the rolling motion of the ship was more pronounced now. In the silence of the dead machinery space, he heard the sound of waves slapping against the hull of the ship, a sound he'd never heard in an engine room before.

Kozlewski's feet hit the corrugated steel deck plates at the end of the ladder, and he stopped, looking around cautiously, as Robertson and Tobin collided behind him.

"Get off my tail," Robertson said over his shoulder.

"Knock it off," the chief said. He stood motionless, looking with his flashlight, listening, his senses on high alert. Sparks's vomit, mingled with the other smells in the compartment, created a stench that made his stomach turn. He could hear the rasping, openmouthed breathing of Robertson and Tobin behind him. The only other sound was the muffled slapping of waves against the hull. "Come on." He pointed with the beam of his flashlight toward the glow of the lantern Sparks had dropped.

Kozlewski looked down at the dim lantern lying on its side, illuminating the face of the corpse whose blank eyes stared vacantly back. Black blood flowed from the corpse's mouth in a congealed river of nourishment for a pair of bilge rats. Red eyes sparkled in the beam of the flashlight as the rodents backed away and disappeared in the darkness. The seaman's blue chambray shirt had been chewed through. Kozlewski could see two tails sticking out of the cavernous belly like wire ropes, twitching with enjoyment. His foot came down on the tails with all the force he could muster, triggering muffled squeals from inside the corpse. The bilge rats exploded from within the belly, covered with blood and soft organ tissue, and stood hissing like snakes. The chief reached for his service pistol, then thought better of it as the rats waddled into the darkness.

"Filthy little beggars."

"Holy shit is right," Robertson said in a whisper.

Tobin softly chanted a whispered mantra that sounded on the verge of hysteria. "Oh God, blessed be Thy Name, Oh Jesus, protect us sinners—" Suddenly he let out a shriek. "*Jesus!*"

Sparks jerked his hand away from Tobin's shoulder. "It's just me."

"Don't come up behind me like that, you idiot."

Sparks edged Tobin aside and stood breathing hard, the stain of vomit down the front of his shirt. "I knew this ship was trouble. I knew it the minute I laid eyes on it. What have we got ourselves into here, Chief?"

Frank Kozlewski squatted beside the corpse and shined his flashlight into the white face. "This guy's tongue has been cut out."

Sparks screwed his face up in a grimace. "How do you know? I mean . . . where is it?"

Kozlewski aimed his flashlight down through the deck grate

into the bilges. "It was probably breakfast for our furry friends down below."

"What do we do now?"

"What do *we* do? You're going to get that emergency diesel running. I'm going to go find the lieutenant."

Seaman Luis Alvarez struggled forward on the windswept deck behind Doc Jones and Sergeant Rivero, heading for the number three cargo hold, which lay just forward of the bridge.

"How many more of these things we got to look at, anyway?" Alvarez said over the whistling wind.

"Well, we just did number five and number four," Doc Jones said. "And this is number three. That leaves two and one, by my count."

"Yeah, and we ain't seen nothing but truck batteries, and car tires, and bags of coffee."

"Don't forget the ingots of tin," Doc said.

"It's all a waste of time, if you ask me."

A huge, rolling wave broke over the weather rail, pushing them back, soaking them to the waist. "Oh, man, I just started to dry out." Alvarez's wet dungarees, swaddled tightly around his legs, made it difficult to walk on the pitching deck.

"Just don't get too close to the weather rail," Doc said, "or you're liable to get a lot wetter."

Alvarez felt a cold shudder go through him. For a moment he could actually see himself bobbing up and down, disappearing behind the swells, waving frantically as he was swept farther into the distance, while the others looked on helplessly. He shook the thought out of his mind and offered up a silent prayer to Saint Elmo, the patron saint of the sea, to protect him.

They approached the number three cargo hold, struggling to keep their balance against the rolling ship. Sergeant Rivero kicked the small hatch used for customs inspections and nodded to Alvarez.

"What am I, the official hatch opener?" Alvarez loosened the dogs on the manhole-sized hatch and slid it to one side, making just enough room to squeeze through. Sergeant Rivero went down first. Alvarez could hear Rivero's combat boots echo down the steel rungs of the ladder into the cavernous hold. Doc Jones followed, then Alvarez, grateful to be out of the weather that could sweep a man to his death in an instant.

The ladder led down about fifteen feet into the rusty-smelling air of the first level in the cargo hold. Alvarez thought it appeared to be considerably larger than the two previous holds. He stood shivering in his wet dungarees, watching Sergeant Rivero play his flashlight over what appeared to be thousands of bags marked "Winter Wheat." Rivero walked over to a pallet and unsheathed his combat knife. He plunged the Parkerized blade into the end of a random bag and stood back as a river of red wheat poured out, cascading down to the thick wooden planks supporting the first level of the hold. The slit in the bag widened, and the river of grain picked up speed, piling up on the planks and sifting through the spaces between, filtering down to the next level. A faint purring sound, like course sand hitting metal drums, rose from the second level. Alvarez noticed Sergeant Rivero cock his head and listen intently. His black eyebrows rose almost imperceptibly over narrowed eyes. Rivero made a final pass at the cargo, giving the bags a cursory up-and-down look. Jones and Alvarez followed behind, punching random bags, and headed down the ladder to the next level.

The air in the second level of the hold seemed thinner and slightly humid to Alvarez as they stepped off the ladder. He smelled a faint, pleasant scent and noticed Doc Jones wrinkle his nose and sniff in a quizzical way. He watched Sergeant Rivero beam his flashlight around at hundreds of shiny metal containers stacked on pallets. The reflections from the square containers bounced back in a kaleidoscope of colors. Alvarez yawned and stretched. The close air and pleasant scent were making him sleepy. Maybe if he showed some interest, moved around, did something. Rivero had the only flashlight, and he was tired of standing around doing nothing. He withdrew his Zippo from his pocket and stepped toward the containers.

''Put that away,'' Sergeant Rivero said.

Alvarez jumped. He hadn't heard this many words from Rivero since they'd left the *Carlyle*. ''Why? What is this stuff anyway?''

''Ether.''

''Of course,'' Doc Jones said. ''I should have recognized it right off. One flick of that lighter could blow us out of the water.'' He gave out a low whistle. ''There must be tons of this stuff. No hospital in the world could use this much ether.''

''This ether won't see the inside of a hospital,'' Sergeant Rivero said, squinting at the label of one of the containers.

Alvarez looked over his shoulder. '' 'Diethyl Ether—Highly Flammable.' So what's it for?''

Rivero ignored him and walked over to the other side of the compartment where black fifty-five-gallon drums were strapped together on pallets and stacked to the overhead. He beamed his flashlight at one of the labels and nodded his head.

Doc Jones stood behind Sergeant Rivero, reading the label over his shoulder. ''What's 'Dimethyl Ketone'?''

''Acetone,'' Rivero said after a pause.

''What's all this stuff for?'' Alvarez said.

Sergeant Rivero glanced at Alvarez with a look of contempt and started for the ladder leading down to the third level of the hold. Jones and Alvarez trailed behind. When they reached the ladder, Rivero turned and said, ''Wait here.'' They looked at each other as Rivero disappeared down the ladder into the inky depths.

With the flashlight gone, the only light filtering in to the second level of the hold was from the hatch cover Alvarez had opened on the main deck. Dusky light from the first level drifted through the cracks of the deck planks, casting weak lines of light and shadow across their faces.

''What's he doing down there, Doc?'' Alvarez could see the beam of the flashlight dart around, stride across the hold, then disappear completely.

''Beats me,'' Jones said, peering down the ladderway. ''But he seems to know what he's doing. Best do like the man says.''

"I don't like the son of a bitch. Thinks he's hot stuff, struttin' around with that knife on his ankle. I know some guys in my neighborhood, make him eat that knife." Alvarez hunkered down on the deck with his back against a pallet of ether.

Jones said nothing.

After a few minutes of silence, Alvarez said, "How come they call you Doc? They don't call the other corpsmen Doc."

Jones pointed a thumb toward the name stenciled above his shirt pocket.

Alvarez squinted at the initials. "I'll be. 'Jones, M.D.' I never noticed that. What does it stand for?"

"Mohammed DuWayne. My old man was a Black Muslim. My mother liked the name DuWayne. It was a compromise." Jones looked at Alvarez and smiled. "How come they call you Muskrat?"

"They don't, if they know what's good for 'em." Alvarez looked at Doc Jones and saw the friendly smile. He looked down at his feet. "I went over the side once on maneuvers. When they fished me out they said I looked like a drownded muskrat."

They sat in the near darkness making small talk. It suddenly seemed to Alvarez that they'd been sitting there for a long time. "How long's he been down there, Doc?"

Jones squinted at his watch, holding it up to a slit of light. "I don't know. Fifteen minutes, maybe."

"Corpsman," Sergeant Rivero called out from below.

"Yo," Jones shouted down the ladder.

"Down here." Rivero played his flashlight on the ladder.

Jones swung his canvas medical bag over his shoulder and started down the ladder. Alvarez followed close behind.

The final level of the number three hold was pitch-dark except for Sergeant Rivero's flashlight and the weak beam of a single battery-powered emergency lantern in a far corner. Jones and Alvarez stepped off the ladder and turned to face the white beam of light coming from Sergeant Rivero, standing about ten feet away.

"Over here." Rivero directed the corpsman with the beam

of light. The air was close and warm, and Alvarez could feel the heat that radiated from Sergeant Rivero's back as he followed behind.

Alvarez stared down, fascinated. A crumpled, dark mass lay on the deck near stacks of what appeared to be some kind of baled cargo. Jones bent over the body and rolled it over. The flashlight beam hit the corpse full on in the face. Alvarez recoiled at the open mouth, full of clotted blood.

"Jesus," Jones said after he'd examined the body. "This guy's really messed up. Broken neck. Broken back. Looks like he's been hit by a truck." He asked Sergeant Rivero for the flashlight and looked into the gaping mouth. "Somebody gave this guy a tonsillectomy, and then some. His tongue's been sliced out, clean as a whistle."

Alvarez had seen a few drive-by shootings in the streets of East LA, but he'd never seen anything like this. The corpse had a look of horror frozen on its face that he knew he'd never forget. His stomach flirted with the idea of getting sick; it had started to rise at one point, but he had willed it back down. No way was he going to show his ass in front of these guys, especially that *macho* prick Rivero. He took a few casual steps backward and drifted away from the scene, toward the flickering lantern in the far corner of the hold.

He walked down a narrow passageway created by stacks of palletized cargo. Running his hand along the sides of the passageway, feeling his way, he felt the contours of small pillow-shaped bales behind heavy sheets of plastic. The dying glow of the lantern emerged from behind the pallets at the end of the passageway, casting a yellow glow over the cargo and the entrance to what appeared to be a steel vault.

Alvarez adjusted his eyes to the dim light. The cargo was clearly visible now as he got closer to the lantern. Behind the blue plastic sheets were small bundles, each wrapped in clear plastic over heavy, brown paper. Alvarez unsnapped a key ring hanging from his dungarees and opened his pocketknife. He made a small cut through the outer layer of plastic, and inserted the long blade of the knife into one of the packages. He carefully withdrew the blade with a tiny pyramid of white, crystalline powder drifting over the sides. He stuck his tongue to the powder and spit, his stomach rebelling at the bitter taste.

"Well, kiss my ass," he whispered to himself. Alvarez was no stranger to coke—he'd been a small-time dealer at one point in his juvenile career—but this was big-time, more kilos than he could count of the purest shit he'd ever tasted. One or two of these could set him up for life. It was like nothing he'd ever seen or imagined.

He turned his attention to the steel vault with renewed interest. The heavy door was standing ajar. He pulled it all the way open on smooth ball bearings, allowing the weak beam of the lantern to push back the darkness several feet into the vault. Beyond the penetration of the lantern, the vault was pitch-black. Removing the emergency lantern from its brackets on the bulkhead, he crept inside.

Alvarez could feel that the vault was huge. The fading light of the lantern could only penetrate a short distance, but his muffled footsteps echoing up to the steel ceiling and outward to the steel walls indicated that it was much bigger than it had appeared. It felt cool and humid inside, something like being in a cave, he imagined, although he'd never been in one. He turned his light toward the cartons stacked neatly in rows. Waxy cardboard boxes were stacked floor to ceiling, and left to right as far as he could see. Marked only with a serial number, the cartons offered no clue as to their contents. He pulled one down from the top and guessed its weight at twenty-five or thirty pounds. Snapping open his pocketknife, he slit the strip of duct tape running down the center. Alvarez pulled the flaps up and stared in amazement at rows of green-and-black United States currency.

"Holy Mother of God," he said in a whisper, his eyes transfixed by the numerals "100" flanking the round face of Benjamin Franklin, whose eyes twinkled out from behind an orange currency band. Hesitating for a moment, he reached for one of the bundles as though it was a mirage that would disappear if he tried to touch it. His fingers on the silken paper told

him it was real. It even smelled real. Holding the small bundle
in his sweating hand, he riffled the bills with his thumb. Ben
Franklin's eyes twinkled out from his oval portrait, smiling
at him one hundred times. The orange currency band said
"$10000."

"Ten grand," he breathed in a whisper. He looked around.
As far as his light would travel, the cartons were stacked.
Hundreds of them. His numb fingers stuffed the small bundle
equal to a year's pay inside his shirt. He stood up and walked
deeper into the vault. He couldn't see an end to it. There must
be hundreds of millions of dollars here, he figured. How could
he even count it? The boxes were going by faster now. He
wondered if all the boxes contained hundred-dollar bills, and
if they did, how to calculate twenty-five or thirty pounds of
$10,000 packets. How many packets to a carton? How many
hundreds of cartons? His brain grew numb, then giddy at the
thought.

His calculations stopped when his foot came down on the
spongy inner wrist of a forearm. The fingers of a huge hand
curled around his ankle, locking it in a viselike grip, each finger
a band of steel. Alvarez tried to scream, but his throat was
paralyzed. He tried to pull away, but the more he struggled,
the tighter the bands constricted. His bowels grew warm and
turned to sludge. Pure adrenaline surged through his veins as
he stomped crazily on the fleshy human trap with his free foot.
The grip tightened. He kicked at the arm, then backward into
the barrel chest with his heel, flailing wildly, nearly falling
over. Regaining his balance, he stomped at the head, grinding
his foot into the face. Feeling the grip loosen for an instant, he
wrenched free and ran for the exit like Satan himself was behind
him. He tripped over a carton and fell flat, his lantern skating
across the steel deck of the vault like a frozen pond. Flickering
from the blow, the lantern nearly went out, then recovered with
a tiny beam. He pulled himself up and stumbled forward, toward
the lantern lying facedown on the deck. Scooping it up, he ran,
following its beam wherever it would take him, as long as it
was away from this place, out of this nightmare. The echo of

his own footsteps reverberated behind him, gaining on him. He was sobbing now, pleading with the Holy Virgin, begging Her to save him, when he collided against the solid frame of a man.

"You have no business in here," Sergeant Rivero said.

Alvarez stared up at him, openmouthed, gasping for breath. "Somebody grabbed my ankle in there."

"Where?"

"Over there . . . over there in the corner."

Sergeant Rivero pushed Alvarez aside and started into the vault, shining his flashlight down the narrow pathway between the stacked cartons. Doc Jones followed close behind and Alvarez scampered to catch up.

The darting beam of light gave Alvarez a truer picture of the size of the vault. It appeared to be twenty-five or thirty feet square and perhaps twelve feet high. Stacked cardboard cartons left just enough room for narrow, mazelike passageways between them. In the far corner of the vault, a crumpled form was sprawled like a pile of dirty laundry. The beam of the flashlight bathed the figure in a pitiless, white light. Rivero stood, stoically staring at the still form, with Alvarez standing on tiptoes, trying to see over his shoulder.

"Is he dead?" Alvarez said.

Sergeant Rivero stood sideways in the passageway, allowing just enough room for Jones to squeeze by with his medic kit.

Jones took the L-shaped flashlight and knelt beside the body. The head was turned at an awkward angle from the trunk, the eyes staring dully through slits. He pressed his fingers against the bull neck and shook his head. He paused for a moment, then shined the light into the open mouth and stood up.

"What's the matter with him, Doc?"

"Appears to be a broken neck."

Alvarez looked down at the outstretched hand that had held him in a death grip just minutes before and shuddered. Suddenly fascinated from his vantage point of safety, he stared into the face of the corpse, a face that looked strangely familiar. Alvarez thought he looked like Sergeant Rivero; same high cheekbones, faintly reddish brown complexion, thin beard . . . clearly some kind of Indian-Spanish mix. Alvarez had heard Sergeant Rivero called a mestizo, and he figured that this guy must be the same thing. But whatever he was, he was one big dude. It was hard to tell how big, looking at this crumpled pile of flesh, but he appeared to be at least six-five, maybe more, and built like a wrestler. Whoever or whatever had dispatched him, Luis Alvarez would want no part of.

"Is he dead?" Alvarez asked again.

"Yeah," Doc said. "But that ain't the scary part."

"You mean his tongue—"

"I mean this guy's fresh. Let's get the hell out of here."

Chapter Six

Jorge Cordoba ran a hand through his hair and paced across Don Gallardo's study, glancing at the door, waiting for the latch to turn. What would he say to Don Gallardo? What could he say? Ayala had already implicated him. It would only make things worse to deny it.

He looked at his watch. Thirty minutes had passed in the silence of the room since Don Gallardo had told him to wait. He shook his head and resumed pacing, trying to fight off the feeling of numbness. He would never have guessed in a thousand years that his godfather would be capable of murder. He'd heard talk of killings in the organization, of course, but actually to see one, and one done by Don Gallardo himself. . . . He could still see the look of terror on Rafael Ayala's face just before the impact. He reached for a cigarette and noticed that his hand trembled.

He took a deep drag, told himself to relax, and glanced around the Don's study. It was a man's room. Shafts of sunlight drifted in through the French windows behind the massive oak desk. Big-game trophies hung like monuments to death on one suede-covered wall. On the opposite side of the room, oak bookcases were lined with leather-bound classics that looked as if they'd never been opened. Beams of sunlight splashed through glass cases filled with dazzling displays of pre-Colombian gold artifacts. The gold pieces made Jorge's stomach churn. The plan was in ruins, and so, he knew, was his appointment as chief of finance.

But loss of a title was the least of his problems, after what he'd just seen. Loss of this shipment would place the entire organization at risk. If he was linked to that disaster, and he had been, he knew his status as Don Gallardo's godson wouldn't save him.

Jorge lit another cigarette and drew the smoke deep into his lungs, trying to calm the churning in his stomach. He exhaled a thin stream of smoke and resumed pacing. The only thing that could save him now would be for him to recover the ship, but to take an active role in that would take him farther into a side of the organization he'd been able to avoid until now.

He thought about his parents, and how they'd fought to keep him out of it. Before the rift, Don Gallardo and Jorge's father had been family friends and business associates, senior vice presidents in one of Colombia's largest banking houses, until the Don had seen the potential in another line of business. But the real falling-out came when he saw Jorge's talent as a young bond trader and offered him a wonderful opportunity within the new organization. His parents had strenuously objected to his involvement until their deaths eight years ago. Jorge was only twenty years old at the time, and had been devastated by the tragic accident, but that had ended the debate.

He knew it was an unsavory business, but he needed a home, and Don Gallardo had convinced him that he would be protected from the dark side of the business; he only wanted his financial expertise, he said, his genius for making strategic investments that would take the organization where it needed to go. He rubbed his eyes, cursing himself for being such a fool. He had no choice now but to take the next step. He had to convince the Don to put him in charge of the task force to recover the ship.

His pacing was interrupted by a commotion outside the window. Steel gates were clanging, men were shouting, the big cats were snarling and fighting. He walked over to the French windows behind the desk and looked down. The compound had been situated so that Don Gallardo could swivel his chair around and watch his prized African lions feed on their daily ration of horse meat. He knew that Don Gallardo occasionally sent live horses in for the cats. Broodmares from his stable of purebred Paso Finos that were too old to breed, or foals that had been born with genetic defects. It satisfied their natural instincts to kill, he said. He enjoyed putting on these shows for the board members after their monthly meetings. Jorge had never forgotten the first one, and the only one, he had ever seen. The pathetic old mare, nostrils flaring, eyes bulging in terror, prancing back and forth, neighing pitifully while the cats lay quietly, grooming themselves, seemingly oblivious to the mare, taking their time. Then slowly, the females sauntering into formation, two on each side of the mare, edging her into a corner, the lightning spring, the claw marks raking her sides, the numbing bite on the back of the neck that brought her down, the throat being torn out while she bleated like a lamb being slaughtered. Then the male sauntering over after the kill, going for the soft underbelly and the choice parts of the rump, his muzzle red with blood. Jorge had been repulsed by it, but he'd noticed the expression on Rafael Ayala's face. He had looked orgasmic. After that experience, Jorge had always made it a point to leave for some prearranged business immediately after board meetings.

From above, the big-cat compound looked like a small island, landscaped with boulders and tropical plants, surrounded by a concrete moat. The African lions, one large male and four females, were the crown jewels in Don Gallardo's collection. The big cats were fighting over bloody chunks of meat. Odd, he thought. He knew they were fed once a day, in the evening. Looking closer, he saw the big male licking at a long, slender piece of meat—white meat—while two females were shredding what appeared to be the remains of a dark suit. He heard the door click behind him and swiveled around.

"Magnificent, aren't they?" Don Gallardo said.

Jorge felt his stomach turn. The musky feline smell of the lion compound coming in through the open window suddenly seemed repulsive. He stared at Don Gallardo as though seeing him for the first time.

"What's going on down there?"

"Did you know that on the African plain it is the lioness that makes the kill?" Don Gallardo removed his coat and hung it up. "The lions are like males everywhere. They eat, sleep, and fuck."

Jorge stared down on the compound. *"Madre de Dios."* The words escaped from his mouth in a dry whisper. "What have you done?"

Don Gallardo raised his eyebrows. "What have I done to deserve such disrespect from my godson? Come and sit down, Jorge. We have a problem."

"How could you put him in there like a piece of meat? I didn't like him, but he was a human being."

"Who?"

"Rafael Ayala."

Don Gallardo's face grew dark, a hint of the raging mask Jorge had seen before in the executive committee meeting. "I only hope my cats don't get sick from eating his filthy flesh."

Jorge stared down at the compound. He felt the blood drain from his face. "Was he . . . Was he dead?"

"What difference does it make? He is now. Sit down."

Jorge walked around to the front of Don Gallardo's desk and sat down, grateful to ease the quaking in his legs. He gripped the arms of the chair and gazed at his godfather, trying to reconcile the man seated before him with the man he'd seen standing behind Rafael Ayala.

Augusto Gallardo cut the tip off a Cuban cigar as big as a sausage and lit it, watching Jorge out of the corner of his eye. He exhaled a stream of blue smoke and pitched a gold Dunhill lighter onto his desk. "I can see that you have no taste for the realities of business.'' He leaned back in his chair. ''I've recommended you to the confederation for the position of chief of finance. Perhaps I've made a mistake.''

''This isn't what I bargained for when you hired me away from the bank. You assured me I would never be involved in anything like this. Perhaps my parents were right.''

Don Gallardo's eyes flashed. ''Yes, let's talk about your parents. Who took you in when they died? I did. And this is the way you repay me.'' He paused and leaned back in his chair. His tone softened. ''You disappoint me, Jorge. We've struggled for the past eight years to build an organization, to wrest control away from the Ramirez butchers—''

''The *Ramirez* butchers!''

''. . . to develop a plan that will ensure our long-term survival. Now that we're ready to make the first move, you allow this to happen.''

''I don't see how I can be blamed for this—''

''You alone in the organization knew what it meant if we lost this shipment. Yet you stood idly by while Ayala made a decision that placed not only the confederation but the entire organization at risk.''

''But you know that fool. He's always shooting his mouth off about some scheme or another. No one thought he'd actually—''

''Knew him, Jorge. Past tense. He is no longer with us. And he will have company very soon if that shipment is not recovered. Do you understand?''

Jorge's mouth suddenly felt dry. The icy look in Don Gallardo's eyes sent a chill through Jorge that seemed to still his blood. It was time to replace righteous indignation and denial with self-preservation. ''Yes, Godfather.''

Don Gallardo snorted with disgust, tapping his cigar. ''Godfather. Yes, I'm your godfather. And have I not been your godfather in every sense of the word? Have I not met my obligation to your parents since their tragic deaths? Have I not provided you with a place in the organization? Have I not provided you with the finest education, even at the cost of a

five-million-dollar endowment just to get you into that arrogant
school in North America?''

"You've been more than generous. I'm grateful for all
you've done—''

Don Gallardo held up his hand. "It's not about money. It
goes way beyond that. I've tried to teach you things, Jorge,
important things about the history of our country, about the
higher purpose of our organization, and about the dangers we
face from outside. But you still don't understand." He leaned
forward and steepled his fingers under his nose, staring intently
at Jorge. "When I was a boy, my father took me to the world-
famous National Gold Museum, to see the remains of Colombia's once-fabulous treasure. It was housed in the basement of
the *Banca de la República,* in downtown Bogotá. I was struck
by its simple beauty: ear and nose ornaments of the *Sinu* people,
decorative pins from the *Calima* tribe, necklaces and breast-
plates made by the *Chibcha* Indians from as early as 300 A.D.
The pieces were exquisite, but I was saddened at the pathetic
remnants. Look around you, Jorge." Don Gallardo waved his
hand at the glass cases around the room. "What you see here
is the largest collection of pre-Colombian gold outside the
Museo del Oro. These few trinkets are the pitiful remains of
the incredible wealth our country once had before it was looted
by the Spaniards. And when the country was stripped of its
gold, it went into a decline that lasted for centuries, while Spain
dominated much of the world. I keep them here in my study
as a daily reminder of the power of gold.''

Jorge had heard the stories before, but nodded.

"You nod as though you understand, Jorge. But I don't think
you do. I've tried to teach you, but I can see that I've failed.
Perhaps it's my fault. I've spoiled you just as I've spoiled my
natural children." He looked at Jorge's blank expression and
slammed his fist on the desk. "We're in a war, damn it. The
Norte Americanos wish to destroy us. The lessons of the past
are clear; in the long term there is only one defense. I have
studied history, Jorge, and I know. Gold is the one constant,
the one thing on earth with inherent, intrinsic value, the one

true form of wealth. This is the only way we can ever be free of foreign tyranny. And we have a plan to achieve it, a plan brilliant in its simplicity, a plan based on the systematic conversion of the world's lowest-level commodity into the highest.'' Don Gallardo launched into his well-worn litany, ticking off each point on a thick finger. "We will convert the leaf of the humble coca plant into paste, the paste into white powder, the white powder into paper, and the paper into gold. And with the gold will come the power to bring the *yanquis* to their knees.''

"I understand—"

"Even assuming you do, understanding is not enough,'' Don Gallardo said, standing up. "Execution is everything, and you, quite simply, have failed.'' He walked around the desk and stood, looking down on Jorge.

Jorge stiffened at the word "execution.'' Used with the word "failed,'' it had an ominous ring. He decided that now was not the time for moralizing. He sat motionless and carefully chose his words.

"All right, I have to admit that everything you've said is true. I'm not going to make any more excuses. But given all that you concede that I've done for the organization, I think I should have a chance to redeem myself.'' Jorge glanced up to test the reaction and noticed a slight softening of the steel-blue eyes.

"What did you have in mind?"

"Let me do it. Let me recover the ship.''

"You?'' A smile crossed Don Gallardo's face.

"Why not? I see it as a management problem, like any other.''

"You wouldn't know where to begin.'' Don Gallardo looked at him like an amused father watching his child try for something over his head.

"This isn't brain surgery. The first step is to find out the status, where it is, whether it's still afloat or not.''

"And how would you do that?''

"We've got more than a dozen planes. We'll begin a search

immediately, a systematic sweep of the entire route of the ship if necessary."

"The route of the ship covers the area from Buenaventura to Montevideo. It would take days, weeks, to sweep such a territory."

"We can narrow it down. We can estimate the position of the ship, based on the length of time it's been at sea, its approximate speed."

Don Gallardo shook his head. "We only know the time of the last radio contact. We don't know if the ship has stopped or is still under way. If the *mudo* has disabled the ship's officers, it could be steaming unmanned in circles or in any direction. Even a slow cargo vessel could steam hundreds of miles in forty-eight hours. It could be anywhere. No, we would have to have at least an approximate location if we are to have any chance of finding it."

"Do you remember that admiral from Bogotá? You introduced Isabella and me to him and his wife at a party, right here on the estate. His name started with a C."

"Cuartas."

"That's right, Admiral Cuartas. From the amount of gold on him, he can get us the information we need."

Don Gallardo stood rubbing his chin. He looked down at Jorge and smiled. "Perhaps your stay in North America did you some good, after all. It must have been all those Rambo movies. He leaned across his desk and held down the button on his intercom. "Get me Admiral Cuartas in Bogotá."

"Good morning, Admiral," Don Gallardo said into the telephone. He swiveled around to face Jorge. "I apologize for calling at so early an hour."

Jorge watched anxiously as Don Gallardo leaned back in his chair, and spent a full five minutes smoothly engaging in the polite chitchat necessary before any business can be discussed in Colombia. The status and health of wives and children was covered in great detail on both sides before he got down to business.

"Admiral, I'm sorry to trouble you with something so trivial," Don Gallardo said, switching on the speakerphone, "but an awkward situation has developed within one of my shipping companies. It seems that one of our cargo ships has ceased radio contact."

"Oh? I'm sorry to hear that," Admiral Cuartas's aristocratic voice came through the speaker, reviving Jorge's memory of their meeting. Jorge had been introduced to the admiral and his wife at one of Don Gallardo's weekend extravaganzas. He remembered him as an impressive man, a patrician with the elegant manners of one born to wealth and privilege, but Jorge thought he now detected a note of caution in his voice.

"I'm sure there's a logical explanation," Don Gallardo went on, "but we hesitate to announce that it's missing; a public search for it would be a source of embarrassment for our company. I'm sure you understand."

"Of course. What is the name of the ship?"

"The *Latin Star,* a cargo freighter registered in Panama."

"Its route?"

"Buenaventura to Montevideo, with scheduled stops at ports in Peru and Argentina."

"And its cargo?"

"The usual commerce between countries; truck batteries, grain, machinery, the usual things."

"Then, of course, it's fully insured."

"For the most part," Don Gallardo said. "However, the ship does contain some special cargo—I won't bore you with the details—for which we were unable to obtain insurance."

"I see," Admiral Cuartas said. "How can I help you?"

"I wondered if you could provide us with any information that may have come across your desk as to its status and position."

The pause that followed stopped just short of being impolite, Jorge thought. "Just a minute," Admiral Cuartas said. "We received a dispatch this morning from the Pacific Command

Headquarters in Buenaventura about an incident involving a freighter.'' The sound of muffled commands came through the speaker.

Don Gallardo tapped his cigar against a lead crystal ashtray. Jorge stared at him, amazed at his calm demeanor.

''Yes,'' Admiral Cuartas said over the rustle of paper. ''The Pacific Command relayed a radio transmission from a US Navy destroyer early this morning. Here it is. An unidentified cargo freighter of the C-2 class, found dead in the water 250 miles off the coast of Peru. Picked up by radar at 0430 hours this morning.''

Jorge felt a film of cold sweat on his forehead. If the Americans had impounded the freighter, the game was over. Processing plants throughout Latin America would be shut down for lack of chemicals to process coca paste. Trade routes supplying the finished product to Europe would be disrupted. Much needed cash flow would dry up. The short-term commitments he'd made in Uruguay and Argentina to finance Don Gallardo's aggressive plan would be in default, placing holdings worth billions at risk. The future viability of the confederation would be in serious doubt, and so, Jorge knew, would be his own existence.

''Did the American ship take the freighter into custody?'' Don Gallardo's voice was as calm as if he were inquiring about the weather.

''No. Apparently they dispatched a boarding party—the ship's engineering officer and a small group of support people—to lend assistance.''

''And?''

''The destroyer became disabled shortly after—an explosion of unknown origin in the engine room. They've requested a tow from the Colombian Navy.''

''And the US Navy people?''

''Still aboard, apparently. 'Unable to recover due to high seas,' according to the dispatch.''

''Do you have a location?''

There was another long pause. ''Approximately 10 degrees

35 minutes south latitude and 82 degrees 14 minutes west longitude,'' Admiral Cuartas said. "We're preparing to dispatch the frigate *Padilla*."

"To what end?"

"To take the destroyer under tow."

"And the freighter?"

"The captain of the frigate is under orders to impound the freighter and return it to Buenaventura, if he can do so safely."

"And if not?"

"If he deems it a hazard to navigation, he is cleared to sink it, at his discretion."

Jorge felt his stomach tighten.

"Obviously, neither event would be in our best interests," Don Gallardo said, making notes.

"I'm sorry, my friend," Admiral Cuartas said. "I hope your loss is not too severe, but there is really nothing I can do."

"The frigate could be delayed."

"Obviously I cannot do that. The destroyer is in the path of a tropical cyclone. The frigate will have to steam at flank speed to reach it in time, as it is."

"I see."

"I have tried to be helpful in the past with small requests, Don Gallardo, but there are limits."

"I understand."

"I hope you do. Our friendship goes back many years, but you must understand there are some things I cannot do."

"Of course. Forgive me for asking," Don Gallardo said. "I apologize for imposing on you."

"Not at all. I'm glad you appreciate my position."

"Certainly."

Jorge watched with a sinking feeling as Don Gallardo acquiesced, leaning back in his chair, launching into small talk for the next several minutes, bringing the conversation to a close. Warm good-byes had been exchanged when Don Gallardo said, "Oh, by the way. I meant to ask you. How is your youngest daughter?"

There was a pause. "She's very well."

"She's now eleven?"

"Twelve."

"Has she given her debut yet?"

"Yes, with the Philharmonic in Bogotá," Admiral Cuartas said, warming to the subject. "Mozart's Piano Concerto number 22 in E flat major, a very difficult piece." His voice swelled with pride.

"She shows much promise for one so young," Don Gallardo said. "Take good care of her. It would be a tragedy if anything kept her from reaching her full potential."

The speakerphone hummed in the corner of the desk for what seemed a full thirty seconds before Admiral Cuartas spoke.

"Twelve hours." His voice was dead with contempt.

"And your son," Don Gallardo said. "I understand he is in his final year at the Naval Academy in Cartagena. Perhaps he will follow in your footsteps one day. You must be very proud."

"Eighteen hours. No more."

"I don't wish to impose."

There was another pause. "Not at all."

"You've been extremely helpful, Admiral. It will not be forgotten." Don Gallardo switched off the speakerphone and looked at Jorge.

Jorge felt the blood return to his face. He stared at Don Gallardo with a look of astonishment. "I can't believe you did that."

"Did what?"

"Threatened the man's children."

"I threatened no one," Don Gallardo said. "All men have priorities. I merely probed a bit to determine his."

Jorge stared at him without speaking.

Don Gallardo's face flushed. "Grow up, Jorge. You've lived a fairy-tale existence for too long, cavorting around the world in your four-thousand-dollar suits, hobnobbing with your investment banker friends, keeping a blind eye to the realities of the business. You can't be a Boy Scout if you're going to survive in this world. The lives of a few mean nothing compared with what's at stake here." He tore off a sheet of notepaper with the location of the ship and handed it to Jorge. "We have an eighteen-hour lead to locate the ship and retake control before the arrival of the frigate. All operations have been canceled. Our fleet of aircraft is standing by. I've named Enrique Lopez acting director of security, replacing Rafael Ayala. He's in Peru, at the Command Center in Campanilla, waiting for your instructions."

Jorge gulped down his cold coffee and stood up. "I've got some fires to put out in Montevideo. Quintero's not cooperating."

"Fine. Get down there and handle it, but get Lopez started before you go. I want all our jet aircraft in the air immediately. I want that area screened in a crisscross pattern, grid by grid. When the precise location of the ship is determined, our helicopters will go in; the first wave will land security people aboard to secure the ship, the second will land a replacement crew to get the ship under way and sail it to the nearest friendly port. I want you to board in the second wave and take personal charge of the shipment from that point forward."

"What about the destroyer?"

"A disabled destroyer won't pose any threat. Our American-made helicopters will provide all the support necessary."

Jorge had approved the purchase of the two UH-60 Blackhawk helicopters from Israel, purchased through an Iranian intermediary. He'd thought the expense for the combat-ready helicopters and pilot training was excessive, and had tried to dissuade Don Gallardo, but now saw the wisdom of being prepared. The helicopters could prove to be the key to their survival. His godfather was right. He had much to learn about the business.

"And if the Americans are still aboard the freighter?"

Don Gallardo's eyes smiled. "It's time to use your newfound *cojones* for something besides pleasure," he said. "You can preside over their burial at sea."

Chapter Seven

Daniel Blake descended the ladderway to the passenger deck and paused at the door of the captain's quarters. The smell coming through the louvers of the door confirmed the scrawled entry he'd read in the ship's log. He sucked in his breath and glanced at Kelly.

"Brace yourself."

"I'm braced."

Leaving his side arm holstered, he pushed the door inward and stepped over the coaming. The smell pushed him back. He steadied himself and adjusted his eyes to the light. Fighting back the urge to vomit, he covered his mouth and nose with his hand and made his way across the room. Twisting open the brass dogs over a porthole, he swung it open and locked it back. A thin stream of light filtered in through the algae-covered glass.

His eyes took in the room at a glance: gray metal desk, safe with peeling green paint welded to the bulkhead, wooden bunk, faded green bedspread, small round table. A porterhouse steak and baked potato covered with cheese sauce sat half-eaten on a bamboo tray. A nearly empty beer bottle rolled around the table with an eerie droning sound. The lime green walls were decorated with yellowed posters, curling with age. Over the bunk, a bikini-clad beauty smiled from the swimming pool of a Cartagena beach resort. On the bulkhead over the safe, the St. Pauli Girl served up frothy steins of beer with a gaiety that seemed absurdly out of place.

The captain of the *Latin Star* lay near the open safe door, glassy eyes staring up at the buxom redhead. Blake recoiled. Knowing what to expect hadn't lessened the impact of seeing it. He instinctively turned away and winced at the unfinished meal on the tray. He forced himself to look back and felt his stomach move. The captain's severed tongue matched the color of the steak; the black blood in his mouth was the consistency of the cheese sauce on the potato. His outstretched hand lay just a few inches from a revolver and box of spilled cartridges near the open safe door. Steeling himself against a feeling of nausea, Blake picked up the revolver and looked at it. It was a .38 caliber Smith & Wesson with a two-inch barrel, a Chief's Special. The five-cartridge cylinder was loaded, but still open. Snapping the cylinder back in place, he hefted the stainless-steel piece and slowly shook his head. ''Looks like he lost the race.''

Kelly didn't say anything. She was staring down at the body, her face the color of bread dough. Blake noticed her eyelids begin to flutter. Jamming the revolver in his hip pocket, he pulled the bedspread from the captain's bunk, twirled it over the corpse, and edged her toward the bed.

''Come over here and sit down.''

''No.'' Kelly pulled away, glassy-eyed. ''I'm okay.''

''Just sit for a minute.'' Blake eased her down on the edge of the bunk and removed her radio backpack. Stepping into the bathroom, he turned the water on full blast. The pipes rattled and hummed, and coughed out water that looked like lemonade. He waited for it to clear and filled a plastic cup. Kelly was sitting in the same position when he returned.

''Here, drink this.''

Blake closed her hands around the cup and thought they

felt cold. She stared blankly across the room without saying anything, while he removed her helmet and loosened her life jacket. He opened the porthole above the bunk. Wet, cool air whistled into the stateroom, blowing wisps of her hair around. The organic smell of the sea gradually displaced the smell of death and decay. He knelt down, looking into her face. Neither spoke for a moment.

Kelly took a deep breath and looked at the cup in her hand. "Sorry. I thought I'd be better at this."

"You're doing fine."

"Sure. I see a dead body and nearly faint."

"Don't worry about it. This isn't something we see every day."

Kelly looked at him and screwed up her face. "I get the feeling we're going to see more of it."

Blake nodded. "I'm afraid so."

"I'll try to get my act together." She stared over at the covered body as if to steel herself. "It's just that . . . that tongue business."

"Forget it. The only thing that kept me from barfing was you."

"Me?"

"Sure. How would it look for an officer to toss his cookies in front of an enlisted type?"

Kelly laughed. "I can see that Melinda was right."

"Melinda?"

"Davidson, the new radar tech who came aboard with me. She was excited about me being picked to go with you. Finally, the women get in on a little action."

"What was she right about?"

Kelly shook her head. "Forget it. I shouldn't have said anything."

"Suit yourself."

"She said you're not like most officers."

Blake laughed. "That's part of my problem."

"She meant it in a nice way. Just that you're not a stuffy type."

Blake looked at her. It was the first time he'd seen her uncovered. Her reddish brown hair was cut short in a feminine version of a military haircut. Strands of auburn hair skittered around her forehead. He hadn't paid that much attention before, but now that he looked at her, he could see what all the fuss had been about when she'd reported aboard. Large brown eyes, widespread under arching eyebrows, set off by a straight nose, white teeth, and full mouth. He knew she wasn't wearing makeup—she'd been roused out of the sack like they all had—but she was pretty, Blake thought. Not drop-dead beautiful like Vicki, but pretty. The blood returning to her face brought her cheeks back to their normal glow. The first time he'd seen her on the boat deck of the *Carlyle,* he'd thought she had a well-engineered tan, but seeing her up close it was obvious that the slightly golden cast of her skin was natural. He wondered if she had some Spanish or Italian blood somewhere in her history.

"Just sit here for a minute," Blake said. "I need to find the manifest." He walked over to the open safe, pulled the door back, and secured it to a hook welded to the bulkhead. Kneeling, he reached inside and retrieved a sheaf of paper from the top shelf.

He thumbed through the stack. The documents appeared to be routine shipboard paperwork for the most part: customs declarations, payroll records, copies of memoranda. On the third shelf down he found a thin folder marked *Manifesto*. He turned it over in his hands and looked at it skeptically; it was too clean to be a working manifest. It wasn't unusual for merchant ships carrying illicit cargo to carry dual manifests: one to be handed over to knowing port officials with a wink, and one that reflected the actual cargo for the owners. Odd that the real manifest wouldn't be here, he thought, looking at the empty floor of the safe. He started to get up and did a double take. Tiny scratch marks lined the base of the floor. He ran his thumb along the edge. The scratches felt fresh. Glancing around, he picked up a knife from the captain's dinner tray and pried up the floor. A manila envelope with *Confidencial* stamped across it in red letters lay in a shallow compartment. Bingo.

He carried it over to the table where the beer bottle was still weaving its monotonous pattern and shoved the moldering food to one side.

He ran his eye down the official list of cargo and started to whistle, but his mouth was suddenly dry. Thirty-six tons of ether. Twenty-four tons of acetone. A total of sixty tons of highly flammable chemicals that could blow a crater in the ocean a mile wide and a mile deep. They were sitting on a floating bomb with a storm coming that would toss them around like a chip of wood. If that cargo ignited, the storm would be the least of their worries. A film of cool sweat broke out across his forehead. He didn't think they could be in more trouble than they were until he turned the page.

A list of pallets loaded with cocaine ran down the page by serial number, with the number of kilos each contained. He flipped back through the pages to get to the total: thirty tons. *Good God.* He remembered reading somewhere that the price for a kilo of cocaine was $40,000. He tried to compute the value of thirty tons of cocaine at that price and was so overwhelmed by the arithmetic he had to stop. They were sitting on a bomb, all right. A time bomb, and it was ticking loudly. He turned the page.

The next page began with a list of numbered cartons and the amount of cash each contained. The list of cartons ran for thirty pages, segregated in descending order by the US dollar denomination of their contents. The list of one-hundred-dollar-denominated cartons ran several pages, followed by a list of fifty-dollar cartons for nine or ten pages, then page after page of twenty-dollar-denominated cartons. He turned to the last page and stared at the grand total. It had to be a mistake. There wasn't that much money in the world. He read it again: 350 million US dollars.

Head spinning, he flipped through the manifest, piecing together the route of the freighter and the destination of the cargo. The ship had been en route from Buenaventura, Colombia, to Montevideo, Uruguay, through Drake's Passage with stops scheduled for Peru and Argentina. The chemicals were destined for a cocaine processing lab in the Peruvian jungle, someplace called Campanilla, near the source of the coca leaf. The finished product was destined for Argentina for repackaging and transshipment to Europe, with Spain as the intended port of entry. The cash was bound for Montevideo, Uruguay.

He laid the manifest facedown on the table and looked off into the corner, his heart racing in his chest. They were in trouble. Big trouble. The owners of this cargo had to be one of the major players in Colombia, and they wouldn't just walk away from it. They were probably prepared to write off an occasional loss—that was part of the game—but not one like this. They would be coming, were probably on their way at that very minute. He thought about the helicopter landing pad on the fantail. What would he do with the *Carlyle* disabled? One marine with a rifle and a pair of pistols in the hands of two engineers who couldn't shoot straight would be laughable against the kind of assault those people could launch.

He became aware of Kelly's eyes on him and stuffed the manifest back into the envelope. He looked at his watch. It was eleven-thirty. He glanced at her and smiled. "Feel better?"

"I'm okay." She brushed her hair back self-consciously with a graceful sweep of the hand. The color which had been returning to her cheeks seemed to accelerate under his gaze.

"How's your Spanish?" Blake asked, looking at a page in the ship's log.

"The log's in Spanish?" Kelly asked. "I thought I saw you reading it."

"No, it's in English, most are, it's the universal language of commerce. But there are some Spanish words here I don't understand."

Kelly looked at him suspiciously. "What makes you think I speak Spanish?"

"Just a guess."

"Actually I do, a little. My grandmother on my mother's side. Plus some in college."

"You went to college?"

"San Jose State." She shrugged. "Just a year."

"Why'd you quit?"

"Ran out of money. My Volkswagen died in front of a Navy recruiting station."

"Any idea what '*El Callado*' means?" Blake asked, looking at a page in the log. He pronounced it "El Cal-a-doe."

"How's it spelled?" Kelly asked, wrinkling her brow.

Blake spelled it out.

"Two L's in Spanish has a Y sound," Kelly said. "That would be pronounced '*Ky-yad-o,*' with the emphasis on the second syllable."

Blake nodded. He should have remembered. He'd learned the "Lladro" lesson from a stuffy salesclerk at Macy's when he'd bought one of the Spanish artist's figurines for Vicki. "What does it mean?"

Kelly frowned and rubbed her chin. "*Callado, callado.* 'Quiet,' I think."

"Quiet?"

"No, wait." Kelly narrowed her eyes. "*Callado* means 'silent, mysterious.'" She looked at Blake. "I guess the most literal translation of *El Callado* would be . . . 'the silent one.'"

Blake stared at Kelly, then down at the log. He felt a tingling sensation on the back of his neck. The words seemed to come alive on the page. *The silent one.* Whatever it was, it had murdered the entire crew, one by one. Out of the corner of his eye, he saw something move. Adrenaline roared through him like a freight train. He slapped the Beretta out of its holster, snapped the safety off, and spun on the door.

"Whoa, don't shoot." Frank Kozlewski's round face peered through the door, his wide eyes looking down the barrel of the automatic.

"Christ," Blake said, thumbing the safety on. "Scare a man to death." He holstered the pistol and felt his knees tremble slightly.

"Why so jumpy, Lieutenant?" Kozlewski stepped into the captain's stateroom with Robertson and Tobin stumbling in behind. "Jesus. Another one?" He picked up a corner of the shroud and grimaced at the yawning mouth. "Good thing Sparky's not here."

Blake felt the deck vibrate. The overhead light in the stateroom flickered and came on with a white steady glare. He let out a long breath. The sense of relief he felt wasn't just from the light flooding the cabin; it was from the vibration pulsing through the hull of the ship, bringing her at least partially back to life. A dead ship was a dangerous place to be on the high seas.

"I didn't think it'd take him long to get some lights on," Kozlewski said, looking down at the body. "There's a guy looks just like this next to the emergency diesel. I told Sparky he couldn't come out of the engine room 'til he got some power going."

"You shouldn't have left him alone," Blake said.

"We secured it first. Ain't nobody down there alive except Sparky, and I'm not so sure about him." Kozlewski chuckled and rubbed his belly. "The men'll be getting hungry, sir."

"There should be plenty of food in the galley," Blake said, wondering how anyone could eat after what they'd seen. "See if you can find a volunteer."

They all looked at each other.

"I ain't no cook, but I did some pearl diving once," Robertson spoke up. "Little place down in Mobile. I watched the cooks fry eggs and stuff. Don't look too tough to me."

"You've got the job," Blake said. He motioned Kozlewski over to the side. "Send someone down to get Sergeant Rivero."

"Sure. What's up?"

"We've got big problems. The deeper we dig, the bigger they get."

"We've got a radio. Let's call home. Get some help out here."

"I need to know for sure what we're up against before we push the panic button. Get Rivero up here. I've got a feeling he knows more about this stuff than any of us."

* * *

The friendly smell of freshly brewed coffee wafted through the compact galley, which separated the officers' dining salon from the crew's mess, and served both. Blake breathed in the aroma and filled his cup with a steaming brew the color of molasses. He blew across the coffee and smiled at Robertson dancing over the inky black grill with sweat pouring off his forehead, frying steak and eggs, the sailor's traditional favorite. The nearly thawed steaks from the frozen-food locker hit the grill with a sizzle, sending up vaporous clouds of steam and a slightly burnt aroma, dissipating the smell of cold grease and stainless steel that hovered over the galley.

Blake stood at the coffee urn and nursed his coffee, collecting his thoughts. Frank Kozlewski had just given him a report on what they'd found in the engine room. The chief had discovered two additional bodies, one near the control-room console, the other near the high-pressure steam turbine. Both had suffered the same fate as the corpse found near the emergency diesel generator. He had also checked out the main-propulsion machinery and opined that it ought to be in a museum somewhere, but appeared to be undamaged.

Rivero hadn't said a word during the chief's report, which wasn't too surprising. Blake had never heard more than a handful of words out of him at all. He felt sure the Colombian could shed some light on what they were up against if Blake could find a way to make him open up. He walked back over to the table in the far corner of the dining salon where Frank Kozlewski and Sergeant Rivero were seated, hoping he could get the Colombian to respond in words of more than one syllable. The others were scattered about, two or three to a table, chattering in hushed tones.

"Hey, Chief," Robertson shouted over the hiss of the grill. "How you want your eggs?"

"Just warm 'em up a little," the chief yelled over his shoulder.

"Now there's a man knows how to eat eggs." Robertson cracked a brown egg in each hand and dive-bombed them across the grill.

Blake sat down at the table and glanced at Sergeant Rivero. He was struck by the inky depths of his eyes, peering out from under his combat helmet. Eyes so dark they were almost black. "What about the cargo holds, Sergeant? Find anything interesting?"

Rivero loosened his chin strap and tilted his helmet off, exposing a haircut that Blake thought must be the standard for marines all over the world. A narrow strip of black bristles not more than a quarter of an inch high ran down the top of his head, fading into white sidewalls. Rivero gave his report in a surprisingly articulate monotone, a straight reporting of the facts. It was what Blake had been afraid of. He let Rivero run through the inventory of cargo to verify what he'd read in the manifest. When he'd finished, Blake hadn't learned anything he didn't already know, except for the two additional dead bodies, which were no surprise under the circumstances.

Blake looked at Rivero sitting stiffly upright in his chair and decided it was the old bugaboo between officers and enlisted men that was getting in the way. He'd always been able to get around that with his own people by making self-deprecating small talk and by showing respect. It wasn't an act. He firmly believed that many enlisted people were just as smart as he was; the only difference was that he'd had the opportunity to get a commission and they hadn't. He decided to probe a little, try to draw him out. He leaned back in his chair and took a sip of coffee. "What do you make of all the chemicals?"

Rivero sat stiffly. "They're used in the extraction process."

"I assumed it had something to do with the manufacture of drugs," Blake said. "How does it work?"

Rivero shrugged. "It's a fairly simple process. The coca leaves are harvested by hand by local farmers, then taken to processing plants in their village, where the process of extraction begins."

"That's where the cocaine is made?"

Rivero smiled indulgently and seemed to loosen up a little. "Not exactly. The first step is to prepare coca paste by the process of maceration—they soak the leaves in a mixture of kerosene, water, sodium carbonate, and sulfuric acid. Depending on the quality of the leaf, it takes between one and two hundred kilos of leaves to extract one kilo of paste."

Blake raised his eyebrows, stuck his bottom lip out and nodded. The Colombian obviously knew what he was talking about. "What do they do with the paste?"

"The paste contains up to 90 percent pure cocaine. It's easier to transport than huge quantities of leaves would be. The paste is then flown to central processing plants in the jungle, where it's converted into pure cocaine hydrochloride, the white powder your people seem to love so much."

Blake stiffened. "My people?"

"The people in America."

Tactful son of a bitch, Blake thought. He felt a tinge of red creeping up the back of his neck but told himself not to react. He needed Rivero's cooperation. "And how do they convert it?"

"By adding various chemicals to the paste. Hydrochloric acid, ether, acetone, sulfuric acid, sometimes kerosene."

"Sounds like real healthy stuff."

Rivero's face grew dark. "Coca leaves have been chewed by my people for at least fifteen centuries without any problems." His eyes focused on Blake. "It has been foreigners who have exploited the coca leaf."

"Take it easy," Blake said. "That wasn't meant to be a dig."

Rivero went on as though he hadn't heard. "It started with the Spanish conquerors. They were opposed to its use at first; they thought it would make conversion of the Incas to Christianity difficult. But when they discovered it enabled the Indians to work long hours in their gold mines with little food or sleep, they quickly had a change of heart." He snorted with disgust. "It wasn't long before the king of Spain declared that the coca habit was essential to the health of the Indians. They even had the gall to start paying them with coca leaves for their labor.''

Blake stared at Rivero, stunned by his diatribe, wondering how he was going to establish any kind of rapport with this guy. "Well, that was a long time ago."

"Nothing has changed. Even now, your country creates the demand, then punishes the poor peasants for filling it."

We're off to a great start, Blake thought. Obviously, xenophobia wasn't limited to Americans. He decided to take another tack. "Those problems are a little beyond our scope," he said. He leaned back in his chair and mentally formed the words the way Kelly had taught him. "Tell me, Sergeant. Does the name *'El Ky-yad-o'* mean anything to you?"

Rivero's eyes flashed. *"El Callado?"* He pulled his face into a smile, but his eyes weren't smiling. "Where did you hear that?"

"Why? What does it mean?"

Rivero held his counterfeit smile and shook his head. "Nothing."

"What do you mean, 'Nothing'? It has to mean something."

"Peasant superstition, Lieutenant." The Colombian dismissed it with a wave of his hand. "Nothing you *Americanos* would be—"

"Let me be the judge of that," Blake said. "What does it mean?"

"Literally? 'The silent one.' ''

Blake folded his arms and studied Rivero's copper-colored face, wondering just what he had to work with here. The Colombian appeared to be somewhere close to his own age, maybe a few years older, but he had the telltale marks of one who had lived a hard life: a deep gouge above his left eye, a ragged scar down his right cheek, smaller scars on his hands. His black-onyx eyes were surrounded by laugh lines that Blake was sure were not from laughing. "Tell me everything you know about this 'peasant superstition.' ''

Rivero rolled his coffee mug between scarred brown fingers and shrugged. "As you wish. I first heard the story from the peasant children in the village of Vicenzio, near the Colombian jungle, when I was a young *muchacho*.''

''Is that where you're from?''

''No. I'm originally from Bogotá. I went there to live with my grandmother after my parents were killed.''

''I'm sorry,'' Blake said.

Rivero drank off the dregs of his coffee and grimaced. ''The story has been around so long, it has become something of a legend. He is called *El Callado,* 'the silent one,' because he is a *mudo,* a mute. He is said to be a mestizo, one of mixed Spanish and Indian blood. According to the peasants, he was a *huerfano,* how do you say . . . an orphan, abandoned in the jungle. He was found near a processing lab hidden deep in the jungle as a young man and taken in by one of the drug cartels. The story says he grew up wild in the jungle, where he developed great physical strength and cunning. The legend among the peasants is that his senses are highly developed; it is said that he can hear a leaf drop in the forest, can see the mites on a hawk, can smell the wild clover high in the Andes mountains—but he cannot speak. All these things made him valuable to the cartel leaders, especially his inability to betray them, and he was trained to protect their interests. According to the story, he has been trained by the cartel's *sicarios,* their trained assassins, to kill silently, using only his hands. He supposedly has been used for acts of terrorism against government officials waging war against the cartel. The peasants are terrified of him, and he is said to guard cocaine-processing labs in the jungle and, on occasion, important shipments of cocaine and cash. This is the legend of *El Callado.*''

''And you don't believe it?''

Rivero shook his head. ''The National Police in Colombia believe it's just a story concocted by the cartel to keep the peasants away from their operations.''

Blake tapped his cup, looking at Rivero, trying to read those inscrutable black eyes. He had the feeling Rivero wanted to say something more, but was holding back. ''What else can you tell me about this 'legend'?''

Rivero hesitated. "There is one thing I perhaps should mention . . ."

"What's that?"

Sergeant Rivero hesitated, shaking his head. "I wouldn't read too much into this, *Teniente,* but . . . the peasants believe that he is jealous of the ability to speak and always . . ."

"Always what?"

"Always removes the tongue of his victims."

Frank Kozlewski's jaw dropped. "Are you saying this El . . . this nut is aboard this ship?"

Blake smiled to himself. The chief had a way of cutting through the crap.

"It has to be just a coincidence," Rivero said. "There have never been any documented sightings—"

"Maybe them that saw him didn't live long enough to document it," the chief said.

Rivero scoffed. "We've run down every lead for the past ten years. There's nothing to suggest that it's anything other than a *leyenda,* a legend, a story designed to keep the peasants at bay."

Blake thought Rivero protested too much. "Most legends have some basis in fact," he said, twirling the coffee grounds in the bottom of his cup, studying Rivero's face.

Rivero said nothing. A light film of sweat appeared on his forehead.

"Well, it don't make any sense, even if it's true," Chief Kozlewski said. "Why would he go on a rampage and do in half the crew of the ship he was supposed to be protecting?"

"It may not make sense," Blake said, "but according to the ship's log, that's exactly what happened."

Kozlewski gaped at him. "That's what the log says?"

Blake nodded. The chief knew what any sailor knew; the ship's log was as close to a sacred document as you could find on a ship at sea. You didn't enter anything into it unless it was gospel.

"But it don't make sense. Why would he . . ."

"I don't know," Blake said. "Maybe the crew came across

the money and tried to high-jack it. Who knows? But for whatever reason, if you believe the log, someone or something called
El Callado began to eliminate every member of the crew, one
by one, after the ship had put to sea.''

"And a whole crew couldn't protect itself from one lunatic?''

"With what?'' Blake said. "It's basically an unarmed mer-
chantman. The crew's spread thin, scattered around the ship,
standing watch in remote areas twenty-four hours a day. It
wouldn't be hard to pick them off one by one, especially if
you're trained to do that sort of thing. After he worked his way
through the chief engineer, and the first mate, and the captain,
my guess is the remaining crew panicked, rang up 'All Stop,'
and abandoned ship.''

"I can't believe they'd do that,'' Kozlewski said. "They
had to know there was a storm moving this way.''

"I'm sure they did,'' Blake said. "The storm probably
seemed the lesser of two evils.''

"Good God.'' Kozlewski started to take a drink of coffee
and stopped, his coffee mug poised in midair. A puzzled look
wrinkled his forehead. "So where'd he go?''

"Hard to say,'' Blake said. "All the lifeboats and life rafts
are gone. He could have taken one of them. Or, for that matter,
if he was as crazy as he appears to be, he could have jumped
over the side. Or . . .'' Blake raised his eyebrows.

"Or, what, sir?'' Kozlewski stared intently into Blake's face.

"Or, he could still be aboard.''

"Holy Mother of Christ!'' The chief banged his coffee mug
down on the table. He looked at Rivero, then back to Blake.

"Hold it down, Chief.'' The calmness in Blake's voice belied
the turmoil in his stomach. "We don't want to panic the crew.''

Robertson approached with two sizzling platters, and Blake
waved him off. "Serve the others first.'' The Alabaman made
a U-turn, struggling to keep his balance on the heaving ship,
and headed for the table where Kelly was seated.

"So what do we do now?'' the Chief said in a raspy whisper.

"As soon as the crew has had some food, we'll form search
parties led by those of us with side arms. We'll sweep the ship

starting at the lowest deck aft and work our way forward. We'll go deck by deck and hold by hold. If he's on board, we'll find him. But in the meantime, I don't want anyone to go wandering off.'' Blake looked across the room and watched Robertson approach the table where Kelly sat. He'd caught a glimpse of Robertson's creation—two globes of yellow liquid quivering in a pool of white slime atop a nearly raw steak—and it had made his stomach roll. He wondered how Kelly would react to it after what they'd just seen.

''Ladies first,'' Robertson said. He slid one of the platters across the table to Kelly and the other to Sparks, then stood looking down like a proud parent, wiping greasy hands on his apron.

''Just the way I like 'em,'' Sparks said loudly. Blake could see the electrician staring greedily down at his plate. He watched Kelly's reaction. She looked down at the sunny-side up eggs shimmering atop her steak, then at Spark's platter. The freighter pitched up, then rolled sharply to port as Sparks sliced into the mess, puncturing an egg yolk. A look of disbelief came over Kelly's face. She pushed away from the table and stood up.

Blake caught her halfway to the door. ''Kelly?''

''I . . . I just wanted to get some air, sir.'' Her eyes were wide, pleading.

Blake glanced at the platter where she'd been seated and cursed Robertson for being so stupid. ''Sure,'' he said. ''Just don't go far.'' He looked at Doc Jones and nodded toward Kelly's back as she wheeled and headed for the door. The corpsman nodded and followed her out.

Blake shoved his coffee cup aside and rubbed his eyes. The lack of food and sleep was beginning to get to him. He had to keep his head straight, think the situation through, establish some priorities. The possibility that some headcase might be lurking aboard worried him a lot less than the probability that his keepers were just over the horizon. He felt vulnerable, not knowing who these people were, how they operated, how far they'd go to recover this shipment. It was a world he knew nothing about, and now he realized his ignorance made him vulnerable. He had to get up to speed and do it quickly. He couldn't count on any help from the *Carlyle*. He had to learn who the players were, which ones owned this cargo, what their reaction was likely to be when they realized it was missing, and, if it came to war, how the war would be fought. And, he knew, his only resource for doing this was the stoic Colombian marine sitting across the table. It was time to make a clean start.

"How long have you been in the Marine Corps, Sergeant?"

"Twelve years, sir."

"And you're a staff sergeant?"

Rivero nodded. *"Sargento vice primero."*

Chief Kozlewski raised his eyebrows.

"The equivalent rank of a petty officer first class in the US Navy."

"I hate to admit my ignorance," Blake said, "but I didn't even know Colombia had a marine corps."

"It's quite small," Rivero said. "Five battalions. Two under the Atlantic Marine Brigade and two under the Pacific. The fifth is under the jungle battalion, part of the Western River Forces Command, where I'm from. About a three-thousand-man force, total."

"With a group that small, I guess they can afford to be picky."

Rivero smiled, acknowledging the compliment. "They are."

"There's a lot about this business I don't know," Blake said. "You've been at this game a long time. Maybe you can help me sort things out."

"Of course, *Teniente.* I'm here as an advisor. That's part of my job. What would you like to know?"

The importance of being important, Blake thought. The merest touch of flattery could do it. "For starters, I need to know who the probable owners of this cargo are. I also need to know what they're likely to do about it when they realize it's missing."

Rivero looked down at the platter of steak and eggs sliding to a stop in front of him, the eggs rippling in little waves.

He pushed it over to Frank Kozlewski. "There are only two organizations large enough to control a shipment of this size, Lieutenant. One we need to worry about and the other we probably don't."

Blake ignored the platter Robertson shoved in front of him. "Which one owns this shipment?"

Rivero shook his head. "I thought I knew; now I'm not sure."

"Why? Are they that different?"

"As different as two groups of people could be." Rivero let out a breath. "The first group, the one we need to worry about, was formed twenty years ago in northern Colombia by a thug named Miguel Ramirez." His eyes grew dark and glossy.

Frank Kozlewski sliced into the steak, severing an egg yolk, sending a stream of amber liquid flowing down the side of the steak, pushing its way into a crimson pool of *au jus*. He forked a pink morsel of steak dripping with egg yolk into his mouth. Blake felt his stomach turn. He pushed his platter away and shifted to face Rivero.

"Ramirez was first arrested twenty years ago with two hundred kilos of cocaine," Rivero went on, "the largest amount ever seized in the country. For unknown reasons, the case was quickly dismissed. The police officer who made the arrest was killed several years later."

The Colombian got a distant look in his eye. "He was a *capitán* then, a captain of police. He had a wife, a son, a daughter. The family was going to mass on a Sunday morning in the spring. At the last minute the boy got out of the car and ran back into the house to get his catechism. The father turned the ignition. The boy was knocked to the ground by the explosion. He rolled over in the wet grass to see his father, his mother, and his five-year-old sister engulfed in a ball of fire." His eyes grew shiny, glasslike.

My God, Blake thought. *He's talking about himself.*

Rivero blinked his eyes and swallowed, as if coming out of a trance. "I've devoted my life to destroying these animals."

No wonder this guy is a little off-the-wall, Blake thought.

His suspicions about Rivero began to evaporate; it would be impossible to fake the look of pain and hatred he saw in his eyes. He felt a guilty sense of relief. *If this Miguel Ramirez and his boys decide to come after the ship with Sergeant Rivero aboard,* he thought, *I wouldn't want to be the first one out of the helicopter.*

"They were the first to make massive shipments of cocaine into the United States, and became incredibly wealthy almost overnight. When their wealth and power grew to astronomical heights, the government tried to crack down. Miguel Ramirez responded by declaring war against the state. His *sicarios,* his trained assassins, murdered hundreds of police officers and high government officials on the streets. Thousands died in bomb blasts. Even the Bogotá headquarters of the DAS, our version of your FBI, was bombed out. Our cities became war zones."

"And the government couldn't stop them?"

"They waited too long; Ramirez and his people were out of control by then."

Rivero went on for a full ten minutes, describing the open warfare that had evolved between the Colombian government and the Ramirez cartel. Once he had started, he couldn't seem to stop. Blake gazed at Rivero, at the wild look in his eyes, the small drops of white forming in the corners of his mouth, shocked at the level of obsession he seemed to have with Miguel Ramirez. Hatred for the man radiated from him like a furnace.

"You said there were two organizations," Blake said, trying to get him focused. "What about the other one?"

Rivero seemed to come back from a long way off. He nodded. "Because of his violent methods, Ramirez was on the defensive, and a new organization headed by Don Augusto Gallardo, a businessman from Cali, was formed to challenge him."

"Is this the 'Cali' cartel you hear about all the time?"

"No," Rivero said. "The so-called Cali cartel gets all the press coverage while Don Gallardo's organization, which is much larger, operates quietly behind the scenes."

"Tell me about him."

"Don Gallardo is a member of the aristocracy, an astute

businessman. He rejected the violent methods of the butcher, Ramirez. He knew it was bad for business. Instead of murdering officials who stood in his way, he cooperated with them. He even joined the Colombian government in the fight against Miguel Ramirez by raiding his processing labs and, later, helping to track him through the jungle."

"Hold it a minute," Blake said. "Are you saying the Colombian government used one drug cartel to wage war on another?"

"They had no choice," Rivero said. "The Ramirez cartel brought it on themselves when they murdered a popular candidate for president at a political rally outside Bogotá. The government had to use every resource at its disposal to bring it to an end. The Colombian people were sick of the endless war, the endless bloodshed."

"So, what does that mean?" Blake asked, eyeing Rivero warily.

"It means that my government has come to realize that fighting a drug war just isn't worth it. It's too costly for everyone concerned. They will have no more of it. Miguel Ramirez competed with the state, tried to become the state. The Gallardo organization cooperates with the state. They have donated money to build neighborhood police stations in the cities in a drive to suppress street crime, for example."

"I may be a little slow," Kozlewski said, "but what are you saying here?"

"I'm saying that the government now knows the only way to defeat Ramirez is to quietly support the Gallardo organization, to leave them alone and let them run the Ramirez cartel out of business. They're well on the way. The Ramirez cartel's share of the country's $6 billion in annual cocaine exports has fallen substantially. The market share of the organization headed by Don Augusto Gallardo has already surpassed it."

"All that from just being nonviolent?" Blake asked.

"That, and being good businessmen. While the Ramirez cartel was on the defensive, the Gallardo organization concentrated on developing new markets in other parts of the world, most notably Europe, because of the price advantage. A kilogram of cocaine goes for as much as $90,000 in some European cities. Athens, for example.''

Blake let out a low whistle. It was clear now that the value of the cargo they were sitting on was such that the owners, peaceful or not, wouldn't let it go without putting every resource at their command into the fight to recover it, even if it meant taking on the entire Western Pacific Fleet.

"In order to serve their European markets," Rivero went on, "the Gallardo organization expanded production into other countries, most notably Bolivia, Peru, Ecuador, and Venezuela. The governments of these countries are more tolerant, tend to look the other way, not only because of the revenue the cocaine traffic brings in, but because they are not under the watchful eye of the United States, which remains focused on Colombia, even though the game there, so to speak, is over.''

"Jesus," Blake said. "Are we behind the times.''

"The game changes quickly. Only a few years ago, the major worldwide routes for cocaine traffic were from Colombia, through Mexico and the Bahamas, into Florida. Today, the major flow of cocaine in the world is from Colombia, Ecuador, Peru, and Bolivia—these are now the major producers—into Brazil, Argentina, Venezuela, and Suriname—these are now the major repackaging and transshipment centers—for shipment to the Netherlands and Spain, as ports of entry into the European markets. Spain is surrounded by so much coastline, it's impossible to monitor it all. It is now called The Florida of Europe.''

Blake shook his head. "Sounds like they're taking over the world.''

Rivero nodded. "The Gallardo organization has not only displaced the Ramirez cartel as the largest drug organization in Colombia, it is the predominant cocaine-distribution organization in the world. But it is a peaceful group, and the government has made it clear that it does not intend to challenge it so long as it remains peaceful and cooperates with the authorities.''

"You mean the Colombian government just lets them have a free hand?'' Blake asked.

"For the most part," Rivero said. "The government makes

a show of a few seizures from time to time, but it is understood that they will not touch the leaders. No charges have ever been filed against Don Augusto Gallardo or any of his senior officers.''

''You're saying that the drug war is over in Colombia and everyone knows it except the United States government?'' Blake asked.

''Governments are sometimes slow to react to policy changes in other countries,'' Rivero said. A condescending smile crossed his face.

Frank Kozlewski finished the last bite of his steak and shoved his platter out of the way. ''So there's a group of good guys and bad guys out there. Which one owns this shipment?''

''At first I thought it was the Gallardo organization,'' Rivero said. ''They prefer shipment in a low-key manner, usually in freighter cargo holds, like this, unlike the Ramirez cartel, which generally prefers shipment by plane or high-speed motorboat.''

''And now you don't?'' Blake asked.

''I don't know.''

''Why are you confused?''

Rivero looked at him. ''The presence of *El Callado.*''

''Well, I'll be damned,'' Frank Kozlewski said. ''So it is true.''

''I didn't say that,'' Rivero said. ''But if it is, he has long been thought to be a puppet of the Ramirez cartel.''

''And this doesn't look like a Ramirez shipment?'' Blake asked.

''No. If this shipment were owned by the Ramirez cartel, it would be bristling with armed guards.''

''So you're saying that this is a Gallardo shipment?''

''I'm saying that this shipment has all the hallmarks of the Gallardo organization, which prefers quietly to buy their way into ports, not to call attention to themselves.''

''Then how do you account for it?'' Blake asked. ''What would this character be doing on board a Gallardo ship?''

''There is one possible explanation,'' Rivero said. ''During the war on the Ramirez cartel, the Gallardo organization participated in raids on Miguel Ramirez's processing labs in the jungle. It's possible that they captured him there and tried to convert him to their own use.''

''And his true loyalties surfaced after the ship put to sea?''

''That is the only explanation that makes sense.''

''So it's the Gallardo cartel that owns this little shipment of dynamite we're riding on,'' Blake said.

''That is my best guess,'' Rivero said.

''Ain't we lucky,'' Frank Kozlewski said. ''The good guys.''

Blake ignored him and stared at Rivero. ''And you're saying that they won't be coming after it?''

''They don't operate that way,'' Rivero said. ''In the first place, they are extremely wealthy and can afford to write it off as a cost of doing business. And in the second, according to our intelligence, they do not own the necessary offensive equipment, no helicopters or gunships that they would need for a recovery operation like this. No. If it is theirs, they will accept the loss. They won't like it, but they will accept it. We have nothing to worry about from them.''

''What's the matter, sir? Didn't you like it?'' Robertson asked, picking up the platters.

''I guess I'm not hungry,'' Blake said. ''Thanks, anyway.'' Robertson went bustling off to the galley, loaded down with half-eaten platters, mumbling to himself. Blake stared at Rivero. He didn't buy his foolish optimism for a minute, no matter how much he wanted to believe him. No one would walk away from a shipment like this, no matter how rich, or how ''peaceful'' they were. There was no doubt in his mind that they were coming. The question was, what to do about it. Something his father had taught him years before began to surface in his mind. As important as it was to know your friends, he had said, it was even more important to know your enemies. He looked at Rivero. ''What can you tell me about these people?''

''Why? I've already told you they pose no threat to us.''

''Just call it curiosity.''

Rivero shrugged. ''Don Augusto Gallardo is considered to

be the Godfather of the cartel. Unlike Miguel Ramirez, a high-school dropout who rose from petty thief to head of the Ramirez cartel, Augusto Gallardo is a well-educated man with a respected background. He was an executive of a major banking house. He is prominent in social circles in Colombia. He is known as a brilliant tactician. Because of his aggressive moves into worldwide cocaine markets, he is thought to be a billionaire, many times over.''

Blake studied Sergeant Rivero's face. His dark eyes were glowing, and his monotone had increased in pitch and intensity. There was a tone of approval, even enthusiasm, in his voice that bothered Blake. It was suppressed, but it was there. He wondered if it was for the demise of the Ramirez cartel, which he could understand, or if it was for the emergence of the ''peaceful'' Gallardo cartel as Colombia's dominant drug organization. Depending on which one came after this shipment, the distinction could be important.

''You sound like you approve.''

''The Gallardo family is much admired in Colombia. Don Gallardo has three sons and a godson who have attended university outside of Colombia, in training to help ease the family fortune into legitimacy for the next generation.'' Sergeant Rivero paused for a moment, then added, ''Not unlike your Kennedy dynasty.''

''What do you mean by that?''

Rivero smiled. ''It's well-known that the patriarch of the Kennedy family established the family fortune through questionable transactions involving large amounts of alcohol, the drug of choice for Americans. His fortune ensured that his children were trained at Harvard, and at other prestigious institutions overseas. The second generation has brought legitimacy to the family through careers in public service. Two of his sons were American naval officers, like yourself,'' he said. ''One was later an American president.''

Blake stiffened at the comparison but stopped short of challenging Rivero. He needed his cooperation to work his way out of this, and couldn't risk jeopardizing it over a trivial argument. Straightening the sergeant out would have to wait.

He looked at his watch. "Thanks for the briefing, Sergeant," Blake said with a nod in Rivero's direction.

Sergeant Rivero made no effort to move.

"That's all for now, Sergeant."

"Yes, sir." Sergeant Rivero pulled himself to attention, slung his M-16 over his shoulder, saluted, and stalked out of the dining room. Blake watched him walk away, wondering who he really was, knowing he would probably never know. He wondered why Sergeant Rivero wasn't commissioned—he was clearly an educated man—and guessed that his single-minded obsession had gotten in the way.

"See if you can find Doc," he said to Frank Kozlewski. "I want to talk to him before we contact the *Carlyle*."

"Aye aye, sir." The chief started to push himself up from the table, paused, and cocked an eye at Blake. "You don't buy that good-guy, bad-guy stuff?"

"Not for a minute," Blake said. "Not with 350 million in cash aboard. They're coming, all right." He nodded toward the door. "My only question is, is he going to be with us or against us when they get here?"

"Yes, sir, Lieutenant," Doc Jones burst out from halfway across the dining room. Blake watched the hospital corpsman come paddling toward him in that whimsical gait that belied his ability.

"Have a seat, Doc. Coffee?"

"No thanks, sir. That stuff Robertson brewed will keep me awake for a month."

Blake smiled. "How's the patient?"

"Kelly? She's okay. Tossed her cookies over the rail. I took her to one of the passenger cabins and gave her something to settle her stomach, made her lie down for a while—"

"You didn't leave her alone?"

"Oh, no, sir. The Koz grabbed Tobin and posted him outside

her door when he came to get me. The stuff I gave her made her sleepy. She was still sawing 'em off when I looked in on her.''

Chief Kozlewski came walking into the dining room. He scratched his belly and strolled over to the coffee urn, glancing around in search of a clean cup. ''Coffee, Lieutenant?'' he said, glancing over his shoulder.

''No, thanks.''

The chief filled his cup with a tepid brew the color of tar and joined them at the table.

''You've had a chance to inspect all the bodies?'' Blake asked.

''Yes, sir. Robertson and Tobin went with me.''

''Give me a full report on what you found—cause of death, approximate time of death, any patterns or any inconsistencies.''

''They were all pretty consistent,'' Jones said. ''All died of broken necks and spines snapped like twigs. My guess is that the neck was broken first, then the spine. The final part . . . the tongues being cut out came after. . . . Must have been done by one crazy dude.''

''How long have they been dead?''

''I'd say a range of twenty-four to forty-eight hours, something like that, all except . . .'' The corpsman pursed his lips and squinted his eyes into the far corner of the room.

''Except what?''

''Except that guy in the vault. The vault with all the money.'' Doc Jones shuddered. ''Big creepy-looking dude with a tattoo on the back of his hand. Blue star.'' He looked at Blake. ''I ain't no doctor, but that dude was fresh.''

''What makes you so sure?''

''Well, Alvarez came running out of the vault like all the demons in hell were after him, screaming that someone grabbed him by the leg, by the ankle,'' Jones said. ''I thought he was nuts, but when I checked this guy for a pulse, he was warm, as warm as I am. I think there's a chance he really did grab

Alvarez by the ankle, maybe when he stepped on him or something, maybe a last, dying reflex.''

"Notice anything else different about the guy in the vault?''

Doc Jones thought for a minute. ''He still had his tongue.''

Blake felt cold sweat on the back of his neck. ''Okay, Doc.
Thanks for the update. Will you check on Kelly and see if you
can put her and her radio back together? I'd like to report in
to the *Carlyle* as soon as possible.''

"Sure thing, Lieutenant. I'll wake her up.''

"Oh, and one more thing, Doc,'' Blake said, as the corpsman
stood up to leave.

"Yes, sir?''

"Let's keep what we've discussed here to ourselves.''

"You got it, sir.'' Jones turned and paddled out of the dining
room.

Blake watched him depart through narrowed eyes.

Chief Kozlewski blew little ripples on the surface of his
coffee, studying Blake's face. ''What do you make of it, Lieutenant?'' he said after Jones was out of sight.

"It's not good,'' Blake said, glancing at the chief. ''*El Callado,* or whatever you want to call him, is still aboard. Alive
and well.'' He looked off into the distance.

The coffee mug trembled slightly in the chief's hand. ''How
. . . how do you know?''

"It's pretty obvious, isn't it?'' Blake said. ''Sergeant Rivero,
Doc, and Alvarez must have interrupted him in the process of
killing the last member of the crew during their inspection of
the number three hold.''

"What the hell was this guy still doing on board after everyone else abandoned ship, anyway?'' Chief Kozlewski asked.

Blake shook his head. ''My guess is that he got left behind
somehow in the panic.''

"But what was he doing in the vault?''

"Where would you hide if a lunatic like that was after you?''

"Yeah, I guess you're right. I'd want as much steel between
him and me as I could get.''

"Exactly," Blake said. "He must have tried to bar it from the inside. Poor devil."

"But why didn't he make himself known to us when we came aboard?"

"I doubt if he knew. In fact I doubt if either one of them knew we were aboard until they heard Sergeant Rivero's troops scrambling down the number three hold. They were probably locked in a game of cat-and-mouse in the vault, oblivious to everything else."

Kozlewski was staring at Blake intently. Beads of sweat were forming across his forehead. His face looked puffy and gray. "So what happened?"

"After breaking this guy's neck he must have dropped him and disappeared into the hold when he heard them coming down the ladder. He didn't have time to do the rest of it. He was probably watching Sergeant Rivero and his people the whole time they were down there."

Chief Kozlewski ran his tongue over dry lips. He put his cup down and mopped his brow with a red bandanna. "It's hot in here."

"Stick around," Blake said. "It's about to get a lot hotter. We're in way over our heads. We need to get some help out here. Where the hell is Kelly?" He glanced at his watch and looked up as Dana Kelly appeared in the door of the dining salon. She paused at the door, hesitating. Doc Jones stood behind her in the narrow doorway, eyes wide. Blake watched her advance on the table with the hospital corpsman close behind. She stood looking down at Blake, breathing hard. Her face was white.

"What is it?" Blake said.

"It's the radio, sir."

"What about it?"

Kelly blinked her eyes and swallowed hard.

"It's gone!"

Chapter Eight

The Learjet 55C accelerated down the runway and lifted off with a shudder, leaving the city of La Paz in the distance. Jorge Cordoba gripped the armrests and closed his eyes, trying to keep his stomach synchronized with the motion of the plane. He leaned his head back and kept his eyes tightly shut until the jet reached its cruising altitude and leveled off, banking southeast toward Uruguay.

He rubbed his eyes and gazed out the window. The sun slipping away in the west cast an orange glow over the Bolivian capital. The brief refueling stop had given Jorge a chance to stretch his legs, but the welcome whisper of the jet now lulled him with a feeling of distance. The farther away he got from Don Gallardo, the more relaxed he felt. Still, he knew that a reprieve was only temporary. If he couldn't produce results quickly in the form of restructuring the debt and recovering the ship before the Colombian Navy got to it, there would be no going back. He'd been on the phone most of the trip down talking to Ayala's replacement, the acting security director at Campanilla, and had been assured that a dozen planes were in the air, sweeping the coordinates Admiral Cuartas had given them, and that they would soon have a sighting. The helicopters were being prepared and would be ready for him to board in the second wave when he got there. Jorge felt his pulse quicken at the thought. He rubbed his face in his hands, distressed at the frightening speed with which he was becoming enmeshed in the side of the business his parents had warned him about. He'd wanted desperately to avoid it, but now he had no choice.

He closed his eyes, trying to shut out the memory of that morning. He couldn't shake the question that kept hammering at him: Had Ayala still been alive when he'd been thrown into the lion compound? The fool deserved it for putting that cretin aboard the ship. Still, Jorge knew that unless he got some results, he could find himself in the same position. His hand trembled as he reached for the call button.

The flight attendant, a brunette with the longest legs he had ever seen, was there in an instant, smiling down on him. "Yes, Señor Cordoba?"

"Bring me a whiskey. Straight."

"Yes, Señor."

Ernesto Rodriguez looked up from his papers. "Since when do you drink?"

"There's a time for everything."

Jorge tilted his head back and poured the twelve-year-old Scotch down his throat. It seared all the way down, like liquid fire. He made a face that looked as though he had taken medicine.

"*Madre de Dios.* This stuff is poison. *Veneno.*" His face flushed from the burning in his throat and the memory of the subtle insults he had endured during his two years of graduate school in the United States. Arrogant *yanquis,* strutting in their cloaks of legitimacy. How could anyone who sold poison like this sneer at him for the business he was in?

The flight attendant handed him a glass of mineral water. He downed it in three swallows. "Bring me another."

"Better take it easy with that stuff," Ernesto Rodriguez said.

The chief accountant sat heavily beside him, quietly laboring over a debt-restructuring plan. Jorge glanced at Rodriguez, reassured with the older man's presence. He'd asked him to come along specifically for his negotiating skills and his coolness under fire. Negotiating was never Jorge's strong point—he had too short a fuse—and negotiating with a snake like Quintero in his present state of mind would, he knew, be especially dangerous. With his plodding, disarming style, his chief accountant could be a formidable opponent across the conference table.

The Learjet hit an air pocket and bucked with turbulence. Rodriguez dropped his pencil and gripped the armrests, his sagging face the color of the spreadsheet on his tray. "You're a pilot, aren't you? Why don't you go up there and fly this thing?"

Jorge laughed. "I just got licensed to fly single-engine props. One step at a time."

The plane lurched and took a sickening drop. "You couldn't do any worse than these gorillas," Rodriguez said, clinging to the armrests. "I still don't see why we have to go flying off to Montevideo in this flea of an airplane."

"We can't risk negotiating over the phone," Jorge said. "You know that. If Quintero gets antsy about the delay, we've got a problem."

"I told you we were moving too fast," Rodriguez said. "Buying over a billion dollars' worth of bullion in thirty days with borrowed money, for Christ's sake. What's the hurry?"

"You know what the plan is," Jorge said, probing. It was becoming important to know just how much Rodriguez knew, or how much he would admit to knowing.

The plane stabilized. Rodriguez picked up his pencil and flicked eraser dust off the spreadsheet. "I just keep the books. I don't know anything."

Jorge tensed at the dismissive tone. A cavalier attitude toward a problem of this magnitude was something he couldn't afford. If they were to have any chance in the negotiations with Quintero, the chief accountant would have to be as committed as Jorge was, would have to understand fully what was at risk. The only way to incentivize him, Jorge thought, was by telling him enough of the plan to show him what was at stake. He wouldn't tell him about the confederation that had just been formed, that was forbidden under penalty of death, but he felt he had no choice but to reveal enough about Don Gallardo's plan in general terms to make him understand the consequences if they failed.

Leaning back into the leather seat, he watched Rodriguez out of the corner of his eye. "How's it coming?"

Rodriguez stopped punching numbers into his HP-12C and wiped his forehead with the back of a thick hand. "Almost there. Revising the plan is the easy part." He dropped his glasses down on his nose and peered over the rims at Jorge. "But getting it approved will take the full cooperation of the lending consortium, which, as you know, just happens to be lead by Fabio Quintero's private bank."

"I've been meaning to talk to you about that," Jorge said. "I want you to take the lead on the negotiations. It's better if I don't act too eager."

"I don't mind, but how do you get on a level playing field with a guy like Quintero?"

"He's a duplicitous bastard," Jorge said, "but I think we'll find some common ground for negotiation."

"Like what?"

"Everyone wants something."

"He wants something all right. He wants all of our real-estate holdings in Uruguay and Argentina."

"There's something else he wants even more," Jorge said. "All we have to do is find it." He thought of Admiral Cuartas. It hadn't taken Don Gallardo long to find what he wanted.

"You can't buy everyone," Rodriguez said.

"Sure you can." Jorge gave Rodriguez a knowing look. The chief accountant was middle-aged, with a fat, doting wife and a houseful of children. For a paltry two hundred thousand dollars per year, they owned him, mind, body, and soul. "Everyone has a price. It's been proven so often it's no longer a theory. It's a fact, a natural law, like the sun rising in the east."

Rodriguez went back to laboring over his papers, jabbing

numbers into his calculator, muttering under his breath. "More gold bullion. Don Gallardo's already got warehouses full of the stuff. What the hell does he think he's going to do with it all?"

Jorge smiled, pleased that the chief accountant couldn't grasp the significance of what they were doing any more than the others. It was a good sign. "Before we're done, we'll have warehouses full of the stuff from New York to Geneva," Jorge said.

"But what are you going to do with it? It's just metal, for Christ's sake."

Jorge glanced at Rodriguez, grateful for the opening. "Metal to you. In the hands of a man like Don Gallardo, it's power."

"Power to do what? He's already the most powerful man in Colombia."

"We're not talking about personal power, Ernesto. We're talking about a global shift in power."

Rodriguez raised his eyebrows. "Oh, really?"

"Don't scoff at things you don't understand," Jorge said.

"Well, it'll take a hell of a lot more than we've got to do that."

Jorge took a sip of Scotch. "You're forgetting what we've already stockpiled."

"I know. Two thousand tons of the damned stuff," Rodriguez said. "Twenty-five billion dollars tied up in gold bars sitting around in bonded warehouses in Zurich and Geneva and God-knows-where, not earning a dime's worth of interest. Every time the price of gold falls a penny on the world market, our balance sheet goes into convulsions. The whole thing's crazy to me. I say we sell off enough to pay off that bloodsucking bastard Quintero, and take it slower from now on."

Jorge shook his head. "Don Gallardo is a buyer, not a seller. Selling is forbidden. Ever. Under any circumstances. If he has to resort to selling, you and I won't be around to see it. He has a timetable to keep."

"Two thousand tons of gold just ties up all our capital,"

Rodriguez said. "It's a lousy investment, number one; and number two, it's not going to shift any balance of power."

Jorge chuckled to himself. He hoped that Rodriguez's naïveté was typical of the general populace. "It's more significant than you think." He drank off the remainder of his Scotch and motioned the flight attendant for a third drink. He was beginning to feel comfortable for the first time since Rafael Ayala had burst into his office. He smiled indulgently at the accountant. "Do you have any idea what the total gold holdings of all the world's central banks combined is, Ernesto?"

Rodriguez shook his head. "No idea."

"About twenty-eight thousand tons," Jorge said. "That's it."

"So what?"

"So our two thousand tons represents a big chunk of that. Nearly 25 percent of the gold the *Norte Americanos* hold in their fabled reserves in Fort Knox, Kentucky. It's more than twice as much as the Bank of England holds."

"But that doesn't mean we're going to be able to keep doing this forever. At some point, the *Norte Americanos* are going to wake up—"

"Let them. There's nothing they can do to stop us," Jorge said. He picked up the fresh drink and spun the amber liquid around in the glass. "Well, there is one thing. But they'll never do it."

"What's that?"

Jorge threw his head back and downed half the Scotch. "Legalize cocaine." He grimaced. "That is the one thing that could stop us and the one thing they will never do."

"I wouldn't be so sure," Rodriguez said. "Some government official said something about it the other day in a speech."

"Yes, and you saw the reaction. All hell broke loose. No, my friend. The stupid *yanquis* believe all you have to do is pass a law against something, and it will go away. Don't like something? Prostitution? Drugs? Liquor? Make it against the law. There. We've solved that problem. You would think the dumb bastards would have learned their lesson from the Volstead Act in the twenties, but they didn't. We have nothing to worry about.''

''Two thousand tons or not, there's no way even Don Gallardo can accumulate all the gold in the world,'' Rodriguez said.

Jorge smiled at the accountant, amused by his insight. After accumulating twenty-five billion dollars' worth of gold on his own, that was exactly the conclusion Don Gallardo had come to, and the reason for forming the confederation, but he couldn't tell Rodriguez that.

''He doesn't need it all. A simple majority will give him all the leverage he needs to bring the *Norte Americanos* to their knees.''

''And just how does he plan to do that?''

''We won't have to do anything,'' Jorge said.

''You're not making sense.''

''Over time they will do it to themselves. The policies that will bring them down are already in effect. Policies which can't be changed because of their liberal Congress, voted into office by those who demand more and more. Their decline as a world power is certain, fixed, inevitable. It's happened over and over again throughout history. All we have to do is continue to accumulate gold and sit back and watch while the American government prints unlimited quantities of paper currency to finance their insane social policies. We will help them along a little, by withholding gold from the world markets and forcing them to print ever-increasing quantities of worthless money, and over time, we will see them fall. And when they do, it will trigger a chain reaction that will bring down the other industrialized nations of the world. We will see the paper fortunes of the world crumble into ashes, victims of hyperinflation, while Don Gallardo's fortune, based on gold, grows to astronomical heights.'' Jorge drank off the third Scotch and pressed a finger around his mouth, feeling for his upper lip, which had started to go numb from the alcohol. ''They're doing it to themselves, Ernesto. We're simply taking advantage of their stupidity. Those with the wisdom and the capital to accumulate gold will be the new elite, at the top of the new social order. Don Gallardo has studied history, and he knows. Gold is the one constant, the one true form of wealth on earth." He looked at Rodriguez through fogged eyes. "Believe me, Ernesto. It will happen."

Rodriguez squirmed in his seat. "If you can see this, why can't they?"

"Because the world is full of ordinary, greedy men, Ernesto. Men who can't see past lining their own pockets. Men who will sell their souls to get elected and reelected to public office. Men who don't give a damn about future generations."

"It's a mistake to underestimate the *Norte Americanos,*" Rodriguez said. "They have a history of waking up at the last minute and raising all kinds of hell. Ask the Japanese."

"You give them too much credit," Jorge said, smiling up at the brunette who picked up his glass. He motioned away an unspoken offer of another drink. "That 'sleeping giant' theory may have been true once, but no more. They're a weak country. They have no cultural solidarity, no moral fiber, no direction. They're drifting on a sea of confused liberal policies that will eventually drown them all."

"Maybe, but whatever else they may be, they're not stupid," Rodriguez said. "It's not going to take them long to see what we're up to."

Jorge shook his head. "They won't see it until it's too late. Like all great ideas that have changed the world, Don Gallardo's plan is simple. So simple they'll never see it." Jorge laid his head back to keep it from spinning and closed his eyes. "It's the simple conversion of the world's lowest-level commodity into the highest," he said, launching into Don Gallardo's credo. He had heard it so many times he could recite it in his sleep. "We will convert the leaf of the humble coca plant into paste, the paste into white powder, the white powder into paper, and the paper into gold." He looked at Rodriguez. "All it will take is this simple formula, and the passage of time, and I can guarantee you that the world will fall under the economic, political, and cultural domination of Don Augusto Gallardo and his descendants, as surely as winter follows autumn, as surely as night follows day.''

"Something like that would take a lifetime," Rodriguez said. "If it ever happens, we won't be around to see it."

Jorge stifled a yawn and laid his head sideways on the pillow, peering at Rodriguez through blurred eyes. "It won't take as long as you think. You saw the amazing speed with which the Soviet Union crumbled into ashes. It festered for years, like the US, then collapsed within a week. But the timing isn't important. What is important is that it will happen. All we have to do is maintain our market share and our timetable. We have a network of holding companies in place all over the world to do the acquisition. Companies that are controlled by the Gallardo family. With our cash flow, it's only a matter of time before we control a majority of the world's gold reserves. And, whoever controls the world's gold, controls the world. It's the Golden Rule, as Don Gallardo is fond of saying: 'He who has the gold, rules.' ''

Rodriguez looked skeptical. "That's a pretty ambitious plan, even for Don Gallardo."

Jorge folded his arms and embraced the warm glow of the alcohol. "Don Gallardo is no ordinary man. He's a man of vision. His children are being trained in the leading universities of the world to assume their rightful places in the new order. His family's influence will someday reach into every corner of the globe, just as the Rothschild family reached into and influenced every corner of Europe during the eighteenth and nineteenth centuries."

"Aren't you forgetting the source of this wealth?" Rodriguez said. "How influential can people be who . . ."

"Sanitizing his fortune won't be a problem," Jorge said. "History has shown that memories are short where great wealth is concerned."

"This is dangerous talk," Rodriguez said. "Why are you telling me all this?"

"Because we're both at risk, old friend," Jorge said. "It's important for you to know."

Rodriguez stared at Jorge in the dark. "What happens if we don't succeed?"

Jorge didn't answer for a long time. "Let me put it this way. If we don't get this loan agreement renegotiated successfully and recover that ship, you and I won't be going home again."

Jorge awoke to the chirp of tires on asphalt. He stretched and glanced at his watch, not sure how long he'd been asleep. Nearly eleven. His neck throbbed with a dull ache, and his mouth was dry. After nearly seven hours on the plane, he couldn't wait to get off. He glanced at Rodriguez as the jet taxied down the runway. The chief accountant was sitting in the dark, passing the beads of a rosary through his thick fingers.

"Did you sleep?"

"Who could sleep on this damned thing?"

The jet taxied to a stop, and white overhead lights flickered on. Jorge glanced at his companion's face. He looked haggard and gray, older than his fifty-three years. Fear etched his eyes. Perhaps he'd overdone it. Now that Rodriguez really understood what was at stake, he looked terrified. It hadn't occurred to Jorge that it might work against him.

"Don't worry about what we talked about," Jorge said. "Just relax and do the best you can."

"No problem."

Jorge looked out the window at a black limousine pulling alongside the plane. He gathered up his coat and briefcase and stepped off the plane into a moonless night. A cool breeze floated across the tarmac, lifting his collar. The chauffeur, a squat man in a dark business suit, got stiffly out and held the rear door of the limousine open as he and Rodriguez approached. Jorge stopped and squinted into the dimly lit passenger compartment. It was empty.

"Where is Quintero?"

"Señor Quintero sends his compliments and his regrets that he is unable personally to meet you," the chauffeur said in a monotone.

Jorge climbed into the compartment and slid across the seat, the air-conditioned leather crumpling stiffly beneath him. He flung his briefcase against the door. "This is outrageous. The nerve of that bastard. Who the hell does he think he is?"

"This is just part of his negotiating tactics," Rodriguez said after the chauffeur closed the door. "He smelled blood when you refused to take his call this morning."

"How did you know that?"

"I was standing by Elena's desk. I heard her tell him you were out. That was a mistake."

"I know," Jorge said, embarrassed that he'd panicked.

"He's just trying to rattle you. Don't let him."

Jorge glanced at Rodriguez and nodded, grateful for his calm presence. "You're right, old friend."

They fell silent when the chauffeur opened the front door and got in. The limousine drove through a private exit, bypassing customs, and wound through deserted streets. Jorge looked over his shoulder at the city lights fading into the background. He peered out the window into the darkness of the countryside. "Where the hell are we going?"

"He wanted to meet in some resort hotel he owns," Rodriguez said. "A place called El Dorado." He looked out into the darkness. "He said it's because it's near the airport, but it's not that close. He just wants us to see how they bow and scrape around him. Wants us to see what a big man he is. Thinks that will help him in his negotiations."

Just before midnight, the limousine pulled into a gated resort hotel that sprawled over the rolling Uruguayan countryside. A winding drive cut through the grounds to the lobby of the main hotel, which was flanked on both sides by white cottages with red-tiled roofs. Muted lights glowed from fountains and plants shaped like animals. *Very impressive,* Jorge thought. He could see why Quintero would want to meet here, not that it would do him any good.

Fabio Quintero was standing under a glittering crystal chandelier in the main lobby, surrounded by his entourage, when Jorge walked in. He was a tall thin man with Germanic features, who appeared completely bald from a distance. The black frames of his glasses gave him an owlish look. He took off his glasses and flashed an exaggerated smile. "Ah, Jorge. How nice to see you."

Jorge. The nerve of the bastard to call him by his Christian name. His face flushed. Rodriguez threw him a cautionary glance. Jorge forced a smile. "Señor Quintero." They shook hands coolly, properly. "It's nice to see you." Jorge fixed him with a level gaze, and said, "Finally."

Quintero laughed. "Please forgive me for not meeting you. The pressures of running a business." He swept his hand around the empty lobby. "I'm sure you understand."

Jorge's jaw muscles rippled. The arrogant pig. If Don Gallardo had come, Quintero would have been standing on the tarmac with his hat in his hand when he stepped off the plane. He forced a tight smile. "Of course."

Quintero raised his hand and snapped long thin fingers, still smiling at Jorge.

The hotel manager, a small pink man in a waistcoat, stepped forward. "Yes, Señor Quintero?"

"Please escort my guests to the Viennese Room. We will meet there. See that they are comfortable."

"Time is of the essence," Jorge said. "I have a plane waiting—"

"I will be along shortly," Quintero said, bowing slightly. He turned and walked away.

Jorge started to say something, and Rodriguez shook his head. They turned and followed the diminutive manager down a long corridor. "To hell with him," Jorge said under his breath. "We'll start the meeting without him."

"This way, gentlemen." The hotel manager opened a gilt-covered door into a conference room decorated in the palatial style of eighteenth-century Vienna. The opposing walls were covered with gilt-framed mirrors. Blue-and-gold tapestries hung on the opposite walls. There was no one in the room.

"What is this?" Jorge said. "Where is everyone?"

The manager shrugged. "I know of no others."

"Goddammit!" Jorge moved toward the manager. "Where are they?"

Rodriguez put his hand on Jorge's arm. "He doesn't know."

"There is food and drink on the sideboard, gentlemen." The manager was backing out the door. "Please ring if there is anything else you need. Enjoy your stay." The door eased shut behind him.

"That son of a whore will pay for this." Jorge threw his coat and briefcase across the long table.

Rodriguez walked over to the sideboard and picked up the lid of a silver chafing dish. Cubes of steak were simmering in a rich brown sauce.

"Put that down," Jorge said. "We didn't come here to eat."

"This could be our last meal," Rodriguez said, picking up a plate. "You'd better eat, too. We might be here awhile."

"I'll be here exactly five minutes," Jorge said. "Then I'll solve the problem my own way."

The door swung open and Fabio Quintero walked in. A tall, thin man Jorge had never seen before walked in behind him.

"Where are the others?"

"They're not coming," Quintero said.

Jorge stared at him. Fabio Quintero had a smug expression on his face. His immaculate appearance contrasted sharply with Jorge's rumpled look. The private banker looked as though he'd spent the day preparing for this moment.

"What do you mean, they're not coming?"

"There's no need for them to be here," Quintero said, smiling. "As the lead bank, the others have authorized me to speak for them." The other man stood awkwardly by his side, clutching a file folder.

"What's going on here? Who is this?"

"My director of accounting," Quintero said. "Please, sit down, gentlemen." He nodded to Rodriguez, who had skewered a cube of steak on a toothpick. "I see you've discovered the excellent food."

"I insist that the full consortium be represented at this meeting," Jorge said.

Quintero flashed his professional smile. "That's quite unnecessary. We discussed it over a conference call this afternoon and are all in agreement." Quintero took a seat at the head of the table and glanced at his accountant. The thin man pulled a single sheet of paper from his folder and placed it in front of Quintero.

"And now, gentlemen, if I may summarize. You have arranged for us to purchase one billion, three hundred million in gold bullion for you. As collateral you have put up commercial real estate in downtown Montevideo and Buenos Aires, Argentina. We have accepted this on the strength of your stated cash flow from your . . . business operations."

"Our cash flow is as strong as it ever was."

"I'm very glad to hear it," Quintero said. "The first payment is due in ten . . ." He glanced at his watch. "Make that nine days. Three hundred fifty million dollars." He smiled quickly and said, "US."

"It's on its way," Jorge said.

Quintero held his smile. "The check is in the mail, so to speak?" He paused and his smile seemed to slip. "Then why the meeting?"

"As I explained to you when I called you back, operational difficulties may prevent us from making the first payment in ten . . . nine days. We need more time—"

"That, unfortunately, will not be possible," Quintero said quickly.

Jorge felt a twist in his stomach. "What do you mean, not possible? You said—"

"I said I would look into it, and I did. A purchase of that size strains the resources of even a group like ours. You are in a high-risk business. The feeling is that if we grant an extension this time, we will be asked to grant another and another. Our cash flow will be strained to the breaking point. We must have payment on the date promised."

"And if we don't?"

"Now, just simmer down a little," Rodriguez spoke up.

"It's a little early in the meeting to be making ultimatums. I'm sure we can work out a compromise without—"

"There's nothing to work out," Quintero said. "If the cash is not here by noon of the ninth day, the full amount becomes immediately due and payable under the terms of the agreement. The lending group will have no choice but to take possession of the real property on this list—"

"That real estate is worth billions," Jorge said.

"So it is. We would not have made a loan of such gargantuan proportions without the finest collateral as security."

"I'm sure it's sheer coincidence that that list contains a half dozen of the major properties you've tried to acquire for the last eight years," Jorge said.

"Properties on which I have been outbid each time. Unfortunately I have to earn my cash legitimately. You'll find it's much more difficult."

Jorge stood up. He could feel the heat creeping up his neck, into his face. Rodriguez was staring at him, moving his head almost imperceptibly back and forth, flashing a warning message with his eyes. Jorge took a deep breath. "We're asking for a two-week extension. For which we're willing to pay a substantial fee. Am I to understand that it's being refused?"

"Our relations go back a long way, Señor Cordoba. If it were only me, I would do so in a minute. But the others have spoken." Quintero examined his manicured nails under the light. "I'm sure even you can see their point. Business is, after all, business."

Jorge stared across the table at him. Quintero was smiling peacefully, steepling his fingers. Now it was Señor Cordoba, now that he thought he'd won. There was only one way to handle an arrogant pig like this.

"Very well," Jorge said. "In that case we will have to draw on an alternate source of capital we keep in reserve for cases just such as this. You may tell the others that you will receive payment in full on or before the due date."

Quintero's eyebrows raised. "Oh?"

Jorge watched Quintero's eyes flashing back and forth, considering this turn of events, trying to figure out what it meant. He walked to the end of the table and extended his hand. "Good-bye." He smiled and added, "Fabio."

Quintero stood up. "An alternate source of capital? But if you have that, why the need for—"

"It's an expensive source of capital," Jorge said. "We only use it when we must."

Quintero's eyes darted around. "I'm sorry to put you to this trouble—"

"It's no trouble at all," Jorge said, fixing him with a steady gaze.

"Perhaps if I talked to the others again, asked them to reconsider—"

"No," Jorge said. The word hung heavy in the room. "We have asked, and you have answered." He looked at his watch. "I have no more time for talk."

"But surely, it can't do any harm to ask—"

"My plane is waiting," Jorge said. "But first I need to make a call."

"Of course," Quintero said. "Please use my office."

"That won't be necessary," Jorge said. "A public telephone will do."

Quintero ran his tongue over his lips and swallowed. "I sincerely hope there are no hard feelings, Señor Cordoba. You know that I have the utmost respect for you and Don Gallardo—"

"None whatever." Jorge smiled, watching him squirm. "As you have said, 'Business is business.' " He turned and walked out the door.

Rodriguez hustled to catch up with Jorge, who was walking deliberately down the hall. "What's all this stuff about an alternate capital source?" he said over Jorge's shoulder, struggling to pull on his coat. "What do you think you're doing?"

"Buying time," Jorge said, stopping at a bank of public telephones. "I've got to make a call. Find me some transportation back to the airport."

"Where are we going?"

"You're going home," Jorge said, picking up the phone. "I'm going to Peru. The Command Center in Campanilla. I've got to find that damn ship."

"Don't you want me to go with you?"

"No," Jorge said. He looked at the fat accountant. He would be useless in the jungles of Peru. "We're beyond the need for accountants now. You go on home to your family. Take a commercial flight. And don't worry. We're not out of the game yet."

Jorge watched the bearlike accountant shuffle out the door, then stood facing the telephone with his heart pounding. He had never had to resort to anything like this before in his eight-year affiliation with the organization. He had convinced himself that he was above such thuggery. He took a deep breath and dialed the number Don Gallardo had given him. He hadn't wanted to use it, but now it couldn't be avoided. The arrogant son of a bitch had brought it on himself. He got through on the third ring. A soft female voice answered. Jorge read a numbered code from the piece of paper Don Gallardo had given him. He had a job for them. An immediate job.

The hotel was quiet when Fabio Quintero closed and locked his office just after 2:00 A.M. He walked quickly through the lobby, ignoring the fawning gestures of the staff. He normally enjoyed the stir his presence created, but his mind was locked on Jorge Cordoba. What was that Harvard-educated thug up to? If he'd used the phone in his office to make his call, he would have been able to monitor it. All this double-talk about an "alternate source of capital." Was it a veiled threat or would he really be able to pay him off? In either case it was a problem.

The doorman scrambled to open the front door of the hotel, bowing with a sweeping gesture. Quintero stepped out into the night air and looked up at the moonless sky, breathing deeply. As if on cue, his black 500 SEL pulled up to the entrance. The parking valet swung out of the car and stood at attention, holding the door. Quintero rounded the hood, admiring the lines of the Mercedes. The lacquered finish gave the car a jewellike quality under the lights of the portico. He slid in behind the wheel. The valet closed the door firmly, and Quintero immediately pressed the door-lock button. All four locks snapped shut with German efficiency. Safe now, he settled into the leather seat and ran his hand over the wheel, breathing in the smell of the interior, allowing the new car to take his mind off business. He had just taken delivery on the Mercedes, his twelfth. Or was it his thirteenth? He had lost count. The financier had a standing order for a replacement every twelve months. It was his one indulgence.

Quintero pressed the accelerator and pulled away from the entrance, gratified with the surge of power. No chauffeur for him. These Germans knew how to build cars. Not surprising. Germans did everything well. Music, literature, science, commerce, even war, if the meddling Americans had stayed out of it. Not many people knew it, but his father had been German. A banker from Munich who had met his mother on a business trip to Montevideo. The fact that they had never married was a source of embarrassment, but he was grateful for the leg up his Germanic blood gave him in Uruguay.

He drove out of the compound and headed east toward his villa on the coast, reassessing the risk of what he'd done. Foreclosing had been a huge gamble, one he normally wouldn't have attempted, but he couldn't resist the temptation to acquire some of the finest commercial real estate in downtown Montevideo and across the river in Buenos Aires. If he lost, the consequences would be severe, but he had looked carefully into the cartel's finances and he'd been sure they would have no choice but to go along. The others in the consortium were frightened of the Colombians, but he wasn't afraid. He could outmaneuver these thugs any day of the week. He knew they were overextended, but made the loan anyway. With the collateral they had, he couldn't lose. He would disappear until the deadline passed, then he would reemerge and start the foreclosure proceedings.

He pulled onto the expressway that ran east and west along

the coast and quickly accelerated, frustrated at not being able to go over eighty miles per hour without risking the nuisance of a speeding ticket. Such a waste. The Germans had the right idea with their Autobahn. He slid a compact disc into the player and settled back. Mozart's Flute Concerto No. 1 in G came gliding through the speakers, soothing him. He glanced up in the rearview mirror. The same headlights that he'd seen shortly after leaving the compound of the resort were behind him. The left headlamp was out of alignment, glowing yellow. He watched it for a mile or so. It hung back far in the distance, making no attempt to close the gap. He decided it was nothing.

As the concerto's *adagio* spun to a close, Quintero saw the familiar four-way traffic signal shining like a star in the distance, signaling the end of the expressway. The light glowed red. Damn traffic lights were a nuisance on a deserted expressway. He braked and prepared to stop. The car behind him gradually closed the distance.

Quintero pulled up to the light. The car behind him shifted into the left lane and came to a smooth stop beside him. He glanced to his left. The car was empty except for the driver. He looked again. The driver was wearing a black hood over his head. He felt his blood run cold. Frozen with terror, Quintero stared at the dark figure. The man was sitting, calmly staring at him through white slits in the hood. He made no attempt to move. Quintero gripped the wheel, his heart hammering, unable to move. The man sat motionless, staring. What does he want? Is this a joke? Slowly, Quintero began to see it for what it was: an attempt to frighten him. If he'd meant to do him any harm, he'd have acted by now, done something. His heart rate began to subside. He swallowed, breathing easier. It was just a cheap trick. One that wouldn't work. Anger replaced his fear. He'd call that Colombian thug first thing in the morning and tell him he couldn't be intimidated. The green light in the opposite direction shifted to yellow. He looked straight ahead and prepared to accelerate.

Quintero felt something press against the back of his head, a gentle nudge against the base of his skull, something small and hard and cold. He glanced up in the mirror and saw a black hood rising from the rear seat. The dull glint of a nine-millimeter automatic shone in the yellow streetlight. He gasped and started to cry out just before a clap of thunder exploded in his head.

He slumped forward, his face resting against the steering wheel, amazed that he could actually feel the bullet crash through his skull, tear into his brain. His senses faded quickly. He felt the warm flow of urine below his waist turn cold, followed by a numbing paralysis that spread throughout his body. For a few seconds he saw faint shadows and heard distant sounds. The rear door opened and closed. The light turned green. A car drove slowly away.

Chapter Nine

Daniel Blake stood on the bridge of the *Latin Star,* peering through the rain with binoculars. A wave of desolation swept over him, watching the tiny speck that was the USS *Carlyle* fade over the horizon, blown by the capricious wind patterns of Tropical Storm Bruce. He lowered his binoculars and steadied himself against the binnacle.

"No way to signal her now. She's out of sight." He glanced at Frank Kozlewski, who was peering into the rain with a pained look on his face.

"Ain't this ship got a radio?" the chief asked.

Blake shook his head. "It was trashed along with all the navigation equipment."

"Let me take a look at it," Dana Kelly said. "Maybe I can fix it."

Blake looked at her eager eyes. She was trying to redeem herself for something that wasn't her fault. He felt like a bastard for not telling her the truth, but he didn't know how to tell her without scaring them all to death. The last thing he needed now was a panicked crew. He bit his tongue. "You can look, but I don't think so. There's not much left."

"Without a radio, we're screwed," the chief said.

"I don't know what happened to it," Kelly said. She ran through the explanation again, as if trying to understand it herself. "It was in the stateroom with me when Doc gave me that stupid pill. Sitting right by my bunk. I lay down for a minute. When I woke up, it was gone."

"Forget it," Blake said. "It's not your fault." He couldn't bring himself to tell her how close she'd come to buying the farm. The thought of that lunatic being in the same room with her, looking down on her while she slept, made his blood run cold.

"I thought Tobin was supposed to be watching her," Chief Kozlewski said.

"Said he stepped away for a cup of coffee," Doc Jones put in. "Said he was only gone a few minutes. One of the guys took it, that's what I think. Thinks he's being funny. Ain't that right, Lieutenant?"

Blake didn't answer. In his mind's eye he could see the radio drifting down through the undercurrents, settling onto the ocean floor as clearly as if he were watching it from an underwater camera. He cursed himself. There was no one else to blame. He knew from Doc's report that *El Callado* was still aboard, but he hadn't thought he would make a move until nightfall, if he'd move at all against an armed boarding party. It was a mistake that had almost gotten Kelly killed. The wind rose to a high-pitched howl and blasted through the superstructure. He looked out at thick sheets of rain whipping the bridge. The weather was deteriorating by the minute. He looked at the anxious faces. He couldn't keep them in the dark much longer.

"This weather ain't getting any better," the chief said, holding on to a handrail. His face was drawn. "When's that frigate due?"

"Forty-eight hours, hopefully sooner," Blake said. It was the first time he'd seen fear in the chief's eyes.

"That ain't gonna cut it," the chief said, clinging to the rail, blinking his eyes, looking out at sea. The wind was gusting, blowing the tops off waves. "We ain't gonna be here in forty-eight hours."

"What do we do now?" Kelly asked, leaning into a roll.

"Yeah," Doc Jones said. "How we gonna get off this bucket?"

Blake looked at the expectant faces. They were looking to him for answers. Answers he didn't have. He glanced out at the mountainous waves forming and the empty place on the horizon where the *Carlyle* had been. There was nothing to do now but level with them. He had a plan in the back of his mind, but it would take everything they had to pull it off. He couldn't shield them from the realities of the situation any longer.

"The first thing we do is secure the ship." He nodded to Frank Kozlewski. "Let's get everyone together."

"It's him, ain't it?" Frank Kozlewski said, drawing coffee. "That headcase Rivero was talking about." He and Blake stood alone by the coffee urn, leaning into a steep roll, waiting for the others to assemble in the dining salon. "He took the radio and threw it over the side. Trying to cut us off, isolate us."

Blake nodded. "I'd say that's a pretty safe bet." He took a sip of coffee and winced at the acid in his stomach. He hadn't had anything to eat since noon the day before. His stomach felt like it was full of ground glass.

"What are you going to tell the others?" The chief's face was drawn up into a worried look.

"The truth," Blake said. He grabbed a stanchion as the freighter pitched up and yawed to starboard. The ship rolled upright, groaning loudly. "They have a right to know."

Sparks came drifting in, rubbing his eyes, followed by Robertson and Tobin a few moments later. Luis Alvarez and Sergeant Rivero were the last ones in. They joined Doc Jones and Kelly at the urn and drew steaming mugs of coffee.

"All right," Blake said, motioning, "gather 'round." He leaned against the edge of the table and watched them without seeming to, trying to gauge their mood. He motioned for them to stand easy.

They clustered around the adjacent table, finding corners to sit on or lean against, looking at Blake, sipping coffee, finding comfort in familiar movements.

"We've got some problems we need to talk about," Blake said. He paused and took a drink of coffee, trying to set a relaxed tone. He could tell by the look in their eyes he hadn't. "Let's deal with the most pressing one first."

"What's that, Lieutenant," Alvarez said, holding on to the edge of the table. "Robertson ain't gonna cook no more?"

A few chuckles, then silence.

Blake smiled. "I wish it were that simple. The truth is, we have reason to believe there's someone else aboard." He paused to let it sink in, watching for reactions.

"Like who?" Sparks said.

"We're not sure, but we think there's a good chance that whoever killed the ship's officers and crew is still aboard."

"I knew it," Sparks said, glancing over at Kelly.

Dana Kelly raised her hand. "Wait a minute. Are you saying that's who took the radio?"

Blake nodded. "Probably."

Kelly blanched. "Are you telling me that I was asleep alone in a cabin with some lunatic murderer running around the ship?"

"You weren't alone," Blake said. "We posted a watch outside your door." He shot a look at Tobin, who looked down at his shoes.

Sparks was muttering in the background, "There ain't nobody aboard. She lost the damn radio. She's a Jonah. A goddamn Jonah. I knew it the day she came aboard."

Blake fixed the electrician with a withering glare. "That's enough."

Sparks breathed out one last "Jonah," and fell silent.

Blake settled back against the table. "Now there's no need to be unduly concerned. We're going to form search parties led by those of us with side arms. We'll go over the ship with a fine-tooth comb. If someone's aboard, we'll find him." He made it sound matter-of-fact, but it was a confidence he didn't feel. He'd sailed aboard merchant ships during sea year at the Academy, and for two years after, and knew it would be impossible to find someone on a cargo ship if he didn't want to be found. He'd heard apocryphal stories of stowaways living aboard freighters for months before finally being caught.

"Search parties?" Tobin said. "With all due respect, Lieutenant, shouldn't we stick together? If we find this guy, he isn't exactly going to welcome us with open arms."

"We'll have a better chance of catching him if we split up," Blake said. "He'd hear nine people coming, if we sweep one deck at a time. All he'd have to do is pop up on the next deck and wait for us to pass below him."

"Who is this guy, what does he look like, what are we looking for?" Tobin asked, his voice rising to a reedy pitch.

"We don't know much about him," Blake said. "All we know is he's a mute."

"A Mute?" Alvarez asked. "What the hell is that? Some kind of South American Indian tribe?"

"Are you for real?" Robertson said.

"Well, my grandmother was a Ute," Alvarez said.

"It means he don't talk," Robertson said. "He's a dummy, like you."

"That's not exactly right," Blake said. "He hears, but he doesn't speak. And he's no dummy. Don't underestimate him."

"Does he have a name?" Tobin asked.

"They call him *El Callado*," Sergeant Rivero spoke up.

"I don't think I like the sound of that," Tobin said. He screwed his face up into a painful squint. "What does it mean?"

" 'The silent one,' " Kelly said.

"Oh God," Tobin said.

"He'll be silent if he fucks with me," Alvarez said, fingering his bosun's knife.

"Yeah, you're a real bad hombre," Robertson said.

"Knock it off." Blake glanced at his watch. "I want to get started before it gets dark. Chief Kozlewski will lead the first party, consisting of Sparks and Robertson, through the third deck and below." He nodded to the Colombian marine. "Sergeant Rivero will lead the second party, consisting of Alvarez and Tobin, through the cargo holds. Doc, Kelly, and I will take the second deck and above, including the superstructure. Any questions?"

"What do we do if we find him?" Frank Kozlewski asked.

"Try to subdue him without any fireworks," Blake said. "We're sitting on a cargo of highly flammable chemicals."

"What about the radio, sir?" Tobin asked.

"We'll deal with that later," Blake said. He knew what had to be done next, but it was an ambitious plan, and he wasn't sure how much they could handle at once. He decided to reveal it one step at a time, on a need-to-know basis. "The first priority is to secure the ship. We'll start aft and work forward. When you're finished, muster back here. Remember to stick close to your leader and keep your eyes open."

Blake paused at the entrance to the narrow compartments under the forecastle and looked at his watch in a thin stream of daylight leaking in from the deck above. The search had taken longer than he'd thought, and he was eager to finish up before it got dark. Doc Jones and Dana Kelly stood behind him, dogging his heels. They had searched every compartment of the second deck, from the freshwater tanks aft to the area just forward of the number one cargo hold, without finding anything. He glanced at their faces to see how they were holding up. Kelly seemed calm, although she stuck close to him, while Doc Jones seemed to get edgier the longer they went without finding anything. Blake wiped the sweat out of his eyes and motioned for Kelly to hold the flashlight while he twisted the dogs open on a watertight door. She handed it back and he stepped over the shin-buster and stopped, shining the white beam down the murky passageway.

"How much more, Lieutenant?" Doc Jones asked behind him, his voice a dry whisper.

"This is it," Blake said. His voice rang hollow in the narrow passageway, louder than he'd intended. Instinctively, he toned it down. "The forwardmost compartment. We're directly beneath the fo'c'sle." Blisters of peeling green paint dotted the bulkheads like acne. Black water trickled in from a loose hatch on the main deck above. The weather outside made a muted backdrop for the sounds of heavy breathing and water sloshing across the passageway. Blake took a few cautious steps forward and stopped, aiming the flashlight at the last watertight door going forward at the end of the passageway. The beam of light came spiraling back from a brass nameplate marked BOSN'S STORES.

Blake began to feel a sense of unease. He didn't like confining places. He also didn't like guessing what was on the other side of a door. The ship was rolling heavily now. A film of cool sweat began to form on the nape of his neck. He steadied himself against the bulkhead and approached the door, which was dogged down tight. It was a standard watertight door, with heavy welded hinges on the right and three swivel latches on the left at the top, center and bottom. The latches, called dogs, had long handles for leverage. They were identical on each side of the door, enabling it to be secured from either side. He shoved the top latch upward with the heel of his hand, screeching it open. He could see by the shiny contact points that it had been used recently. The latch in the center easily gave way. As he reached down for the bottom latch, the top latch swiveled back in place with a resounding clang.

He jumped back as if he'd been shot.

"Oh my God, he's in there," Kelly said.

Blake felt the hair bristle on his scalp. He fumbled with the flap of his holster, cold sweat breaking out on his back.

"I'll go get the chief and Sergeant Rivero," Doc Jones said.

"No," Blake said. "It's too confining in here, somebody'll get hurt."

They stood in the semidarkness, breathing heavily, staring at the steel door as the center dog swiveled smoothly back into place. Blake snapped the safety off the Beretta with a metallic click that echoed down the passageway. He motioned for Doc and Kelly to stand back against the bulkhead. Approaching the door again, he took a deep breath, shoved the top latch upward and almost simultaneously swiveled the center latch open only to be greeted with the sound of the top latch being snapped back in place. He stepped back, breathing hard. "This is getting us nowhere."

He felt Kelly's hand on his arm.

"Doc's right, Lieutenant," she said. "This is crazy. Let's go get the others."

Blake stepped back from the door, motioning with his head for them to follow. "I can't risk letting him get away," he said. "We might not get another shot at this guy."

"Ain't there another way out of there?" Doc asked.

"No," Blake said. "This is it. It's shaped like a V. The bulkheads are the hull of the ship, the bow. He can't be too smart to let himself get trapped in a compartment like that. We won't have another chance like this."

"How are we going to do it?" Kelly asked. Her golden complexion had paled.

Blake looked at the door and let out a long breath. "We've got more hands than he has." He motioned them back over by the door. "Doc, you take the top, Kelly you take the center and I'll take the bottom. We'll open on three." He looked at Doc. "When it opens, pull the door all the way back and shield yourselves with it. I'm going in."

"Lieutenant, this is crazy," Kelly said. "If anything happens to you—"

"I'll be okay," Blake said. "Let's go."

They approached the door as if it were electrified. Blake crouched and nodded. They each took a firm grip and waited for the signal.

Blake looked up from his crouched position, cocked pistol in his right hand, flashlight tucked under his right arm, left hand on the bottom latch. "Okay, on three. One, two, *three.*" Latches clanged in unison, Doc Jones wrenched the door open and slammed Kelly back against the bulkhead, the steel door shielding him as he shielded her. Blake rolled over the coaming into the compartment. He came to his feet and shifted the flashlight to his left hand. Heart thudding in his chest, he flashed the beam of light around the V-shaped space, straining to see everything at once.

The steady white beam played over an array of maintenance supplies and equipment jumbled around the compartment, casting moving shadows that made him flinch. He swiveled his head around, expecting to be hit from behind. Stacks of coiled lines, wire rope, tarpaulins, cans of paint, wire brushes, chipping hammers, holystones, mops, and buckets were everywhere. He hesitated, then stepped around a pile of coiled rope. A faint shuffling sound came from the corner. The hair stiffened on the back of his neck. The adrenaline was pumping furiously now. He stood there, wondering if he could really kill someone, knowing he'd probably have to. He took another step. A scrambling sound. More shuffling. His heart hammered, pumping extra blood throughout his system, preparing him to fight or run. Beads of sweat rolled into his eyes, blurring his vision. He took another step around the pile of rope and froze.

The beam of his flashlight caught a dark huddled form, like a giant bat, crouching close to the deck. The form froze. The sparkle of a pair of eyes was caught in the beam of light, like an animal caught in headlights. Blake raised the automatic and aimed at a spot between the eyes, concentrating on holding his hand steady. He didn't want to kill it, whatever it was, but if it moved it was dead. They stared at each other, neither blinking, neither moving, for what seemed like a full minute. The pistol grew heavy in his hand. He elevated the flashlight with his other hand and leaned forward, squinting for a better look.

"Well, I'll be damned." His knees were suddenly weak.

Doc and Kelly came scrambling into the compartment. They stood behind Blake, looking over his shoulder.

"What is it, Lieutenant?" Kelly asked.

A laugh came from his core, a release of tension from the deepest part of him, that echoed in the close compartment. He stared down at the form, huddled under a blanket between two coils of rope. "It's a kid," he said in a wondrous tone. He said it again as though he didn't believe it. "A little kid."

"You're lyin'," Doc said from behind. He raised up and peered over Blake's shoulder at the dark form. "Well, kiss my granny," he said. "Damned if it ain't." He squinted into the shadows. "But what is it?"

"I don't know," Blake said. He raised the flashlight. Stringy black hair cascaded around a smudged face emerging turtlelike from the blanket. "I think it's a girl."

"Well, don't just stand there like idiots," Kelly said. She shoved her way around the two men and held out her hand. "Come on out, honey. We won't hurt you."

The child didn't move, eyeing Kelly warily, looking at her uniform.

Kelly knelt down. "Come on, sweetheart. I promise we won't hurt you."

The child looked past Kelly at Blake and Doc.

Kelly glanced over her shoulder. "Are you afraid of them? Don't be. They're ugly but they won't hurt you."

A weak, desperate smile crossed the girl's face.

Kelly moved closer and held out her arms. "Come on, darling."

The girl fell into Kelly's arms and began to cry. Softly at first, it became a wailing animal sound, a release of the grief and terror she must have suppressed for the last forty-eight hours.

Kelly rocked the little girl, stroking her matted hair. "It's okay, honey. After what you've been through, you can cry all you want to." She kissed the top of her head.

"That's just great," Blake said. He holstered his pistol and glanced at the corpsman. "That's all we need."

"Do me a favor, will you, Lieutenant?" Kelly said softly. She sat on her knees with her back to Blake and Doc, holding the sobbing child, caressing her gently.

"What's that?"

"Be quiet."

* * *

Blake carried the child into the dining salon and sat her down on a table. She felt weightless in his arms, but sitting upright she was taller than he had thought, seeing her huddled under the blanket. Also older. He guessed she must be somewhere around eleven or twelve. Under the grime and matted hair, she was a cute little kid, large brown eyes, sculptured face, porcelain skin. It was bizarre, but something about her looked familiar. He tried for a brief second to think where he'd seen her before and shook it off, knowing it was impossible.

Doc brought his medic kit over to the table and convinced her to open her mouth long enough for him to shove a thermometer under her tongue. She sat precariously on the edge of the table with her sneaker-clad feet dancing nervously on the bench, lolling the thermometer around in her mouth, clutching the blanket around her neck, eyeing Doc suspiciously.

Kelly emerged from the galley with a steaming mug. "Here you go. Tomato soup. Campbell's finest. What my grandmother used to give me. Drink this, you'll be good as new."

Doc slid the thermometer out of the child's magenta-colored lips and studied it in the light. "Ninety-eight point six," he said, shaking it back down. "She's a little dehydrated, and she's probably lost some weight, but she seems healthy enough."

"That's it?" Kelly said. "That's all you're going to check? Some doctor you are. She could have a broken bone, or something."

The corpsman spread his hands. "Look, I don't know anything about little kids."

"Well, at least look at her, for God's sake."

Doc shrugged and reached for the blanket.

The child clutched it tighter around her neck and drew back.

"It's okay, honey," Kelly said. "He's a doctor." She threw a dubious glance at the corpsman and lifted her eyebrows. "Sort of." She peeled the child's long thin fingers away from the blanket and lowered it from her shoulders.

Blake thought she was all arms and legs. She was wearing

faded blue jeans and a tank top, with red and blue stripes, that hung from her thin torso like a flag. Her collarbones protruded as if she'd been shrink-wrapped in her skin. Smooth round shoulders flowed into thin downy arms that seemed to go on forever. Long thin fingers made her hands seem too big for the arms they were attached to. She hugged herself and danced her toes on the bench, eyeing the hospital corpsman.

Doc took her left hand and gingerly stretched her arm out-right. He looked at her eyes, watching for a reaction as he ran his fingers down her arm, gently applying pressure along the way. He let it drop in her lap and repeated the process with her right arm. "She's fine," he said.

"Oh, for God's sake, Doc," Kelly said. "You act like she's a leper. Stand up, honey." The child allowed Kelly to lead her down from the table. She stood quietly while Kelly looked her over with a critical eye. Kelly ran her hands down her ribs, squeezing gently. Her hands nearly encircled the girl's torso. The child didn't flinch.

"I told you she was fine," Doc said.

"What's your name?" Kelly asked.

The girl looked at her.

"*¿Como se llama?*" Kelly asked again.

"The child swallowed. "Maria," she said in a soft dry voice.

Kelly leaned down with her hands on her knees. "Hi. I'm Dana Kelly." She brushed a finger against the girl's cheek and smiled, nodding over her shoulder. "This is Lieutenant Blake and Doc Jones." Kelly studied her eyes.

The girl looked past Kelly at Blake and Doc, but said nothing.

"*¿Habla Inglés?*" Kelly asked.

Maria tugged at her tangled hair and shrugged. "*Un poco.*"

Kelly smiled at her. "That's all you need. 'A little' is all these guys speak."

Maria laughed weakly.

Kelly gave the child a knowing look and bent close. "Let's speak English so these dummies can stay up with us."

Maria smiled and nodded.

"What are you doing aboard?"

Maria brushed the hair out of her eyes. *"Mi padre . . .* my father . . ."* She bit her bottom lip, fighting back tears.

Kelly put her arm around her. "Just take it slow."

". . . was taking me to visit *mi tía* Louisa . . . my aunt . . . in Buenos Aires . . ."

"And who was . . . who is your father?" Kelly asked.

"Numero dos . . ." Maria said, looking down.

"I don't understand," Kelly said.

"Number two," Blake said. "Second-in-command." Now he knew where he'd seen her. He studied her face. He'd seen her picture in the first mate's wallet. Poor little kid. He wondered how much she'd seen. He hoped she hadn't seen her father like that. It all made sense now. From the bridge, the bosun's locker would be a logical place to try to hide her while the first mate manned the helm and tried to radio for help. It could be dogged down tight from inside and, if you were quick enough, you could frustrate the hell out of someone on the other side trying to get in. The way she'd handled those dogs, it looked as though she'd had some practice. Blake felt his ears getting warm at the thought of that demented bastard trying to get to a little kid. He secretly hoped that Sergeant Rivero would be the one to find him. He doubted that the Colombian marine would be as genteel with him as Americans would be.

Kelly was smiling up at him. She stuck her lower lip out and nodded. "Very good, Lieutenant."

A cold blast of wind and spray swept through the dining salon. Kozlewski, Sparks, and Robertson stumbled in through the open door, dripping seawater. Robertson leaned into the door, slamming it shut against the wind.

Maria jumped behind Kelly.

"Any sign?" Blake said to Kozlewski.

The chief shook his head. "Not hide nor hair." He walked up to Blake, wiping water out of his eyes.

Maria peeked around Kelly's arm.

Kozlewski's eyes grew wide, looking at the child. He glanced at Blake. "Looks like you found something."

Blake nodded. "Not what we were looking for."

Sparks came around from behind the chief's broad shoulder, wiping salt water from his face. His eyes narrowed. "Well, now, what do we have here?"

"Nothing that concerns you," Kelly said.

"Ah, now, Sweetie, don't be like that," Sparks said, not taking his eyes off the child. He walked over to Kelly and tried to look around her.

Kelly stood blocking his way with her arms crossed, staring at him. "Did you lose something, Bozo?"

He glanced over his shoulder at Blake. "You gonna let her talk to me like that? I'm just trying to be friendly."

Maria peeked around Kelly at Sparks.

Sparks flashed a smile exposing crooked yellow teeth.

Blake thought he looked like a weasel in a henhouse. "Find something for that creep to do," he said quietly to the chief.

"Sparky," the chief said. "Go make some fresh coffee."

"Me? You gotta be kidding. I'm a first class. She's only a third class, and a woman to boot. Tell her to make coffee."

"A first-class jerk," Kelly said, looking him in the eyes.

"You heard me," the chief said.

"Fine, fine. I'll make coffee." He peered around Kelly's shoulder and flashed his yellow smile at the girl. "I'll see you later."

"Where in God's name did you find the kid?" the chief asked, scratching his head.

Blake filled Kozlewski in on the details, watching Sparks walk into the galley. If what he'd heard about Sparks was true, he was going to be a problem. "Excuse me for a minute, will you, Chief?"

Blake pulled the door closed that separated the galley from the dining salon and walked up behind Sparks as he was drawing water from the tap. Sparks glanced up and started filling a container with coffee grounds.

"Hey, Lieutenant, where'd you find the little cutie? Reminds me of a little doll I had in Buenaventura before we deployed. Couldn't a been more than twelve, thirteen. These bastards always lie to you, but you could tell this kid wasn't no more'n—''

Blake grabbed him by the arm and spun him around, sending the coffee reservoir clattering across the stainless-steel counter.

"What the hell's the matter with you?" Sparks said. His face was drained white.

"That little kid's been through hell," Blake said. "And I don't want to see you bothering her." His eyes narrowed. "You got that?"

Sparks stared at him, white saliva forming in the corners of his mouth, and nodded.

Blake gently released Sparks, smoothing his shirt, looking at him. "Good," he said. "I hope you do."

Sparks pulled back, straightening his shirt. "You're crazy. What are you so up tight about? Who gives a fuck about some little bean kid?"

Blake's eyes flashed.

"Okay, okay. Jeez. You can have it all to yourself. I get the message."

Blake stared at him, shaking his head. "How'd you get in the Navy?"

The chief pushed the galley door open and stuck his face through. "Lieutenant. Rivero's back."

Blake threw a final warning glance at Sparks and followed the chief into the dining salon. Rivero, Tobin, and Alvarez came stumbling in over the coaming, dripping water. Blake looked at Rivero's face, searching for some good news. The plan he had in mind was a long shot that would require an almost superhuman effort on everyone's part. He couldn't afford having a loose cannon like *El Callado* aboard to complicate things.

Rivero laid his M-16 across a table and wiped salt water from his face. He looked at Blake and shook his head. *"Nada, Teniente."*

"That's good news, ain't it?" the chief said. "That means he ain't aboard."

"No," Blake said. "That means we didn't find him. We'll

try again later.'' Blake looked at his watch and the dusk settling over the heaving sea. ''We've got just enough time left to get these guys buried before it gets dark. Better do it now, we won't have time tomorrow.'' He nodded to the chief. ''Let's put together a burial detail.''

The chief raised his eyebrows. ''A burial detail?''

''We can't leave these bodies lying around much longer,'' Blake said. ''We're too close to the equator.''

''Hell, let's just pitch 'em over the side,'' the chief said.

''We can't do that.'' Blake looked across the room at Maria, standing with Kelly. ''Let's try to make it as dignified as we can.''

The chief followed Blake's eyes across the room to the frail child standing with Dana Kelly and nodded. ''Yes, sir, we'll do our best.''

''Looks like we've got a break in the weather,'' Blake said, looking out the window. ''Have your people assemble all the bodies on the quarterdeck as soon as possible. Find some planks and some sheets for a burial at sea. Place all their possessions in envelopes marked with their names, if you can find them. We'll turn them over to the authorities.''

''Aye aye, sir,'' Kozlewski said.

Blake motioned Tobin over. ''I understand that you're a minister of some kind, or were, is that right?''

''Well, not exactly, sir,'' Tobin said. ''When I was sixteen, I was named a deacon in the Church of the Holy Gospel back home in Fort Wayne. Some thought I had the calling, but . . .'' He grinned sheepishly. ''After I preached a few sermons, the girls started to hang around and I kind of fell by the wayside. It didn't go anywhere.''

''I wondered if you'd like to say a few words over these folks. I believe I saw a Bible in the captain's stateroom.''

''Well, yes, sir. Like I said, I'm no preacher, but . . .''

''You'll do fine,'' Blake said. He looked at the chief. ''Best get started. I don't know how long the weather will hold. Kelly had better stay here with the girl. Call me when you're ready. I'll be in the chart room, behind the pilothouse.''

* * *

Blake was hunched over the chart table, writing on a pad of yellow paper, when Kozlewski walked in. "We're about ready, sir," the chief said, glancing down at the tablet.

"Everything in place?" Blake asked.

"All except the guy in the vault. They're bringing him up now."

"Let's do it." Blake tossed the pencil down and closed the cover.

Blake and Kozlewski stepped out of the superstructure onto the port quarterdeck, where six bodies lay neatly aligned, feet splayed out at a forty-five-degree angle, soles facing the weather rail. The bodies lay on sheets of plywood which had been stripped from packing crates by Robertson and Alvarez. The silhouette of the bodies could clearly be seen under thin white sheets, which Doc Jones had taken from the ship's laundry. A clear plastic envelope containing their possessions lay at the head of each victim, like a headstone. Inside the envelopes could be seen wallets, coins of various nationalities, pocketknives, keys, a few family photographs.

Blake looked up as Sergeant Rivero and Doc Jones walked quickly toward him, breathing hard, faces drawn. "What is it?"

"That body in the vault," Doc Jones rasped in Blake's ear. "It's gone."

"Gone? What the hell do you mean it's gone?" Blake said. "I thought you said the guy was dead."

"I thought he was," Doc said. "But I gotta tell you, I didn't take the time to look at him real close. I wanted to get the hell out of there."

Blake felt a cold tremor go through him. What the hell was going on here? Dead people didn't walk. Either the guy got up and walked away, or somebody moved him. Either way, it sent a chill through him. He looked at the others, staring at him curiously. "Let's get on with it," he said to Doc. "We'll sort it out later." He glanced up at Kelly and Maria watching from the window of the dining salon and nodded at Tobin to begin. The group stood solemnly, hands folded, heads slightly bowed. Tobin stood at the center of the formation of bodies, looking down on the six sheeted figures, clutching a small black Bible. He opened it to a place mark and began to read in a soft steady voice that was barely audible over the howl of the wind:

"The Lord is my shepherd; I shall not want. He maketh me to lie down in green pastures: He leadeth me beside the still waters . . ."

The ship took a roll to port as a huge wave crashed against the starboard side of the freighter and rolled across the quarterdeck, shifting the positions of the bodies.

"He restoreth my soul; He leadeth me in the paths of righteousness for His name's sake. Yea, though I walk through the valley of the shadow of death, I will fear no evil: for Thou art with me; Thy rod and Thy staff they comfort me . . ."

A gust of wind buffeted the group, snapping the funeral shrouds into puffy, elongated balloons. Dungarees, khakis and fatigues whipped and snapped in the wind. Blake struggled to keep his balance, hoping Tobin would keep it short.

"Thou preparest a table before me in the presence of mine enemies: Thou anointest my head with oil; my cup runneth over . . ."

The skies opened up with a torrential rain that came down in a solid sheet of water, drenching the dead and the living equally. Blake looked up and squinted. *Come on, Tobin.*

"Surely goodness and mercy shall follow me all the days of my life: and I will dwell in the house of the Lord forever."

Blake glanced impatiently at Tobin, hoping he wasn't going to launch into a lengthy sermon.

Tobin reverently closed the book, clenched his eyes tightly, and bowed his head. Water poured off the end of his nose as if coming from a spout. His voice seemed to rise an octave in an attempt to be heard over the wind.

"Oh, God," Tobin said in a singsong voice, "we commit the earthly bodies of our brothers of the sea, to the sea, and we pray you to accept their souls into heaven; and to keep them and comfort them, until the glorious day of Christ's coming on Earth, when the dead shall rise from the earth, and the sea shall give up her dead.'' He threw his head back in the rain, eyes tightly clenched, and said, ''Amen.''

A chorus of *Amen*'s rose from the group, followed by the sign of the cross, with dripping hands, from Chief Kozlewski, Sergeant Rivero, and Luis Alvarez. Tobin took a deferential step backward as the first body, the one next to Blake, was gently tilted up by Alvarez and Robertson. It slid from its packing crate bier into the sea with an audible ''ka-whump'' and disappeared, pulled down into the black water by ingots of tin Robertson had tied around its ankles. Images of six mutilated corpses floating upright in a macabre dance of death flashed across Blake's mind as each body was in turn launched from the quarterdeck into its watery grave. As the last body disappeared, a blast of cool wind against his shirt sent a shiver through him.

They all stood in the rain, heads down, dumbly looking at the now-empty deck before them. Then, with an awkward glance at one another, they turned and walked toward the superstructure with darkness assembling around them.

The solemn walk toward the shelter of the superstructure became a sprint as the rain intensified, drenching them with gusting sheets of gray water. They dripped single file up the ladder without speaking. The slightly burnt aroma of the coffee Sparks had made greeted them as they stepped into the dining room. Sheets of water from the driving rain swept the windows in a staccato of rapid fire gusts.

Kelly and Maria had turned away from the window. The girl was rubbing her eyes, huddled against Kelly. Blake handed the clear plastic envelope containing the first mate's possessions to her. ''This should go to you,'' he said, wiping water from his eyes. He looked into the child's grief-stricken face and put his hand on her thin shoulder. ''I'm sorry.''

Maria accepted the envelope and moved closer to Kelly. Kelly put her arm around the child and gave Blake a warm look.

Blake stepped away with Chief Kozlewski. "Anything of interest turn up in their personal possessions?"

The chief shook his head. "Just the usual stuff. Wallets, keys, pocketknives, different kinds of currency, stuff like that."

"Have you been able to identify who they were?"

"The three guys in the engine room were the chief engineer, the second engineer, and the ship's electrician. The guy down in the number three hold was an AB, an able-bodied seaman. I forget their names . . . all Spanish-sounding."

"It's not important," Blake said. He stared off in the corner. "With the captain, first mate, and chief engineer gone, it's not hard to see why the rest didn't want to stick around."

Kozlewski frowned. "It sure as hell ain't."

A huge gray wave came crashing down over the superstructure, rolling the freighter sharply to port. The ship righted itself with a tortured groan while the chief and Blake struggled to keep their footing. The howling wind whipped the superstructure with blankets of black water, covering the windows of the dining salon with an opaque haze. Gray water bubbled in around the windows and trickled down the bulkhead.

"Like I been telling you, sir, this weather ain't getting any better," the chief said.

Blake looked out at the weather and let out a deep breath. He couldn't avoid it any longer. "I know." He glanced at the chief. "Let's get everyone together."

"What's up?" the chief said.

Blake looked at the chief. "When I talked to the exec he said there was a good chance Tropical Storm Bruce would be upgraded to a tropical cyclone." He glanced out the window. "This weather seems to bear him out. I checked the barometer in the pilothouse again. It's fallen a point in the last hour. We can't rely on that Colombian frigate finding us before it hits. This old ship won't survive a full-blown tropical cyclone without power to the main engines and some expert ship handling. Maybe not even then."

The chief swallowed. "What are we going to do?"

"It's not like we have a big choice," Blake said. "We've got to get her under way."

Kozlewski's mouth fell open. "Are you kidding, sir? We ain't got half enough people to get a ship this size under way."

"We've got a crew of nine," Blake said. "Modern merchant ships don't have much more than that. A ship this size would have a crew of nineteen or twenty. But we can get by with half that."

The chief stared at Blake. "But, sir. Our crew of nine includes people like Doc, and Kelly, and Sergeant Rivero, and Alvarez. They don't know anything about getting a ship under way."

"We'll have to teach them," Blake said. "We don't have any choice. We'll just have to make do with what we've got."

"But hell, sir," the chief said, "even if we could get her under way, where would we go? What would we do?"

"It's not a question of going anywhere." Blake nodded toward the window. "If we can't maneuver when that cyclone hits, this ship will break up like an old house. We can't just sit here and wait for it to happen." He nodded toward the quarterdeck. "Unless we want to join those guys."

"This is crazy. The only seaman we've got is Alvarez, and he's never conned anything bigger than a twenty-foot motor whaleboat."

"I'll take the conn."

The chief looked at him and shook his head. "I don't know how to say this nice, Lieutenant, so I'll just say it. You ain't qualified as a deck officer. You're an engineer. You've never conned a ship before in your life." He looked at Blake's eyes and his voice took on a gentler tone. "Hell, that ain't nothing against you. I know that asshole Hammer won't let you qualify. Everybody knows."

Blake stiffened. He hadn't realized his personal frustration was common knowledge. "You got any better ideas?"

Kozlewski rubbed his face with a thick hand. He looked at Blake, then out at the weather. He nodded and managed a smile. "No, I guess not. Skipper."

"Very funny," Blake said, breathing out a sigh of relief. It would be an engineering miracle if they could really pull this off, but the chief was with him. At least they had a chance now. The next step was convincing the crew. He motioned for the others to gather around.

They came sauntering up, trying to keep their balance against the motion of the ship, looking apprehensive.

"Gather around," Blake said. "We don't have a lot of time, so I'm going to give it to you straight. Tropical Storm Bruce is probably going to be upgraded to a tropical cyclone. It's moving this way. There's a good chance it'll hit within the next twelve hours, before the Colombian frigate can get here."

"Cyclone?" Tobin said. "Is that anything like a typhoon?"

Blake nodded. "They go by different names depending on where you are in the world. In the China Sea, they're called typhoons. East of longitude 160, where we are, they're called cyclones. But whatever you call it, without power to the main engines and the ability to maneuver, the ship probably won't survive."

"Don't hold back, Lieutenant," Tobin said.

"I know that's a little cold," Blake said, "but we're out of time. That's the bad news. The good news is, we're going to get the ship under way."

They stared back at Blake without speaking for what seemed a full minute.

Finally Robertson spoke up. "A cold-start? Sir, that ain't no small job, even with a full crew that knows what they're doing."

"Five of us are engineers," Blake said. "The chief, Sparks, you, Tobin, and myself. It'll be up to us to teach the others what they need to know."

"We may be engineers," Robertson said, "but this here's a merchant ship. That's a whole different power plant than a destroyer."

"Not as different as you think," Blake said. "A steam turbine's a steam turbine. A boiler's a boiler. There are more similarities than differences."

Sparks raised his hand. "Even if we could get her under way, who'd take the conn?"

"I will," Blake said.

"You don't just drive one of these things all by yourself, like a car," Sparks said, looking doubtful.

"After we get up a head of steam, Doc Jones will man the helm. Dana Kelly will man the engine-order telegraph," Blake said.

Doc Jones put a hand against his chest. "Me?" He looked at Dana Kelly. "I'm going to drive this thing? Man, I'm from New York. I don't even drive a car. You must be joking."

"Some joke," Sparks said under his breath.

Blake glared at Sparks. "Doc will follow the headings I give at the helm. Kelly will relay the orders for engine speed to the engine room. Chief Kozlewski and his team will answer the bells."

"What about the kid?" Kozlewski asked.

Blake looked over at Maria, sitting on a table shivering, resting her feet on the bench. She looked like a bird that had fallen out of its nest. He hadn't counted on her when he'd made his plans. He'd have to find a way to keep her safe and out of the way. "She'll be with us on the bridge."

The light had begun to fade in the dining salon. Blake looked at his watch. It would be dark soon. "The thrust of the storm won't hit for several hours, probably not before morning. We'll begin the cold-start at 0300 and get under way as soon as we get up a head of steam. In the meantime I want you all to get some sleep."

"Where?" Sparks asked.

"There are eight passenger staterooms aboard," Blake said. "Pick one."

"Yeah, but there's nine of us," Sparks said. "Ten, with the kid."

"Some of you will have to double up," Blake said. "For security reasons I want us all to stay close together."

Sparks took a drag on his cigarette and flashed a yellow smile at Dana Kelly. Smoke streamed out of his nostrils like gray tusks. He leaned over and whispered, "How about you and me? You can bring the kid."

"You disgusting jerk," Kelly said.

Blake looked at Sparks, wanting to yank his cigarette out of his mouth and put it out on his forehead. The dumb bastard still hadn't gotten the message.

"Why all the security?" Tobin asked. "We turned the ship upside down looking for this *El Callado* and didn't find anything."

"It's just that it'll be easier to communicate if we're all together," Blake said. "Any questions?"

The sailors stared at him.

"The chief and I will be in the number one stateroom working up an engine-starting procedure," Blake said. "I want the rest of you to get some sleep. We've all had a long day, and tomorrow's going to be even longer. I want you to stay in your staterooms," he said, remembering the disappearing radio and now the disappearing body. "You're all critical to getting under way. We can't afford to lose anyone."

Chapter Ten

"Madre de Dios." Jorge Cordoba gaped out the side window of the Learjet as it descended through the trees, hovering over its shadow like a hawk over prey. It touched down with a puff of smoke and quickly reversed its engines, pitching him forward. He pulled his seat belt tighter and blew out a long breath. From the air, he hadn't seen the opening through the trees until the last minute and had thought they were going to crash. He glanced out at the tangled vegetation flashing by and gathered up his coat and briefcase, feeling limp with relief. The scream of the engines subsided, and the jet taxied toward a low building sheltered by overhanging trees. The plane swung around, bright moonlight reflecting on silver wings, and rolled to a stop in front of a row of crude hangars. He peered out through the fogged windows at the pole construction and corrugated tin roofs. So this was Campanilla.

The door cracked open with a sucking sound, and a rush of air smelling of wet asphalt rolled into the passenger compartment. The copilot pulled the door back, and Jorge stepped out onto the tarmac, happy to be alive. A light rain had transformed the landing strip into a shiny black ribbon. He stood in the rain, breathing deeply, and glanced around at his new surroundings.

The row of hangars at the near end, which housed the fleet of jets, was empty except for a Sabreliner crawling with mechanics in khaki uniforms. At the far end of the landing strip, two light green Blackhawk helicopters with the distinctive blue stars on their fuselages crouched under tin roofs like giant grasshoppers. Jorge had tried to dissuade Don Gallardo from displaying the blue-star insignia of the confederation so blatantly, but the Don had insisted, arguing that a visual symbol would help build unity. *Perhaps,* Jorge thought, smiling at the solid blue stars. Privately, he thought the real reason was because Don Gallardo took a perverse delight in flashing the confederation's symbol in the face of the *yanquis,* who wouldn't realize its significance until it was too late.

Adjusting his eyes for distance, he could see the deep green leaves of the Peruvian coca bush on the surrounding hillsides. A detachment of antiguerrilla forces based in nearby Punta Arenas patrolled the perimeter of the compound. The price for Army protection came high, but it would be impossible to move such vast quantities of crude coca paste to Colombia for refining without it.

He looked back toward the hangars and saw a squat figure in shirt-sleeves standing in the shadows next to a white Ford pickup truck, staring at him. Sizing up Don Gallardo's godson—just what he would expect from what he knew of Enrique Lopez. He returned the stare. The man flashed an obsequious smile and started across the asphalt toward him, skirting silver pools of water.

"*Buenos días, Señor* Cordoba. Welcome to Peru. I trust you had a pleasant flight?" The squat man smiled at Jorge and glanced past him, admiring the tall stewardess coming down the steps with her black leather flight bag over her shoulder.

"Not unpleasant," Jorge said, turning to glance at the stunning brunette himself. The flight attendant diverted her eyes. She'd done her best to seduce Jorge on the flight and seemed embarrassed that he'd chosen not to take her, but he hadn't been in the mood. His sleep during the two-hour flight from Montevideo had been interrupted with surreal dreams of lions chasing him through the streets.

"Permit me to introduce myself. I am—"

"I know who you are." Jorge stared at the man. "Congratulations on your appointment as acting security director." He made no attempt to conceal his lack of enthusiasm.

"You honor me," Enrique Lopez said, nodding slightly, extending his hand.

Jorge took the swarthy hand reluctantly. It would be hard to imagine an uglier man than Enrique Lopez. He had the body of a troll, with a dark acne-pitted face that looked like the surface of the moon. His black hair receded in a U-shape, exposing a patch of smooth scalp. A ribbon of scar tissue separated the two. He was called *Cara de Piña*, Pineapple Face, behind his back, but he was treated with respect. He had worked for Don Gallardo since the beginning, and his reputation as an assassin was well-known.

Jorge distanced himself from people like Lopez, who had made his name by personally disposing of Don Gallardo's most dangerous challenger in his rise to build the organization. In the process, he had also brutally disposed of the man's wife and four small children. The Don had expressed outrage over the killing of women and children and had made a show of exiling Lopez to the field. But after listening to the phone conversation with Admiral Cuartas, Jorge wondered if the Don hadn't protested too much. Now that he thought of it, no new challengers had risen to the occasion since. Perhaps Enrique Lopez had been Don Gallardo's way of sending a message. Jorge had avoided any knowledge of such things, choosing to focus on the financial operations of the business, but now understood that it was sometimes necessary to eliminate opposition when there was no other way. His order to eliminate Fabio Quintero had been the first time he had ever done such a thing, but Quintero had forced his hand, and it couldn't be avoided. He had found it surprisingly easy to do; still, there were limits.

Women and children. Jorge wondered what made a man like

Lopez tick. He glimpsed into his black eyes for a brief second, trying to see inside him. He saw ruthlessness, which he expected, but he also saw a level of intelligence that surprised him. It was a dangerous combination.

"This way, Señor Cordoba." They walked toward the truck. Four armed guards with AK-47s resting between their knees sat in the back of the pickup, hats pulled low, shielding their eyes from the rain. They looked like common hoodlums to Jorge. "This is Señor Cordoba," Lopez said. "He is Don Gallardo's godson. While he is here, he is under my protection. What happens to him, happens to you." The four scrambled out of the truck and formed a circle around Jorge.

"Get rid of these thugs," Jorge said, suspecting that Lopez intended them to be more constraint than protection.

"As you wish." Lopez nodded, and the men stood back.

Jorge threw his coat over his shoulder and walked with Lopez past the row of hangars to a footpath carved into the jungle. He followed behind, glancing up at the back of Lopez's sweat-stained shirt, picking his steps carefully, watching a layer of debris gather over his Gucci slippers. The thrum of diesel generators grew louder, muffling the tropical sounds of the jungle. He wrinkled his nose at the acrid smell of chemicals hanging on the air. The narrow path sloped down and grew darker, gradually becoming a tunnel through thick vegetation. After a hundred yards, the path opened up to dusky streams of moonlight and a low building of concrete-block construction. The building was small, perhaps fifty by seventy-five feet. Hidden by overhanging trees, it was invisible from the air. Radar and radio antennae bristled from the red-tiled roof.

Lopez paused at the steel door and spoke into an intercom, while Jorge glanced around at raucous tropical birds competing with the noise of the generators. The door latch snapped, and Lopez pulled the heavy door back. Jorge stepped into an area ringed with small offices separated by glass partitions.

"You can put your things in there," Lopez said, nodding to an empty cubicle. Jorge threw his coat over a chair and followed Lopez through a double door. A blast of refrigerated air chilled his shirt. He stopped and adjusted his eyes to the dim light. A bank of technicians glanced up, their faces green from the glow of radar screens. Radio operators at a console looked up with heavy eyelids, then turned back to an array of knobs and dials, making notes on clipboards. The walls were decorated with colored maps. The air was heavy with the smell of stale cigarette smoke.

"This is it," Lopez said, sweeping his hand around the room. "Command and control for our European shipments." He motioned for Jorge to follow him to a map table. The table was backlit, illuminating a vast field of blue. He tapped a hairy finger against a grease-penciled spot a few inches off the coast of Peru. "This is the last known position of the *Latin Star*. Ten degrees 35 minutes south latitude, and 82 degrees 14 minutes west longitude."

"How far off the coast?"

"Two hundred and fifty miles, perhaps less."

"Any communication from the ship?"

Lopez shook his head. "We haven't expected any. I'm sure the ship's radio is out of commission."

"What makes you so sure?"

Enrique Lopez smiled. "Your pet would have destroyed the radio before he got down to business."

"What do you mean by that?"

"I mean the business of killing every member of the crew."

"No, no. You said 'your' pet." Jorge stared at him. "What did you mean by that?"

Lopez smiled. "It's not important."

That goddamn smile again. "I'll decide what's important," Jorge said. "Answer me."

"I did not mean to give offense," Lopez said. "Rafael Ayala boasted that he had taken the one called *El Callado*, the silent one, from the Ramirez organization during a raid on their main processing lab. He said he was training him with your approval."

"That's a lie. I gave no such approval."

Lopez nodded deferentially. "If you say it, then it is so."

Jorge glared. If he heard one more word linking him to this *mudo,* this freak of nature Ayala kept like a pet dog, he was going to explode. He forced himself to concentrate on why he was there. He glanced at his watch. "All right, drop it. We've got work to do. In less than six hours a Colombian Navy frigate will be leaving Buenaventura. We've got to locate the ship before they do."

"Of course. Please forgive any inference that you were responsible. It was completely unintended."

Jorge watched him turn away, smiling. He couldn't read this ugly troll. He had the distinct feeling he was laughing at him, that he was privy to some great secret Jorge didn't know. He shook it off. "How many planes do we have in the air?"

"Twelve. All the jets we have, except for the Sabreliner you saw being worked on," Lopez said, all business again. "We're sweeping the area for several hundred miles around the coordinates you gave us."

"What's wrong with the Sabreliner?"

"Fuel-line problems. It's common in this humidity. It should be flying within the hour."

"What about the weather?"

"Our meteorologists report that Tropical Storm Bruce has now been upgraded to a tropical cyclone."

"Which direction is it heading?"

"Toward the freighter, but it keeps changing direction."

"Will it impact the search?"

"Not for the next several hours. The planes can fly over it, but if it hits, it could sink an unmanned ship."

"Why would you assume it's unmanned?" Jorge asked.

Lopez gave Jorge a condescending look. "I have seen the *mudo* in operation, Señor Cordoba. I can assure you, no one is left alive."

"Perhaps not the original crew, but you're forgetting it's been boarded by the American Navy," Jorge said.

Lopez laughed in a high-pitched squeal that startled Jorge. "And you're forgetting I've seen the *mudo* at work. He will take them one by one. There will be meddling American tongues scattered throughout the ship like leaves from a tree.''

''It would be a mistake to underestimate an armed boarding party from a US Navy warship,'' Jorge said.

''Perhaps,'' Lopez said, flashing his smile.

''What's the range on the helicopters?'' Jorge asked, wanting to change the subject.

''With the added fuel tanks, enough to get there.''

''You mean a one-way trip?'' Jorge asked, incredulous.

''There is a landing pad on the ship,'' Lopez said. ''After the first helicopter has landed, we will make room for the second.''

''How?''

Lopez shrugged. ''When the second wave comes in, we will push the first helicopter over the side.''

Jorge grimaced at the thought of pushing a seven-million-dollar helicopter into the ocean, then caught himself.

Lopez seemed amused at his reaction. ''The helicopters are nothing, Señor Cordoba, compared with what is at stake here.''

That smile again. Jorge wanted to wipe it off his ugly face. He forced himself to concentrate. ''If the cyclone hits full force, could the *Latin Star* survive such a storm?''

''The ship is very old,'' Lopez said. ''It would have a chance, but only if there is power to the main engines and some competent ship handling.''

''According to the information we have, the American in charge of the boarding party is the destroyer's engineering officer,'' Jorge said.

Lopez nodded. ''So I understand.''

''What's the likelihood that such a person could get a ship like the *Latin Star* under way and maneuver it through a cyclone?'' Jorge asked.

''It might be possible for the American officer to get the ship under way with an experienced crew,'' Lopez said, ''but it is doubtful that he would have the experience to maneuver the ship in a storm, although he doubtless will try, unless he is a complete fool.''

"Does it follow, then, that if he survived the storm, he would be able to steer the ship to a port somewhere?"

"I would think it unlikely that an engineer would be able to navigate or conn the ship with any accuracy," Lopez said. "Keep in mind also, that in all these endeavors, the American officer will no doubt have the added complication of dealing with the silent one." He smiled.

Jorge lit a cigarette and leaned back against the table, rubbing his eyes, trying to guess what the American officer would do, how to counter it. So many variables, so little time. A wrong move could be fatal. He told himself to relax and think. The Harvard Business School was famous for its case-study method of analyzing business problems. He had studied complex business situations with the *Norte Americanos*. He understood the *yanqui* mentality. The arrogant bastards thought they could do anything. That would be the underlying assumption.

"Let's think this through logically," Jorge said.

Lopez leaned back against the table and folded his arms. His smile faded into a smirk.

"The first question we need to answer is whether the Americans are in control of the ship," Jorge said. "It's possible that the entire boarding party has been eliminated, and the ship is drifting, dead in the water. But I don't think so. A boarding party from a US Navy warship would be armed, unlike the crew of the *Latin Star,* and would be able to deal with *El Callado*. So it would be prudent to assume that the boarding party is in control of the ship."

Lopez looked amused.

"The second assumption we should make is that the American officer is not a fool," Jorge said. "To underestimate any opponent would be a serious mistake." He looked at Lopez, hoping he got the double meaning.

"I agree," Lopez said, returning the look.

"Given those two key assumptions," Jorge said, "it's safe to assume that the American officer will try to get the ship under way to save it and his crew from the storm."

"And then?" Lopez asked.

"If he succeeds in that, he will simply ride out the storm and wait to be rescued, lacking the necessary skills to navigate the ship to port."

"Your logic is faulty, Señor Cordoba," Lopez said. "When the American officer sees the cargo and realizes who owns the ship, he will know that to sit and wait would mean almost certain death. Therefore, if he could not navigate the ship, he would try to make a run for it and hope he is spotted by friendly forces before he is spotted by our planes."

Jorge nodded, reluctantly. The little troll was right. "But in which direction would he run?" he mused aloud.

"Obviously, he would head toward the nearest land," Lopez said, "and that would be east, toward the coast of Peru. If the ship is 250 miles off the coast, we will have ample time to intercept and land a crew aboard by helicopter. The boarding party will, of course, have to be disposed of, but this can be done cleanly on an isolated ship at sea." Lopez's dark eyes seemed to glow at the prospect.

"Very well," Jorge said. "If we can't locate the ship and take control before the storm moves in, we'll concentrate our search efforts in this area." He drew a circle around the area between the coast of Peru and Lopez's grease-penciled spot on the map.

"As you wish, Señor Cordoba. I will transmit your instructions to the pilots." Lopez walked over to the console of radio operators on the other side of the room.

Jorge remained standing by the map table, looking at the grease spot on the vast field of blue, his mind filled with thoughts about this American naval officer who held the fate of the organization in his hands. With the rank of lieutenant, Jorge reasoned, the American officer must be about the same age as himself. He wondered how the young lieutenant would cope with *El Callado,* the savage *mudo* Ayala had placed aboard the ship. Jorge had advised against using this unproven beast to guard such an important shipment and he had been right. Loyalties ran deep in Colombia.

And if he survived *El Callado,* Jorge wondered what the

reaction of the lieutenant would be when he saw the cash. Three hundred fifty million US dollars. It was more money than a naval officer would see in ten thousand lifetimes. He smiled at the thought.

But most of all, Jorge wondered if the young lieutenant had the skills to keep the ancient ship afloat, to save it for the organization and for the future of Don Gallardo's children. If he succeeded, the descendants of Don Augusto Gallardo would be eternally grateful to the unknown American officer. Candles would be lit for him at mass, and he would be well remembered in death.

Jorge looked up as Enrique Lopez approached. ''Your visit has brought good fortune, Señor Cordoba.'' His scarred face was pulled into his familiar smile. ''We have a sighting.''

Chapter Eleven

Blake unlocked the louvered door to stateroom number one with the ring of keys he'd found in the captain's cabin and leaned into it, cracking it free from what appeared to be a dozen layers of white paint. The wooden door, decorated with an oval porcelain tag bearing a faded number one, gave way with a shudder, releasing a rush of musty-smelling air. He stepped inside and glanced at the 1930s oriental-style decor, struck by how out of place it looked on a cargo ship. He opened a brass porthole, admitting a stream of fresh air, and walked over to a small writing desk affixed to the bulkhead.

"Looks like a Persian whorehouse," Frank Kozlewski said, stepping in behind him. He wrinkled his nose and sniffed. "Smells like one, too."

Blake ignored him. The chief was going to be difficult; he'd been having second thoughts about getting the ship under way since the weather had started to improve. Blake sat down at the desk and flipped to a clean sheet of the yellow tablet he'd retrieved from the chart room. He drew a rough outline of the bow of a ship, followed by a series of connected boxes, four to starboard and four to port. He numbered them one through eight—even numbers port and odd numbers starboard—beginning with the forwardmost cabin on the starboard side and ending with the aft cabin on the port side. He began writing names in each of the boxes, beginning with his own name in box number one.

Kozlewski peered over Blake's shoulder. "Drawing pictures?"

"I need to know where everyone is," Blake said. "You're in number three behind me, Sergeant Rivero's in number five and Doc Jones is in number seven on the starboard side," he said, writing in names as he went. "On the port side, Kelly and the girl are in stateroom number two, just across from us, Sparks is behind them in number four . . ." He paused, irritated that Sparks had managed to finagle himself into the cabin directly behind Kelly and the girl, wondering what kind of mischief he was up to. "Robertson's in six, and Tobin and Alvarez are doubled up in number eight."

"I think we should have doubled everybody up."

"I'm trying not to scare everybody to death," Blake said. "Besides, who'd want to sleep with you?"

"You got a point, but I think we ought to at least post a watch," the chief said.

"The only one I'd trust out there alone tonight would be Sergeant Rivero, and he's standing watch in the engine room."

"What good's the machinery if all our people get murdered in their sleep?"

"They'll be okay if they stay in their rooms," Blake said. "But if anything happens to that plant, we'll never get out of here."

"We got side arms, we ain't exactly helpless. You don't have to be no marine to stand watch."

"Who would you post? Tobin? Robertson? Alvarez? Doc? Even with a side arm they wouldn't be any match for someone lying in wait. If this guy was good enough to pick off almost the entire crew one by one . . ." His voice fell away. "It's too dangerous to expose our people like that."

"But what if this headcase . . . how you say his name?"

"Kelly says it's *'El Ky-yad-o,'* means 'the silent one.'"

"So what if *El Callado* decides to open the seacocks and scuttle the ship while we're asleep?" the chief said. "We wouldn't even know it 'til it was too late."

"If he was going to do that, he would have done it by now," Blake said. "That's not what this guy's about. I get the feeling from talking with Rivero that this joker's guidance system has somehow malfunctioned, that he's on some misguided mission to protect the ship and its cargo for who he perceives his real masters to be, this Ramirez cartel. Sinking it's the last thing he'd want to do."

"And that missing corpse in the vault. Gives me the creeps." Kozlewski looked at Blake. "What you think he's up to?"

"I don't know," Blake said. "I've got a couple of theories, but . . . I just don't know."

The chief gazed out the porthole into the black night. "I wonder where he is, what he's thinking, what he's doing right now?"

"I'd give a year's pay to know that."

"What did you learn from the little girl?"

"Not much," Blake said. "Kelly and I tried to talk to her, but she got upset every time we brought it up. Poor kid. It's not hard to see why."

The chief shook his head. "I'll be damn glad when we find him. A guy like that running around loose aboard a ship can cause a lot of trouble."

"We can deal with whatever he does after the fact," Blake said. "But I'm not going to expose our people trying to prevent it. I'm not going to play the game on his terms. We need every pair of hands we've got if we're going to get under way."

"Too bad you couldn't get the girl to talk. Maybe she could tell us something that would help us find him," the chief said.

"She's bunking with Kelly. I asked Kelly to talk to her later, after she's calmed down. Maybe she'll have better luck alone."

The chief looked out the porthole again and looked at Blake, rubbing the side of his nose. "Weather seems to be getting better all the time, Lieutenant. Maybe we should just wait for that Colombian frigate. The wind's calm now. Maybe that storm'll go right past us. The exec said it keeps changing direction.''

"We can't count on that," Blake said.

"Yeah, I know. But we also can't count on getting this pile of junk under way without blowing it up in the process," the chief said. "We've got an inexperienced crew here. We need to weigh the risks of doing a cold-start and maybe blowing up one of the boilers. Where'd we be then?''

Blake let out a tired breath. He'd heard Kozlewski's arguments on the way down from the dining salon. "We've got a core of experienced hands," he said. "You've got thirty years' experience as a boiler tender. Robertson's a second-class BT. Tobin's a third-class machinist's mate. They're both young, but they're good men. Sparks is a louse, but he knows what he's doing. I sailed as a third assistant engineer for a couple of years. I've done a couple of cold-starts on merchant ships."

"Yeah, sitting next to a dock, with auxiliary power lines coming in to back you up. But not out in the middle of the ocean, not in a storm. And sure as hell not on one as old and beat-up as this." The chief stroked his chin. "I don't know. There's an awful lot that can go wrong. With all those chemicals on board . . . If we had a fire in the engine room, we got no pumps, nothing to fight it with, we could end up blowing this thing sky-high. With no lifeboats, we'd be screwed. I just don't know if it's worth the risk."

"If we wait for the storm to hit, it'll be too late," Blake said. "If we're going to get under way, we've got to do it now.''

"I don't know how you figure we got all this experience, sir. The only real experience we got is you, me, and Sparks. Robertson and Tobin ain't been around that long.''

"Long enough," Blake said. "We're dealing with a basic power plant here. Single screw, turbine-driven through reduction gears. Six thousand shaft horsepower. It's all vintage stuff, but nothing unusual. Pair of GE turbines, one cross-compound

unit, one high- and one low-pressure turbine. Gravity-type lubri-
cating-oil system—''

"Did you get a close look at the turbines?" The chief screwed
up his face. "They look like something out of a museum."

"You don't have to worry about the turbines," Blake said.
"The older ones were built to last forever. But there's piping,
just in case. We can cut over and run either the high- or the
low-pressure turbine as a stand-alone if we have to in a pinch."

"And those boilers . . . Jesus."

Blake struggled to keep his voice level. "They're as good
as any marine boilers you'll find today. Babcock and Wilcox,
oil-burning, sectional header, single-pass type. About 500
PSIG."

"I'd be afraid to go near 'em with a full head of steam."

"Damn it, there's nothing wrong with the boilers," Blake said.
"They're old, but—" He started to say, "They'll be here when
you and I are gone," and stopped himself. "They'll do what we
need them to do." He flipped back to the front page of the tablet.
"I've started to sketch out an engine-starting procedure. It's a
little rough yet, but—"

"Is that what you were working on in the pilothouse?" the
chief asked. "You planned to do this all the time, didn't you?"

"When the *Carlyle* and the weather went south at the same
time, I knew we had to do something."

"Well, I think we're taking a hell of a big risk," the chief
said, looking out into the relative calm of the night, "for you
to play captain—"

Blake stiffened. "Is that what you think this is about?"

"We got no backup, Lieutenant. No place to go. If we shit in
our nest, we ain't got another. I just think it's damn risky—"

"I agree there's risk involved in getting under way," Blake
said, "but in my mind there's a lot greater risk in doing nothing.
Don't be fooled by this lull in the weather. When you're anywhere near the vicinity of a tropical cyclone the weather can
change in a heartbeat."

As if on cue, the ship suddenly pitched up, shuddered, and
rolled sharply to port. The chief grabbed Blake's chair and

hung on with wide eyes, waiting for the ship to right itself. He let out a deep breath. "Well, you could be right. But even if you are right about the weather, I still don't think we've got enough people to pull this off."

"If we had one man less, we might not," Blake said, "but I've worked out all the assignments, at least in my head, and I think we can do it."

"In your head?"

"Sit down. I can show you on paper," Blake said.

The chief stared at him.

Blake threw him a look that said the discussion was over. "We don't have a lot of time, Chief. Let's get started."

"Yes, sir," Kozlewski said. He retrieved the other chair, which was lying on its side against the bulkhead, and pulled it up to the small desk. "But I gotta tell you, I don't know anything about merchant ships. I'm way outta my element here."

"Cut the crap, Chief. You've been a boiler tender for thirty years. You've done cold-iron start-ups on everything that floats in the Navy," Blake said. "Suddenly you've never seen the inside of an engine room." Glancing up at Kozlewski, he saw the fear behind the old man's eyes, and softened. He paused for a moment and said, "What's the problem?"

Kozlewski rubbed his face in his hand. "Tell you the truth, I'm scared shitless."

Blake nodded. "So am I."

"Yeah? Well you sure as hell don't act like it, pushing to get this thing under way. He can pick us off one at a time down there, slinkin' around in that engine room. There's a million places a guy like that could hide, just biding his time waiting for someone to come along to check a gauge or close a valve. You saw what he did to those other poor bastards. I say we stay here, stay together, wait 'til we get picked up."

"I wish that were an option," Blake said, "but it's not."

"You think he'll bother us down there? That many of us, I mean?"

"That depends on how smart he is," Blake said. "If the

weather gets worse, he may be smart enough to figure out that he needs us, that we're his only hope of keeping this thing afloat.''

''You think a whacko's smart enough to figure that out?''

''Crazy doesn't mean stupid,'' Blake said. ''Some of the most violent sociopaths are cunning as hell.''

''And what do you think he'll do if the weather stays like this?''

''If the weather stabilizes and he thinks he doesn't need us, he'll probably go for us, one by one. All the entries in the log said that's his style. But in either case, we should be okay together in the engine room. He's not likely to charge into a group of people armed only with a knife.''

''Well, I guess that's that,'' the chief said with resignation. ''What have we got to do?''

''I've checked off some preliminary stuff,'' Blake said. ''The good news is the boilers were laid up wet.'' He put a check by the first item.

''Not hard to see why,'' the chief said.

Blake nodded. ''They were obviously in one big hurry to get off this thing.''

''No bigger hurry than me.''

''That's two of us,'' Blake said. He turned back to the tablet and checked off the next three items on the list. ''The DC heater is full of water, the distilled-water tank is full, and there appears to be enough Bunker C fuel oil in the settling tank to get us started.''

''What about the stern tube?'' the chief asked.

''I looked at it,'' Blake said. ''The oil-sealing system appears to be okay. No leaks that I could see.'' He checked it off.

''What's next?''

''We'll need to sound all the fuel-oil tanks and water tanks,'' Blake said, writing down the next item. ''After that, we'll cut off all the emergency power going to the rest of the ship''— he glanced up at the single bulb glowing white in the overhead—''and route it to the engine room and boiler room through the emergency electrical bus. Then we begin the process of lighting off one of the boilers.''

"That might take some doing," the chief said.

"Same basic procedure as a destroyer. First step is to make sure the bottom and surface blow valves are closed and not leaking." He wrote it down.

"Better check the steam stop valves," the chief said.

"Right," Blake said, writing it down. "What's next?"

The chief shrugged. "Unless you want to be adding water to the boiler while you're raising a head of steam, you'd better make sure the main feed valves are closed."

"That's right," Blake said, writing faster now. "Just like a destroyer." He glanced at the chief. "What's next?"

Kozlewski squinted into the corner. "I reckon we'd have to make sure the air cocks on the steam drum and water drum are open."

Blake nodded encouragement, writing. "What else?"

"Make sure the root valve and burner valve are closed?"

"We'll make a merchant mariner out of you yet," Blake said. "Next we'll line up the fuel-oil system and recirculate fuel through the heater to get it hot enough for atomization."

"That's got to be at least 150 degrees," the chief said. "What if those old heaters won't get it that hot?"

"They looked okay to me, but if there's a problem, Sparks can handle it," Blake said. "Next, we'll start the forced-draft fan and let it run for a while."

"A helluva while," the chief said. "You're going to have to purge every trace of combustible gases out of those boilers. . . ." The chief paused. "Listen. You hear that?"

"What?"

"Nothing, I guess. I thought I heard . . . a shuffle. It almost sounded like a footstep outside."

"I'll check," Blake said, starting to get up.

The chief stopped him, listening. "No, it's okay, just the waves against the hull, I reckon."

"Okay," Blake said. "We're almost home. We'll need to check the water level in the boilers to make sure we've got enough, then we'll gradually close in on the fuel-oil recirculating valve until we've got a fuel-oil pressure of at least 150 PSIG. Then we're clear to light her off. Got your pipe lighter?''

"Never leave home without it," the chief said, patting the front pocket of his khakis.

"Take care of it. That lighter could be the key to our survival."

"Funny, ain't it?" the chief said. "Without a match, we couldn't move this tub a foot."

"For want of nail . . ." Blake said, writing.

"A nail, sir?"

"Poor Richard's Almanac. Okay. We'll make a torch out of a burning rag, you shove it into the boiler through the peephole, we'll open the root and burner valves. When the burner ignites, we'll close the fuel-oil recirculating line." Blake started on the next page, writing furiously.

"Listen," the chief said. "There it went again. That shuffling sound. You hear it?"

"All I hear is the waves against the hull," Blake said.

The chief cocked his ear. "I guess that's all it is. I'm getting jumpy. How long you reckon it'll take these old boilers to come up to line pressure?"

"It shouldn't take more than an hour." Blake paused and tapped his pencil against the tablet. "Maybe a little longer because of their age, but not that much." He shoved the tablet over to Kozlewski. "That's a pretty simplified list of what we'll need to do."

The chief squinted at the yellow sheet. "Looks easy enough on paper, but timing's critical on some of this stuff. Just hope we've got enough hands to pull it off."

"We don't have any people to spare, but we'll have enough," Blake said. He spent the next few minutes going down the list, writing in names, making assignments, showing the chief how certain jobs could be combined, how it would be tight, but how, with luck, they could make it happen. As he got to the end of the list, he could tell by the grunts and nods that the chief was becoming reconciled to the idea.

"Well, at least we've got the right mix of people," the chief said. "You were right to bring Sparky. There's no way we could get lit off without the emergency diesel. He's a pain in the ass, but we'd be screwed without him."

"He'll be all right if we can keep him focused," Blake said, thinking about Maria and the predatory look on Sparks's face when he was around her. He was grateful that Kelly was here to take care of the girl. She wouldn't take any crap from Sparks, certainly not where Maria was concerned. In spite of the dangers, he was glad she'd come along.

Blake heard a sound outside the door, the soft snap of wire cutters biting through heavy-gauge wire. He spun around, his breath caught in his throat. The silhouette of a large man was clearly outlined against the white louvers, the door handle rattling softly, the door pulsing in and out.

"Mother of God, he's outside the door," the chief whispered.

Blake grabbed his pistol and lunged for the door. Tugging at the handle, he could feel that something was holding it from the outside. He jammed the pistol in his belt and took the door handle in both hands. After several violent yanks, he jerked it open and stepped out into the passageway in time to see the dark figure of a man disappear down the ladder to the deck below. He glanced down at the deck and saw a length of heavy-gauge wire dangling from the bulkhead and a pair of wire cutters. The other end of the wire was tied to the handle of a box containing a fire axe that was adjacent to the door of the stateroom. "The son of a bitch was trying to lock us in."

"And he damn near did it. Come on," the chief said, fumbling with his pistol. "Here's our chance to catch the sneaky bastard, kill him before he can kill us."

"No," Blake said, holstering his pistol. "That's just what he wants us to do. He'd have the advantage in the dark."

Kozlewski stopped short, seeming to come to his senses. "Reckon you're right about that." He let out a visible shudder. "What do you think he was trying to do?"

"We're the only two guys with side arms," Blake said. "He obviously planned to lock us in and go after the others."

"Jesus Christ," the chief said. "What the hell do we do now?"

"I'll check on everyone, make sure they're okay. Right now, you'd better get some sleep."

"I ain't gonna be sleepin' much, after that." The chief blew out a long breath. "What time you want me to wake you up?"

"We'll get started at 0300."

Blake walked the chief to the number three stateroom located just behind his own and waited for him to open the door, looking both ways down the quiet passageway. A single white light glowed in the overhead from the emergency generator, dimly illuminating the black-and-white-tiled corridor. Kozlewski leaned into the door, cracking it open, and looked at Blake over his shoulder. "Sure you don't want me to stay with you?"

Blake smiled. "Neither one of us would get any sleep."

"Reckon you're right. I'll wake you up at 0300," the chief said, closing the door behind him.

Blake waited to hear the click of Kozlewski's lock, then made the rounds to each stateroom, gently rapping on each door and asking through the louvers if everything was okay, reminding everyone to stay in their staterooms. He wasn't surprised to find that everyone was still awake. *No one's going to get much sleep tonight,* he thought. Still shaken, he returned to his cabin, pulled the door closed behind him, and locked it.

Unbuckling his pistol belt, he laid it across a chair and stretched out on the bed. A wave of exhaustion rolled over him. The ship was gently heaving on smooth rolling swells now. He lay with his hands behind his head, the weariness draining out of him, staring up at the overhead, listening to the pleasant murmur of waves lapping against the hull.

He should have been pleased with the sudden improvement in the weather, but in a bizarre way he knew it was the worst thing that could happen. The ship appeared to be in no danger; there was no reason for *El Callado* not to kill them all and wait for his masters to arrive. Almost as bad, the good weather began to make him doubt his own judgment. What if the chief was right? What if the storm did pass them by while they were in the process of getting under way? It wouldn't be that hard for something to go wrong, lighting off an unfamiliar plant with a skeleton crew of inexperienced people. They could end up causing a fire or an explosion that could kill them all, when all they would have had to do is stay together and wait for the Colombian frigate to arrive. But what if he waited and the storm took them by surprise? Then it would be too late. He decided he couldn't take the chance. It was a risk either way, but the odds were with the start-up. He would proceed as planned. He closed his eyes and tried to rest for a few hours, knowing sleep would be impossible.

''So this is how the other half lives,'' Dana Kelly said, glancing around at the stateroom, marveling at the relative elegance of the passenger accommodations. ''Or did, anyway.''

Kelly pitched her helmet on the nearest bed and ran a hand through her hair, shaking it out. She breathed deeply and wrinkled her nose. The room smelled old, like her grandmother's parlor. It was a place she had been forbidden to go as a child, and for a moment she had a sense that she was trespassing. She glanced around, sizing it up. The cabin was surprisingly large, about ten by twelve feet, with furnishings that looked like they were straight out of the 1930s. She'd never cared much about material things, never thought she had the nesting instinct most women seemed to have, but her eyes took a quick inventory: A rich-looking Persian carpet, woven in a complex pattern of blue, green, and ivory, covered the teak deck. Mahogany panels, split and cracked from decades of exposure to the sea air, lined the bulkheads. Teak bookshelves ran the length of the inboard bulkhead. A few faded volumes, some bound in leather, were held in place by a brass rail, tarnished with age. Two single beds with wooden headboards were separated by an ornately carved nightstand in an oriental design. A small brass table lamp with a Tiffany shade was attached to the center of the stand. The beds were covered with faded green velvet spreads, trimmed with gold fringes.

"Not exactly my taste," Kelly said, winking at Maria, "but it'll do." She unbuckled her life preserver and smiled at the girl, who was standing awkwardly by the door, still clutching the dark gray blanket around her throat. Her eyes were sharp and focused, following Kelly's every move. Kelly thought it was the clear-eyed look that comes from food deprivation and fear, the look animals in the wild have. Lieutenant Blake had asked her to talk to the girl to find out anything that might be useful, and Kelly was dreading it. The last thing she wanted to do was make this vulnerable-looking child relive what she'd seen. "Well, let's see if we can get you cleaned up. My guess is, there's a *muy bonita chica* under that grime."

Maria flashed an embarrassed grin.

"With any luck there'll be some shampoo in here," Kelly said, peering into the wooden medicine chest above the sink. "Or something that will pass for it." She rummaged through an assortment of bottles and tubes and retrieved a small shampoo bottle half-filled with a waxy-looking substance the color of rust. She held the bottle under the hot-water tap of the porcelain sink and let the still-warm water flow around the cap. She twisted it off with a grimace and filled the bottle with tepid water.

Maria watched intently.

Kelly winked at the girl. "A little trick I learned in college." She screwed on the cap and vigorously shook the bottle. Gradually the clump of hardened shampoo dissolved into a reddish mixture the consistency of sludge.

"This stuff must be twenty years old, but it'll still work. Freeze-dried shampoo. Just add water."

Maria had a dubious expression on her face.

"Here we go," Kelly said, maneuvering the girl over to the sink. She bent her head down and spooned tepid water over her stringy black hair with a cupped hand, then poured a glob of the rust-colored pulp into the palm of her hand. She added a little more water and worked it up into something that resembled a lather. "Don't worry," Kelly said, rubbing the grainy mess into her hair. "The worst that can happen is your hair will fall out."

Maria's head jerked up.

Kelly laughed, pushing her back down. "Relax. Just kidding." She poked the girl in the ribs. "If it does, I'll loan you my helmet."

The girl started giggling.

"Hey, this is neat," Kelly said, scrubbing Maria's tangled hair. "I always wanted a little sister."

"You have no family?" Maria asked. Her voice sounded garbled under the running water.

"Not really," Kelly said. "I have some early memories of my mother, but I never really knew her. She died when I was three."

"You have no *padre?*"

"Somewhere, I guess, but I don't know who he is. Or where."

"How did you live?"

"I was raised by my grandmother," Kelly said. "She was a great lady. Daughter of a Spanish count who had to leave the country in a hurry for some reason. They emigrated through Mexico and ended up in San Jose, California. No money, but she was so elegant. When she walked into a room, everything stopped. She hated my father, an Irish guy who left when things got rough. She taught me that I had the blood of Spanish kings, that I could do anything. I loved her a lot."

"She is gone?" Maria asked.

"She died five years ago." Kelly cupped her hand and added a little more water to the thin layer of foam around Maria's head. She worked it up into a respectable lather. "I got a job as soon as I could and saved enough money to get me through a year of college. When that ran out I enlisted."

"Why do the *Norte Americanos* have women in their Navy?"

"Why not? Women can do anything a man can do."

"More," Maria said, rubbing water out of her eyes. "But a wise woman does not try to do the things men do. A woman is more powerful when she is a woman."

Kelly looked at her askance. "How old did you say you were?"

"The *teniente,* he is *muy guapo,* no?" Maria said.

"Only if you like tall athletic guys with a tiny little scar over their left eyebrow, a crooked nose, and hazel green eyes that make you melt," Kelly said, pausing to look off into the corner. "Oh yes, he's quite the topic of conversation in the women's compartment."

"You and the *teniente,*" Maria said. "You are his woman?"

Kelly laughed. "That's a hot one. He doesn't know I'm alive."

Maria shook her head and laughed softly. "He knows. I see the way he looks at you when you do not see. You are *muy hermosa.*"

Kelly glanced at herself in the blackened mirror above the sink, grateful for her mother's cheekbones and complexion. Her eyes weren't bad, either, with the right touch of eye shadow. "There were a few guys on campus at San Jose State who thought so." She shook her head. "If they could see me now."

"You like the *teniente?*"

"It's not worth talking about," Kelly said. "He's an officer, and I'm enlisted."

"He is a man, and you are a woman."

Kelly bent down and looked at her. "How old are you, anyway?"

"Next April I will be thirteen years. Then I will be a woman, like you."

Kelly laughed. "It takes more than birthdays. I'm pushing twenty-three, and I'm not sure I'm there yet." Kelly paused. Her mood got somber. "Would you like to talk about what happened?"

Kelly felt Maria's frail body shudder and instantly regretted raising the issue. "I'm so sorry. I don't mean to upset you. It's just that it might help the lieutenant to know what we're up against if you could tell us—"

"The *teniente,* he can get us off this ship?" Maria asked, trembling.

"He can do anything," Kelly said.

"He must get us off the ship," the girl said. "He must."

"Why? What is this thing? Is it a man?" Kelly said.

"He looks like a man," Maria said. "But a man could not do such terrible things."

"What happened? What set him off?"

"I don't know. We had been at sea for two days. My father told me of the silent one in the vault, never to go there. On the third day, something happened. He killed the chief engineer and disappeared. Then others as they stood watch. No one could find him. Soon the whole ship was in a panic; no one would stand watch alone."

"But why?" Kelly said. "What made him do it? What made him kill all those people?"

"I don't know."

"What does he look like?"

The child started to cry softly. *"No mas, por favor."*

"I'm sorry," Kelly said. "I really am, but we have to know."

"He is ugly," Maria said, sobbing now. "He is a huge beast. He stalks like an animal. Unless we get off this ship, he will kill us all."

The terror in Maria's voice made Kelly shudder and look over her shoulder. She looked back at Maria, wanting to say something soothing, but her mouth and throat were suddenly dry.

"The *teniente*, how will he get us off the ship?" Maria asked again.

"The lieutenant said there's a frigate on the way to pick us up," Kelly said.

"When will it come?"

"A couple of days, less now."

"Two days?" Maria said. "He will kill us all before then."

"Hey, stop it. You're starting to scare me, and I don't scare that easy," Kelly said. "Anyway, you're forgetting about that big tall handsome lieutenant we were just talking about. If anyone can find a way to get us out of this, he can."

Kelly wrapped a stiff, musty-smelling towel around Maria's

head and absently dried the girl's hair, glancing around the
compartment, listening to every creak and groan. She'd grown
up a virtual orphan, was used to the feeling of being alone, but
she'd never felt so isolated in her life. She turned away from
the girl; she couldn't let her see the fear in her eyes. She reached
through the curtain behind them and turned on the shower.
Standing with her back to Maria, Kelly went through the
motions of testing the water with her hand while she stared at
the door. It was wooden, with louvers. Designed to keep honest
people out. A few good kicks would splinter it. She wanted to
believe what she'd said about Lieutenant Blake's being able
to get them out of this, but they were just words. He'd have
to get the ship under way and then he'd have to conn it, couldn't
be everywhere at once. And even if the Colombian frigate
found them, forty-eight hours was a long time with a lunatic
running loose on the ship. She told herself to get a grip. She
had to be brave for Maria, couldn't let the girl see the fear in
her face after what she'd been through. She turned around and
forced a smile. "Well, I don't know about you, kiddo, but I'm
going to take a shower while the water's still warm."

"Which rack do you want?" Tobin said, throwing his life
jacket down on the closest bed.

Luis Alvarez stood in the bathroom with the door open,
noisily urinating in the stainless-steel toilet. "Makes no never
mind to me," he said over the noise. He stepped out into the
stateroom, buttoning his fly. "Hey, Tobin, come here."

"What do you want?"

Alvarez stuck his index finger out. "Pull my finger."

"Why?"

"Just pull it. Hurry."

Tobin reached for his finger hesitantly and pulled on it.

Alvarez raised his leg, grimaced, and broke wind. "Thanks."

"That's disgusting," Tobin said.

"Oh, yeah?" Alvarez said, tossing his life jacket on the

other bed. "Well, I'll show you something that ain't." He started to unbutton his shirt.

"What are you doing?"

The seaman reached inside his blue chambray shirt and slowly retrieved the sheaf of hundred-dollar bills he had taken from the vault.

Tobin gaped at the orange currency band. "What is it, play money?"

"Play money, my ass." Alvarez riffled the bills under Tobin's nose. "Smell it."

"Where did you get it?"

"Wouldn't you like to know?"

"No, I wouldn't like to know," Tobin said. "Money is the root of all evil. It says so in the Bible."

"Whoever wrote that didn't grow up in East LA."

"Don't blaspheme," Tobin said. "Look, I don't know where you got that, but you'd better turn it over to the lieutenant."

"I'll be damned. And you better not say anything, either."

"Don't talk to me like that. I'm a petty officer."

"Big deal. Third class."

"You can't just take money like that. I'll have to turn you in. It's my duty."

"Look, don't be a jerk-off. There's boxes of this stuff down there in the number three hold. Enough money down there to live like a king for the rest of your life, and your kids' lives, and their kids'."

"What are you saying?"

"What do you think I'm saying?" Alvarez pulled his bosun's knife from its sheath and began ripping the seams out of the lining of his foul-weather jacket. "This little package right here is ten grand. I figure we can stuff about twenty-five of these inside our jackets. That's $250,000. One quarter of a million bucks. Each."

"You mean steal it? We can't just take it. That's illegal."

"Illegal? How do you think they got it?"

"I don't care how they got it," Tobin said. "I'm not going to have any part of this."

"Look, you're a preacher, ain't you? If you don't want it for yourself, you could use it for your church. I'll bet that little church back in . . ."

"Fort Wayne."

"Yeah, Fort Wayne, I'll bet they've never seen that much money in their lives. You could be the big man back there. Hell, you could probably buy the damn thing."

"Don't talk like that. You can't buy a church."

"The hell you can't. You got enough money, you can buy anything."

"That's stealing. The Lord doesn't want that kind of money."

"Oh, hell, it's drug money. God would probably like to see it recycled to the church. Think what you could do with it."

Tobin shook his head. "Not that kind of money."

"Well, you can suit yourself, but I'm going down with or without you. That frigate will probably be here tomorrow. Tonight is the only chance we'll have, and I ain't going to pass it up. I told you about it because I'd like to have someone to cover my back, just in case, but I'm going, just the same. And you ain't going to say nothing to nobody."

"The lieutenant ordered us to stay in our staterooms. You heard what he said about someone being aboard."

"Ain't you figured that out yet? He's sweet on Kelly. He's just covering up for her losing the radio."

"I don't believe that."

"We searched the ship high and low didn't we? Did we find anything? Yeah, we find a kid hiding out. Well, if we could find a kid, we could find anyone else who was hiding, right? And did we? Hell no. There ain't nobody else aboard."

"I'm ordering you not to go."

Alvarez fingered his bosun's knife, running his thumb down the blade. "You ain't ordering me to do nothing. For that kind of jack, I'd shift your gears." He made a motion of sticking the knife in and moving it up, over and down, like shifting the gears on a car. "I've done it before for a lot less, don't think I haven't." He pulled his foul-weather jacket on and zipped it up. "I'll be back in a little bit." He opened the door and looked back over his shoulder. "Just remember. You ain't saying nothing to nobody."

John Sparks sat in his stateroom and cursed the ten-by-twelve-foot cell that held him prisoner. This ship was trouble; he'd known it when he'd first laid eyes on it, wallowing on the horizon like a fat old whore. And Kelly, the dumb cunt, losing the fucking radio. What the hell were women doing on ships in the first place? He rubbed his palms. He wanted a drink. Wanted, hell. Needed. He could make it from liberty to liberty on the *Carlyle* without a drink, but he'd never been in a mess like this before. He needed a drink, and he needed it now.

He liked the Navy okay, but he hadn't counted on this. He'd made the Navy a career for a very practical reason: it was the only place he could practice his hobby easily and safely. He'd discovered during his first enlistment that the seaports of the world contained brothels with access, for a price, to lovely young nymphets. Sparks didn't consider himself to be abnormal in the least; he never asked for girls younger than fourteen or so. A few had been younger than that, but it wasn't his fault. Language barriers sometimes got in the way.

Age was all relative anyway. In the underdeveloped countries, girls tended to reach puberty quickly. And as far as Sparks was concerned, if they functioned like women, they were women. He lay back on the bed, irritated that he had to defend himself. Whose goddamn business was it anyway? There was nothing wrong with what he did. In fact, it was a good deal; everyone got exactly what they wanted. When he thought about it, he was actually a savior, dispensing greenback dollars, hard currency, to those less fortunate than himself.

The sounds of laughter filtered through the walls. He cocked his head and listened to the faint murmuring of the girlish prattle coming through the thin bulkhead that separated the passenger compartments. He could tell that the lieutenant was pissed off at him for ducking into the room behind the girls.

Fuck him. Officers were always uptight about something. You couldn't please the bastards. Like stepfathers. Beat hell out of you for nothing. Anyway, what was the harm? He just wanted to be close to the girl, that's all. What a little beauty she was. He wished he'd been the one to find her, he thought, rubbing his crotch. All alone in that bosun's locker they said she was hiding in, huddled under a blanket. He forced himself to sit up and think about something else.

He glanced around the room and rubbed the sweaty palms of his hands against his dungarees. Christ, what he wouldn't give for a drink. It was becoming impossible to think about anything else, even the girl. He looked again at the mahogany cabinet in the corner of the room. It looked like a minibar, but he hadn't bothered to look. Now, in desperation, he dropped down on his hands and knees and pulled the sliding doors apart, exposing a dozen dark wells to hold bottles of liquor. Empty wells. He bent down and peered inside, praying that some forgetful passenger from some bygone era had left something behind. Nothing but some old papers and crap littered around. He dropped his head in frustration and started to push up from the deck. Something made him do a double take. A dark form in the far corner of the cabinet, partially hidden by a crumpled paper bag, caught his eye. He groped into the darkness and curled his fingers around the familiar shape. His heart jumped. He tilted the bottle in the well and could tell by the feel it was nearly full. He withdrew it and stared, a smile of disbelief spreading across his face.

It was a bottle of Johnny Walker Red Label Scotch, covered with a gray film of who-knew-how-many decades. He wondered how long it had been mellowing in the dark little corner, gently rocking with the rhythm of the ship as it traversed the shipping lanes of the world. Sitting cross-legged on the deck, he twisted off the cap and held the bottle under his nose, breathing in the musky fragrance of blended Scots whiskey. Wetting his lips, he took a sip of the Scotch and held it in his mouth, swishing it around over his tongue, savoring the taste before letting it slide down his throat. It swirled down like the flush of a toilet, igniting a fiery glow in his belly that seemed to warm the entire cabin. It was the real thing. Sparks sat back and let out a long breath. He could feel his luck changing. Two great passions consumed his life: very old whiskey and very young girls, and he had expected to find neither aboard the *Latin Star*.

He leaned back on the Persian carpet, nursing warm swallows of the Scotch, his head swaying against the gentle roll of the ship. The weather was quiet now. What was the big deal about getting this derelict under way? The Colombian frigate would be here in a day or so. The fucking lieutenant was grandstanding, playing the hero to Kelly and the girl. Let him play his games. Now that Sparks had a bottle he could wait it all out. And all this crap about someone being aboard. They had searched the ship high and low and hadn't found anyone but the girl. That was all crap, too, just Blake's way of covering for Kelly.

The whiskey warmed him. His thoughts returned to his last liberty. The Brazilian girls had cost him over a month's pay, but they'd been worth it. They looked enough alike to be twins, but weren't related. One was thirteen the other fourteen, or so they'd been advertised. You could never be sure, but they were young all right, nymphets of unbelievable beauty, who were available only to true connoisseurs with the right connections— and only then at great price. Sparks had been amazed that two so young could be so skilled in the art of pleasing a man. The warm glow of the Scotch enhanced the memory. He played it through again and again, savoring each detail, until the fantasy began to dim from overuse.

He heard the shower go on, the old pipes banging. He imagined Kelly and the girl in the shower together, laughing, giggling, playing grab-ass. He'd give a lot to see that. Not that he gave a shit about Kelly. She was too old for his taste. But the girl. Christ. He couldn't get her out of his mind. He pictured her frail body impaled on his cock, the taut porcelain skin of her belly bulging out with each stroke, her dark eyes rolling in pain. He scanned the bulkhead, wondering if he could somehow fashion a peephole.

The sounds of laughter coming through the walls were louder

now. They were having a high old time next door. He rubbed his crotch and glanced around the cabin. There had to be a way to at least get a look. If he was going to do it, he had to do it now, before the shower went off. There were two brass portholes on the outboard bulkhead and a louvered air vent in the inboard bulkhead. The girls were in the forward cabin; there was an outside passageway on the other side of that air vent. Thoughts of what he might see through those louvers tantalized him. He clenched his eyes in an alcoholic fog, picturing them both nude. The warm glow of a fire began in his crotch, matching the fire in his belly.

The lieutenant had come around earlier and told them again to stay in their staterooms, but that was just part of the show. If there was anyone else aboard, they would have found him after turning the ship upside down. Capping the bottle, he unlocked his stateroom door and tiptoed down the dimly lit passageway, around the corner of the number two stateroom. He glanced around. The air vent was exactly where he thought it would be. He looked around for something to stand on and found a portable fire hose on a large reel. He dragged it over, trying to make as little noise as possible, into position under the air vent. The shower was still running.

He climbed up on the hose reel and quietly pried open the louvers to the air vent with the screwdriver blade on his electrician's knife. The light in the cabin was dim, but he could clearly see the canvas shower curtain waving gently before him. Where was the girl? Were they both in the shower? He glanced frantically around the cabin and spotted the top of the girl's head sitting in a chair beneath the air vent he was looking through, huddled under that damned blanket in a corner of the stateroom. Shit. He told himself not to panic. Maybe she'd be next. He had a perfect view and settled down to wait for the show.

After a few minutes the shower went off. Sparks saw the towel that had been hanging over the curtain rod disappear into the shower. He heard Kelly singing a little song from behind the curtain. He wasn't all that interested, but hoped she wouldn't dry herself completely in the damned shower. His fears were allayed when he saw a hand reach up and slide the curtain back. Sparks let out a gasp that he was sure she must have heard. His mouth went dry. His heart hammered in his ears. He had no idea she looked like that beneath those baggy dungarees. Her long legs were flawless, running smoothly up to the French-cut bikini tan lines. Her small patch of dark pubic hair was decorated with glistening drops of water. Her waist was tiny. Her breasts, although not large, were perfectly formed with firm, erect-looking nipples. With her golden skin, she looked like a statue he'd seen in a magazine once, part woman, part girl. The sight of her warm flesh amid all that cold steel stirred feelings in him he'd never felt for a grown woman before.

He watched with watery eyes, transfixed, as she dried herself with the towel, the fire below his belt raging out of control. He imagined now that she was much younger, perhaps fourteen or so. Every movement was erotic, the little song she was softly humming, a seductive siren song, like the sea nymphs he'd read about in Greek mythology who lured mariners to their deaths on the rocks surrounding their island.

The hammering in his ears prevented him from hearing the faint rustle of clothing behind him. Too late, he felt the gentle breeze of a hand shooting out of the darkness, expertly covering his mouth and pinching off his nostrils in an airtight, unbreakable grip. The glands in his body were instantly thrown into a painful struggle to shift his body's hierarchy of needs from sexual reproduction to survival. The struggle was mercifully brief. A sharp crack reverberated in his ears. He knew at once what it was. His neck had been snapped like a hickory branch. With a smooth continuity that made the two movements appear as one, he felt the stump of a knee against his back and heard the sickening tear of his spine being wrenched in two. A black-and-white film of his life played backward as his body slipped into a state of paralysis.

Still alive, unable to move, unable to scream, he felt a hand pry open his mouth. A thumb and two fingers stretched out his tongue. He tasted the salt from the thick, sweating fingers first, then the acrid taste of cold steel in his mouth. He felt the blade glide under his tongue, scraping across his lower teeth, flooding his mouth with hot liquid.

He slumped to the deck and stared up at the dark form hovering over him, unable to believe his eyes. He heard a faint wet plopping sound as something hit the steel deck beside him. His head rolled over involuntarily and the small pink object came into focus. Through eyes glazed with shock, he stared at the neatly severed tongue. He thought it looked like a miniature version of the beef tongues he'd seen in butcher shops, except that his had a sickly green cast to it. He lay still, unable to control even his eyelids, and stared at the grisly lump until it faded from sight.

Chapter Twelve

Jorge Cordoba walked the short distance to the VIP bungalow with a spring in his step, despite an earlier feeling of exhaustion. With the discovery of the *Latin Star,* his energy level had bounced back to its normal driving exuberance. If he had lost points with Don Gallardo for his role in the loss of the ship, blameless though he felt he was, he would more than regain those points with its recovery.

In the distance, mechanics worked under the blue-white glare of sodium-vapor lights to get the Blackhawk helicopters ready to fly at dawn. He paused when he heard the first one whine and cough and fire, warming up its engine. In a sliver of moonlight peeking through the trees, he glanced at his watch. It would be light in a few hours. He breathed in the cool night air and let out a deep shudder of relief. It was only a matter of time before they retook the *Latin Star,* and, with the recovery of the ship, he would be solidly in control again. Life would be back to normal, except that he would now be chief of finance, older and wiser from the experience.

He could sense that things were starting to go his way. Everything pointed to it. The weather had improved significantly. The *Latin Star* had been found easily, located within twenty kilometers from the coordinates Admiral Cuartas had given them. The ship was dead in the water, drifting. That meant the crew had obviously heaved to and abandoned ship to escape the *mudo*. And that meant the *mudo* was probably still aboard. Good. He would make their job that much easier. By the time Enrique Lopez's security people landed, the silent one would no doubt have disposed of at least some of the American boarding party. Jorge stretched and yawned. The feeling of relief that swept over him now removed the last barricade against the feeling of exhaustion he'd been fighting. Lopez had suggested that Jorge get some sleep while his people boarded and secured the ship, and Jorge, for once, had not argued. He would be fresh and ready to board in the second wave, ready to take personal charge of the shipment from that point on.

Jorge could feel the tension drain out of him as he paused at the door of the bungalow. He glanced over his shoulder and looked around. He would be glad to leave this place. A dusty, shithole of a town in the Huallaga Valley of eastern Peru, Campanilla lay on the main road skirting the eastern foothills of the Andes mountains, a five-minute march away from Punta Arenas, a Peruvian Army base which housed an antiguerrilla battalion. The government of Peru and the base commander had differing ideas as to what their mission was. The Peruvian government had posted the battalion there to fight Maoist guerrillas of the *Sendero Luminoso*, the Shining Path, but the base commander, Colonel Julio Suarez, had found that it was more profitable to provide security for Don Gallardo's shipments of crude cocaine paste being flown to Colombia and Ecuador for processing. At five thousand US dollars per flight, the cost of security was high, but worth it, Jorge thought, glancing around at the soldiers patrolling the perimeter of the compound. He turned the key and entered the bungalow.

He wanted a drink. A cold beer would cut the dust out of his throat and help him sleep. The Scotch on the plane had been an anomaly and a mistake. He normally drank only beer, specifically Brazilian beer, and hoped there would be a cold one in the minibar. He threw his coat over a chair and peered inside.

"Is this what you're looking for?" a voice said behind him.

He swirled around. The stewardess from the flight stood in the door to the bedroom with a bottle of Brahma beer in one hand, a chilled glass in the other. The tall brunette was completely nude.

Jorge gaped at her. Things were indeed going his way again. She'd seen him coming up the path to the bungalow and had prepared a welcome for him. Obviously she'd done her homework, even down to his preference in beer. He wondered what else she knew about his preferences. He had ignored her on the flight from Montevideo, and she had taken the challenge. Women could stand anything except being ignored, he thought. His eyes took in her small round breasts, her slim waist, the V-line of her crotch, and broke into a smile. She would not be ignored tonight. With the discovery of the ship, he could loosen up. The helicopters were being prepared. There was nothing for him to do now but relax and get some much-needed sleep. And what better way. No sleeping pill could compete with the effect of being completely drained by a woman. He felt a stirring begin in his loins that had been missing since Rafael Ayala had burst into his office. His normally deep hunger for sex returned with an intensity that startled him. He was absorbed by the whiteness of her skin, silhouetted by the soft light coming from the room behind her. He tugged at his tie, not taking his eyes from her, and slowly slid it from around his neck.

"Here. Let me do that."

Jorge stood completely still as she walked slowly toward him. Tall, about five feet ten, Jorge thought, she seemed perfectly proportioned in her bare feet. In the dim light, her straight brown hair looked black. Parted in the middle, it fell gracefully to her shoulders before curving slightly outward. Her hair was dark and shiny, ravenlike, yet her eyes were blue. Jorge guessed she might be Argentinian. Her lips had a wet, soft look, and her chin had the faintest hint of a cleft. Her breasts moved only slightly as she walked toward him. A thin gold chain around her waist shimmered across her navel. Her dark patch of pubic hair was carefully trimmed, surrounded with a faint stubble. Her hands were large, almost masculine, with deep red polish on finely manicured nails.

She poured the beer gently down the side of the glass and raised it to his lips. Without taking his eyes from her, Jorge took the glass and drained it. A trickle of beer ran down his chin. Raising up on her toes, she licked the single drop of beer from his chin with a swipe of her tongue. The sensation was delicate, fleeting, like the lick from a kitten. With a sly grin, she began unbuttoning his shirt. Jorge tossed the glass across the room, where it smashed in a corner. She slowly worked her way down the row of buttons, glancing coyly up at him, the tip of her tongue slipping into the corner of her mouth. Jorge concentrated on the movement of her tongue as she concentrated on each button. She pulled off his shirt and tugged at his belt buckle. Jorge stepped out of his pants and kicked them across the room. Gliding her thumbs smoothly into his shorts, she slipped them down, releasing him. She eased down to her knees and took him gently in her mouth. Jorge gasped and fell back against the coolness of the minibar, holding her head in his hands. He moaned and stroked her hair.

After an indiscernible amount of time, when he thought he could hold back no longer, he pulled her to her feet and carried her over to the table. Laying her back, he lifted her legs and entered her. She rolled her head from side to side and moaned, hooking her ankles over his shoulders. He watched her naked body spread before him, feet up, legs open, the most vulnerable position for a woman. He'd had them all. The impossibly beautiful, the merely attractive, the plain. He marveled at how much women looked alike with their feet in the air.

Although he'd never loved any woman—he'd gotten married only because the Don had required it of all senior officers—he enjoyed giving women pleasure. He stood, grinding into her pelvis, making full clitoral contact, watching her eyes roll back in her head, pleased with the sounds of her. She was under his control now, humping, shrieking, gasping. He felt her shudder to a rapid-fire series of climaxes, and stopped. He stood regaining his composure. Now it was his turn. Time for his pleasure. He watched himself enter her. Some ancient part of his brain took over and he gave himself up to it, hunching, thrusting, copulating like an animal, watching the pink flesh of her labia dragging against his swollen cock. She twisted on the table, emitting little squeaks of pain. The primitive thrill of human domination rippled through him. He was lost now, driving relentlessly to his own release. Somewhere in the distance, he heard a phone ringing. He felt himself erupt with jarring spasms that seemed to go on forever, mercifully releasing him. He fell across her and lay there, gasping, exhausted, cursing the telephone. Ten rings, eleven, the phone was relentless. He slipped out of her and staggered across the room. He flung himself on the couch, grappling for the handset. "What the hell is it?" he croaked into the telephone.

"Jorge, is that you?" he heard Don Gallardo say.

Jorge lay gasping for breath, trying to compose himself. Don Gallardo was a family man who disapproved of his peccadilloes. "Godfather," he managed.

"What's going on there? Are you okay?"

"Fine, fine." Jorge held his hand over the receiver, breathing hard. "Give me a minute. I just woke up."

"We don't have a minute. All hell is breaking loose in Montevideo," Don Gallardo said. "The lending consortium is outraged with what happened to Quintero. They're demanding payment now, refusing to negotiate any further. What the hell were you thinking of?"

Jorge stiffened at the inference that killing Quintero had been his idea alone. Don Gallardo had given him the number to call, in case it was needed.

"I didn't have any choice. The arrogant pig was trying to make an end run for all our real-estate holdings. I thought it would slow the others down."

"It's had the opposite effect. They've got a judge to declare the loan in default under some obscure 'special-circumstances' law and are filing to take possession.''

"Let them file. We've found the ship. I was going to call you in the morning.''

"That's excellent. Where?''

"Within twenty kilometers of the coordinates Admiral Cuartas gave us. The helicopters are warming up now. They fly at first light.''

"Where is the American destroyer?''

"Nowhere in sight of the freighter. The storm has blown them apart. We'll have a straight shot in and out.''

"And the weather?''

"The storm seems to have changed direction. According to our pilots, the weather is relatively clear in the vicinity of the ship.''

"And the replacement crew?''

"They're here now. Just arrived a few hours ago. All licensed merchant marine officers and seamen.''

"The frigate Admiral Cuartas dispatched will be leaving in a few hours. I don't want that freighter to be anywhere in sight when it arrives.''

"We'll be steaming for the coast by the time they get there. They'll never even see us. If they do, we'll be under way in international waters under a Panamanian flag.''

"Excellent.''

"Can you delay the foreclosure long enough for us to get the cash delivered?''

"We're working on it. We've got a judge of our own in Uruguay. We can delay it for a day or so, but not indefinitely.''

"That's all we'll need,'' Jorge said. "You have my personal assurance.''

There was a pause. Don Gallardo sounded almost apologetic. "I'm sorry to get you out of bed in the middle of the night. You've done an excellent job. Now get some sleep. I want you to be fresh when you take control of the ship. I don't want any more mistakes.''

Jorge hung up the phone and lay back on the couch, relieved

that yet another fire had been put out, pleased with his ability
to handle whatever came his way. Sleep began to overtake him.
The flight attendant crept over and knelt beside him. She laid
her head on his chest and gently caressed his groin. He lay
quietly, stroking her hair, wanting to sleep. She twisted the
damp hair on his chest around her finger and gently ran her
tongue around his nipples. He felt himself begin to rise. He
opened his eyes and saw her mount him, easing herself gently
down, taking all of him. He closed his eyes and drifted off,
half-asleep, half-awake, enjoying the femaleness of her above
him. Looking up, he saw her arch her back and throw her head
back as she rode him like a horse, her pelvis gliding smoothly
back and forth. He closed his eyes and drifted in and out of
consciousness, losing all track of time. At some point, he wasn't
sure when, he felt himself come. Slowly, easily, he felt the
seminal fluid leave him, oozing out as if in a wet dream he'd
had as a boy, releasing him. He drifted off into the blackest
sleep he'd ever known.

The hammering on the door woke him. Jorge jerked up and
looked around. He was covered with a gray blanket. The brunette was gone. He looked at his watch and flinched. He'd
overslept, something he never did. He swaddled the blanket
around him and staggered toward the door. Fumbling with the
lock, he noticed the security chain dangling free. He put it back
in place, wondering where the brunette had gone, and opened
the door the length of the chain. "What the hell is it?" He
peered through the space, blinking into the predawn light. His
eyes focused on the shiny brass of an Army officer, backed up
by a cluster of green uniforms and rifles.
    "Jorge Cordoba?"
    "What do you want?"
    "You're under arrest."
    "What?"
    "Open the door."

Jorge slid the security chain free. "Who the hell do you think you are?"

"Major Portillo, Peruvian Army," the officer said, pushing his way past him. Jorge looked out the door and squinted his eyes at the far end of the field. The helicopters were still sitting under the canopy. No one was in sight.

Jorge felt the rage well up within him. "You've picked one hell of a time for your semiannual shakedown." He slammed the door in the face of the soldiers.

Major Portillo cocked his head. "Are you accusing me of taking bribes? That is a serious accusation."

"You stupid son of a bitch," Jorge said, trembling. "You're going to kill the goose that laid the golden egg."

"There is no need for such clichéd theatrics," Major Portillo said. He stood smiling at Jorge.

"Those helicopters should have taken off at dawn."

"All flights from Campanilla have been grounded until further notice."

"Now you listen to me and you listen carefully," Jorge said, clutching the blanket around him. "If those helicopters don't take off—right now—you're a dead man. Your family's dead. Everyone you know is dead. I'll personally see to it."

"You're in no position to be making threats," the major said. His smile faded into a grim, determined look. "You Colombian thugs think you can come down here and intimidate us?"

Jorge stared at him with a sick feeling. "Let me get some clothes on. We can talk."

"You'll do your talking with Colonel Suarez. Get dressed."

"Where are we going?"

"Punta Arenas."

Jorge felt a wave of panic sweep over him. The outcome of the talks was foreordained. It would involve several hours of negotiations, the price would go up, and the flights would be permitted again. But by then the window of opportunity to take the freighter would be closed, either by the weather, the Colombian frigate, or both. He had to do something.

"Look. It's worth one million US dollars in cash to me to get one of those helicopters off the ground. Now."

Major Portillo broke into a bemused smile. "And why would one helicopter be so important?" His expression changed to one of pure greed. "What's on it?"

Jorge shook his head. "No questions. One helicopter, one million. That's all you need to know."

Major Portillo leaned back against the minibar, snapping his riding crop against his boot. "A most interesting proposition, but being a loyal follower of Colonel Suarez, I, of course, could not accept."

"If you're worried about the colonel, this would be a side agreement between you and me. He doesn't need to know."

"He would find out."

"I can guarantee you he won't."

Major Portillo tugged at an earlobe. "And this would be paid how?"

"Any way you want. All cash, wire transfer to a Swiss bank, investment-grade Colombian emeralds, diamonds, anything you say."

The major sat quietly staring at Jorge, reading him. "There is a very high rate of inflation in my country. One million doesn't go far."

"Two million."

Major Portillo's eyes sparkled. "I really would like to see what is on that helicopter. Perhaps we should go look."

"There's nothing on the goddamn helicopter, you greedy bastard," Jorge shouted.

Major Portillo came upright. "I think we shall impound all the helicopters and see."

"No," Jorge said. "You can't do that."

"We can do anything we like."

The realization that the major was right swept over Jorge. This wasn't his game. He took a deep breath and walked toward the bathroom. "Then do it. You will find nothing on the helicopters, we will be out of business, and you will be out two million dollars. Not to mention your head when Colonel Suarez finds out it was your stupidity that shut us down."

Major Portillo stared at him.

Jorge paused at the bathroom door. "Let's see," he said. "Six flights out a day, times five thousand dollars, times seven days a week equals roughly . . . ten, eleven million dollars a year, doesn't it? The colonel has a big payroll to meet. He might not like it if—"

"Even if I agree to let one helicopter fly, we would still have to meet with Colonel Suarez."

"Fine," Jorge said. "We'll take all day. Have a nice conversation."

"And our side agreement will be confidential?"

"What agreement?" Jorge said. He looked at his watch. "By noon today, you will be the beneficiary of an anonymous donor. A wire transfer to a secret numbered account at the Swiss bank of your choice."

Major Portillo swallowed and ran his tongue over his lips. "In my name?"

"No names. You'll be given a number. Two million, tax-free." Jorge looked at his watch. "This offer expires in one minute." He watched him squirming. He had him.

"Done."

Jorge scooped up his clothes and darted into the bathroom. "I want the pilots, mechanics, and security people released. Also Enrique Lopez. Immediately."

"It shall be done."

Jorge emerged from the bathroom, hair disheveled, tucking his shirt in his trousers. He could smell the brunette, rising up from his crotch. He needed a shower, but there was no time. He wondered briefly where she was. The thought crossed his mind that they had used her to keep him occupied while they quietly took control of the camp. He never overslept; perhaps she'd put something in his beer. He'd find out and deal with her later. He opened the door, and the soldiers jumped to attention.

Major Portillo barked some commands, and the troops scattered. Jorge headed for the helicopters. By the time he got there, the pilots, crew, and maintenance men were drifting toward him from various holding locations, rubbing their wrists, blinking up into the floodlights. "You, there," Jorge shouted to a tall man in his thirties with a pencil-thin mustache. He had the swaggering air all pilots seemed to have. "I want this helicopter in the air immediately."

"Anything you say, pal. You're writing the checks."

Jorge blinked. "Are you an American?"

The tall man grinned. "Chief Warrant Officer Michael Gaines, late of the US Army, at your service." He nodded toward the Peruvian soldiers and chuckled. "These boys think they know how to play rough. Guys like these wouldn't last five minutes in my old outfit."

"What are you doing here?"

"The Army and I had a little disagreement about what I could smoke and what I couldn't," Gaines said. "Besides, I didn't like getting my ass shot at for twelve hundred bucks a month. You guys pay a little better."

Jorge stared at him. "Do you understand what this assignment is?"

"Sure. Set her down on an old freighter, then push her over the side. Piece of cake. Shame to lose such a beautiful ship, though." He nodded at the Blackhawk. "Preflight's completed. Get your troops loaded. All we need is a weather update, and we're outta here." He turned and walked toward the Command Center.

Jorge looked around. Enrique Lopez, the acting director of security, was walking briskly toward him from the Command Center, coming past the pilot.

Jorge met him. "Where's the other flight crew?"

"Why?"

"We can't use this guy," he said.

"Why? What's wrong with him?"

"He's an American."

"They both are."

Jorge stared at him. "You must be joking."

"Who else did you think we'd get to fly Blackhawk helicopters? What's the problem?"

"When he figures out what this assignment is, he may not like it."

"It doesn't matter whether he likes it or not. When the helicopter goes over the side, he'll be in it."

They turned and saw the pilot come out of the Command Center. He sauntered toward them, dangling his helmet by his side, shaking his head.

"What is it?"

"Tropical Cyclone Bruce has just shifted again. It's heading for exactly the spot we're flying into. Bullets I can face. But I ain't flying into that. We ain't going anywhere for a while."

Chapter Thirteen

Daniel Blake bolted upright in bed, not sure whether it was the steep roll of the ship or the sound of something crashing against the bulkhead that woke him. He braced himself against the roll and pressed the light button on his watch. Almost one o'clock. He didn't think he'd slept, but he must have. Feeling groggy, worse than if he'd stayed awake, he rubbed his face in his hands and tried to focus on the noise he'd heard. The steep roll hadn't been followed by another, so the weather was still holding, but something was obviously loose on deck. His gut tightened at the thought of going out there alone, but a loose piece of gear on a ship in heavy weather was something that couldn't be ignored. Slipping the Beretta out of its holster, he stuck it in his belt, then scooped up the three-cell flashlight he'd found in the engine room. Cracking the door of the cabin, he aimed the light out into the passageway.

"What was that?" Blake heard a confused, half-awake voice say behind him. Playing the light on the door of Frank Kozlewski's cabin, he saw the chief's puffy face, screwed up into a squint, peering out through the partially opened door. The few remaining strands of hair on his head stood looped over his scalp like McDonald's golden arches.

Blake let out a long breath of gratitude. As irascible as the old chief was, sometimes he loved the guy. He was always there without being asked; if there was trouble in the air, he would sense it and come.

"I don't know," Blake said. "Sounded like it came from out there." He pointed the beam of light toward the forward door that led out onto a narrow promenade deck that surrounded the passenger staterooms. Opening the door into the wind, he stepped out onto the partially exposed walkway and swept the light around. He froze at the sight of a crumpled form lying against the forward bulkhead of stateroom number two. Kelly's stateroom. The instant his beam of light hit the shapeless form he knew who it was. "Get Doc," he said over his shoulder.

Kneeling, Blake beamed the light into Sparks's face and grimaced at the gaping wound that had been his mouth. He felt for a pulse in the carotid artery, though he could tell as he knelt down that it was no use. The feel of Sparks's veallike skin repulsed him. He glanced at the open louvers of the air vent above and knew immediately what the electrician had been doing. Anger boiled up inside him with an intensity that made his hands tremble. The stupid lecherous bastard had jeopardized them all. Getting under way now was less certain than ever, maybe impossible.

Blake stood over Sparks's body, oblivious to the rain slanting into the promenade deck, and told himself to get a grip. He didn't like anger; it made a man lose control, do things he wouldn't normally do. He stepped back into the cabin area and rapped lightly on the door to stateroom number two.

"Who is it?" he heard Kelly say from behind the louvers.

"It's me, Lieutenant Blake."

The wooden door opened with a shudder and Kelly peered out. "What is it? What's happened?" she asked. Maria was standing behind her, looking around her shoulder, trembling.

"Are you two okay?" Blake asked. Kelly's hair was wet, and she appeared to have pulled on her dungarees hastily after getting out of the shower. He told himself his anger toward Sparks was because he'd put them in jeopardy, but he knew now there was more to it than that; the thought of those weasel eyes looking at Kelly nude filled him with a rage that startled him.

Kelly opened the door wider and saw Doc Jones rushing by with his medical kit. "What's going on? What was that crash?"

Blake blocked her passage with his arm. "It's okay. Just go back to sleep."

Kelly looked at him with raised eyebrows. "Lieutenant, I think I have a right to know what's going on."

"Hey, Lieutenant," Doc Jones called from outside.

Blake looked away. Kelly pushed past him, out the door to the open promenade deck. Forgetting about the girl, Blake started after Kelly. He came up behind her as she froze at the sight of Doc Jones bent over the body of John Sparks. She stared down at the body, then at the hose reel, then up at the air vent with its louvers pried open. She turned and looked at Blake with her mouth open, eyes wide. Maria came through the door, walking toward her, coming up behind Blake. "No, don't . . ." Kelly said. "Stop her."

Blake turned and stepped toward the girl, too late. Maria gaped at the body and let out a shriek. Dropping the blanket, she clutched her head with both hands, grimacing as if trying to block out what she was seeing, then spun around and threw herself against Blake. She laid her head on his chest and began to cry with wet, muffled sobs.

Blake awkwardly put his arms around her, feeling helpless. He wanted to tell her she'd be okay, but the words wouldn't come. He nodded to Kelly. "Take her back to your room."

"Come on, sweetheart," Kelly said, wrapping the blanket around the girl, leading her away.

"He's dead, Lieutenant," Doc Jones said after they were out of sight. "I'm sure about this one. Neck's broken. Spine's severed. Must have died almost instantly."

Blake looked up to see Tobin step out into the promenade

deck and start toward him. His face was drawn up into a pale grimace. Blake thought he looked sick.

Tobin stopped and stared down at Sparks's body. He looked at Blake and said, "Sir?"

"What is it, Tobin?"

"I heard the commotion, sir. I thought it might be Alvarez."

"Alvarez? What about him?"

"He's gone, sir."

"What do you mean he's gone? Gone where?"

"He had a packet of money. In his shirt. He said he got it in the number three hold. He said he was going down to get some more."

"When? How long's he been gone?"

"Over an hour, sir."

"Damn it, why didn't you try to stop him?"

"I did, sir. He pulled a knife. I couldn't do anything with him."

"Why didn't you come and get me?"

"I'm sorry, sir," Tobin said, looking down. "I should have. I was afraid to leave my cabin."

"That's just great," Blake said. "If we lose another man, there goes any chance of getting under way."

The corpsman nodded at Sparks's body. "What'll we do with him, sir?"

"Lay him out in his stateroom," Blake said.

"We're in the tropics, Lieutenant," Doc Jones said. "We can't leave him there too long. How about the frozen-food locker?"

"The power's been off for a couple of days," Blake said. "It wouldn't be much better. Just put him in his stateroom for now." He knew what their chances of surviving a tropical cyclone were without the ability to get under way and thought it was a moot point where they stored him; they were all likely to end up in the same place anyway. "Tobin can help you."

Doc Jones and Tobin scuttled off carrying Sparks's body between them, and the chief and Blake stepped back into the stateroom area, out of the rain now driving into the promenade deck.

"Looks like we better get up another search party," the chief said.

Blake shook his head. "There are a thousand places he could hide on a freighter."

"What are we going to do? We can't just let him pick us off one at a time."

"We're not going to go searching for him in the middle of the night," Blake said. "That's just what he'd like us to do. That's why he killed Sparks, to bait us into looking for him."

"Poor Sparky," the chief said.

"If Sparks had stayed in his stateroom, he'd have been okay."

"Well, I reckon that's that for getting under way," the chief said. "Without an electrician, there's no way."

"We might still have a chance," Blake said, "as long as we can keep the emergency diesel running." He glanced up at the small white emergency light in the passageway, secure in the knowledge that Sergeant Rivero was standing watch in the engine room. Blake could see the chief thinking the same thing he was, then he saw the look on the chief's face change. He felt it too; the vibration in the deck was changing, winding down. He heard the diminishing whine of the diesel engine. The tremor in the deck shuddered to a halt as the overhead light flickered to a tiny glow in the filament, then went out entirely. Blake gasped as though all the air had been sucked out of his lungs. He stood in the black silence that followed, the hair bristling on the back of his neck. "Mother of God," he heard the chief say.

Blake stood at the hatch leading down into the engine room, cocked pistol in his right hand, flashlight in his left. He drew in a deep breath and nodded for the chief to follow him.

"You ain't going to fall for that, sir?" The chief was standing behind him, rasping in his ear. "I'm telling you it's him, that son of a bitch is down there. He's killed Rivero, and he's knocked out the generator. He's baiting you, trying to draw you down—''

''What choice do we have? Without that generator, we've had it.''

''Not necessarily. The weather ain't too bad. Maybe that cyclone—''

''It's coming, Chief. Trust me. I can feel it in the way the ship's moving. The barometer's dropping like a stone.''

''Hell, sir, let's get some backup—''

''Who would you get?'' Blake said. ''Doc? Tobin? Robertson? What good would they be? A bunch of unarmed people stumbling around in a dark engine space? That's just what he'd want.'' He shook his head. ''We can't afford to lose anyone else.'' Blake took a deep breath. ''Let's go. All I need is someone to cover my back.''

The chief glanced over his shoulder. ''Who's going to cover mine?'' He pulled the slide back on his pistol, cocking it with a satiny click.

''Be careful with that damned thing,'' Blake said. ''Come on.'' He started slowly down the ladder into the black hole of the engine room, thinking he'd been right about one thing. *El Callado* was obviously insane, but that didn't mean he was stupid. He'd seen the guard posted over the emergency diesel generator and understood that it was important. After killing Sparks, and probably Alvarez, he'd killed Rivero and disabled the generator as a way to draw them out and hunt them down in the dark, on his terms. And the worst part about it was that Blake had no choice but to go along. He stopped on the third step down and listened. The only sounds were the waves lapping against the hull and the chief's ragged breathing behind him. ''Sergeant Rivero,'' he called.

The sound of his voice echoed in the silence.

The knot tightened in his stomach. Every instinct he had told him to get out of there. Blake descended a few more steps down the ladder, beaming his flashlight ahead of him into the cavelike darkness. He paused and aimed his light down into the lower level, trying to see the emergency diesel generator.

"I don't like this one little bit," the chief said in Blake's ear, his whisper pronounced in the deathly quiet.

"Shh," Blake said, straining to see and hear. The beam from his flashlight was nearly overwhelmed by the blackness, the quiet so intense he could hear the faint skittering of rats in the bilges. He descended the remaining steps down to the catwalk that circled the engine space and paused, beaming his light below, straining to see the generator.

The faintest whisper of movement caught his ear, something coming toward him. Fast. He flashed his light ahead. The beam illuminated a dark form flying through the air, arching into him. Turning, he shoved the chief flat and started into a crouch, twisting to one side on the narrow catwalk. Something heavy hit him on the left side, knocking him back over the chief. He heard Kozlewski's pistol fire, the shot ringing in his ears. He felt a dull thud, then a sharp pain in his shoulder. Grabbing his arm, he felt warm blood seeping through his khaki shirt. The chief struggled to get up and Blake pushed him back down as the object reversed itself and flew back over their heads.

"Christ, I didn't mean to fire," the chief said in a choked voice. "Did I hit anything?"

Blake ignored him, struggling to aim his flashlight. He got it in focus as the object made another pass over their heads. It was moving slower now, and he could see what it was: the body of Seaman Luis Alvarez, flying noiselessly through the air, suspended by its ankles.

Blake lay back in the darkness, sweating and clammy, gripping his arm, listening to the whisper of the body traversing over their heads, waiting for it to slow. He reached up and struck it a glancing blow with his foot. It wobbled to a stop, dancing at the end of the ropes that held it. Blake steadied the body and beamed the light on its face. The yawning hole that had been a mouth was stuffed with crisp hundred-dollar bills, stuck together with dried blood like a paper flower. Alvarez's bosun's knife was embedded up to the handle in his chest.

"That sick son of a bitch," Frank Kozlewski hissed in Blake's ear. "Why would he do a sick thing like that?"

"He's sending a message for us to stay away from the money," Blake said, grimacing. "He wanted to make sure we got it."

Blake sucked in a deep breath and called, "Sergeant Rivero."

There was no answer.

"You're hurt, sir," Chief Kozlewski said, staring at the field of dark red spreading around Blake's upper arm.

"Yeah, you shot me, you bastard," Blake said, his voice tinged with irony.

The chief's face fell like a mud slide. "Oh, Christ, no." Kozlewski ripped Blake's shirt open and gaped at the wound. "You're bleeding like a stuck pig, sir." The chief pulled his red bandanna out of his rear pocket, twisted it around Blake's upper arm, and tied it into a square knot. Reaching into his front pocket, he retrieved his pipe lighter, stuck it through the loop in the bandanna and twisted it tight.

"Don't drop that lighter into the bilges, or we'll really be finished," Blake said, grimacing.

"When you going to get it through your head that we ain't going to be getting under way?"

"Don't give up yet. Rivero could still be alive."

"Yeah, and the Pope could be married." Kozlewski released the tension on the bandanna and bright red blood oozed out of the hole in Blake's biceps. The chief twisted it tight again. "It ain't slowing down none. You're going to have to hold it while I go for Doc."

Blake felt the vibration of footsteps coming down the ladder. He motioned for Kozlewski to be quiet. Lying back, shielding the chief, he aimed the Beretta at the part of the ladder he could see, holding it steady on his knee, ready to blow apart the first thing that moved. A flashlight beam flickered.

"Lieutenant Blake," Doc Jones called down in a tremulous voice. The beam of his flashlight hit Blake in the face. "Are you all right, sir? I heard a shot."

"Doc," Blake said, breathing out, "you're a welcome sight,

but that's a good way to get shot." He eased the hammer back down on the automatic, awed by the courage it must have taken for the corpsman to come down into this black hole looking for him. "Come join the party."

Doc Jones stood over them, looking at Alvarez's body suspended in the air, his dark face drawn. He bent down and looked at Blake's arm. "Jesus Christ, sir, what happened?" Without waiting for an answer, he pulled a bottle of something purple out of his medic kit and began swabbing out the wound.

Blake grimaced at the sting of the antiseptic.

"It went all the way through," Doc said. "Who shot you?"

"Never mind. Just clean it up," the chief said.

"It's clean," Doc said, swabbing it out, "but you really need some stitches to close that up properly."

"Ain't you got any?" the chief asked, holding the light.

Jones shook his head. "It's one thing I didn't bring. There might be something in the ship's infirmary."

"We don't have time for that, Doc," Blake said. "Just tape it up and dress it tight."

The corpsman looked at him questioningly.

Blake nodded encouragement. "It'll be okay. I heal fast."

Jones closed the wound and placed a layer of gauze over it. "Stretch your arm out and relax it as much as you can." The corpsman ripped off a length of tape with his teeth and bound it tight. "Now don't move that arm any more than you have to." He smiled and added, "Sir." He looked up at Kozlewski. "Help me get him back to his cabin, Chief."

"Negative," Blake said. "I've got to get the diesel running. Help me get down to it."

"Excuse me, sir, but I can't let you do that," the corpsman said. "You're in shock, you've lost a fair amount of blood. You need to get some rest, sleep would be even better."

"I will, just as soon as we get the diesel up and running. Help me down."

The corpsman looked at Kozlewski.

"Ain't no use arguing with him," the chief said. "He's under the delusion we're going to get this thing under way."

Kozlewski and Jones helped Blake to his feet and walked him down the ladder to the next level below. Blake leaned against the corpsman and beamed his light over the emergency diesel generator. He could feel the heat of the engine rising up from the deck grids.

"Where the hell is Sergeant Rivero?" the chief said, glancing around.

Blake didn't answer, certain they'd find the Colombian marine's mutilated body when they got the power back on, hoping against hope they'd find him alive. With the beam of his flashlight, he traced the fuel lines coming in and the exhaust lines going out. He retraced the lines and stopped at a gate valve in the fuel line about chest high. Layers of paint around the valve stem were twisted free. Normally open, the fuel-line cutoff valve had obviously been closed, shutting off the fuel supply to the engine. The chief saw it at the same time and stepped forward to open it. Blake held his light on the valve as the chief twisted it counterclockwise.

"Let's fire it up, Chief."

"Aye aye, sir." Kozlewski bent over the control panel and engaged the starter. The batteries spun slowly. "That ain't a good sign," the chief said.

"Let them rest for a minute and try it again," Blake said, leaning against Doc Jones, his arm throbbing. He felt light-headed.

"You ought to be in bed, sir," Doc Jones said.

Blake felt the blackness closing in on him. He slumped against the corpsman.

"All right, that's it," Doc Jones said. "I'm taking you out of here."

"Wait," Blake said, shaking away the darkness. "Try it again."

The chief bent down and spun the engine. The batteries ground slower and slower until only the clicking of the solenoid could be heard. Blake sagged against the corpsman.

"Come on, sir, let's go," Doc said.

"If we don't get this running, we aren't going anywhere," Blake said.

"We ain't going to get it running with these batteries," the chief said. "They're shot."

The ship took another steep roll and Blake knew the storm wasn't that far behind. He could feel it in the way the ship was moving. He didn't know when it would hit, but he knew that it would. He'd checked the barometer in the pilothouse, and it was continuing to fall. The erratic behavior of the weather was typical of the lull before a cyclone. If it caught them like this, they wouldn't last an hour before going down. Fading fast, sick with fear and frustration, he lunged toward the generator and reached for the cutoff valve. He spun it counterclockwise and found to his amazement that it was not even halfway open. The chief had given it the standard three and a half turns, but the ancient valve must have had a different ratio. Blake opened it all the way and fell across the control panel. He hit the start switch, and the rested batteries spun the engine with a dying surge. The engine caught and clamored to life with a deafening roar, shattering the silence in the engine room.

"Way to go, Lieutenant!" he heard Chief Kozlewski bellow. Doc stood with his mouth open, then leapt forward to help him. He and the chief pulled him to his feet.

"You're going to open that wound up and bleed to death if you aren't careful," Doc Jones said. He held Blake up and looked at him. "I know I'm only an E-5, but now I'm going to give you some orders. You're going back to your cabin. You've got to get some rest, build your blood back up."

"I will in a minute," Blake said, slumping against the generator, holding his arm. "You guys fan out and see if you can see any trace of Sergeant Rivero."

Jones went to the left and Kozlewski went to the right, playing the beams of their flashlights around the machinery space. After a few minutes, Frank Kozlewski called out, "Here's his helmet and there's blood on it. In fact it's lying in a pool of blood. There's drag marks. It looks like the bastard killed him and dragged him off somewhere."

The chief walked back over to Blake and pitched Sergeant Rivero's helmet down. It clattered to the deck in front of him.

Blake grimaced at the dented helmet covered with blood. He reached down and picked it up, feeling guilty for having doubted the Colombian. The metallic smell of blood mixed with the human smell of Sergeant Rivero made him retch. Christ. If a guy like Rivero was no match for this animal, what chance would the rest of them have? He rubbed his face with his hand, the rage building in him. With three men dead, their chances of getting under way were nil. Suddenly he felt unblinking eyes on him, watching him. He looked out into the dark shadows of the engine room, his eyes searching. Rage and frustration welled up inside him.

"I know you're out there," he shouted. "Nice going, you stupid bastard. You may think you've won this round, but the joke's on you. There's a typhoon coming. It'll be here in a few hours and without engines we all go down together. This old tub will break up and sink like a stone. I thought you were smart enough to see that, but I can see now that you're just a stupid fucking animal!"

"Take it easy," the chief said. He grinned. "Ain't never heard you use such language."

"Sorry about that outburst." Blake gripped his shoulder, grimacing, then shouted out into the darkness, "But this moron needs to know what he's done."

"Well, it's done now," the chief said. "With three men dead we ain't going anywhere."

Blake tuned him out, thinking. Getting under way didn't require a bunch of rocket scientists, just enough bodies to follow orders and enough hands to do the right thing at the right time. Only six people left, seven counting Maria. The only chance he had now of pulling it off was to press Kelly and even little Maria into service. He hated the thought of endangering a child by putting her to work in the engine room, but knew she would be in much more danger if he didn't.

"You give up too easy," Blake said.

"You gotta be realistic, Lieutenant," the chief said. "Sparks and Alvarez and Rivero are dead. That's three men gone. That just don't leave enough bodies to get the job done."

"That leaves seven of us."

"Seven? How you figure that?"

"You, me, Tobin, Robertson, Doc, Kelly and Maria."

"Maria? You counting that little girl? What the hell do you think she could do in an engine room, for God's sake?"

"She's a pair of hands," Blake said. "We'll have to use her."

"Come on, sir," Doc Jones said. "You need to get some rest."

Kozlewski stood shaking his head, staring at Blake. "Doc's right," he said. "Maybe some sleep will get your head straightened out. Come on, I'll help you."

"Doc can handle it," Blake said. "I want you to stay here, Chief. Someone's got to stand watch over the generator, keep it running."

"What about *El Callado?*"

"He won't bother you now that he knows why we've got to get under way." Blake cupped his hand and shouted into the darkness, "Unless he's a complete moron, unless he wants to lose the ship for his bosses, unless he wants to go down with the fucking ship!" After the words stopped echoing, he said in a more normal tone, "The guy can't be that stupid or that bloodthirsty. Now that he understands what we're doing, he'll leave us alone until the storm passes. If we're still afloat after that, it'll be business as usual, but we'll deal with him then."

"You think he heard all that?" Kozlewski said in an awed voice, glancing around.

"He heard, all right," Blake said, his eyes sweeping the machinery space, probing the dark shadows. "He's right here in the room with us. Watching us. I can feel the son of a bitch, feel his eyes on me."

"You think he understands English?"

"He'd better understand, or he's as dead as we are."

The chief shuddered. "What you reckon he's done with Rivero?"

Blake shook his head, remembering the disappearing body in the vault. "I don't know. Apparently he likes to play games." He glanced up at Luis Alvarez's body, swaying with the motion of the ship. "I expect the guy in the vault and Rivero will show up in some dramatic way when it suits our deranged friend." He leaned his arm on Doc Jones's shoulder and nodded at Alvarez's body. "Cut him down, Chief. I'll send Robertson down to relieve you in a few minutes. Give him your side arm." Blake glanced at his watch. "It's almost two o'clock. Wake me in an hour. We'll begin the cold-start at 0300."

Blake leaned heavily on Doc Jones and shuffled up to the door of his stateroom, weak and exhausted from the climb back up the ladder. Almost no food or sleep in the last twenty-four hours, combined with the shock and loss of blood from the gunshot wound had begun to take its toll. He twisted the latch and found that the door was locked from the inside.

"What the hell is this?" He hammered on the door.

"Just a minute." He heard someone fumbling with the interior lock. The door opened and Dana Kelly stood there with an embarrassed look. "It's Maria," she said. "She insists on staying here with you."

Blake walked in, leaning on Doc's shoulder. "You know that's not possible. Take her back to your room."

Kelly's eyes grew wide when she saw the blood-soaked bandage around Blake's upper arm. "Oh my God, you're hurt. What happened?"

Maria saw it at the same time and let out a shriek, wailing, *"El Callado, El Callado."*

"No, no. It's all right," Blake said. He sat down heavily in a chair, clutching his arm, numb with pain, and looked at Maria. She was huddled in a corner of the room with the same gray blanket wrapped around her, trembling. "I'm sorry, honey, but you can't stay here."

The girl's soft weeping turned into sobs. She came up out of the corner and threw herself at Blake's feet. Rising up, she laid her head in his lap, hugging his legs. Blake touched her hair awkwardly and looked up at Kelly, the irritation showing in his eyes. "Dammit, you should know better."

"I tried to explain it, sir, but she doesn't understand." Kelly moved toward them and reached down for Maria. "Come on, darling, let's go."

Maria clung tighter to Blake's legs, refusing to budge.

Blake let out a long breath. There was only an hour left to get some sleep before getting under way. After that, it was anyone's guess when he would sleep again. "Okay, okay, you can stay." It seemed ridiculous to worry about regulations when there was a good chance they'd never get off the ship alive anyway.

The girl looked up with wide eyes and snuffled.

"You'll have to stay with her," Blake said, glancing at Kelly.

"The lieutenant's been hurt," Doc Jones said. "He needs to get some rest. How's he going to sleep with you two chatter-boxes in here?"

"I promise we won't make a sound," Kelly said.

"I'll give the girl something to make her sleep," Doc said, opening his medic kit. "Poor little kid's about over the edge."

Doc went off into the bathroom to get some water for Maria, and Kelly came over and started fussing with Blake's bandage. "What happened, sir? Was it him?"

"Just an accident," Blake said.

"How bad is it?"

Blake felt himself relax a little, moved by Kelly's look of concern. "I'm okay," he said.

Doc Jones came back with a large white tablet in one hand and a plastic cup of water in the other.

"Better make it a mild one," Blake said. "We're going to need all hands."

"Sure," Doc said. He snapped the tablet between his thumb

and two fingers and offered half to Maria. "Here you go, little one. Drink this down and you'll feel a lot better."

Maria looked at Kelly. Kelly nodded her approval.

The corpsman slung his medic kit over his shoulder and walked to the door. "I hope you can get some sleep, Lieutenant." He glanced dubiously at Kelly and the girl. "I'll check that dressing again before we go back down."

Locking the door after Doc Jones, Kelly led Maria over to the inboard bed. Shaking out a gray blanket, she covered the girl and tucked it around her chin. She sat on the edge of the bed, smiling down on Maria, stroking her hair. Within minutes the sedative had infiltrated the child's slender body, and she was snoring softly.

"Flip you for the bed," Blake said, nodding to the other single bed in the stateroom.

"I can squeeze in with Maria," Kelly said, shaking out another blanket. "You take it."

Blake didn't argue. Snapping out the light, he collapsed on the bed and whistled out a long, tired breath. He laid his head back on the pillow, clutching his arm. The pain in his arm was throbbing now, pulsing up into the side of his neck and shooting down to his elbow as the natural anesthesia produced by shock began to wear off. Doc had tried to convince him to take something for the pain on the way up from the engine room, but Blake had refused, wanting to be alert for the cold-start. He was beginning to wish he hadn't. He heard the rustle of damp clothing squirming down between dry bedclothes.

"Lieutenant?" Kelly whispered after a few minutes of silence.

"Yes?"

"I don't even know your name."

"Daniel . . . Dan."

"Like Daniel in the lion's den?"

"Not a bad analogy."

"Are you married? Do you have a family?"

Blake didn't answer for a long time. If there had been anything good about what had happened over the last twenty-four hours, it had been that it had suppressed all memories of his last night at home with Vicki. "Not anymore."

"What happened?"

"Two people going in different directions," Blake said, his thoughts drifting back. He'd met her at Lincoln Center when he was a midshipman at Kings Point. He was standing around in the lobby during intermission, feeling out of place in his ice-cream whites, savoring a rare break from the Academy. She walked up with an impish grin and asked for an ice-cream bar. Blake didn't know what to say until she flashed that soon-to-be-famous smile, and he knew she was kidding. She was a junior at Columbia, majoring in communications. She wanted to be the next Jane Pauley, she said, but after a promising start in broadcasting, paying her dues in small regional markets, she'd given it all up for him. All he'd ever wanted was to go to sea, maybe be captain of his own ship some day. He'd always known it would never work; deep down he knew that someone like Vicki could never be satisfied with a guy from San Diego with nothing to offer except a life as a sailor's wife, and he'd been right. They'd made it work for a few years, through sheer animal magnetism, but after she'd choked down the loneliness of uncountable six-month absences, first in the merchant fleet, and now this, she'd decided that was not the way she wanted to spend her life. They both knew it was over, but her timing was impeccable. On his last night at home, she had announced that she had taken a job as coanchor on a six o'clock news show at an ABC affiliate in New Orleans, and wouldn't be back. She had given up all rights to Laurie, dropped her with Blake's mother, and walked out of his life, just like that.

"Do you have any children?"

"A girl," Blake said. "Almost three."

"I'm sorry. I shouldn't be talking to you."

"It's all right. I can't sleep anyway."

After a pause, Kelly said, "I bet she's cute."

Blake slid his wallet out of his pocket and retrieved a picture from the plastic insert. A grim smile crossed his face. She was way beyond cute, he thought, with her blond curls and sparkling blue eyes. He wondered if he'd ever see her again. He replaced the wallet in his pocket and handed the picture across to Kelly.

Kelly groped for the picture in the near dark, touching Blake's hand. She raised up and squinted at the picture in the dim light coming from the door of the bathroom. "She's beautiful," Kelly said, handing it back.

Blake shoved the picture in his shirt pocket and lay back, breathing out. The pain in his arm was still throbbing, pumping blood to the wound.

After a minute of silence, Kelly said, "We're not going to make it out of this, are we?"

"Not if I don't get some sleep," Blake said.

"Sorry, sir."

"It's okay." Blake twisted in the bed, knowing that this would be the last chance he'd have to sleep for a while, but sleep wouldn't come. He heard Kelly stirring in bed. His mind flashed on the picture of her standing in the rain after Sparks had been killed, her damp shirt stretched across her breasts. She apparently wasn't wearing anything under her dungarees then, and he wondered if she was now. Shifting in the bed, he tried to blot the image out of his mind.

Outside, the wind picked up, and Blake concentrated on the long swells that were gently heaving the ship. He had timed the rate of swell earlier. The crests were passing at the rate of four per minute, about half the normal rate. He knew from the copy of Bowditch he'd found in the chart room that this was one of the earliest signs of a tropical cyclone.

With the gentle heaving of the ship on the long swell, he gradually drifted off into a troubled sleep, punctuated with bizarre dreams. He was being chased by a faceless creature wielding a combat knife similar to the one Sergeant Rivero carried, only much longer. He had managed to make it safely into a room and lock the door behind him, just ahead of the flashing blade. In the room stood Dana Kelly with a blanket wrapped around her, bathed in the glow of moonlight coming through the open window. A soft summer breeze gently blew the curtains inward. Beautiful, gentle music he couldn't identify filled the air. The violent pounding on the door was forgotten as she slowly let the blanket fall and stood before him with outstretched arms, completely, beautifully nude. The sight of her took his breath away. She looked like a goddess, smiling at him in the pale, yellow light. Blake stepped toward her and she reached out to him, smiling broadly, her eyes shining. He took her face in his hands and moved down to kiss her. Inches away from her mouth, her face suddenly turned into the dead face of John Sparks, the mouth an open wound, filled with clotted blood. He drew back in revulsion, then the face fast-forwarded through all the mutilated faces he had seen during the last few hours, like a grisly, black-and-white film. He awoke with a violent start and sat up, gasping for air. His shirt collar, soaked with sweat, felt cold on the back of his neck.

He rubbed his eyes and looked at his watch, wondering how long he'd been asleep: 0245. It seemed like seconds. He heard murmurs from the bed next to him and remembered that he was not alone. Kelly was mumbling in her sleep. He sat still, listening to the unintelligible sounds. She was obviously having her share of bad dreams, too. Standing up, he made his way into the bathroom with the flashlight. His arm throbbed with pain. Propping the flashlight up on the sink, he filled a plastic cup with water and downed it. It had a rusty taste that made him retch. He looked at his reflection in the faded mirror and noticed deep circles under his eyes.

Startled by a scream from the stateroom, Blake rushed in and saw Kelly in the dim light, flailing her arms. Afraid she'd injure Maria, he leaned over the bed and held her arms. The child stirred but didn't wake. Kelly heaved violently, and the blanket slipped away. Blake released her arms and covered her with the blanket as she shot upright and stared into his eyes.

"You were having a bad dream," Blake said.

Kelly threw her arms around his neck. "Oh God, I'm so scared," she said, almost whimpering. Blake gently tried to pull her arms away, but there was almost no strength in his left arm and he was surprised at her grip. He smelled the clean, fresh scent of her hair, felt the heat of her body through her shirt as his hands left her arms and groped painfully in the air, then came to rest on her back. The warm touch of her body made his hands come alive with a tingling sensation that reached up into his chest, overshadowed the pain in his arm. Kelly responded to the touch of his hands on her back with a tighter grip around his neck. Blake tried to break the grip, tried to pull away, but the feel of her cheek against his, her warm breath on his neck, conspired to sap his strength from him.

They sat locked together in a one-sided embrace. Animal feelings were surging in him he hadn't felt since the early days with Vicki. He summoned all the strength he could muster and wrenched Kelly's arms from around his neck, letting her fall gently back onto the bed. She pulled the blanket up around her chin, looking up at him with a smile that seemed to say they had shared something that would forever change the way they saw each other. Blake looked down on her for a minute without speaking, astonished at how beautiful she was, wondering why he hadn't seen it before, fighting off an overpowering urge to take her back in his arms and kiss her. "Go back to sleep," he said finally. "It's okay."

Stepping back into the bathroom, he washed his face in cold water and told himself to forget it. Everything about it was wrong. He was an officer, she was enlisted, under his own command. Captain Hammer would have a field day with that one. They were from two different worlds, and this could never be allowed to happen. Stretching out on the bed, he lay back and tried to put it out of his mind. He laid his arm across his eyes and squeezed them shut, trying to blot out the smell of her hair, the warmth of her body. *This can't be happening,* he thought. *People must go a little crazy when they know they're about to die.*

He drifted off again into an uneasy sleep with vague dreams that were undefined but decidedly pleasant. He knew it was only a few minutes until 0300, but the dreams seemed to last for hours. Suddenly he heard a loud crash and found himself sprawled across the deck, the chairs tumbling over him, the pain in his arm excruciating. He tried to stand but couldn't get up. Kelly and Maria went flying out of their beds against the bulkheads, screaming. He heard a violent pounding on the door. Crawling on his hands and knees, he reached the door and pulled himself up by the door latch. He opened it and Frank Kozlewski fell into the stateroom.

The chief stood clinging to the brass door handle, his face drawn. "Time to get this hunk of cold iron under way, sir," he said, glancing around with wide eyes. "That cyclone you been talking about? It's here."

"Rouse the others, Chief," Blake said, struggling to regain his footing. "I'll be down in a minute."

"Aye aye, sir." The door closed behind the chief, and the ship stabilized momentarily.

Blake looked at Kelly in the diffused glow of the flashlight, wondering if he'd see what he'd seen earlier. She held the blanket around her neck, framing her face in a way that set off her high cheekbones, golden skin, dark eyes, auburn hair. He hadn't been deluded by the passion of the moment; she was indeed beautiful, even in a clear frame of mind. He stared at her, amazed he hadn't seen it until now.

"We're going to need your help to get under way," he said. "Maria's, too."

Maria sat on the deck, her head lolling against the bulkhead. "I don't know if I can revive her," Kelly said.

"I've got to get down there," Blake said, rummaging in his right rear pocket. After his outburst in the engine room he was certain that even a bloodthirsty animal like *El Callado* would understand the seriousness of the situation and not interfere with them getting the ship under way, but just to be safe he retrieved the snub-nosed .38 caliber revolver he'd found in the captain's cabin and handed it to Kelly. "Here, you'd better take this. Bring her down as soon as you can."

"Wake up, little one," Dana Kelly said, patting Maria's face. She sat on the bed beside Maria, holding on while the ship pitched up and yawed to starboard. "We've got to go help."

She pressed the light button on her Timex while Maria rolled over. It had only been five minutes since Blake and the chief had left, but the lieutenant said he needed them to get under way, and she was getting anxious. The weather suddenly seemed worse.

Maria moaned and covered her eyes with a thin arm.

"Come on, sweetheart, we women have to pull our own weight." Kelly looked down on the sleeping child, moved by her innocent beauty, feeling guilty for waking her up. She retrieved a rag soaked in cool water from the bathroom and mopped the girl's face. "Come on, honey. Wake up. The men need us."

Maria allowed herself to be pulled groggily to a sitting position, then blinked her eyes open. "What time is it?"

"Time to get up. The guys need our help in the engine room."

Instantly awake, Maria's eyes opened wide with fear. "We're going down there alone?"

"Not to worry, kiddo," Kelly said, patting her hip pocket.

Maria's eyebrows raised. "You have a *pistola?*"

"You bet your boots." Kelly grinned. "If that clown shows his face, I'll fill him full of lead."

"No, señorita." Maria grabbed Kelly's shirt. *"El Callado* has eyes that see in the dark. We must not leave this room."

"We've got to, honey. The men need us, they're counting on us." Kelly smiled gently. "But more important, all the women in the world are counting on us. You don't want to let them down, do you?"

Maria nodded.

Kelly laughed. "You don't mean that." Pulling the child close, she hugged her and kissed the top of her head. "Don't be afraid. Let's go."

Kelly opened the door a crack and cautiously peered out into the dimly lit passageway. "Come on, pal. All clear."

Maria hesitantly followed her out of the room, glancing around like a doe in a field full of hunters. "Let us go quickly."

"We'll be there in two shakes," Kelly said, taking her hand.

They stepped around the linen closet and walked toward the open stairwell that led down to the main deck. Pausing at the opening, Kelly peered down into the shadows of the deck below, some instinct telling her to stop.

Maria pulled at Kelly's hand. "Listen. Did you hear that?"

Kelly shook her head. "I didn't hear anything," she said without conviction, knowing something had made her hesitate.

Holding her breath, straining to hear, Kelly heard a faint sound, catlike footsteps on the deck below.

"It's him, he's down there," Maria whispered in Kelly's ear, terror constricting her voice.

Heart pounding, Kelly placed her finger across her lips in a shushing motion, listening.

Staring down the stairwell, eyes adjusting to the gloom, Kelly saw the composition of a shadow change, something moving back into the protection of the darkness.

"It's him, it's *El Callado*, the silent one," Maria rasped in Kelly's ear. "We must go back."

"We can't," Kelly said in a whisper, her mouth suddenly dry. "They need us down there."

Fumbling in her hip pocket, she withdrew the revolver Blake had given her and tightened her fist uncertainly around it, her damp palms sticking to the varnish on the wooden grips. She'd never fired a revolver before, but the Chief's Special was small enough for her to hold comfortably, and she thought she could handle it. She studied it in her hand. It looked like all you did was snap the safety off, point it, and pull the trigger. Hands trembling, she pushed the safety off with her thumb, and stepped toward the stairwell.

"No!" Maria screamed.

Kelly saw the dark figure of a man break from the shadows below, then disappear. "Come on. We've got to get this guy before he kills someone else, or we'll never get out of here."

"No!" Maria shouted again. "Let the men do it. Killing is not for women."

"The men have their hands full. Remember what I said about, 'Women can do anything men can do'?" She took a deep breath and swallowed hard. "Well, now's the time to prove it."

Maria dragged behind, tugging at her, whimpering, while Kelly cautiously started down the ladder, eyes flashing in every direction, peering down into the semidarkness.

"Por favor, señorita," Maria said behind her, crying with muffled sobs. "Do not go down there, I beg you."

"Shh," Kelly said. She took one step down the ladder and heard the rusty screech of a light bulb being twisted out of its socket. The dim light on the deck below faded into darkness.

"Look. He has removed the light. He can see in the dark," Maria hissed in Kelly's ear. "I beg you, do not go down there."

Kelly peered down into the shadows, the only light now coming from the deck they were standing on. "We don't have any choice," she whispered. "The men can't get under way without us."

"If we go back to the cabin and wait, the *teniente* will come for us."

"Yeah, and that guy will just sit there in the dark and wait for him to come." She thought of the intense closeness she'd felt with Blake's arms around her and desperately wanted to feel him close to her again. She knew there was no chance of that happening—it was a relationship that could never be—but she'd never felt like this about a man before, and wasn't about to let this creature get to him. "We can't just sit in our cabin and let this guy ambush the lieutenant when he comes to get us. You wouldn't want that to happen, would you?"

"No," Maria cried, snuffling, wiping her eyes.

"Then it's up to us. Come on."

Kelly started down the ladder, pausing on each step, eyes alert for any movement below. Maria lagged behind, tugging at her, not wanting to go forward, not wanting to lose contact. On the third step Kelly heard a shuffling sound below and paused, straining to see into the darkness. She heard it again, directly beneath her, and looked down. From behind the stairwell, a hand reached through the open rungs of the ladder and tightened around her right ankle. A surge of adrenaline shot through her as a smooth pull backward jerked her off-balance. She pitched forward, desperately trying to catch herself. The next few seconds were a blur, the feeling of flying noiselessly through the air with the sure knowledge that she was going to die. The last sound she heard, before the crushing sound of her head against the deck, was the high keening sound of Maria's anguished scream.

Chapter Fourteen

Jorge Cordoba stared at the tall helicopter pilot. The knot in the pit of his stomach tightened. "What do you mean, you're not flying?"

"Am I talking too fast for you?" The pilot stared back.

Jorge swallowed, struggling to keep the panic out of his voice. "Listen, my friend. We've got to get aboard that ship. Now. You've flown into dangerous situations before. We'll pay you a bonus."

The pilot shook his head. "Only a fool would fly into a Pacific cyclone. And Michael Gaines's mama didn't raise no fools."

"How does five hundred thousand sound to you?"

"No way."

"All right, I don't have time to quibble, let's make it a million."

Gaines laughed. "You don't get it, pal. You can't fly in that stuff."

"Don't be ridiculous. It's just a weather condition. How bad can it be?"

The pilot gave him a wilted smile. "It's just a weather

condition, all right. But there's not a worse one in the world. When God made cyclones, at least He had the kindness to keep them over water. If something like that hit on the land, there wouldn't be anything left, and there won't be anything left out there when it's gone, either.'' He looked at his watch. ''We might as well be heading back for Lima. You aren't going to be needing me to land on any freighter. By tonight, that sucker's going to be hull-deep in whale shit.''

Major Portillo came walking up, cracking his riding crop against his boots. ''Now that you've taken care of your business, Señor Cordoba, we have an appointment to keep. Come, we are late.''

Jorge shook his head, staring at the pilot. ''The pilot says he can't fly.''

Major Portillo raised his eyebrows. ''Oh? And why is that?''

''He doesn't like the weather,'' Jorge said, not taking his eyes off Gaines.

The Peruvian officer frowned. ''And if he doesn't fly, what happens to our . . . agreement?''

''It's off,'' Jorge said, looking at the pilot. He would see how serious this loudmouthed *yanqui* was about not flying into a little bad weather.

''I have a vested interest in that particular flight,'' Major Portillo said, stepping up to the American pilot. ''I suggest you consider carefully the consequences of not flying.''

''And I suggest you butt out,'' Gaines said. He glanced around at the soldiers in green camouflage fatigues. ''You and all your little tin soldiers aren't going to squeeze me into a ride like that.''

Major Portillo's hand flashed out, startling Jorge with the crack of the riding crop across the American's face. Gaines reeled backward with a stunned expression. He raised his hand to the welt rising across his face. The look of disbelief in his eyes narrowed into rage. Ignoring the clack of a dozen bolt-action rifles being cocked, he lunged forward, only to be met by a row of fixed bayonets. Major Portillo nodded to two soldiers who stepped up behind the pilot. One bound his hands behind his back with a leather thong, the other forced him roughly to his knees. Unbuckling his holster, the major withdrew a nine-millimeter Browning automatic pistol. Smiling at the American, he pulled the slide back on the automatic with great deliberation and screwed the muzzle into the pilot's left ear.

"Perhaps now the weather doesn't look so bad to you, eh, *compadre?* Perhaps now you would like to get into your helicopter and fly away?"

"We fly when I say we fly," Gaines said. "Kill me, and we don't fly at all. Go fuck yourself, General."

Major Portillo bristled and thumbed the safety off the pistol with an audible snap.

"Hold it," Jorge said. He stood looking down on the pilot, satisfied that it was pointless to continue. It was clear that nothing would make him fly into a tropical cyclone. And if by some miracle the ship survived the storm, they would need him later. "He's right. Release him."

Jorge turned and kicked a clod of dirt, exploding it into the sultry air. Because of these bumbling Peruvian fools, and that treacherous *puta* of a flight attendant, he had missed his one window of opportunity to recover the ship. He knew he should call Don Gallardo with the bad news, but he couldn't bring himself to do it.

There might still be a chance, he told himself. His last hope now was the American officer who was aboard. It all came down to him, a faceless stranger who held the fate of the organization in his hands. Jorge knew he was grasping at straws, but the tantalizing idea that the American might somehow get the ship going and maneuver it through the storm, seized him. He knew it was wishful thinking; the chances were slim, almost nonexistent, that any young officer would be able to keep an ancient ship like the *Latin Star* afloat through the kind of storm the pilot had described. Still, the will to survive was man's strongest instinct.

He decided to wait until the storm had passed, and he had a definitive answer about the ship before he called Don Gallardo. He would use the talks with Colonel Suarez as an excuse to delay the call. Hopefully, the storm would have dissipated by then. If the ship survived, they would simply revert to their original plan. If not, nothing else would matter anyway.

Major Portillo removed the automatic from the pilot's ear and stood looking at Jorge with the pistol dangling at his side. "And our agreement?"

Jorge nodded. "You'll be taken care of." He wasn't disposed to quibble over the relatively small sum of two million dollars with an agitated man who had a loaded gun in his hand.

He glanced at Enrique Lopez, who had been watching the ruckus with a look of anticipation on his pockmarked face. Jorge thought the director of security looked disappointed that he would not see the American's brains splattered in the dust.

"Continue to monitor the storm closely," Jorge said. "As soon as it passes, determine the status and location of the ship, assuming it's still afloat. I'll be back as soon as possible." He nodded toward the pilot. "I'm leaving him under your protection. See that he is made comfortable."

The five-minute march to the Peruvian Army base at Punta Arenas took fifteen minutes by Humvee over the potholed road. Jorge sat in the rear seat next to Major Portillo and looked around at the dense jungle overhanging the road as the all-terrain vehicle lumbered along. Needles of sunlight flashed through the vegetation like laser beams, blinding him. Laboring to breath in the humid air, he wrinkled his nose at the smell rising up from his crotch, and thought about the flight attendant. If it hadn't been for that *puta,* he could have avoided this, headed it off. No matter how this came out, he thought, he had a score to settle with her.

The four-wheel-drive vehicle labored up a hill, and from the crest Jorge could see the Army base sprawled out below. It was bigger than he had imagined. A ten-foot-high chain-link fence topped with spirals of concertina wire surrounded the entire compound. On the perimeter, a pair of Caterpillar tractors worked ceaselessly to hold the jungle at bay while armed guards watched idly from atop wooden towers. The hum of diesel engines grew louder as the Humvee bumped its way down the hill and ground up to the main gate.

Two sentries in green uniforms snapped to attention and saluted with their rifles while soldiers in camouflage fatigues scrambled to open the gate. Major Portillo touched his helmet, and the vehicle proceeded through the gate down a wide boulevard that cut through the center of the base. Jorge glanced at the unpainted wooden barracks and soldiers slumped around in the stifling heat. Near an open water tower, a sprawling one-story brick structure stood nestled in a landscaped area of the base. It looked like a combination office building and luxurious private residence. Guards were everywhere. The Humvee pulled into a curved driveway, and, before it came to a halt, a young officer wearing the silver bars of a first lieutenant stepped up with his hand on the door. He came to attention and saluted.

"Good morning, Major."

Major Portillo touched his helmet with his riding crop. "Lieutenant."

"The colonel is waiting for you, sir."

The young lieutenant escorted Jorge and Major Portillo through wide mahogany doors into a large air-conditioned reception area. Jorge glanced around, amazed at the luxurious decor. The lieutenant stopped and turned to Jorge with his hands outstretched. "With your permission, sir."

It took Jorge a minute to realize what the lieutenant wanted. He looked at Major Portillo. "Is this really necessary?"

Major Portillo smiled. "I'm sure you would take similar precautions with any visitor not personally known to Don Gallardo."

Jorge exhaled a long breath. He raised his arms slightly as the lieutenant stepped forward and ran his hands down his sides, feeling a twinge of embarrassment that his armpits were soaking wet. The lieutenant knelt down and ran his hands down Jorge's legs, from his crotch to his ankles. Jorge flinched at the touch of another man. The lieutenant stood and looked

Jorge in the eye for a brief second, a clear look of warning, that said, "I think you're clean, but we'll be watching."

"This way, please." The lieutenant turned and pushed through another set of double doors that led into a large office area partitioned off with glass enclosures. Two dozen sleepy-looking clerks in green uniforms pounded typewriters and shuffled papers. No one looked up as they passed to the rear of the room, where two guards with machine guns stood at the sides of a solid-looking mahogany door. The guards snapped to attention and opened the door into a wide hallway that ran past rows of private offices on either side. Jorge looked down the long corridor to a set of double doors with yet another set of sentries posted, amused at the extent of the buffer between the colonel and the outside world, wondering when it would end. Something about it reminded him of a film he'd seen on American television about a group of bizarre characters going to see a wizard. As they walked down the hallway, Jorge glanced at the names on the private offices and noticed Major Portillo's name on the office closest to the double doors. The doors opened into an alcove where a bullnecked sergeant with a shaved head sat behind a desk. The sergeant stood without coming to attention, seeming to ignore the two officers. He wore a pistol belt around his thick waist. *Not your typical secretary,* Jorge thought.

The sergeant looked Jorge up and down before he turned to Major Portillo. "The colonel will be with you shortly."

Jorge stood flanked by an officer on each side and glanced around the alcove, aware of the unwavering gaze of the sergeant. He noticed a red light on the telephone console. After a minute the light went out.

"You can go in now." The sergeant nodded toward the door, not taking his eyes off Jorge.

The lieutenant stepped to the door and held it for Jorge and Major Portillo, then closed the door behind them, remaining outside.

Jorge stood quietly with Major Portillo, looking at the rear of a high-backed swivel chair. He could see a thatch of short, neatly combed gray hair over the top of the chair. Whoever it

belonged to was staring out the window behind the desk. Major
Portillo cleared his throat and the chair swiveled around. Jorge
tried not to smile. The figure in the chair bore a vague resem-
blance to the actor who played the wizard in the film: medium
height, dark gray mustache, short gray hair, sallow complexion,
owlish thick dark eyebrows, slightly paunchy, grandfatherly
look. Without the well-pressed khaki uniform and the insignia
on his collar, he would look like any other middle-aged man.
So this was the great Colonel Julio Suarez. Jorge began to relax
a little.

"Gentlemen, please come in." Colonel Suarez stood and
walked around his desk to greet them, his slight paunch straining
lightly at his tailored khaki shirt. Jorge noticed that he was
sweating in the cool room.

"Colonel Suarez, may I introduce Señor Jorge Cordoba,
emissary from Don Augusto Gallardo."

"Don Gallardo sends his compliments," Jorge said,
extending his hand.

The colonel nodded. "I trust your godfather is well." They
shook hands correctly.

Jorge blinked, startled that Colonel Suarez would know such
an intimate fact about him. His estimation of the kindly-looking
man went up a notch. "Quite well, thank you."

"Please," Colonel Suarez said, sweeping his hand toward
a door on the side wall of his office. "I thought you might enjoy
a decent brunch. Good restaurants are scarce in the Huallaga
Valley."

Jorge walked through the door into a formal dining room and
stopped, taken aback with the display of opulence. A rectangular
table, at least fifteen feet in length and covered with a glowing
white Damascus cloth, dominated the room. Gold-trimmed
place settings sparkled beneath a glittering chandelier. On the
perimeter of the room two servants in white coats stood staring
straight ahead. The scene looked completely out of place in a
military installation. *This character's living like a king,* Jorge
thought, *on our money.*

Colonel Suarez seated himself at the head of the table and

gestured for Jorge to be seated at his right. Major Portillo sat opposite. Jorge took his seat and glanced around the room with a slightly bemused look, feeling out of place in his wrinkled suit, needing a shower and a shave.

"We don't have many creature comforts here in Punta Arenas," Colonel Suarez said, seeming to pick up on Jorge's expression. "We indulge ourselves in small ways. Food, wine"—he smiled up at the young waitress who had entered the room carrying a tray—"and other harmless distractions." He hoisted his wineglass. "Your health, gentlemen."

"And yours," Jorge said, raising his glass, thinking it a bit early in the day for wine. The acrid bouquet and the inky legs suggested a vintage French wine, probably very old. *Perhaps a Rothschild,* Jorge thought. He took a polite sip and held it in his mouth, admiring the character of the wine. Nodding his approval, he swallowed, igniting a pleasant glow in the back of his throat. Jorge replaced the glass; there would be no more drinking until after the negotiations.

One of the waiters began pouring coffee while the other served bowls of chilled soup from a tray carried by the young waitress. Jorge waited for Colonel Suarez to begin, then sampled a small taste. It appeared to be a smooth blend of tropical fruit, icy and delicious.

"Our association with Don Gallardo has been long and mutually profitable," Colonel Suarez began, sipping on the chilled soup. He broke open a muffin. "I'm sorry to see it come to such an abrupt end."

Jorge stopped with his spoon poised in midair and looked at him. "Come to an end? You mean temporarily."

"I mean for the foreseeable future," Colonel Suarez said. "At least a year, perhaps longer."

Jorge smiled to himself. A year's gap in production would literally put them out of business, and the colonel knew it. The kindly-looking old gentleman was going to start out playing hardball.

"And why is that?" Jorge said in a controlled voice, playing the game, knowing where it would end. The outcome was foreordained; he had participated in these negotiations before via conference call, listening to the sob stories of how the government was bearing down, clucking their tongues in sympathy, then agreeing to pay what the colonel wanted.

"The situation is becoming unstable. My government has launched an investigation into drug trafficking in the Huallaga Valley and the Army's possible involvement. We have learned that the American Drug Enforcement Agency, the DEA, has put pressure on the Peruvian government to bring a halt to the flow of raw cocaine paste coming through Peru, which is, as you know, the world's largest source of paste."

Jorge stifled a yawn. He'd heard all this crap before. The colonel would go on for hours about the difficult situation they were in before hitting him with the punch line. Wanting to cut to the chase and get back to Campanilla, he decided to open the negotiations. He would agree to anything to get out of here. If the ship were lost, they would be out of business anyway.

"We both agree you're in a challenging environment, Colonel," Jorge said. "In recognition of that, Don Gallardo has authorized me to grant a modest increase for the security services you provide, say six thousand US dollars per flight."

Colonel Suarez laid his spoon down and looked at Jorge for a long minute under his owlish eyebrows. "You would be well advised to curb your youthful impatience and listen carefully."

Jorge felt something tighten in his stomach. He didn't like the sound of this. Something told him to back off. "Forgive me, Colonel. It's been a long trip, and I've forgotten my manners. Please continue."

The colonel went back to his chilled soup. "Within a few days a raid will be conducted on your facility at Campanilla by the government of Peru in a joint effort with the American DEA. According to our sources, the government assumes that those arrested, under threat of life imprisonment, will be willing to make a deal and link certain Army officers to the trafficking."

Jorge swallowed. "A raid? We've been able to avoid those before. There must be something we can do about it."

"The situation has escalated to the level now where there

is only one thing we can do,'' Colonel Suarez said, glancing at the scrambled eggs being served. ''We will beat them at their own game. We will conduct a preemptive raid of our own under the pretext of breaking the drug traffickers. We will give them a high-ranking official of Don Gallardo's organization, along with enough lesser-ranked people to make it appear authentic.''

Jorge suddenly lost his appetite. Now he knew why he didn't like the sound of this. He was the highest-ranking official of the organization they would ever be likely to get in this godforsaken place. Glancing around the room, he felt a surge of blood rush through his limbs. He wanted to bolt for the door, but knew there was no way out.

''You'll never get away with it,'' Jorge said, trying to keep his voice level. ''Don Gallardo is a very powerful man, when he finds out what you've done . . .''

Colonel Suarez looked at Major Portillo, and they both laughed. He glanced at Jorge with an impish look. ''Relax, my dear fellow. No one is talking about you. After all, you are a member of Don Gallardo's immediate family, so to speak.''

Jorge let out a long breath and shuddered in the coolness of the room. That explains how the colonel knew about his relationship with Don Gallardo. The son of a whore had looked into it, with the idea of setting him up. It chilled him to think that he had been a candidate to take the fall, prevented only by the colonel's realization that he was Don Gallardo's godson. His face flushed at the thought of what might have been. The rest of his life in a Peruvian military prison! Sweat appeared on his forehead. He could see now that his parents had been right. When he'd accepted Don Gallardo's offer over their objections, he'd never envisioned himself being exposed to this kind of risk.

''Then who?'' Jorge slumped back in his chair, intensely relieved that it wouldn't be him.

''The next-highest-ranking member of Don Gallardo's orga-

nization in Peru is your acting director of security, Enrique
Garcia Lopez, who has the added advantage of being a Peruvian
national. He will do very nicely, if you agree.''

That was an easy decision, Jorge thought. He didn't espe-
cially like the ugly little man with the scarred face and the
''I've got a secret'' look that he kept flashing at Jorge. He was
Don Gallardo's oldest employee, his chief assassin, but the
Don wouldn't quarrel when he understood the circumstances.
Besides, anyone who would murder women and children had
no redeeming qualities.

''You've got him, but what's to prevent him from implicating
you in the drug trafficking? He might make a deal with the
Peruvian government and the DEA.''

Colonel Suarez smiled. ''You are familiar, of course, with
the *Sendero Luminoso,* the Shining Path?''

''Of course,'' Jorge said. ''They've tried to overthrow every
government in Latin America.''

Colonel Suarez nodded and forked a wet mound of eggs into
his mouth. ''Maoists. Misguided fools still following the failed
policies of Mao Tse-tung down the 'shining path.' But it's a
large Communist organization manned with well-trained guerrillas intent on overthrowing the lawful government of Peru,
and the government takes it seriously. Seriously enough to
prompt it to issue an antiterrorist decree in 1992 establishing
the crime of 'treason against the fatherland.' Conviction carries
the automatic penalty of life in prison.''

''I don't see the connection,'' Jorge said.

Colonel Suarez smiled. ''The decree granted the Army broad
powers to investigate, arrest, charge, and prosecute such crimes
under a military tribunal.''

''So?''

''While conducting our preemptive raid on Campanilla,''
Colonel Suarez went on, ''we will find a significant cache of
arms and military information. We will charge your acting
director of security with supplying arms and military information to Maoist guerrillas of the *Sendero Luminoso.* He will

be charged with 'treason against the fatherland,' which takes precedence over the crime of drug trafficking. It also allows for a military tribunal and, if convicted, a penalty of life imprisonment. He will be held incommunicado and tried in a closed courtroom by an anonymous military judge, all allowed under the decree. After his conviction he will be sentenced to life in a military prison and confined on the same Navy base where the head of the *Sendero Luminoso* is now being held." The colonel smiled at Jorge. "He will not be in a position to talk to anyone."

"The Army has the power to do this?"

Suarez nodded. "Under the decree, the Army not only has the right but the responsibility." He sliced into a thick slab of ham. "With the conviction of a high-ranking officer and the closure of your operation the pressure will be off and we will return to play another day. But to make it look as though you had no advance notice, everything must remain in place; no more flights will be permitted for the foreseeable future except for one aircraft to take you out of here. Our raid will come tomorrow morning at dawn. You must leave before then."

Jorge shifted in his seat, his mind racing. This changed everything. If the flow of coca paste was going to be shut down for a year, they needed to recover the ship now more than ever if they were going to survive as an organization. What if the storm didn't pass until morning? If the ship survived, he would need both helicopters and crews to recover it and sail it to a friendly port. Survival of the organization without the ship had been questionable; with the added blow of the shut down of Campanilla it would be impossible.

"If we're going to have the capital to resume operations in a year, Colonel, there is something I must do before I go," Jorge said. "I can't be specific, but I must have the two Blackhawk helicopters and their specialized crews available to me."

"I have plans for those helicopters," Colonel Suarez said, sipping coffee. "You can do with your crews what you will."

Jorge looked across the table at Major Portillo for support.

The major seemed to sense that his Swiss bank account was on the line.

"Colonel, with all due respect, would it not be in our own best interests to ensure that Don Gallardo's organization has the capital it needs to resume operations when this is over?" Major Portillo said. "Surely we should do nothing that would jeopardize that, for whatever reason."

Colonel Suarez looked at Major Portillo for a long minute, fingering his coffee cup. He looked back at Jorge. "This . . . operation that you don't want to talk about, does it involve any activity in Peru?"

Jorge shook his head. "No. You have my word. There's a possibility we won't need them at all, but if we do, it will be on an assignment out of the country."

Colonel Suarez nodded. "Perhaps you're right, Major. Perhaps it would not be a good business decision to do anything that would deprive our Colombian friends of their livelihood." He looked at Jorge. "Out of respect for Don Gallardo, I will allow you to keep the helicopters. However, the raid will come early tomorrow, just after dawn. My advice is for you to be well clear of Campanilla by then."

Jorge sat in the backseat of the Humvee as it bounced its way back to Campanilla, feeling strangely elated by his narrow escape from being railroaded into a Peruvian military prison. He breathed deeply, savoring his freedom, and congratulated himself on his negotiating skills. Don Gallardo would be proud of him. Not only had he avoided being the sacrificial lamb, but he had also saved the critically important helicopters. The shutdown of Campanilla was a serious setback, but they were not out of the game yet.

He stared at the back of the young soldier fighting the wheel over the rutted road, his elation giving way to a deep sense of anxiety. He had saved the helicopters, but from now on timing would be everything. It was unlikely that the ship would survive, he reminded himself. Still, it was possible. The raid on the camp at dawn tomorrow was another unexpected complication, but if the storm passed before then, if the ship survived, if they found it quickly and got the helicopters launched, they would still have a chance. All he needed from this point on was luck, something he'd always had in abundance.

The Humvee pulled into the compound at Campanilla, and Jorge starting walking toward the Command Center to see if there had been any change in the weather. He glanced around as he walked. The Learjet was still there, parked under the makeshift hangar, and no other flights had been allowed to take off, so the treacherous bitch of a flight attendant still had to be there. Stepping around the building, he saw her walking down the path from the commissary toward him, eating a mango. She started to turn away, then turned and started walking toward him.

"Señor Cordoba," she said, smiling nervously. "How nice to see you."

"I missed you when I woke up," Jorge said, returning the smile.

"I had to do something. I hope you're not mad."

"Of course not."

"I asked about you. They said you had gone to Punta Arenas. I didn't expect you back so soon."

Or at all, Jorge thought. "It was nothing, just a little business to take care of. I see you've had breakfast."

She flashed an embarrassed look at the half-eaten mango and shrugged. "I'm not very hungry."

"I have some business to take care of in the Command Center," Jorge said. "Wait for me in my bungalow."

"You're sure you're not mad?"

Jorge brushed her cheek gently. "How could I be angry with someone as beautiful as you?"

She flushed and looked down. "Don't be long."

Jorge watched her walk down the path to the bungalow. She turned at the door and waved. Jorge smiled and waved as she disappeared inside. "Count on it," he said.

* * *

Jorge walked into the refrigerated air of the Command Center and adjusted his eyes to the dim light. The air stank of stale cigarette smoke. The American pilot was slumped across a leather sofa against one wall, smoking a cigarette, while one of Enrique Lopez's goons stood over him with a machine gun. The acting director of security was standing next to the radar scopes, staring down on a small television screen.

Jorge walked up and stood beside him without speaking. A white, circular, rotating mass was inching its way across the eastern Pacific in a northeasterly direction.

The director of security glanced up at Jorge and answered the question that was in his eyes. "Weather satellite courtesy of the *Norte Americano*'s National Weather Service," he said. "They feed it to about forty countries around the world, including Peru, who provides it to the Peruvian Navy, who provides it to Colonel Suarez, who provides it to us."

"How does it look?" Jorge said.

"Bad," Lopez said. His pitted face looked ghoulish under the green glow of the radar scopes. He nodded to the commercial television set mounted on the wall. "CNN's doing an update every hour. Tropical cyclones don't usually get this far east in the Pacific. They're worried that it might hit the coast of Peru. Major disaster if it comes ashore."

"What chance do you give the ship?"

Lopez shook his head. "Not much. It's doubtful anything could survive that." He nodded at the white spinning mass moving almost imperceptibly across the blue background of the Pacific.

"Where are our planes?"

"I've got three jets circling in a fifty-mile radius above the storm. The minute it clears, we'll be in a position to know what happened to the ship."

Jorge felt Lopez staring at him while Jorge studied the screen.

"What happened in Punta Arenas?"

Jorge's stomach tightened. "The usual," he said, concentrating on keeping his voice relaxed. "They wanted more money."

"That's all?" Lopez asked.

"Sure," Jorge said. "Why do you ask?"

"I've heard rumors of a raid."

Jorge felt a tinge of red flush his face. He shook his head, grateful for the semidarkened room. "Not likely. Not while we're under the protection of Colonel Suarez. There's too much at stake for him to allow that to happen."

"You'd better be right."

"Trust me," Jorge said in a calm voice. It was critical to keep Lopez from suspecting anything until the storm had passed, and they knew the status of the ship. After that, the Peruvians could have him. The lie came easily, but the question had shaken Jorge. He decided to leave lest he give anything away with his tone of voice or body language. He knew it wouldn't take much to spook the wily assassin, who had evaded police in a dozen countries. "Call me at once if there's any change in the weather," Jorge said. "I'll be in my bungalow."

Jorge walked back to the VIP bungalow, clearly worried now. Was Lopez wise to the raid? Who planted that seed? It had to be the flight attendant. If he suspects he's being set up, will he run? He knows his way around here, he's a Peruvian national and he's no fool, he must have an escape plan. Yes, he would run, Jorge concluded, he'd be a fool not to, and that would leave Jorge standing here alone to take the fall. If Lopez got away, Jorge was the only other officer of Don Gallardo's organization at Campanilla. And if he was the only choice, Jorge knew the kindly-looking colonel would order his arrest in a heartbeat, devotion to Don Gallardo or not. Lopez's availability as the pigeon was the only thing standing between Jorge and a life sentence in a Peruvian military prison.

Lopez's suspicion changed everything. That bitch of a flight attendant. He stood on the path to the bungalow and stared at the windows, noticing that the shades were all drawn. He imagined her standing inside the door, nude, with a cold Brahma in her hand, or lying back on the couch with her legs spread, a soft light coming from the bathroom. He wanted to kill her for her treachery, but knew that if he did, Lopez would suspect something for sure. He decided he could wait, and in the meantime, he would use her as she had used him.

Chapter Fifteen

Blake stood in front of the engine-room console with Frank Kozlewski, going over the cold-start checklist. Looking up, he saw Maria come flying down the ladder, wild-eyed, sobbing, awkwardly clutching the stainless-steel revolver he'd given Kelly. A wave of fear passed through him. Passing the clipboard off to the chief, he ran to meet her.

"Where's Kelly?"

"*El Callado,*" Maria said, choking back sobs, gasping. "The *señorita,* she went after him. She fell down the ladder and hit her head. I think she is dead. I could not wake her. I picked up the *pistola,* and pointed into the darkness, and screamed at him to stay away. Then I ran, ran for my life."

"Give me that," Blake said, grabbing the revolver away from Maria, cursing himself for leaving them to come down alone. He thought *El Callado* had gotten the message, would leave them alone while they got under way. He hadn't bothered Kozlewski or Robertson while they were standing watch over the generator. Why would he attack Kelly? It didn't make sense.

"I am so ashamed," Maria sobbed. "I should not have run, I should have stayed."

"No, you did the right thing," Blake said. "Show me where you left her."

"On the main deck, just inside the superstructure."

"Chief, let's go!" Blake shouted over his shoulder and ran for the ladder. Clambering up to the next level, he emerged onto the deck and started for the ladder that would take him up to the main deck. A few steps from the engine-room shaft he tripped over a fleshy pile of something soft lying in the dark, and knew instantly what it was. Stumbling, he flashed his light on the dark form as Chief Kozlewski came puffing up the ladder behind him. Maria shrieked at the sight of Dana Kelly bathed in the white glare of the flashlight, her face covered with streaks of blood, her hair matted to a glistening wound on her forehead.

Blake let out a gasp and felt a sharp pain in his middle, a body blow as brutal as if he'd been struck in the stomach with a sledgehammer. The massive amounts of blood streaming down Kelly's face told him she couldn't possibly be alive. Slumping down beside her, he felt something die inside him. Unable to let her go, he picked her up and cradled her in his arms. Her head lolled to the side. Frank Kozlewski stood over them with a light, shaking his head. Blake softly brushed the matted hair out of her wound and rocked her gently, knowing it was the end of the line. To hell with the damned ship. Let it go down, let that stupid animal go down with it. They would all go down together. His backup plan required seven pair of hands to get under way. With five men and a child left, there was no way out of here. And somehow with Kelly gone he no longer cared.

An almost inaudible moan came out of Kelly's parted lips.

A surge of energy shot through him. "She's alive. Get Doc!"

"Back in a flash," Frank Kozlewski said, stumbling back down the ladder.

Blake cradled Kelly's head in his arms and gently felt for the extent of the wound. He looked at Maria. "I thought you said she was on the main deck."

Maria stared back, eyes wide. "She was, that's where I left her."

"How did she get here?" Blake said, knowing the answer before he finished the question. He glanced around in the darkness, knowing *El Callado* was there, grateful that he had spared Kelly and Maria. The good news was that he knows now that he needs all of us, Blake thought, even the girl, to keep this nightmare afloat. The bad news was that there was no telling what form his pent-up thirst for blood might take after they got through the storm, if they got through, but he'd deal with that when it came.

Doc Jones came scrambling out of the engine-room shaft, with Chief Kozlewski panting behind him. He knelt beside Kelly and shined the chief's flashlight on her forehead.

"Head wounds bleed a lot," Doc said, wiping the blood away from the wound. "They usually look a lot worse than they are."

Kelly eased her eyes open and jumped, startled at the scene crowding around her.

Blake held her tightly. "It's okay, it's just us. Relax. Doc will have you fixed up in no time."

"How did I get here?" Kelly asked, bewildered. "The last thing I remember was . . ."

"Don't think about it," Blake said. "It's okay now."

"Wait, I remember now. The bastard tripped me. I fell. Then I dreamed you were carrying me." She smiled at Blake. "I guess it wasn't a dream after all."

Maria started to say something, and Blake stifled her with a look. "Never mind that. Let's get you back to a stateroom, where Doc can get a better look at you."

"No, no. I'm okay," Kelly said. The ship pitched up and sent them sliding across the deck. "We've got to get under way."

"There's no way you can handle that," Blake said.

"Sure I can," Kelly said, shaking her head.

"What do you think, Doc?" Blake asked.

The corpsman shrugged. "She knows how she feels better than we do."

"*No problema,*" Kelly said, touching the wound on her forehead, grimacing. She looked out into the dark. "But first I want my gun back. That bastard's still out there."

"No chance," Blake said.

"Bullshit. It wasn't a fair fight. The bastard tripped me."

"He tripped you so he wouldn't have to kill you," Blake said.

Kelly looked at him blankly.

"You didn't leave him much choice, going after him with a gun."

"What are you saying?"

"He's finally figured out that we're his only hope of keeping this bucket afloat."

"And that's why he didn't kill me or Maria?"

"That's right."

Kelly screwed her face up. "Are you saying *he* carried me here?"

Blake nodded.

Kelly shuddered. "I don't care. If he's still out there, I want my gun back."

Blake looked at her and grinned. "All right, hardhead, but no more chasing this guy." He handed the revolver back to Kelly, butt first. "The next time you might not be so lucky."

Blake raised his arm and motioned for everyone to gather around the engine-room console. The sailors glanced nervously around the machinery space, struggling to maintain their balance against the violent rolling of the ship, their usual banter noticeably absent. Maria looked at all the faces, then at Kelly. "Where is the *sargento* and *Señor* Alvarez?" she whispered.

Kelly shushed her and put her arm around her. Maria moved in closer, her face grim.

"All right, listen up," Blake said, rocking on the balls of his feet. The ship took a steep roll to port and slowly righted itself, groaning. "I don't have to tell you what the weather's like. We've got to get under way as soon as possible."

"How bad's it going to get, Lieutenant?" Tobin asked.

"I don't know anyone who's ever been through one," Blake said, "but a Pacific cyclone's as bad as it gets."

"I knew this old boy that was in a typhoon once," Robertson said. "On a tin can. He said you don't want no part of that."

"Your friend was right," Blake said. "We're pretty far east of where they normally occur according to the book, but I guess this one didn't read the book." He grinned back at the few weak smiles, wanting to prepare them without scaring them to death. He couldn't get the clinical words he'd read in the copy of the *American Practical Navigator* he'd found on the bridge out of his mind. The words had chilled him: *The rapidity with which the weather can deteriorate with approach of the storm, and the violence of a fully developed tropical cyclone, are difficult to visualize if they have not been experienced.*

"How we going to go about this?" Robertson asked.

"The chief and I have worked up an engine-starting procedure," Blake said. "It's important to listen carefully and follow the instructions we'll give you. There's no margin for error here. If we don't get under way quickly, we're in serious trouble. We may not get a second chance. Any questions before we start?" His eyes went from person to person. Kozlewski, Robertson, Tobin, Doc, Kelly, Maria. He could see what they were thinking, even little Maria. Could this sleepy-looking bunch really get this enormous ship under way and, more importantly, could Blake maneuver it through a storm, the likes of which they could only imagine?

"I'm game to give it a try," Doc Jones said, "but with Sparks, and Alvarez, and Sergeant Rivero . . ." He glanced at Maria staring intently at him. "Well, you know, do we really have enough people to do this, sir? I don't know about Kelly, but I feel kind of worthless. This is about the first time I've ever been in an engine room in my life."

"We'll team you up with experienced people," Blake said.

"Tobin and Robertson are old hands at this. Don't worry. If everyone does their job, we'll have enough people."

"What happened to your arm, sir?" Robertson said.

Blake glanced at his shoulder, and the dull pain surged back. He had forgotten about it in the excitement. "An accident. It's fine now."

Another steep roll pushed them back like a wave, then pulled them back in.

"How about Kelly? What happened to her?" Tobin said, staring at the white bandage around her head.

"I got my feet tangled up coming down a ladder," Kelly said. "No big."

Blake smiled to himself, proud of her gutsiness. "Some of the preliminary stuff has already been done," he said, "but let's run through the checklist to see if we've missed anything." He nodded to Frank Kozlewski.

The chief retrieved a pencil stub from his shirt pocket. He held up a grease-stained clipboard and ran his eye down the yellow tablet paper scribbled in Blake's hand. The list spilled over onto several pages. "Okay," the chief began, "we've already checked the main boilers, and they were laid up wet. The DC heater is full of water and the distilled-water tank is full and ready to go. The emergency diesel fuel tank is full enough to get us going. And we've checked the stern tube oil-sealing system, and it appears to be tight and properly filled." He ticked each item off the list. "The emergency diesel's running and the emergency electrical bus has been energized," he said, checking off the next two items. "That brings us up current, Lieutenant."

"Okay," Blake said, nodding to Tobin. "The next step is to sound the fuel-oil tanks and water tanks."

"I know how to do that," Maria spoke up, rubbing her eyes. "The chief engineer showed me."

"Good," Blake said. "You can help Tobin." Tobin walked off, motioning with his head for Maria to follow him.

"Robertson, prepare to light off the starboard boiler," Blake said. "Take Doc and show him how to open the steam-drum vent and superheater vent and drain. Kelly can handle the main and desuperheated steam stops at the boiler. Make sure they're all open.''

''And make damn sure their drains are open,'' the chief said.

As Blake called out orders and the sailors scrambled to complete each procedure, he could see a sense of excitement begin to build over bringing the dead ship back to life. He could also see fear and uncertainty gradually replaced with a feeling of comfort in the frenzied activity, a sense of doing something, of taking their fate into their own hands. He expected that. What he hadn't expected was the feeling of ownership in the beat-up old ship he could see developing. He welcomed the transition, knowing that the feeling of ownership would be invaluable when it came time to defend themselves.

In spite of the gathering storm, Blake began to ease up a little for the first time since they'd been aboard, feeling comfortable in the setting of the engine room, fussing with the aging machinery. He glanced around, certain that *El Callado* was watching them, and smiled at the raucous howl coming from behind the starboard boiler. Robertson was bellowing something that resembled a country song as Blake came up behind him. Doc Jones was staring at him with an incredulous look.

''Man, you better stick to tending boilers,'' he heard Doc say. ''Hank Williams be turning over in his grave.''

Robertson narrowed his eyes and looked at Doc. ''How you know about Hank Williams?''

''Black people have radios, too, you know.''

''Yeah, but y'all don't listen to good music,'' Robertson said, turning back to the boiler. ''Worked for this cook down in a little place in Mobile. All day long he'd be playing Muddy Waters, Howlin' Wolf, Screamin' Jay Hawkins. Great God Almighty. Never heard such noise in all my life.''

''Modern jazz is more my style,'' Doc said.

''You like that stuff?'' Robertson said. ''Never know where those guys are going to end up, once they start, wandering all over the place like that. Me, I like music with a tune to it.'' He squinted to check the water level in the steam drum. "Starboard boiler ready to light off, sir."

"Very well," Blake said. He nodded to the chief. "Let's get to it."

"Robertson," the chief said. "Let some diesel fuel out of that gravity tank into the booster pump. Tobin, show Kelly how to turn that forced-draft fan. Keep it dampered nice and slow." Kozlewski wrapped a rag soaked in diesel fuel around the end of a four-foot-long metal pole.

"Make sure you've had the fan on long enough for the furnace to purge itself," Blake said.

After a while, Kozlewski sniffed the air. "I think she's ready, sir," he said.

"Very well, chief. Light her off."

"Aye aye, sir." The chief touched the oblong blue-and-yellow flame from his pipe lighter to the end of the oil-soaked rag. He studied the flaming rag with a practiced eye before injecting it into the depths of the oil-burner assembly. The burner tip ignited with an orange flame.

"When the steam pressure reaches fifty psi, make sure you close the steam-drum vent," Blake said. "But leave the super-heater vent open."

They stood around the boiler, making small talk, struggling to keep their footing, waiting for the pressure to build.

"Robertson, what's your line pressure?" Blake said.

"Coming up on four hundred psi, sir."

"When it reaches four-four-zero, secure the superheater vent and stand by to start the main turbines."

"Aye aye, sir."

"Chief, let's activate the lube-oil purification system," Blake said. "When the temperature reaches one-o-five degrees Fahrenheit, start the main lube-oil pumps and start applying oil to the main-propulsion turbines and reduction gears."

"Aye aye, sir," the chief said.

By 0430, Blake and the chief had gone over the checklist twice, meticulously calling out each item, and were satisfied that all systems were go to start the main engines. Blake held his breath as Robertson engaged the jacking gear, spinning the main turbines to life. The ship trembled and surged beneath them with a steady vibration. Blake blew out a long breath and looked at Robertson. "Okay," he shouted over the noise. "Let's get the other boiler lit off."

"Aye aye, Cap'n." Robertson mopped his face with a damp shirt-sleeve.

Blake smiled at the title but let it pass. "Chief, can you finish up here?" he asked, looking at his watch.

"Yes, sir, I think so. After we get the port boiler up to speed, all that's left is to fire up the steering gear and stern tube lube-oil system," he said, flipping to the last page of the checklist. "Then we'll be able to answer a bell."

"Good," Blake said. "I've got some work to do in the pilothouse. I'll call down for Doc later to break him in on helm watches, along with Kelly and the girl. I'd like to be under way by 0500. Stand by to answer."

The chief turned to Blake, saluted smartly and said, "Aye aye, Cap'n."

"Let's not get carried away with this, Chief," Blake said, ignoring the salute.

"Like it or not, that's what you are, sir," the chief said. "A ship under way on the high seas has got to have a captain. It's the oldest law of the sea."

Blake chuckled at the absurd notion, but saw the serious look in the chief's eyes. "Call me anything that makes you feel better," he said. "Just be ready to answer a bell."

Blake emerged from the engine room into a dawn that had broken on a sky nearly as black as the night that had preceded it. Dawn. He was jolted by the realization that it had been nearly twenty-four hours since they'd left the *Carlyle*. He wondered if he'd ever see the old gray lady again.

He glanced up at the sky. Red and green running lights on the mast traced wide arcs against the black skies, now churning with fast-moving stratocumulus clouds. He steadied himself against the hatch cover as the ship shuddered from an explosion of green water across her forecastle, pushing her bow deep into solid water. Awed by the thunderous display of white foam, he held on to the hatch cover and waited for the bow to surface. He took a deep breath. The fresh sea air cut deeply into his lungs, clearing his head from the stuffy confines of the engine room.

As the bow surfaced, spewing frothy sheets of green-and-white water back into the sea, he quickly made his way across the pitching deck, struggling head down against the wind. He stopped and blew out a deep breath when he reached the safety of the superstructure.

He paused near the place where Kelly had been tripped by *El Callado* and glanced around, wondering which bulkhead he was hiding behind, which crack he was watching him through. He could feel his presence, his eyes on him, watching, waiting to kill him when he was no longer needed. He wanted to shout out in frustration, but knew it would be pointless.

He glanced around at the huge ship, shaking his head. He suddenly had what he wanted, something he'd thought would take twenty years to achieve. Command at sea. He smiled bitterly. When the Gods want to punish you, they give you what you want. He thought about Kelly and the girl, the chief, Doc, and the others. They were counting on him to get them through this, and he didn't have the first clue. He was no more qualified to conn this ship than was Alvarez, the coxswain. In fact, the seaman had probably been more qualified. At least he had conned something before in his life. He took a final look around, shaking his head. His first command, he thought with a sardonic smile. He turned and walked up the ladder to the bridge, hoping it wouldn't be his last.

"This is the engine-order telegraph," Blake said to Kelly, raising his voice to be heard over the wind shrieking through the pilothouse. "It sends a signal to the engine room with the direction and speed we want."

Dana Kelly stared at the brass handle and nodded. "Okay."

"Straight up, it's at 'All Stop,' " Blake said, gripping the handle. "If you push it forward, it's back. If you pull it toward you, it's ahead."

"That's backwards," Kelly said.

"That's a good way to remember it," Blake said. "If I give the command, 'dead slow ahead,' you pull it toward you to the first position. The next position is 'Slow Ahead,' then 'Half Ahead,' then 'Full Ahead,' which is maximum engine power."

"Got it," Kelly said.

"If I say, 'Full astern,' you push it forward all the way," Blake said. "In heavy weather fast execution of those orders is critical to the safe handling of the ship. You sure you've got it?"

Kelly glanced out at the raging seas, and nodded. "Yes, sir, I've got it." Her voice sounded tense, but firm.

"Good girl. When I give you a command, give it back to me so I'll know you heard it," Blake said.

Kelly nodded again. "Aye aye, sir. When do we start?"

"Right now," Blake said, glancing up as Doc Jones appeared in the doorway to the pilothouse. The corpsman's face and hands were smudged with grease from the engine room. Blake motioned him over to the ship's wheel. "Doc, you take the helm."

"Sir, I don't know anything about this." The corpsman walked up and stood before the wheel, rubbing the palms of his hands on his dungarees.

"Nothing to it," Blake said. "It's just like driving a car."

"Hell, sir, I told you, I'm from Queens," Doc said, looking at the mahogany wheel. "I've never driven a car in my life."

"This is even easier," Blake said. "Hold the wheel like this. If you turn the wheel to the right, the ship will turn to starboard. If you turn the wheel to the left, the ship will turn to port."

"How do I know which way to turn?" Doc asked.

"This is the compass," Blake said, pointing to the bronze, liquid-filled bowl mounted on the binnacle. "It's a standard seven-and-a-half-inch magnetic compass. Think of it as a circle with 360 degrees. I'll give you the heading when we get under way. It's your job to hold her steady on that course until I give you another one. Got it?''

''Yes, sir, I think so,'' Doc said. He squinted at the compass dubiously and gripped the wheel. ''But what's *El Callado* going to be doing while we're doing this?''

''Hanging on for dear life. He won't bother us,'' Blake said, looking over his shoulder. ''At least I don't think so.''

''Did something suddenly give him religion?'' Doc asked.

Blake nodded. ''The storm did.''

''If this wouldn't put the fear in you, nothing would,'' Doc said, looking out into the dark skies. ''I just hope you're right, Lieutenant. Hope that dude stays away, lets us be.''

''He's our biggest fan right now,'' Blake said. ''We're the only hope he's got to save the ship, not to mention his own hide. He'll leave us alone, long enough to get through the storm, anyway.''

''And after the storm?'' Kelly asked.

''That's another story.''

''Well, it's nice to know we have something to look forward to,'' Kelly said.

Blake glanced at Doc and Kelly. Behind them, Maria was watching intently from the window of the chart room, where Blake had placed her for safekeeping.

''Everybody straight?''

Doc and Kelly nodded and said, ''Yes, sir,'' almost in unison.

''All right, let's do it,'' Blake said. ''Dead slow ahead.''

''Dead slow ahead, aye, sir,'' Kelly repeated in a high-pitched voice. She pulled the handle on the engine-order telegraph back to the first position with a muffled clang.

Blake held his breath, waiting for Chief Kozlewski and the engine-room crew to respond. Outside, rain squalls rattled the bridge windows with pellets of water. The ship pitched and yawed, seemingly oblivious to the order to move. Blake clung to an overhead stanchion, waiting, not daring to breathe. A full minute passed. ''Come on, girl,'' he said under his breath. He started to reach for the sound-powered phone to the engine room. Then slowly, like a sleeping giant being prodded awake, the vibrations in the wheelhouse began to intensify.

Blake's heart began to beat faster, responding to the growing vibration in his feet and in his hands. The *Latin Star* shuddered, then eased forward, cutting into the sea.

"Well, kiss my granny," Doc said, wide-eyed. "You did it, Lieutenant. This big mother's really moving." The corpsman gripped the wheel with a look of amazement and turned it a few degrees to starboard. The freighter groaned, slowly coming around to starboard three degrees by the magnetic compass. His burnished features spread into a broad grin. "How you doing?"

Blake started to breathe again, feeling the thrum of the turbines and the bite of the screw through the water, grateful that the steering gear was still operable, something he hadn't really thought of until now. "Our course is zero-eight-one degrees," he said. "Bring her around."

"Zero-eight-one, aye, sir," Doc said.

Blake grinned at the instant comeback. "I thought you'd never done this before, Doc."

"Who, me? I'm an old hand," Doc said. "I was called to the bridge once when the *Carlyle* was leaving the San Francisco Bay. Telephone talker passed out. Combination of bad liquor and choppy seas. Heard the OOD and the helmsman talkin' that trash."

"You've been holding out on us," Blake said, scanning the horizon with binoculars. "Slow ahead."

"Slow ahead, aye, sir," Kelly repeated, pulling the lever down to the next position. The ship vibrated and gradually picked up speed.

Doc continued to twist the wheel to the right, staring at the compass, the tip of his tongue appearing in the corner of his mouth. The ship eased slowly to starboard, coming around to a heading of 081 degrees. The corpsman let out a deep laugh. "Piece of cake. I can drive the shit out of this thing."

Blake smiled at the expression on Doc's face, a kid riding his bike for the first time without training wheels.

Kelly emitted a doleful laugh, looking out at the sea. "How about driving it to California? Drop me off in San Jose."

"No way," Doc said, staring at the compass. "I'm gonna take this sucker through the Panama Canal, drive it all the way to New York City, run it aground on the first pier I see. We'll grab some of that loot in the number three hold and hail a taxi for the Topper Club on Forty-third Street. Best modern jazz in the city. You guys'll love it."

"Sounds like more fun than we're likely to have here." Blake hung from the stanchion with one hand and continued sweeping the horizon with the binoculars draped around his neck. The line where sea and sky met appeared sporadically, then fell away, hidden by huge waves. Elevating the binoculars slightly, he focused on a mass of white cirrus clouds converging over the southern horizon.

"Half ahead," Blake said, wanting to put as much distance between the ship and those clouds as possible. He wanted to get up to full speed quickly, but had agreed with the chief to ease into it. It made sense with a plant they knew nothing about, but he was nervous about taking any longer than he had to to get there.

Kelly repeated the order and pulled the lever down to the third position, clinging to the telegraph stand to keep her balance. The ship shuddered and surged forward. "What are we going to do, Lieutenant? What's the plan?"

"First, we're going to try to outrun this thing," Blake said.

Kelly brightened. "Do you think we can?"

Blake shook his head. "Not very likely. Cyclones can travel at twenty or thirty knots. But it makes sense to try."

"How fast will this thing go, Skipper?" Doc asked. "Balls out."

"Design speed's fifteen knots," Blake said. "But we'll be lucky to get half that in this weather."

"What if we can't outrun it?" Kelly asked. "What do we do then?"

"Depends on which half of the cyclone we're in," Blake said.

"Which half?" Kelly asked. "What difference does that make?"

"One half is called the navigable semicircle; the other's called the dangerous semicircle," Blake said.

"Which half do we want," Doc said, "or do I need to ask?"

Blake laughed. "Neither, if we can avoid it. Cyclones spin in a clockwise direction below the equator, so the navigable semicircle should be on the right of the cyclone as we face the direction it's moving toward. If we're lucky enough to catch that side of it, we'll bring the wind on the port quarter at a relative heading of 225 degrees and apply all the power we've got."

"What do we do if we're caught in the other side?" Kelly asked.

"Pray," Blake said.

"I don't get how one side can be worse than the other," Doc said. "Same storm."

"It has to do with the rotation of the cyclone," Blake said. "The other side's more dangerous because the wind speed's greater, compounded by the forward motion of the storm. Add the two speeds together, the speed of the wind and the speed of the storm, and you've got an 'E' ticket ride. Also, the direction is such that it would carry us into the forward part of the semicircle, directly in front of the storm. We don't want to be there."

"But what if we do get caught in it?" Kelly asked.

"If we can't avoid it, we'll maneuver in the opposite direction," Blake said. "We'll head her into the wind, bring the wind on the port bow, hold a relative course of 315 degrees, and give it all the power we can muster."

"I'm sure glad you know a lot about this stuff, Lieutenant," Doc said.

Blake stared through the binoculars, feeling a warm flush creep up his neck. The maneuvers he was glibly quoting had come from a quick reading of the chapter on tropical cyclones in the *American Practical Navigator* not more than an hour ago. He wasn't sure he knew what half of it meant. Even if he did, he had no idea whether he could make any of it happen in the chaos and confusion of a tropical cyclone. "All I know is what I read in the book."

"Don't be modest," Kelly said. "If anyone can get us through this storm, you can."

"Right on," Doc said. "Everybody knows you used to be on merchant ships before you were a Navy officer. Bet you've been through lots of these."

Blake smiled wryly, touched at their eagerness to believe in him. He hated pretense, especially in himself, and wanted to confess his ignorance, but doubted if he could convince them. And even if he could, what purpose would it serve? If they knew how little he knew, they'd be as terrified as he was.

Kelly looked nervously out the fogged bridge window. The seas were pitching violently. "How do we know it's really a cyclone? Maybe it's just crummy weather."

Blake nodded to the instruments mounted on the bulkhead behind the ship's wheel. "Three hours ago the barometer stood at 29.29. Now it's at 29.14. That's a fifteen-point drop in a few hours. It doesn't take a meteorologist to figure that one out. It's a cyclone all right."

"It doesn't look bad so far," Kelly said.

"You haven't seen anything yet," Blake said.

"Everybody talks about 'em, but I don't know anyone who's ever actually seen one," Doc said.

"They don't occur that often," Blake said, "and they're not that hard to avoid with modern weather satellites and navigation equipment."

"So how come Captain Hammer got so close to this one?" Doc asked.

Blake didn't answer. Why did Captain Hammer do anything? He hoped the Colombian frigate had at least been able to find the *Carlyle* and tow her clear of the area, even if she hadn't been able to find them.

"For something that doesn't happen much, people sure do spend a lot of time talking about them," Doc said. "Everywhere I go on the *Carlyle,* people are laid back telling sea stories, typhoon this and hurricane that."

"Sailors have always been a little paranoid about cyclones," Blake said. "Not hard to see why. They always originate over water, and they're the most destructive type of storm on earth."

"You've been through 'em before, right, Skipper?" Doc asked.

Blake shook his head. "The closest I ever came was two hundred miles from a typhoon in the South China Sea." *And that was close enough,* he thought, remembering the experience. In six years at sea on merchant ships and naval vessels, he had never steamed through a tropical cyclone. There weren't many people around who had. The smart ones avoided them, and the dumb ones were dead.

The ship pitched up and took a sickening cant to starboard, sending everyone teetering to keep their balance.

"I can't imagine what it's like, if it's worse than this," Kelly said, clinging to the telegraph stand.

"It's a lot worse than this," Blake said. "Much worse." He wanted to prepare them for what was coming but didn't know how to do it without terrifying them. From the look of the clouds forming over the southern horizon, they would see for themselves soon enough.

"I thought they weren't even supposed to be in these waters," Kelly said, sounding a little indignant.

"It's rare to find one this far east in the Pacific," Blake said. "But it happens. They can pop up anywhere over a tropical ocean. The only place they've never been seen is the South Atlantic."

"Wonder where they come from, what causes them?" Doc asked. The corpsman seemed a little crestfallen, Blake thought, with his disclosure that he'd never been through one.

"I could tell you the theories, but I don't think anyone really knows for sure," Blake said, remembering the textbookish words he'd read in the *American Practical Navigator.* Something about warm air and cold air colliding, causing the warm air to rise and the cold air to rush in to fill the void. The earth's rotation gave a spin to the cold air in the process, and a potentially lethal cyclone was born.

For reasons the book didn't enumerate, the direction of the spin was counterclockwise in the Northern Hemisphere; clockwise in the Southern. They were below the equator, so he knew the cyclone would be spinning clockwise. That meant that the navigable semicircle, the less violent half of the cyclone blowing in the direction opposite to its movement, would be on the right, where they could run before the wind.

But having information was one thing, Blake thought, being able to use it was another. In order to take advantage of that phenomenon, he'd have to know both the direction and the location of the center of the storm. And without a radio, he had no way to know. All he could do now was use the visual sighting methods he'd read about in the book, the same methods the ancient mariners had used.

Blake stood out on the bridge wing in a spitting rain and focused his binoculars on the massive formation of glistening cirrus clouds that had formed high over the southern horizon. According to the book, the point where the white silky clouds converged would give an indication of the direction of the center. His stomach tightened when he saw the point of convergence. They were directly ahead of the storm track; the center lay not more than two points off the port quarter.

"Full ahead," Blake shouted through the open door. "Let's get the hell out of here."

"Full ahead, aye, sir," Kelly said, pulling the handle down to the final position.

The horn on the sound-powered telephone blared. Blake came in dripping with water and picked it up. "Yes, Chief?"

"You trying to blow this thing up, or what?" Kozlewski's raspy voice sounded like pebbles being thrown against a tin roof. "Going to full in—"

"Storm track's on a straight line for us," Blake said. "Closing fast. We need everything you can pull out of those turbines."

There was a pause. "Aye aye, Skipper," the chief said.

For the next four hours Blake paced nervously between the pilothouse and the bridge wing while the *Latin Star* steamed in a northeasterly direction at full speed. The old freighter labored up over huge white-crested swells, shuddered with her screw out of the water, and crashed down into foaming black troughs. He stepped out onto the bridge wing in the yellowish daylight and stood with his khakis whipping in the wind, staring hopelessly through binoculars at the black wall of heavy cumulonimbus clouds forming across the southern horizon. He knew from the description in the book that he was looking directly at the bar of the storm. He grimaced at the speed with which it was closing the gap.

Stepping back into the wheelhouse, he continued to watch through his binoculars as large pieces of the dark wall of clouds broke off and drifted overhead. A rain squall appeared out of nowhere and rattled the bridge windows with pellets of water that sounded like hail. The wind alternately rose from an eery whistling sound to a piercing scream, then fell to a low howl. He checked the barometer again and saw to his shock that it had dropped another nine points.

Over the next two hours, the wind speed picked up, the seas became raging, and Doc began having difficulty keeping the freighter on course. Squall lines swept past the ship as though it were dead in the water. As Blake paced across the bridge, watching the bar of the storm approach from the stern, the day became nearly as dark as night. Rain squalls began to slam by at an almost continuous rate, and the barometer fell a point every few minutes. The outer fringes of the wind began to push toward the bow of the ship, pushing the freighter back like a bug caught in the swirl of a drain. Blake thought the center of the storm was still at least a hundred miles away, but it was clear they were losing the race.

"We're not going to be able to outrun it," Blake said. "We've got to turn her around, bring the wind on the port quarter. Hard right rudder, Doc. Bring her around to a heading of two-two-five degrees."

"Two-two-five degrees, aye, sir," Doc said, twisting the wheel to starboard.

Midway through the turn, a gale force wind whipped against the port side of the ship, heeling it sharply to starboard, sending the compass spinning. "What do I do?" Doc said, staring at the spinning compass. "This sucker's going crazy."

"We're broaching to," Blake said. "Just stay calm and hold your position. She'll come around."

"I'm turning the wheel but nothing's happening."

Blake struggled to keep his voice even. "We're broadside to the wind. Give her a minute, she'll come around," he said, praying that it would.

The wind diminished and the lumbering freighter slowly righted itself. Doc's forehead was burnished with a layer of sweat. He mopped at it with a shirt-sleeve and glanced at Blake. "This ain't as much fun as I thought it would be."

"The best is yet to come," Blake said. He knew that the sudden blast of wind that had caused the fully loaded freighter to broach to like a toy boat in a bathtub was only a small sample of what lay in store. He picked up the sound-powered telephone and rang the engine-room console.

"Yes, sir?" Chief Kozlewski's voice rattled through the earpiece.

"We can't outrun it, Chief, we're going to have to ride it out," Blake said. "How's the plant?"

"Seems to be stable," the chief said. "Biggest danger is keeping the fires from going out on those steep rolls."

"We can't let that happen," Blake said.

"I hear that," the chief said.

"It's going to get rough," Blake said. "Secure anything loose in the engine room and don't let anyone come topside until I give the word."

"You don't have to worry about that, Skipper. These guys are scared shitless."

"I don't think it'll come to that, but if we have to abandon, I'll let you know in plenty of time," Blake said, nearly drowned out by the sudden high-pitched scream of wind blasting through the wheelhouse. "But in the meantime give me everything you can pull out of those turbines."

"Aye aye, Skipper, we'll do our best." Kozlewski paused and said, "Lieutenant . . ."

"Yes?"

"You were right about getting under way. I hope I didn't slow you down any."

"That's never been one of your problems, Chief."

"We're counting on you, sir," Kozlewski said. "Good luck."

"Thanks, Chief. We'll need all we can get." Blake replaced the black phone in its bracket, now shiny with a fine spray that was blowing through the wheelhouse. The ship yawed sharply to port. He turned to see Doc spinning the wheel.

"Skipper, she's falling off course," Doc said. "I can't hold her."

"Hard right rudder," Blake said, struggling to keep his footing. His voice was nearly drowned out by a sudden shriek of the wind.

Doc's feet went out from under him and Blake lunged for the wheel. The corpsman skidded across the wet deck, crashing against the port bulkhead of the wheelhouse in a heap as Blake spun the wheel sharply to the right, pressing down on the spokes with all his strength. The freighter groaned, then heaved up on the crest of a huge swell which held it suspended in midair for what seemed a full half minute. Sitting astride the swell the ship vibrated heavily, as the nineteen-foot propeller spun futilely out of the water, before crashing back down into a trough, shooting tons of black water up from her bow in a V-shaped spray.

Doc fought his way to his feet and staggered across the room, throwing his arms around the binnacle as the ship yawed to starboard. "Heading is zero-six-six, sir," he said, peering wide-eyed at the compass, reading it upside down.

"Keep calling out the heading," Blake shouted over the wind as he held the wheel hard right, blinded by the stinging spray that was swirling through the wheelhouse.

"Zero-nine-zero. One-one-five. She's coming around, sir," Doc shouted.

A gigantic wave appeared on the starboard side of the ship, looming high above the superstructure. Blake stared up with his mouth open as the huge gray wave hung there, suspended by the wind. It came crashing down on the bridge in slow motion, ripping off the starboard door of the wheelhouse and flooding it with three feet of sticky salt water. All three were swept to the port side of the wheelhouse in a jumbled pile under the window as the wheel spun out of control. The ship rolled sharply to port, pinning Blake on the bottom of the pile. Salt water swirled around him as he struggled to open his eyes. He blinked his eyes open and saw to his horror that his face was pressed against the window and he was looking straight down into the sea. He didn't think it was possible for a ship to roll over that far and right itself. As the ship hung there suspended for what seemed like an eternity, Blake knew they were all going to die. But slowly, slowly the fully loaded freighter rolled upright with an anguished groan. Blake thought it was the sweetest sound he had ever heard. Kelly and Doc washed away from him, tumbling across the deck like marionettes with broken strings. He glanced up at Maria in the chart room and saw her flailing around, trying to get back on her feet, and knew that she was okay for the moment. Struggling to his feet, he staggered across the room through two feet of water. The green water swirling around his ankles felt thick and amazingly warm. He threw himself over the wheel and hung there, gasping for breath, spitting salt water. Doc Jones got to his feet first, then pulled Kelly up. Blake glanced over and saw that their eyes were wide with fear.

"Doc, what's our head?"

"I . . . I don't know, sir."

"Well, get over here," Blake shouted.

"Aye aye, sir." Doc blinked dumbly and slogged his way through a foot of swirling water to the binnacle.

"Kelly. Man your station."

"Are we going down?" Kelly asked as if coming out of a dream.

"Not if we keep our heads," Blake said, blinking salt water from his eyes. "Doc, what's our heading?"

"One-two-five, sir."

"Take the helm and bring her back around to two-two-five

degrees and hold her there,'' Blake said. He pulled the black
telephone off the bulkhead and rang the engine room console.
A frown crossed his face after the fifth ring with no answer.
He started to hang up and head down to the engine room when
he heard the rasping voice of Frank Kozlewski.

"Yes, sir,'' the chief said.

"Chief, what's going on down there?''

"All hell is breaking loose, sir. We're shipping water, number two boiler went out—''

"Shipping water? "Where's it coming from?''

"One of the seams opened up on that roll that nearly sank
us,'' the chief said. "Water spurted in like a high-pressure fire
hose. That's what put the number two out.''

"How much is coming in now?''

"We managed to shore it up with some four-by-four beams
we found. We're rigging up a sump pump now. Water's still
coming in, but I think the pump will stay up with it.''

"Can you relight the number two boiler?'' Blake asked.

"I'm not sure, sir. We're a little shorthanded. Tobin broke
his leg—''

"Broke his leg? How did he do that?''

"It was that big roll, sir. Everybody grabbed onto something
except Tobin. He went flying like a rag doll. Hit the bulkhead
with a crash you must've heard on the bridge. Wonder it didn't
kill him.''

"Chief, if another roll puts out the number one boiler, we're
in a lot of trouble.''

"If we get another roll like that last one, this old tub is going
to crack like an egg.''

"Do you want me to come down?''

"Negative, sir,'' the chief said. "I expect you've got your
hands full on the bridge.''

"When we get through this, Doc can set Tobin's leg,'' Blake
said. "In the meantime, try to get the number two lit off.''

"Aye aye, Skipper,'' the chief said.

Outside, the day was as dark as a moonlit night. Rain squalls
swept by in a continuous pattern, making it impossible to distin-

guish one from another. The velocity of the wind increased geometrically, buffeting the ship with gusts that threatened to rip the superstructure from the shelter deck.

"What's your head?" Blake shouted.

"One-seven-zero, sir, but it's all over the place," Doc said. "I can't hold her steady."

Gargantuan waves rose and hovered menacingly over the ship as gale force winds ripped their tops off and filled the air with swirling water. Torrential rains as thick as blood covered the wheelhouse in a heavy gray shroud. Blake squinted and tried to look out the windows. Visibility was zero. He glanced at the barometer. It had dropped to 28.96. He knew the worst was yet to come.

"She's falling off hard, sir," Doc said, as the ship yawed sharply to port, caught broadside by a wave as tall as a skyscraper.

"Hard right rudder," Blake said.

Doc spun the wheel to the right. "The wheel feels like it's broken, it's not doing anything."

A blast of gale force wind picked up where the wave left off and caught the ship broadside, sending it skidding across the swells sideways, like a wet kite trying to be airborne.

"What's your head?"

"Zero-nine-six."

Blake lurched forward and gaped at the compass, stunned. In a matter of seconds, the force of wind and wave had shifted the five-thousand-ton freighter's heading from southeast to due east as easily as a puff of wind would blow a leaf across a pond. It was the much-feared weather-vane effect. If the ship continued to blow sideways, the fires in the engine room would be extinguished and the ship would founder.

"We've got to bring her around, get stern to the wind," Blake yelled, spinning the wheel as far right as it would go, wrenching it away from Doc. "What's your head? Keep calling out your head," he shouted over the screaming wind.

"Zero-four-two," Doc shouted. "She's still falling off."

"The rudder's out of the water. The wheel's not holding,"

Blake shouted, bearing down on the spokes with all his strength. He knew he could use the engines to get her around if the freighter had had twin screws like the *Carlyle*. He'd studied the manuals enough. He would simply order standard speed on the port screw and reverse the starboard engine in combination with an emergency right rudder. The shaft horsepower of the *Latin Star* couldn't compare with a destroyer's, but eventually this maneuver would bring them around with the wind on their stern. But with a single screw, he knew they had only one choice. "We'll have to back her down." He spun the wheel to port. "Full astern!"

Kelly stared vacantly, clinging to the engine-order telegraph, her face as white as death.

"Kelly. Reverse your engines!"

Kelly blinked and seemed to come awake. She shoved the brass lever of the engine-order telegraph all the way forward. Clouds of thick black smoke swept past the bridge. The *Latin Star* shuddered violently, rattling the windows in the wheelhouse.

"Keep calling your heading," Blake shouted to Doc.

"One-one-zero. One-three-five. She's coming around, sir," Doc said. "I don't know what you're doing, but it's working."

"The engines won't bring her around," Blake said, "so we'll use the wind. We'll back her down with a hard left rudder and bring her around with her stern to the wind."

"One-five-five. One-seven-five. It's working." As Doc yelled out the increasing heading numbers, Blake slowly eased the wheel to the right, as though he were backing his car into a driveway, then straightened it out. The ship slowly came upright, now heading in a southeasterly direction, still pitching violently, but with her stern to the wind.

"You did it, sir," Kelly said.

"Full ahead," Blake said.

Kelly pulled the lever on the telegraph all the way toward her, staring at Blake with her eyes shining. "Full ahead, aye, *Captain*. I knew you could do it."

"We're not out of this yet," Blake said.

The ship picked up speed with its stern to the wind and plowed through the mountainous seas for the next thirty minutes, seeming to find its head. Without warning, the wind whistled down to an eerie silence, like a siren coming to rest, as the monstrous waves subsided and rolled gradually to a stop. The sky cleared, and rays of sunlight shone brilliantly through holes in the thin cloud cover. The rain came to a dripping halt as though shut off by a celestial hand. A warm breeze floated through the open doorway into the pilothouse. Blake stared out through the dripping bridge windows, stunned by the beautiful sight.

"It's over. We did it," Kelly shouted.

"Praise God," Doc said. "Never prayed so hard in my life." He wiped his eyes with a wet shirt-sleeve.

"No," Blake said, staring out at the wall of mountainous seas surrounding the ship. "It's the eye of the storm, the calm center. It's passing directly over us."

"Oh my God, look," Kelly said, pointing to the massive wall of water approaching from the port bow. "You mean we're going to go through that?"

The seas surrounding their calm setting appeared to be in total confusion. Blake looked on, dumbstruck, as the colossal waves forming the black wall of water encircling them twisted, turned, leapt up, plummeted down, exploded violently in every direction.

Blake glanced at the barometer. It had fallen to a new low, almost two inches below normal. The eye of the storm. The beauty of it took his breath away. Few people alive had ever seen one, he knew, but he had no time to gape at the sight.

"Slow ahead," Blake said. "We have a little while to catch our breath and get her headed into the wind before the other side hits." He looked at his watch. It was after five o'clock. They'd been fighting the storm all day without realizing it. Blake spun the wheel around to starboard. The freighter gradually responded, wallowing around into the wind, which had fallen to a gentle breeze.

"Take the helm, Doc." Blake picked up the black telephone and rang the engine-room console.

"Yes, sir," came the raspy voice.

"Chief," Blake said. "How's it going down there?"

"We're still shipping water, but not as fast as we were. What's happening? Are we through it?"

"No. We're in the eye of the storm. The other side will hit us in an hour, maybe sooner. How about the number two?"

"Still too wet. We're wiping it down now."

"And Tobin?"

"In a lot of pain. His leg is flopping around."

Blake covered the phone and turned to Kelly, wondering where their silent friend was riding out the storm. He hoped he'd gotten his head bashed in on the roll that fractured Tobin's leg. "Can you secure the bridge?"

"I can secure the bridge," Kelly said, patting the stainless-steel revolver in the hip pocket of her dungarees. "After going through this nothing will ever scare me again."

"We're coming down," Blake said into the phone, smiling at the grim set of her jawline and the decisive look in her eyes. He jammed the phone back into its bracket. "Let's go, Doc."

A blast of humid air hit Blake in the face as he dropped down the ladder into the engine room and quickly cast his eyes over the scene. Thin streams of water shot in around the temporary shoring that had been jammed into place. Panels of plywood had been rigged up to deflect the streams of seawater from hitting the number two boiler. Two submersible pumps hummed in the background. Tobin lay groaning on a narrow steel catwalk, placed there to stabilize him during the worst rolls.

The chief and Blake exchanged nods as Blake walked up to the number two boiler and squinted inside. Robertson was furiously wiping down the burner assembly. "How's it going?" Blake asked.

"Getting there," the chief said, glancing at his watch. "How much time you think we've got?"

"An hour, maybe less," Blake said.

Robertson withdrew a grimy arm from the oil-burner assembly. "That should do it," he said, mopping his face with a shirt-sleeve.

Blake squinted into the burner assembly. "Okay, let's do it," he said as Tobin let out a loud wail behind him. "Make sure the blow valves are secured."

He turned to see Doc Jones hunched over Tobin, twisting a roll of black electrician's tape tightly around two lengths of pipe flanking his leg as the machinist's mate threw his head back and howled.

The chief ran through the checklist with Blake's prompting, lit an oil-soaked rag attached to the end of a metal pole, and thrust it into the burner assembly. The burner ignited with a "whump." An orange flame glowed through the observation port.

"I want this boiler up to line pressure within thirty minutes, Chief," Blake said.

"If we try to bring her up that fast, she might blow all to hell," the chief said. "The manufacturer recommends—"

"The manufacturer isn't about to get hit with a wall of water as high as a mountain," Blake said. "We're going to need all the power we can get, as soon as we can get it. Watch it closely, but bring it up fast."

"Aye aye, sir," the chief said, as Blake walked over to the catwalk, where Doc Jones was kneeling over Tobin, smiling at his workmanship. Tobin glowered back.

"How do you feel?" Blake asked.

"He like to killed me, sir." Tobin gripped his pipe splint with both hands and grimaced.

"You'll live," Doc said with a grin.

"I'm heading for the bridge," Blake said. "Join me as soon as you're done here, Doc."

"Aye aye, Skipper," Doc said, wrapping another strip of tape around Tobin's splint.

Blake turned to the chief. "When it hits this time, we're going to be on the wrong side of the storm. It's going to be even worse. Keep those boilers burning, come hell or high water.''

"We'll do our damnedest, Skipper.''

"I know you will.'' Blake looked into the chief's eyes and knew that this might be the last conversation they would ever have. There were things he wanted to say to the man, but knew he couldn't. Finally, he put his hand on the older man's shoulder and held it there for an instant. "Stand by to answer a bell.''

Chapter Sixteen

Blake ascended the ladder to the bridge wing two steps at a time, surveying the damage as he went. The two five-ton cargo booms forward of the number one king post had been ripped cleanly off and were nowhere to be seen. The stack was crumpled, leaning to starboard like an old top hat. The cluster of navigation lights and antennae mounted at the top of the mainmast now dangled over the side, a tangled mess suspended by wires. Looking aft, he could see that three of the five-ton booms over the number four cargo hold were missing; the fourth hung limply over the port quarter, swaying gently, creaking with the slight motion of the ship. The starboard door to the pilothouse had been torn from its hinges. He vaguely remembered seeing it go during the storm.

No sign of *El Callado*, Blake thought, glancing around, but he knew he wasn't far away, unless he'd gotten his head bashed in or been swept overboard. That wasn't likely; the silent one knew his way around the ship, would stay secure belowdecks in one of his little hiding places until they got through the second half of the storm, and then make his move. Blake knew he should be making a plan to deal with him then, but looking at the storm they were about to go through, he wasn't that optimistic.

On the surface the plucky old ship appeared to have survived the first half of the storm with only superficial damage, but Blake knew she was bleeding from wounds that wouldn't heal. He stared across at the raging wall of water that surrounded the ship and shook his head. There was no possible way she could survive what was coming; the sea would find her wounds and rip her apart.

He stood gripping the rail in the ominous hush, mesmerized by the haunting beauty of the scene. The eye of the storm. They appeared to be at the center of a gigantic coliseum twenty miles in diameter. The walls were formed by a funnel of black clouds that slanted thousands of feet upward, then flared out, fading into the blue sky. At the crest, rays of late afternoon sunlight shone through wisps of white clouds. The sea was glasslike, a luminescent green the color of emeralds, pulsing with gentle, conical swells. The wind was still. At the base of the funnel a barricade of white water surrounded the ship, a hundred thousand Niagara Falls gathered in an immense circle. He turned slowly around in a complete orbit, wanting to see it all, fascinated with the means of his own destruction. From every direction he heard the deep, distant roar of the water, like blood roaring in his ears, and the baleful howl of the wind.

A shudder swelled up through him. So this was how it would end. His own death had always been impossible to imagine. Now he knew it was imminent. He took a deep breath. All men had to die sooner or later, he told himself. At least he would die doing what he wanted, and seeing something few men would ever see. Accepting his own death should have given him a sense of peace, but instead it left him with an angry sense of betrayal. The ocean floor was lined with the bones of men who had treated the sea with contempt, but Blake had always treated it with respect.

Looking back, he saw Kelly and Maria huddled together in the pilothouse and felt something twist in his stomach. Not only the bones of men, but women and children, too. The sea was no respecter of flesh.

Glancing up, they saw him and flashed relieved smiles. The look of hope in their eyes stirred something within him. Curiously, he could accept his own death, but not theirs. Looking at their eyes filled him with a sudden resolve to fight the sea with his last breath.

"El ojo," Maria said, walking out onto the bridge wing. The girl's voice was full of wonder.

Blake looked at Kelly.

"The eye," Kelly said. "The eye of the storm. Her father told her about it." Kelly turned slowly around in a full circle as if in a trance. "What an unbelievable sight."

"Not many people will ever see this," Blake said.

"It's so peaceful, so calm."

"Enjoy it while it lasts."

"When are we going to get under way?"

"Right now," Blake said. "Now that our helmsman is here." He glanced over his shoulder as Doc Jones came up behind them. The corpsman's face looked drawn.

"How's Tobin?" Blake asked.

"Compound fracture of the fibula," Doc said. "Got him bound up pretty tight. He'll be okay. As okay as any of us, I guess."

Blake took one last look around, wishing he could freeze this moment in time. The sun was shining brilliantly. A few wispy white clouds formed against the powder blue sky. The wind was almost still. *A beautiful day to die,* he thought.

"Let's do it," he said.

Maria pointed overhead excitedly. *"Pájaros."*

"Look," Kelly said.

A cloud of seabirds appeared overhead crying mournfully. Mingled with the seabirds were land birds, lost and confused. Exhausted, the more aggressive among them began to land on the freighter. Within minutes, the deck was covered with hundreds of shuddering, squawking birds.

"Let's go," Blake said, turning to walk into the pilothouse.

"We must be close to land," Kelly said, walking in behind him.

"There's a small island," Blake said, "just a dot on one of the charts I found in the chart room. The land birds are probably from there, swept up in the storm."

"How far is it?" Kelly asked, taking her place at the engine-order telegraph.

"Forget it," Blake said. "It's about fifty miles southeast of where we were before the storm hit. God knows where it is now." He glanced at his watch and looked out at the black wall, trying to estimate how fast it was moving. "We need to keep our minds on business. This is going to be a rough one." He looked at Doc and Kelly. "Everybody straight?"

They both nodded, and chorused, "Yes, sir."

"Slow ahead."

Kelly repeated the order and pulled the telegraph handle into position.

The vibration in the deck started almost immediately, and the ship eased forward into the calm sea.

"Hard right rudder," Blake said. "Let's bring her around into the wind."

"Hard right rudder, aye, sir," Doc said, twisting the wheel to starboard.

"But couldn't we find it?" Kelly asked.

Blake stared through the binoculars at the dark wall. "Find what?"

"The island," Kelly said.

"In the first place, it's not an island," Blake said. "It's an atoll, made out of coral. It may not even be there anymore. It was an old chart." Blake looked at her curiously. "What is it with you and that island?"

Kelly shrugged. "Given the fix we're in, it seems like a good idea to know where the nearest land is."

"The first thing we have to worry about is getting through that," Blake said, nodding at the slowly moving wall of the cyclone. "If we do, we'll wait for the Colombian frigate to take us off. If we go wandering around, it'll make it harder to find us."

"I hear the Colombians have beer on their ships like the Brits do," Doc Jones said. "Is that true, Lieutenant?"

Blake shook his head. "No idea."

"But what if they don't find us?" Kelly asked. "God knows where we are right now. You said it yourself."

"They'll find us," Blake said. "We can't be that far from our last reported position. If we make it through the storm, we'll drop anchor and wait for the frigate. It'll be easier to find us if we're not moving around."

"I can't wait to be picked up and have one of them cool Colombian beers," Doc said to himself. His eyes seemed to glaze over.

"But—"

"Let's stay focused on business," Blake said, cutting her off. He stared at the black wall of clouds surrounding them. "We've got bigger things to worry about right now than finding an island."

"How much time do you figure we've got before it hits?" Kelly asked.

"Not much," Blake said. "Just about enough time to get up a head of steam and get her headed against the rotation of the cyclone."

Doc gripped the ship's wheel and looked across the shimmering water. "Man, I can't believe the other side of this mother is going to be worse than what we went through."

"The wind should be higher by a factor of two at least," Blake said.

"I guess that means the waves will be higher, too," Kelly said.

Blake nodded. "A lot higher."

"Jesus," Doc said. "We'll never make it. The hull's already—"

"We'll make it," Blake said.

"What about the hull?" Kelly asked.

"We've got some problems, but they're under control," Blake said. He threw an irritated glance at Doc.

"What kind of problems?"

"A break in the hull in the engine room, but we've got it shored up."

"My God," Kelly said, looking off at the ring of white water that surrounded them. "We're going into that with the hull cracked open? I think that's a pretty good argument for knowing where the nearest land is."

"Knowing where it is is one thing," Blake said. "Finding it is another. We'd have to be able to navigate with pinpoint accuracy to hit it."

"But you're an officer, you know how to do that," Kelly said.

"The radio direction finder and all the other navigation equipment was trashed along with the ship's radio," Blake said. "You know that."

"But can't you do it by the stars, or whatever?" Kelly asked. "You know, like the old seamen did it?"

Blake ignored the question and said a little prayer that the Colombian frigate would find them and he wouldn't have to try. He was an engineer. His navigation skills had never been very good. After two years of being stuck in the engine room of the *Carlyle*, they were practically nonexistent.

Kelly stared at the solid curtain of water moving closer and shook her head. "Oh, Sarah," she said. "You were right."

"Who's Sarah?" Blake asked.

"My roommate at San Jose State."

"What was *she* right about?"

"Joining the Navy. She told me I was crazy. I should have listened to her."

Blake flashed a wry smile. "If it helps any, you're having an experience very few people will ever have."

Kelly shook her head. "It doesn't."

"Think of the stories you can tell when you get back home," Blake said.

"*If* we get back," Doc said. "No shit, Lieutenant. You really think we can make it through that?" They both stared at him.

"The first hit will be a jolt," Blake said. "There won't be a gradual buildup like we saw with the first half."

"Oh, God," Kelly said.

"But if we make it through that, we might have a chance." Blake looked at Maria, and said irritably, "Where's your life jacket? Don't you have one?"

The girl shook her head.

"Here." Blake unbuckled his life jacket and slipped it off. He pulled it around Maria's slender frame and cinched it tight. It hung on her like a sack. He glanced at the missing door to the pilothouse and motioned for Maria to go inside the chart room. She pulled the door closed behind her and stood with her face pressed against the window, watching Blake intently.

"Half ahead," Blake said.

Kelly repeated the order and pulled the handle down. The vibration in the deck increased, and the ship cut cleanly through the glasslike water. "Won't we need more speed than this, Lieutenant?"

"We'll want to be at full speed when we hit the perimeter," Blake said, staring through binoculars at the barrier of water moving toward them. "But not before. We'll ease her into it. I'm not eager to rush into that any sooner than we have to."

As the gap narrowed between the ship and the roaring waterfall that encircled them, Blake began to feel powerful blasts of wind buffeting the starboard side of the ship through the open door to the bridge wing. "Right standard rudder, Doc," Blake said. "Ease her into the wind. We're getting close now."

"Aye aye, Skipper," Doc said, twisting the wheel to starboard. "What do we do once we're in it?"

"Keep her headed into the wind and give her all the power we can muster," Blake said. "That's all we can do."

As they approached the perimeter of the eye of the storm, the roar of the water grew louder. The wind rose to a high, shrieking sound. The wall of black clouds loomed over them, spreading a dark shadow across the green water. A gradual darkness fell over the ship as it moved into the shadow of the clouds. The wind shrieked through the superstructure, and black rain fell in torrents, rattling the bridge with marbles of water.

"Full ahead," Blake shouted over the tumultuous clatter before his voice was drowned out by the roar of water that enveloped the ship.

Instantly, the whole world turned to water. Tons of white water boiled against the bridge windows, as though the ship had been submerged, then shot into the pilothouse through the missing door, filling it to the overhead with warm, sticky brine. Maria watched openmouthed through the windows in the chart room for a few seconds before the thin wall separating the chart room from the pilothouse collapsed against her. Blake heard her garbled scream dissolve amid the roar in his ears. He tumbled about underwater until he thought his lungs would explode. Suddenly the ship pitched upward, and the water in the pilothouse was forced out with a loud sucking sound. Blake and Doc dived for the ship's wheel at the same time and hung on as the force of the withdrawing water pulled at them, drawing them toward the open door. Kelly clung to the telegraph stand. Maria spun around in the far corner of the pilothouse like laundry in a washing machine before being caught up in the current. She washed past Blake toward the door, too terrified to scream.

Coughing and sputtering, blinking water out of his eyes, Blake lunged for her and missed. "Grab her, Kelly!"

Kelly opened her eyes, reached out with one hand, and caught a strap on Maria's life jacket just as the girl's feet were at the door. Kelly clung to the telegraph stand with her right arm while the fingers of her left hand gripped the strap. The ship canted sharply to starboard. The effect was like being in a water slide. "I can't hold her! God, help me."

"Hang on, I'm coming!" Sliding down the length of Doc Jones's legs, Blake clung to the corpsman's ankle with one hand and reached for Maria with the other. She slipped from Kelly's grasp just as Blake grabbed for the child, catching her by the hair. The ship heeled to port, and they all tumbled back away from the open door long enough for Blake to get a grip on her life jacket. He pulled her back into the pilothouse.

Blake struggled to get to his feet, pulling the girl up with him. She seemed conscious, but in a daze. Doc and Kelly managed to pull themselves up before the ship plummeted down again, engulfed in water. Within seconds the pilothouse was submerged.

Blake held Maria tightly to him, instinctively trying to protect her, as they were tossed violently around in the roaring, churning foam. His lungs were bursting. He became completely disoriented. He wondered if anyone had ever drowned *aboard* a ship before. He felt a great darkness growing over him, and a feeling of peace that was unlike any sensation he had ever known. His arms loosened their grasp on Maria and he felt her slip away, floating to the top of the pilothouse in his life jacket. He faded from consciousness as the ship pitched sharply up, creating another suction of water from the pilothouse. Water sluiced out with the same intensity it had poured in, pulling them along. His slide toward the open door was blocked by the binnacle. Maria's body slammed up against his. He gasped for air, coughing up warm salt water as the water receded. Blinking the water out of his eyes, he saw Kelly out cold, crumpled in a corner. Another gigantic wave struck the pilothouse, flooding it through the open door. He felt the pull of the water as the ship pitched to starboard. He blinked his eyes open and saw an unconscious Doc Jones sliding toward the open door of the pilothouse.

"No!"

He lunged forward, his strength gone. Maria was like a bag of sand against him. Gathering all his strength, he shoved her away and scrambled across the deck. He grabbed for Doc's ankle and missed it by an inch. He stared in horror as Doc Jones disappeared through the door, out into the mountainous seas.

The ship pitched to port again, sending him flying against the opposite bulkhead. Blake instinctively raised his arms, tried to break the impact, but felt his head slam against a watertight

cabinet. A hazy darkness fell over him. The last sensation he
had was of the ship pitching violently upward. In the shadows
of his mind he felt himself slipping, sliding, tumbling toward
the open door, a free fall into oblivion. In his dreamlike state
he felt a huge pair of hands under his arms, gripping him,
pulling him back with superhuman strength. He felt himself
being dragged across the deck, his back being slammed against
something hard and cold, a stiff rope being wound around and
around, jerking him violently, cutting into his arms, his chest,
his neck. His last thought before losing consciousness was the
vague realization that *El Callado* was going to kill him now.
Too tired to care, he faded into darkness.

A blast of cold air screamed through the pilothouse, jerking
him awake. Blake shook his head and blinked his eyes. The
interior of the pilothouse and the surrounding sea blurred into
one. Gray water raged around him, stinging his eyes, penetrating
his nose and mouth. There was no way to tell how long he'd
been out. It seemed like an instant, but the weather pattern
seemed different now. The ship pitched up, down, whirled
around in a nightmare of motion and water, but compared with
the initial surge of the cyclone it was an improvement. He
looked down at the hemp rope that bound him to the binnacle
and flinched. It wasn't a dream; *El Callado* had pulled him
back from the brink. He could still feel the grip of those steellike
hands under his arms. He shuddered at the thought that the
silent one had been here, had had him in his grip, had tied him
up, could have killed him easily. His gratitude gave way to a
feeling of resentment at being used, being kept alive a few
hours longer until the storm was past.

He glanced frantically around for Kelly and saw her crumpled
body in a corner of the pilothouse. The ship was pitching crazily
now, but the water wasn't reaching the bridge. He worked his
way loose from the wet ropes and slogged over to her in the
ankle-deep foam and held her head out of the water. Propping
her up in a corner, he pulled Maria's body over and leaned
them together. Kelly gave out a queer, gagging sound, and
Blake knew she was alive. He lifted Maria's head up. It sagged

against her chest so limply Blake couldn't tell if she was dead or alive. He placed her on the deck, cleared her mouth, and began to give her mouth-to-mouth resuscitation. He heard Kelly say something incoherent. Blake checked Maria's carotid artery and found a pulse, then opened her life jacket and started pressing rhythmically against her chest. Dribble ran from the child's mouth, then a geyser of water from her lungs. She hacked and coughed, and opened her eyes.

They were through the leading edge, but the storm was in control now. It was impossible to tell what direction they were headed. He'd heard some old sailors say that when a storm situation was hopelessly out of control, and the ship became completely unmanageable, it was sometimes best to stop the engines and give the ship her head, let the ship ride along with the storm rather than fight against it. His instincts told him it was the only chance they had.

Scrambling over to the engine-order telegraph, he shoved the handle up to "All Stop" and reached for the sound-powered telephone. Before he could pick it up, the horn blared. He grabbed the handset and slumped against the bulkhead, wedging his feet against a cable strap to hold himself in place. "Yes, Chief."

"What's going on?" Chief Kozlewski's worried voice came rasping through the telephone. "Why are we going to 'All Stop'?"

"We've lost it, Chief. We can't control it. Best to cut the engines and give the ship her head, let her ride it out the best she can."

"Just as well," the chief said. "We're losing the load. Number one boiler's out and the water's lapping at the number two."

"How bad's the flooding?"

"Worse than before. We're trying to get some shoring in place. The pumps are staying up with it, but if we lose the load completely, we've got a problem."

"How about the emergency diesel?"

"Underwater."

"Do you want me to come down?"

"No, sir, we can manage. It would only scare these guys all the worse if they see you're not on the bridge. You'd never make it anyway, the way this ship is riding."

"How's the crew holding up?"

"Knocked around pretty bad. Tobin's howling about his leg again. Maybe Doc can look at it."

Blake felt an anguished pain swell up in him. "Chief?"

"Yes, sir?"

His throat tightened. "We lost Doc."

"Lost Doc? How? Where?"

"Over the side."

"But how could he—"

"It was like nothing you've ever seen," Blake said. "The entire ship was submerged. He was sucked out the door of the pilothouse." He choked back a sob, barely able to speak. The lump in his throat felt as big as a baseball. He felt responsible. If only he'd moved a little faster. If only . . .

"Mother of God," the chief said. After a pause, he said, "Was he wearing a life jacket?"

"Yes. But he was unconscious." *Thank God for that,* Blake thought. He was glad that Doc had been spared the terror of seeing his own death. He was also glad that he would not know how badly Blake had failed him.

"Well, if he had his life jacket on, maybe we can look for him after the storm passes."

"Sure," Blake said. But he knew in his heart that Doc was dead. The chief hadn't seen what he'd seen. No one could survive being buried alive in a tomb of solid water. Even if he'd been able to breathe, he would have been crushed from the concentrated force of that many tons of ocean.

The ship pitched up and spun violently around, trying to find its head. Blake heard the dull thud of flesh and bone against steel, Kelly's unconscious body slamming against the bulkhead in the opposite corner of the room. Maria was struggling with her, trying to hold her steady, tears running down her cheeks.

"I've got to go, Chief. All we can do at this point is shore

up the hull, hang on, and ride it out. It's out of our hands now.''
He slammed the phone in its bracket and crawled across the
deck to where Kelly and Maria were huddled together. He had
to find a way to stabilize them to keep them from flying around
the deck. The rope *El Callado* had used to tie him down was
slithering around the pilothouse like a dying snake. Sliding in
between them, he gathered them up in his arms and tied them
together, then wedged himself between the bulkhead and a row
of steel cabinets along the port side of the pilothouse. He pulled
them to him and locked his legs into position. Maria buried
her face in his chest and sobbed, saying something he couldn't
understand.

"Don't cry, little one. It'll be all right."

He looked at Kelly. Her head rolled back and sagged limply
against his shoulder. There was a dark bruise down the left
side of her face. On the back of her head, he could see a circle
of blood the size of an egg seeping through her matted hair.
His mind flashed on Doc, Doc could fix it . . . A wave of
anguish tore at him. Doc was gone. He looked at the wound
again. The stain was spreading. He choked back a sob, his grief
for Doc overshadowed by his fear for Kelly. Head wounds
could be fatal, but for now there was nothing he could do but
hang on and protect them the best he could from any further
injuries.

In his years at sea, he had never seen anything like this.
Riding free on the open sea now, the ship roared up, crashed
down, spun around crazily, seeking its own position relative
to the storm. He struggled to hold his position. The missing
door to the pilothouse was a constant menace. Even with the
rope binding them, Blake used every ounce of strength he had
to keep them together while the storm tossed the ship in every
direction. He held Maria so tightly she began to whimper.

He heard a sudden wrenching sound, a combination of wind
and wave that sent the ship into a steep roll to starboard. It
rolled nearly horizontal to the sea and stayed there. Blake
looked down through the pilothouse door into the sea and knew
that this was the end. No cargo ship could roll that far over

and recover. He hung there, heart pounding, gradually losing his grip on Kelly and Maria. The rope had worked itself loose. There was no point in hanging on, they were all going to die, but he couldn't let go, couldn't watch them plummet to their deaths, was determined they would all go together. Maria looked up at him with wide, questioning eyes, and he felt the pain of tears welling up behind his eyes.

"I'm sorry," he said.

Suddenly the ship lurched up and began to right itself. The power of the storm was working for them now. The venerable *Latin Star* slowly came upright with an agonized groan. A rush of euphoria swept over him. In that instant, he knew what it was like to be born again.

He felt his hopes begin to rise. After all they'd been through, they were still afloat. If the stout old ship could recover from a roll like that one, she just might make it.

The last remnants of daylight faded to black. Realizing he'd lost all track of time, he glanced at his watch. Unbelievably, more than four hours had passed since they'd entered the dangerous semicircle of the cyclone.

He wanted to get to the telephone and see how the others were doing in the engine room. He wondered if the shoring was holding, if the boilers were out, if the flooding was worse, but the pitching was too violent to leave Kelly and Maria alone. He imagined that Frank Kozlewski and the others were doing exactly what he was doing. Holding on to whatever they could find and praying like they'd never prayed before.

Clinging to Kelly and Maria, trying desperately to stay awake, he drifted off into a tenuous sleep. He felt the ropes cut into his chest, jerking him awake. It was pitch-black outside. He guessed it was well after midnight. He could feel Kelly and Maria slumped against him, but couldn't tell if they were asleep or unconscious. He noticed a slight change in the wind. The pitch was lower now, softer. The ship seemed to be riding better. She'd found her head, was being blown along with the storm. He cinched the ropes tighter, then faded into darkness.

Drifting in and out of sleep, Blake felt the night pass in a confused jumble of motion and sound. After what seemed like hours, he felt the sensation of light behind his eyelids. He opened his eyes and squinted into the weak light of daybreak. Through the open door of the pilothouse, he could see the dark wave formations. The mountainous seas had receded. He lay back against the bulkhead and watched the dawn break over a cloudless sky.

Numbed and exhausted, Blake relaxed his grip and shook Kelly by the shoulder.

Kelly moaned and opened her eyes. "When will it hit?"

Blake tried to laugh, but nothing came out. "It's over. We're through it. How do you feel?"

"Like I was hit by a truck," Kelly said, feeling her head, wincing. She looked around the shambles that was the pilothouse. "Where's Doc?"

Blake didn't answer, suddenly sobered.

Kelly sat up, holding her head. "Where is he?"

"We lost him."

"What do you mean, 'lost him'? What are you talking about?"

"Over the side. In the storm."

"God, no," Kelly said, and slumped back against the bulkhead. Her eyes filled with tears.

"We'll try to find him," Blake said.

Blinking back tears, Kelly pulled the rope over her head and looked at it. "Where did this come from?"

"You wouldn't believe me if I told you," Blake said.

Kelly stared at him with an incredulous look. "*He* tied us up like this?"

"Something like that," Blake said.

"Hey, I'm beginning to like this guy."

"I wouldn't get too attached. Now that the storm is over, he'll be back, maybe any minute now," Blake said, looking over his shoulder.

"God, is it really over?" Kelly said.

Blake nodded. "I think we're through it."

Maria jumped from Blake's side, shouting something in

Spanish, dancing around the deck. Turning, she leapt into his lap and threw her arms around him, chattering something Blake couldn't understand.

"What's with the kid?" Blake asked, astonished.

"She said she belongs to you now. Her father is dead, and you saved her life. She's chosen you to be her father."

"That's ridiculous."

"Not to her it isn't. She says she will never leave you." Kelly was smiling at him. "Congratulations, Dad."

Blake got to his feet and helped Kelly up. The ship was pitching gently in the relatively calm waters. He cleared his way over to the sound-powered phone. Maria followed him like a shadow.

The horn on the phone blared before he could pick it up.

"Yes, Chief?"

"You'd better get down here, Lieutenant," Chief Kozlewski said. "We've got some serious flooding going on."

Blake felt his heart swell up in his chest. "How serious?"

"The pumps can't keep up with it," Chief Kozlewski said. "She's sinking. It's just a matter of time."

Chapter Seventeen

Jorge Cordoba lay awake with his hands behind his head, staring up at the shadowy ceiling of the bungalow. He counted the dozen beams in the overhead for the hundredth time and glanced at the clock on the nightstand. Ten minutes until 4:00 A.M. Colonel Suarez had said the raid would come just after dawn. It would take at least an hour to get the helicopters launched. He took a deep breath and tried not to think about what would happen if the ship wasn't found soon.

Throughout the night, he'd called the Command Center every hour, then every half hour to check on the progress of Tropical Cyclone Bruce. He resolved to call again at four. Glancing sideways at the sleeping flight attendant whose leg was draped across him, he felt the grittiness and dull ache in his eyes. He closed them, just to rest them for a minute, and drifted off into a thin sleep.

The jarring sound of the telephone brought him upright in bed. He pushed the brunette away and staggered across the room. The window air conditioner cycled, casting an icy breeze across his face and chest, clearing his head. He picked up the phone and blinked into the predawn light creeping in through the window. "Yes?"

"Señor Cordoba? Enrique Lopez here," the acting director of security said. "You'd better get up here. We've found the ship."

Jorge's stomach rolled with a wave of excitement and apprehension. He glanced at his watch. A few minutes before 4:00. Sunrise was at least an hour away. The timing would be tight, but they could make it.

"The storm?"

"Finally dissipated. Headed northeast and blew itself out before it hit the coast."

"And the ship survived," Jorge said, releasing a breath. It was more a statement than a question.

"It was still a little dark, but the pilot buzzed the ship. Superficial damage, according to him. It looks like it's been through a cyclone, but it's still afloat."

"Is it under way?"

"Apparently it's just drifting with the current."

"Where did you find it?"

"Roughly 250 miles off the coast. One of our jets spotted it when the clouds lifted."

"What about the range of the helicopters? Can we make it from here?"

"With the auxiliary fuel tanks, we've got enough for a one-way trip. We can make it out, but there won't be much fuel to spare."

"As long as the ship's there for us to land on, it won't matter," Jorge said. "Any other ships around? Any sign of a Colombian Navy frigate or an American destroyer?"

"Nothing reported."

"Get the crews assembled and the helicopters warmed up."

"I've already done that."

"I'll be right there." Jorge pulled on his shirt and stepped into his shoes. He shouldered into his coat and reached for the doorknob.

"What's going on? Where are you going, lover?"

The whine in the flight attendant's voice stopped Jorge at the door. He glanced over his shoulder. The brunette was sitting up in bed, looking at him. Even in the dark, her silhouette stirred something in him. *As if you didn't know, you treacherous bitch.* He'd learned last night her name was Nita. A dark curtain of brown hair shielded her face from the light drifting in through the window, but he could almost see her pouting in the dark. Perhaps she'd been promised a bonus for keeping him occupied until the raid came.

He'd told himself that he would take care of her when the time came but killing her now would tip the skittish Enrique Lopez that something was afoot. And if the acting security director fled before he could be offered up as a sacrifice for Colonel Suarez, it might leave Jorge holding the bag. No, he would let the faithless *puta* live, for now. If he changed his mind later, he could arrange it with a simple phone call. "Go back to sleep."

He walked out into the cool night air and headed toward the Command Center, exhilarated with the freshness of the morning. The first pink line of daylight was visible across the eastern horizon. It was in every sense the dawning of a new day. The ship had survived. The weather was clear. He could hear the whine of the Blackhawks warming up. There would be just enough time to get the helicopters launched and be out of there before the raid that Colonel Suarez had said would come just after dawn. He was leaving this godforsaken place, and within a matter of hours he would be aboard the ship, solidly in control of his life again.

He couldn't wait to be done with this messy business and get back to his real life in Colombia. As he walked toward the Command Center, Jorge could picture his homecoming in his mind. Don Gallardo warmly greeting him at the mansion. The members of the executive committee standing, applauding as he took his seat near the head of the table. Don Gallardo proudly announcing his promotion to *el Jefe de Finanzas*, Chief Financial Officer of the international operations of *La Confederación Estrella Azul*, soon to be one of the most powerful organizations on earth. And all at the age of twenty-eight. He was sorry that his parents hadn't lived to see it.

Yes, Jorge thought, it was a great tragedy that his parents wouldn't be around to see the fulfillment of his godfather's dream. Then they would know what he knew, and that he had made the right choice.

He tried not to blame them for their resistance. They couldn't have known that Don Gallardo had a plan that would change the world. Only Jorge and a handful of others knew about the plan, had worked closely with Don Gallardo to put it in motion. What they couldn't know, what almost no one knew, was that Don Gallardo had succeeded in bringing the major players in Latin America together in a secret confederation that would shift the global balance of power from North to South America.

It had taken years of individual courtship and one-on-one negotiations to pave the way, but when he was ready, when he knew the time was ripe, when the arrogant *yanquis* had finally gone too far, and he knew what the outcome would be, Don Gallardo had invited the heads of the largest and most powerful organizations in Latin America, except the renegade Ramirez cartel, whom no one could control, to attend a conference at his estate, where he presented them with a proposal.

He began by telling them of a dream he had had—Jorge liked to think of it as a vision—in which a massive blue star was shining over Latin America, flooding it in the light of a new dawn. He proceeded to lay out a plan so simple, yet so powerful, that the delegates sat in stunned silence when he was through.

Jorge would never forget the electric feeling in the room as they all sat there, gazing at Don Gallardo, who calmly sat down when he was finished. The delegate from Peru was the first to stand, then Argentina, then Brazil. Slowly the others came to their feet. Suriname, Uruguay, Bolivia, Venezuela, French Guiana, Ecuador, Paraguay. The applause began slowly, deliberately, then grew to a thunderous ovation, and *La Confedera-ción Estrella Azul,* The Blue Star Confederation, was born. All who had been present at the historic conference had been signatories to what became known after Don Gallardo's stirring speech as the Blue Star Covenant. They pledged to work together, peacefully, to achieve greatness for Latin America and prosperity for all. Only someone with the vision and magnetic personality of Don Augusto Gallardo could have pulled it off, and Jorge loved him for it, was proud to be the protégé of such a great man.

And Jorge was proud to be the architect of the long-range financial plan that was the centerpiece of the Blue Star Covenant, a plan that would bring the arrogant *yanquis* to their knees. His aggressive purchase of gold bullion was the first step in a long-range plan to undermine the currency of the *Norte Americanos,* who were so bent on destroying the Latin countries. It would take decades, of course, but eventually, with the combined purchasing power of all the Latin American signatories to the covenant, they would see them fall.

The plan had wide appeal; there was no real cost to anyone, and no risk involved. It was simply a balance-sheet transaction, exchanging one asset for another. They would exchange massive amounts of cash, most of which ironically came from North American cities, for gold. As the world's gold supplies were removed from the market place, the value of the confederation's holdings would only increase. At the same time, the *Norte Americanos* would help with their own destruction by continuing to print money at an ever-increasing rate to finance their insane social programs. Over time their inflated currency, backed by nothing, would become worthless. A bankrupt nation could not even defend itself, much less be a police force to the world. Everyone had pledged to participate, could see the wisdom of such a long-range plan, a true vision for the future of not only Colombia but all the Latin countries.

For such a grand scheme, it had gotten off to an ignominious start. The first purchase by the confederation had very nearly been a disaster of major proportions, but it had not been Jorge's fault. He pleaded guilty to being overly aggressive on the first buy, but it had been Rafael Ayala's idea to plant that cretin aboard to protect the shipment of the confederation's cash.

Jorge had advised against it. He knew it would take more than a few months of indoctrination and a blue star tattooed on his hand to convert the thug everyone called *El Callado* to their purposes. He wondered how the Americans had handled the silent one. The *mudo* might be the only one left alive on the ship, if what Jorge had heard about him was true. And Jorge had no reason to doubt that it was.

But every cloud had a silver lining. Ayala had paid the ultimate price for his disastrous error in judgment, but Jorge had been given an opportunity to rectify his part in the near disaster. And he was grateful to Don Gallardo for giving him that chance. Perhaps Jorge's handling of the situation would prove to Don Gallardo once and for all that he was more of a son than his own natural sons. They were lazy playboys who had done nothing, amounted to nothing. He had never verbalized it before, but he loved the man, perhaps even more than his own father. It made him feel guilty to think it, but he knew it was true. Pleasing him was the most important thing in his life.

He punched in the numbered code, twisted the knob, and walked into the chilled air of the Command Center. The usual blue haze of cigarette smoke hung over the room. The security team was clustered together in one corner, talking, smoking, checking weapons, while the licensed merchant marine officers and crew that Lopez had assembled were scattered along the opposite wall, looking pleased with themselves. They were usually well paid, but nothing like what they were being paid for this trip. Enrique Lopez and the loudmouthed American pilot who called himself Michael Gaines were hunched over the backlit map table. A man Jorge had never seen before was talking to one of the radio operators. Jorge assumed he was the pilot for the second Blackhawk.

"Señor Cordoba," Enrique Lopez said, nodding, as Jorge walked up to the table. The American pilot stared at him dispassionately. The red mark from Major Portillo's riding crop was still visible down his left cheek.

"How soon can we take off?" Jorge asked.

"As soon as we finish preflight and get a weather update,"

Gaines said. "The ground crews are warming up the birds. Fred's checking the weather."

"Fred?"

"Yeah, Fred Harris."

"The other American." Jorge rolled his eyes.

"Who else did you think you could get to fly Blackhawks?" Gaines said. "Most of these taco eaters down here'd have a hard time driving a pickup."

Jorge looked him hard in the eyes. He would enjoy watching this American pig die. "Keep your arrogant thoughts to yourself."

"Chill out, Pancho," Gaines said, turning back to the map.

"Picnic weather all the way," Fred Harris said, walking up with his helmet in his hand.

Michael Gaines introduced the pilot. He was a short, stocky man in his forties with wispy blond hair, small blue narrowset eyes and a broad nose. Jorge nodded, but didn't shake hands.

"All right, here's the plan," Jorge said, looking at Gaines. "You're flying the lead helicopter with the security team aboard. You will land first and secure the ship. Señor Lopez here will designate a lead man. You're to follow his orders—"

"What's all this about designating a lead man?" Lopez said. "It was my understanding that I would lead the team personally."

"I think you should stay here," Jorge said.

Lopez narrowed his eyes. "Why?"

"After I leave, you're the next senior man," Jorge said.

"That's no reason—"

"I don't have time to argue," Jorge said. "Do as you're told."

Lopez stood staring at Jorge for a moment, then began shifting his eyes around. "What's going on here?"

Jorge ignored him and turned to Fred Harris. "I'll fly in the second helicopter with you and the replacement crew."

"Suits me," Harris said with a shrug.

Jorge looked back at Michael Gaines. "We will hover out of rifle range in the second helicopter while the security team does its work. When the ship's been secured, you are to push your helicopter over the side to make room for us to land. Is that clear?''

''Well, now hold it a minute, Pancho,'' Gaines said. He jerked a thumb toward Fred Harris. ''If you and him are flying out of rifle range, just where does that leave me sitting on the deck of that sucker? Just how much resistance you expecting when we drop in on these folks?''

''Very little, if any,'' Jorge said. ''One of our employees has taken control of the ship and is trying to high-jack it and hold it for ransom. We don't even think he's armed. Securing the ship is just a prudent safety precaution.''

''Maybe so,'' Gaines said. ''But let's you and me just make one other little thing clear, and that is that Michael Gaines don't do no securing. I'm just the bus driver on this route. I'll drop your team of cowboys off, but if any shooting starts, I'll fly away and come back when it stops. Then we'll scuttle the bird. Your money's good, but it ain't good enough for me to get my nuts shot off. That's why I got out of the Army.''

Jorge looked at the tall pilot and snorted. If all Americans were this gutless, they would have no trouble retaking the ship. He motioned to the two groups. ''Let's go.''

The pilots pulled on their helmets and the security team and replacement crew stubbed out cigarettes. Jorge looked away from Enrique Lopez's stare. *The little troll knows something's up,* he thought, glancing at his watch, *but he won't have long to wait to find out what it is.* A shudder swelled up through him. He turned away to keep Lopez from seeing it.

Through the quiet shuffle of men assembling weapons and flight gear, Jorge thought he heard something, the faint burst of a machine gun in the distance. His stomach tightened. He cocked his head and listened. Through the concrete-block walls of the Command Center, he could hear the deadened sound of voices shouting, men running, then another burst of machine-gun fire, closer now. Oh, *Madre de Dios,* no. Not now. His stomach clenched. He could see Enrique Lopez glancing frantically around the room, but there was only one way out. Another burst of machine-gun fire exploded at the door, and everyone hit the deck. The lock blew into the room amid a cloud of smoke and splinters. Jorge looked up in time to see the door to the Command Center fall in. A flood of soldiers in green camouflage fatigues boiled into the room, brandishing semiautomatic rifles.

Jorge watched a young Peruvian officer wearing captain's bars clear his way through the soldiers, who were leveling their rifles at everyone in the room. "Nobody move," he said quietly. "You're all under arrest by order of Colonel Julio Suarez, commander of the Peruvian National Antiterrorist Forces at Punta Arenas. I am Captain Ramon Delgado, and you are all my prisoners."

"There's been a mistake," Jorge said, coming slowly to his knees. He stopped when he felt the cool muzzle of a rifle pressing against the back of his neck.

"Yes, of course," Captain Delgado said, looking down on him, smiling. "There usually has."

"You don't understand. I'm a friend of Colonel Suarez."

"How interesting. So am I."

"You can check it with him."

"And who are you?"

"Jorge Cordoba."

Captain Delgado lifted the top sheet of the clipboard he was holding and scanned some notes. He nodded to the soldier holding the rifle against Jorge's neck, and the muzzle was withdrawn. Jorge came slowly to his feet while the others remained in a prone position.

"You're supposed to be gone," Captain Delgado said.

"You're early," Jorge said, rubbing the spot on his neck where the muzzle had been.

The captain shrugged. "My orders were first light."

"I have clearance for two helicopters and their crews."

"Only if you were gone," Captain Delgado said. "But you are not gone. You are here. I have orders to impound everything I find."

"I have specific approval from Colonel Suarez. You can check it with him."

"Very well. But in the meantime you are under house arrest. Do not attempt to leave the compound." Captain Delgado checked his notes again.

"Where is Enrique Garcia Lopez?"

Lopez lay prone without moving.

"That one," Jorge said, pointing.

"Get up," Captain Delgado said.

A soldier kicked him in the side, and Lopez came slowly to his feet, glaring at Jorge. He looked at the Peruvian Army captain. "What do you think you're doing?"

"You are the Peruvian national, Enrique Garcia Lopez?"

The acting director of security smiled. "I wouldn't advise arresting me for drug trafficking. I have documents that will take all of you with me, from Colonel Suarez all the way down, even as far down as lowly captains."

"I know nothing about any drug trafficking," Captain Delgado said, glancing at his clipboard. "You are charged with treason." A soldier stepped forward and handcuffed Lopez's hands behind his back.

"What are you talking about? You're crazy."

Captain Delgado raised his hand in the air and snapped his fingers. Two soldiers pushed their way through the crowd. One, a private, had an armload of obsolete-looking rifles. The second, a corporal, had a stack of what appeared to be military training manuals. *Secreto* was stamped across them in big red letters. They threw them down in front of Lopez. "These were found in your room."

"You don't even know where my room is."

Captain Delgado flipped to a fresh page in his clipboard and began to read. "I hereby charge you with supplying arms and secret military information to Maoist guerrillas of the *Sendero Luminoso,* the Shining Path," he said in a level voice. "Under the terms of the antiterrorist decree issued by the government of Peru, which granted the Army broad powers to investigate, arrest, charge, and prosecute such crimes, you are hereby charged with treason against the fatherland, a crime which takes precedence over the crime of drug trafficking. The decree further stipulates trial by a military tribunal and, if convicted, a mandatory penalty of life imprisonment. You will be held incommunicado and tried in a closed courtroom by an anonymous military judge. Under the terms of the decree, if you are convicted, you will be sentenced to serve the rest of your natural life in a military prison designated by the judge advocate in this case."

Enrique Lopez looked up at Jorge, his pockmarked face black with rage. "You did this. You set me up to take the fall. You sacrificed me so that you could fly away in your little helicopters and save the day for your beloved godfather."

Jorge stood looking down on the diminutive security director. "It was a small sacrifice to make."

Jorge saw something stir in the depths of Lopez's eyes, something cold, evil, prehistoric. Two soldiers stepped up and took the acting security director by the arms. He shook himself free and stepped up to within a few inches of Jorge's face, his eyes constricted into a reptilian stare.

"There is something you should know before I go."

The hiss of Lopez's voice sent a chill through Jorge, told him he didn't want to hear this. Jorge stared coldly at him. "Get him out of here."

"Wait, I have some information that will interest you a great deal." Lopez was beaming now, enjoying himself.

"There is nothing you could say that would have the slightest interest to me," Jorge said. "Take him."

"I know who murdered your parents."

Jorge stiffened. "Get him out of here. My parents were killed in a boating accident when I was twenty years old."

"So everyone believes," Lopez said. His mouth twisted into an icy grin. "My work is good, no?"

"What are you trying to—"

"Oh, it wasn't just me," Lopez said. "Although I would have done it with greater relish if I had known then what a treacherous son of a whore you would become."

Jorge stood rooted to the spot. A feeling of numbness crept over him.

"No, my friend, not just me," Lopez said, shaking his head slowly, warming to the message he was about to deliver. "I was simply the instrument at hand. It was your beloved godfather, Don Augusto Gallardo, who ordered your parents murdered."

Jorge reeled backwards, as though he'd been kicked in the stomach. "You're insane. Don Gallardo and my father were close friends for thirty years. He worshiped my mother."

"Oh, you're quite right about that. He loved them both. It was their objection to your joining forces with him that he objected to. He was afraid they would talk you out of it. He told me about the alliances he wanted to form, the financial expertise he needed. For some reason he seemed to think you were the only one who could provide it. Shortly after, I fell from favor. I was exiled down here under the pretext that I had indiscriminately killed women and children. I had, of course, but it was under his direct orders. It was simply a ploy to keep us apart. He was afraid that you would read the smile on my face, the look in my eyes, that I would one day make a slip. He wanted to avoid any possibility that you would ever know. He couldn't have foreseen any of this happening, us being thrown together like this. But when we were, he trusted to luck that I would remain silent, and I would have, if not for your treachery."

Jorge felt his knees buckle. "Liar!"

"No, my friend. There is a liar here, but it isn't me. I killed them myself, and I can prove it."

Jorge stood paralyzed, wanting to know, not wanting to hear.

"Don Gallardo loaned your father his boat for the weekend. I remember it clearly. It was a thirty-four-foot Owens cruiser with twin engines and a flying bridge. It was called the *Estrella Azul*, the *Blue Star*. They were planning a fishing cruise out into the *Golfo de Tortugas*. I went aboard and hid below in the bilges until it was under way, and they were well out into the Gulf Stream."

Jorge laughed weakly and shook his head. "You'll have to do better than that. Everyone in Don Gallardo's organization knew about the boat and where they were when it happened. That doesn't prove anything—"

"Your mother was quite beautiful for an older woman. Before I cut their throats, I took her while your father watched. Don Gallardo wouldn't like it if he knew that, by the way. He wanted her for himself, he told me so. She had deep scars across her back. She said it was from a fall from a horse when she was young. The horse threw her, and she fell across a barbed wire fence." Lopez smiled. "She was willing to tell me anything to delay me, but it didn't work."

Bile washed up in Jorge's throat, constricting it, gagging him. His mother had been one of the great beauties in Cali, a city known for its beautiful women. She had been deeply ashamed of the scars, would never wear clothing that would expose them. It was something no one outside the family could have known.

"Then I rigged the explosion to make it look like they had tried to start the engines without first running the exhaust blower to expel the fumes. A Zodiac standing off picked me up just minutes before it went up. You should have been there. The explosion was quite spectacular."

"You filthy scum! I'll kill you!" Jorge grabbed Lopez by the throat. He felt his fingers sinking into the greasy flab around his neck.

"Ah, ah, ah," Captain Delgado said, stepping in between them. "We need him. Unless, of course, you'd like to take his place."

Jorge spit a stream of green bile in Lopez's face before letting go. He turned and began to vomit as Lopez was led away.

Lopez laughed loudly in the distance. "Oh, my dear fellow, why blame me? I was merely following orders. The orders of your glorious godfather!"

The sound of Lopez's laughter rang in Jorge's ears. He stood bent over with his hands on his knees retching, numb with shock and disbelief. Captain Delgado nodded, and two men took Jorge gently by the arms.

"See that he gets to his room and stays there."

The soldiers led him out the door and down the path to his room. As he walked out the door, Jorge dimly heard Captain Delgado say that he would let him know when Colonel Suarez had released him and the helicopters. The statement had as much significance now as saying he would call him for lunch. His life was over, finished. All that he had loved or cared about was gone. The people, the ideals, the goals, the ambitions. Everything was gone.

The sun was up now, but the beautiful morning had been transformed. The sun blazed angrily. The birds in the trees mocked him. Jorge walked along in numb silence, thinking about Don Gallardo, the man he had loved and respected so completely. How could he? How could he?

He entered the door of the bungalow. Nita was still lying in bed. She rose up and looked at him sleepily.

"Back so soon, lover?"

Jorge turned and locked the door. He took off his coat and stared at her without speaking.

"What's the matter, lover? You look sick."

"How much did they pay you, you filthy whore?" His voice sounded dead.

"What in the world is the matter with you? I haven't done anything."

"You're all laughing at me, aren't you?" Jorge reached down and lifted the drape out of the way and unplugged the telephone cord. He stood staring at the flight attendant, slowly wrapping the cord around his hand. When he reached the instrument, he unplugged the other end of the cord and walked slowly toward the bed.

Nita screamed and jumped out of the other side of the bed. She stood there nude, staring at Jorge with terrified eyes, then bolted for the door. She fumbled desperately with the chain as Jorge came up behind her and spun her around.

"I've been betrayed by everyone!" Jorge stood staring at

her with zombielike eyes, so numb with pain they couldn't release tears.

"Please, don't do this, lover. We were real good together. We can be again. Let me show you."

She dropped to her knees and unbuckled his pants. Sliding his shorts down, she released him and took him in her mouth. He moaned and let her take him, eager for anything that would dull the pain. Jorge slumped against the door with a dumb look on his face, breathing hard. He dropped the telephone cord and leaned against the door, grateful for even a momentary release from the mind-numbing pain.

"That's more like it, lover. That's more like it. You just aren't feeling well, that's all. Nita can make it all right." Picking up each leg, she slid his trousers and shorts off, as though she were undressing a child. She came to her feet and led him over to the table. He followed docilely behind with eyes that were dead.

Lying back on the table, Nita opened herself and guided him in. He entered her slowly, then plunged in with deep strokes, savagely losing himself in her flesh. Her moist inner tissues were like a narcotic, deadening the pain. His hands went from her waist to her shoulders, pulling her toward him. He felt his release coming, put his fingers around her throat and began to squeeze. She let out a gasp and grabbed his forearms, tried to say something. His fingers sank deeply into the thin layer of flesh around her neck. Her eyes bulged, and he felt her tighten around him, deadening the pain. He continued to squeeze until he was drained, then slumped across her limp body and lay there, only vaguely aware that the wailing animal sound he heard in the distance was coming from him.

Chapter Eighteen

Daniel Blake half tumbled, half slid down the ladder leading into the engine room and stopped on the bottom rung, jolted by the scene before him. Emergency lanterns blazed around a crude patch of shoring, illuminating streams of white water that shot across the machinery space as if they were coming from a high-pressure fire hose. Overheated boilers hissed and crackled under the assault of thousands of gallons of seawater.

Robertson had stripped to the waist and was driving a wedge in at the base of a massive beam with a sledgehammer, while Tobin struggled to hold the makeshift shoring in place. The stream of water splayed out and appeared to slow, but kept on coming. The air was heavy with the foul smell of bilge water rising up through the deck grating, displaced by the flooding sea. To Blake, it was the smell of death.

Something Doc Jones had said surfaced in his mind. It had been a flip, bizarre statement, but he knew now what he had to do. He shouted to Frank Kozlewski and waved him over to the engine-room console.

Walking up, the chief retrieved a sopping bandanna from

his hip pocket and wiped his neck and face. "Ain't this a bitch. Losing her now after all we went through."

"How long's it been like this?"

"It happened on that last big roll, the one that almost sank us," Kozlewski said. "You could hear the seams popping, opening up with a tearing sound." The chief shuddered. "Never heard a sound like that before in my life. Hope I never do again."

Blake glanced around at the chaotic scene and smiled at the optimism inherent in that statement. In a few hours they wouldn't be hearing anything but the sound of water in their ears. He nodded. "It's a miracle she recovered from that one."

"She righted herself, God bless her, but she's going now." Frank Kozlewski jerked his head toward the stream of water shooting across the engine room. "Knock a man down. There's no way to stop that."

"We've got to slow it down as much as we can," Blake said.

"We need more shoring beams. We've used all we had. I need to send somebody out to hunt for more, but I can't spare anyone."

Blake heard a loud crash behind him. He swiveled and saw a heavy shoring beam come crashing down the ladder into the engine room, then another and another. He and the chief stood back out of the way and counted a dozen beams tumbling down into the engine room, followed by a dozen mattresses.

When the dust settled, they ran over to the hatch and peered up the shaft that led to the upper deck. "Who in the name of God was that?" the chief said, openmouthed.

"Who do you think?" Blake said, peering up the shaft. "I guess he took my little ass-chewing to heart."

"Unbelievable."

"He doesn't have a real big choice if he wants to keep the ship afloat."

"How does he know we're sinking?"

"Probably saw your boys scrambling around looking for packing crates and mattresses."

"Jesus," the chief said, looking around. "You think he's watching us right now?"

"You can bet on it. If we don't get this flooding under control, he's as dead as we are."

"Christ Almighty."

"Every cloud has a silver lining," Blake said. "He won't bother us as long as he needs us."

"That's a great theory," the chief said, glancing around.

"It's more than a theory," Blake said, remembering the steellike fingers that had pulled him back from the brink.

The chief gave him a puzzled look.

"Come on," Blake said. "Let's get this shoring in place."

Blake and the chief each grabbed a four-by-four beam and carried it over to the break in the hull, jammed it into place, and signaled for Robertson and Tobin to bring another round. When the last timber was in place, Blake stepped off to the side and surveyed the velocity of the seawater still shooting across the engine room.

"Still not good enough," he said, wiping his face with a wet shirt-sleeve.

"That's about the best we're going to do, right there, sir," the chief said, shaking water out of his eyes. "We've slowed it some, but the pumps can't keep up with it. Eventually she'll go."

"How much time do you think we've got?"

"Hard to say." Kozlewski looked down through the deck plates at the water rising up in the bilges. "If that seam don't open up any more than it is, and the pumps keep working, ten or twelve hours. If it opens up more, or if we lose a pump, it could go fast."

"The sea's calm," Blake said. "Hopefully that break won't get any worse." He glanced at the boilers. "Can we still get up a head of steam?"

"We can, but what's the point? We got nowhere to go." The chief looked anxiously at Blake. "That Colombian frigate better get here real soon."

"You can forget about that frigate," Blake said, looking at his watch. "It'd be here by now if it was coming."

"Then I reckon the only thing left to do is try to build some life rafts with whatever we can find and abandon ship, pull away and let her go, hope to hell somebody picks us up."

Blake shook his head. "Come on, Chief. What would you build a raft out of? Packing crates? Coming down from the bridge, I spotted a half dozen dorsal fins circling the ship. Big ones. Big enough for me to see without looking. They can sense something's wrong. But even without sharks, we wouldn't last long, floating around on a makeshift raft in these waters. This is storm season. Unless we were picked up right away, our chances of surviving would be slim. And there's no guarantee we'd ever be picked up. We're too far out of the shipping lanes."

"I don't see that we've got any other choice."

"We might have one," Blake said. Doc Jones's comment about driving the freighter to New York and running it aground on the first pier they saw had gotten stuck in his mind. His first reaction when he saw the boilers still operating was to head the ship due east. His navigation skills were weak, but with enough time they could simply run at full speed until they hit the coast of South America and run her aground on the nearest sandbar before she went down. With a target that big, Blake thought, even he could hit it. But in the ten or twelve hours the chief had estimated they had left, there was no way to steam 250 miles toward the coast. But they could steam fifty miles in the opposite direction, if he could figure out how to get there.

"Chief, there's an island."

Kozlewski looked at Blake askance. "An island?"

"It's just a speck on the charts. I didn't even see a name. It may not even be a real island, maybe just an atoll, a coral island, but it's land. Big enough to show up on a chart. If we could make it there, we could beach her, run her aground."

"Where is it?"

"About fifty miles west from where we were before the storm hit. It may be a little farther now, but it can't be more than sixty miles. If we can make six knots, we could be there in nine, ten hours.''

The chief scratched his head. ''How old is the chart?''

''What difference does that make?''

''Coral islands come and go. Might not even be there now.''

''According to the log the ship normally sails in these waters. The charts can't be that old. It's got to be there.''

''But what if it ain't?''

''It's there,'' Blake said. ''I can feel it. That's where all the birds came from.''

Something flashed across Kozlewski's eyes, a fleeting look of insecurity. ''The birds, sir?''

''The birds we saw in the eye of the storm. You weren't up there, but the deck was covered with them. Land birds as well as seabirds. It's got to be there.''

The chief looked relieved. ''Hell, sir, even if it is, trying to find a speck that small will take some pretty fine navigation.''

''I know. It's not exactly one of my strong points, but I think I can get us there.''

''How? I thought the navigation equipment was all trashed along with the radio.''

''Maybe I can find a sextant. There must be one up there somewhere. There's an English-language copy of Dutton in the pilothouse. I think I can—''

Frank Kozlewski's face fell. ''A book? You're going to learn how to navigate out of a book in the next couple of hours and navigate to a little pin speck in the middle of the ocean with a sextant, if you can find one? And hope to hell we get there before this sucker goes down around our ears?''

''I'm not exactly starting from scratch, Chief. I studied navigation at Kings Point. I just need some brushing up.''

''Have you ever done any navigating before, sir?''

''No. But that doesn't mean I can't.''

The chief frowned. ''Jesus. Even experienced navigators don't always hit their targets. What kind of a chance would we have?''

"A better chance than we'd have abandoning ship and hoping we get picked up before the next storm hits."

"How far are we from the coast? If we just sail due east we're bound to hit it."

Blake shook his head. "I've already thought of that. It's at least 250 miles, maybe more. We'd never make it in time. The island is only fifty or sixty miles west of here. It'll be tight, but we can make it."

The chief scratched his head. "If we go moving around, it'll make it that much harder for the frigate to find us."

"Forget the damn frigate. It would have been here by now if it was coming. This is the only chance we've got."

"Pretty goddamn slim chance," the chief said, rubbing his chin. "Water gets too deep, these boilers might blow all to hell."

"I know it's risky," Blake said. "But I'm fresh out of ideas, unless you've got a better one."

Kozlewski frowned and rubbed his eyes. "No, sir, I can't say that I do." He glanced around the engine room and looked at Blake. "I guess maybe you're right. Sitting out there on a raft waiting for somebody to come don't appeal to me much either."

"We'll run at full speed all the way, Chief. Give me everything you can, but don't stay down here any longer than you think is safe. When the water gets too deep, put it on automatic pilot and clear everyone out of the engine room."

"Aye aye, Skipper," the chief said.

Blake reached the ladder and turned for one last look before heading up. Frank Kozlewski was still standing at the engine-room console, staring at him.

The chief pulled his face together in a rubbery attempt at a smile. "Good luck, sir." He gave Blake the thumbs-up sign and nodded to the others fighting to keep the shoring in place. "We're all counting on you."

Blake scrambled back up the ladder, depressed with the near certainty that he had bitten off more than he could chew.

He consoled himself with the knowledge that at least he

knew the general direction of the island. He would get under way immediately and head due west. After he had figured out where they were, and the probable location of the island, he could correct the course as appropriate. As he crossed the main deck, he glanced out at the gray dorsal fins, smooth and glossy, cruising silently around the ship. There were more of them now. He shuddered at the thought of being out there in a raft.

Walking into the pilothouse, he saw a walnut case sitting on the table and shook his head in wonder. One sextant coming up. He glanced out on the bridge wing. Dana Kelly was looking at something with binoculars. Maria was standing beside her, pointing. The silent one had been here and gone, and they didn't even know it. *Aptly named son of a bitch,* Blake thought. He felt a tingling sensation in the pit of his stomach, knowing what they'd be facing after they got the ship beached and were no longer needed. He wondered how he'd feel, trying to kill someone who had saved his life.

"Lieutenant, look there," Kelly said, walking over to him. She lifted the binoculars from around her neck and handed them to Blake.

"We've got to get under way," Blake said.

"Just look."

Blake brought the binoculars up to his eyes and felt the warmth of the eyepieces against his face. He adjusted the focus on the spot where Kelly and Maria were pointing and saw a limp figure in a life jacket, drifting with the swells, three points off the starboard bow.

"It's got to be Doc," Kelly said, almost in a whisper.

Blake estimated the figure to be seven or eight hundred yards off, barely visible to the naked eye. He wondered how Maria had even seen it. The combination of a calm sea and the sharp eyes of a child, he thought. He swept the binoculars in both directions and saw movement circling the figure, gray dorsal fins breaking intermittently through the swells.

Bringing the binoculars into a finer focus, he faintly saw the burnished skin, the black hair glistening with drops of water on the nodding head. A chill went through him. *My God,* Blake thought, *it* is *Doc.* He felt Kelly's eyes on him and tried not to react. There was no way to tell from this distance whether he was dead or alive. If he was dead, they would have to leave him, as distasteful as that was. But if he was alive . . .

They had to try to recover him. Without a boat, they'd have to maneuver the ship as close as they could get without drawing him into the propeller. They still had the Jacob's ladder. Blake was a strong swimmer. He could tie a line around his waist and swim for him, have someone stand by with a pistol to keep the sharks at bay.

But he was standing on the deck of a ship that was sinking. The recovery could take hours, hours they didn't have. How could he jeopardize the ship and everyone on it by taking the time to recover what might be a dead body? More to the point, how could he live with himself if he didn't?

Suddenly, Doc disappeared from sight, pulled down like a lure that had taken a hit from a large bass. After a few moments, the life jacket popped to the surface. The top half of Doc Jones's body hung limply in the harness, drifting on the gentle swells, a dark stain clouding the water around it. Within seconds, a great white mouth burst up out of the sea and closed around the figure, shaking it like a doll. There was a rush of water, then an empty life jacket floating on the surface.

Blake felt his stomach begin to rise. He forced it back down and lowered the binoculars, feeling guilty at the sense of relief he felt.

"It's not Doc," he said.

"It has to be," Kelly said. "Who else would be out there in a US Navy life jacket?"

"It's just an empty life jacket. It's easy to mistake things at sea."

Kelly looked at him with disbelief. "You're not just going to leave him there?" She snatched the binoculars from Blake's hand and focused on the remnants of the life jacket, rising and falling with the swells. She swept the binoculars slightly to widen her field of vision and Blake saw her jaw go slack.

Kelly lowered the binoculars and handed them back. Her

face was pale, drawn up into a tight smile. She glanced at Maria. "I guess you're right, Lieutenant. It was just a life jacket."

"Let's get under way," Blake said. "Kelly, you take the helm. Maria, you're on the engine-order telegraph." He led the girl into the pilothouse and rang up Half Ahead. "¿Comprende?"

The ship vibrated and moved forward through the glasslike sea. Maria nodded and looked up at him with her bright, brown eyes.

Kelly grinned. "I didn't know you spoke Spanish, Lieutenant."

"That's one of about three words I know."

"What are the other two?"

"Taco and cerveza."

Kelly laughed. "That's probably all you needed, growing up in San Diego." She looked at Blake and smiled. "Anyway, you don't need it. Maria speaks very good English."

"I've heard her," Blake said.

"She only speaks it around people she likes, don't you, honey?"

Maria smiled at Blake. "I will speak English for you."

"Good girl," Blake said, patting her thin arm. "Kelly, our course is due west until I give you another."

"Where are we going?" Kelly asked, turning the mahogany wheel, eyeing the magnetic compass. "I thought we were just going to drop anchor and wait for that Colombian frigate to pick us up."

"We've had a little change in plans," Blake said. "Full ahead."

Maria instantly pulled the telegraph lever into position. "Full ahead," she piped, her eyes shining at Blake.

Blake laughed. "You're an old hand at this."

"I have sailed with *mi pa—*, my father, since I was a little girl," Maria said. "He taught me many things."

"I can see that," Blake said. "Let's see how you are on the helm."

Blake ushered her over to the ship's wheel, showed her the course he wanted her to maintain, and nodded for Kelly to follow him out on the port bridge wing, the one that still had a door.

Kelly followed Blake out and closed the door behind her. She stood in the early-morning sun looking at him with a puzzled expression, the sea wind gently lifting her hair. "What is it?"

"A little change in plans," Blake said. "I don't want Maria to know. We're going to make a run for that island."

"The one we talked about? Why? Why shouldn't Maria know?"

"We're going down," Blake said. "A seam in the hull broke open during the storm, and we can't get it shored up completely. The pumps can't keep up with it. It's only a matter of time. We can't risk waiting around for a frigate that may never show up. And you just saw why I don't want to put us off in a raft."

"My God. How much time do we have?"

"We can't be sure. The chief thinks ten or twelve hours. The island is fifty, sixty miles away. If we can make it in time, we'll beach her, run her aground."

Kelly let out a long breath. "You had me worried there for a minute. That doesn't sound as bad as I thought. If we've got enough time, it's just a matter of going there, right?"

"It's a little bigger problem than that," Blake said. He tugged at his earlobe. "You may as well know. I've never really done any navigating before."

Kelly looked at him. "Let me see if I understand this. We're going to head for an island and beach the ship before it sinks, except you don't know how to navigate? Gee, what a great plan."

"I've studied theory. I've just never done it before."

"You really think you can do this?"

"I don't know. I'll have to get a book and figure it out."

"A book? It'll have to be in English, if I have to translate we're liable to lose something—"

"They are. Both Dutton and Bowditch."

Kelly nodded. "That's right. Maria said the owners of the shipping company insisted everything be done in English. Used to grate on her father."

"A lot of international companies do, it's pretty much the standard language for commerce," Blake said. "Can you keep Maria occupied?"

"Well, sure, but she knows a lot about that stuff. She told me that her father taught her everything. She knows how to shoot sun lines, whatever that means."

"Getting a fix on latitude's not that difficult," Blake said. "It's longitude that has me stumped."

"Maybe Maria can help."

"No, I don't want her to know any more than she has to. I can figure it out." Blake turned to go back into the pilothouse and Kelly touched his arm, stopping him.

"By the way, that was a nice thing you did back there."

"What?"

"You didn't want Maria to see," Kelly said. "Or me. Did you?"

Kelly's eyes locked in on him, looking at him as though he were a casual acquaintance who had suddenly sent flowers. Her brown eyes were bemused, questioning.

Blake returned the look and felt the familiar pleasant electricity ripple through his body. He resisted it, tried to break her down into individual components, tried to break the image. He focused on her dirty, oversize life jacket hanging loosely from her slender frame, at her smudged hands dangling at her sides, at her baggy dungarees whipping against her long legs. He looked at her matted auburn hair falling across her forehead, at the sun spots across her nose.

There was nothing about the individual parts of her that would attract any attention, he thought, but the totality of her filled him with the exquisite pain of wanting something he knew he couldn't have. He looked into her eyes, into the smoky depths of this woman who had been a stranger only three days ago, and, to his amazement, wanted her.

He broke free of her gaze and glanced in through the window

to the pilothouse. Maria stood with her legs apart, her tongue visible in the corner of her mouth, conscientiously gripping the wheel, working to keep the ship on course. He smiled at the absurdity of a twelve-year-old girl at the helm of a five-thousand-ton freighter.

"She's a good kid."

"She adores you," Kelly said. "She has no one left except an elderly aunt in Buenos Aires. She was quite serious about wanting you to be her father."

Blake looked through the window at Maria and smiled at the thought. It was a ludicrous notion, but somehow it pleased him to hear it. "If we don't find that rock, it's going to be a moot point," he said. "Come on. We don't have much time."

The wall separating the pilothouse from the chart room was gone, washed away by the cyclone. Blake cleaned out the debris, rigged up a makeshift table near the ship's wheel, and gathered up the scattered charts. He opened a watertight cabinet along the bulkhead and retrieved a heavy, black book with white letters along the spine, that read *Dutton's Navigation and Piloting, Thirteenth Edition.* He hefted the book, which seemed to weigh ten pounds, and flipped it open to the table of contents. The book contained forty-one chapters, a half dozen appendices, and various charts and tables in over nine hundred pages. He turned it over in his hand, wondering how the simple practice of finding two lines on the surface of the ocean could possibly be this complex. To a novice, this much information was almost worse than none at all.

He pitched the book on the table, wishing he'd paid more attention when he'd traded navigation lessons for engineering lessons with his sea partner. He'd done it as a lark and had promptly forgotten most of what he'd learned. He knew he needed some tables. Something to do with the angular position of the sun, or some damn thing. It was all so long ago. Scrounging around in the cabinet, he found a current copy of the *Nautical Almanac,* a hardcover, orange-colored book, containing tables showing the angular position of the sun, the moon, and the stars.

There was something else he needed. Another book of tables of some kind. Looking through the cabinet, he found a bloodred hardcover book, *Hydrographic Office, Publication 214*. Flipping it open, he saw "Sight Reduction Tables," and it started to come back to him in bits and pieces. He threw the book on the pile.

"Does it have to be that complex?" Kelly asked, watching him from the helm.

"The legacy of the Brits," Blake said.

"The British? Why?"

"They were always worried about mutiny," Blake said, scanning the table of contents of Dutton. "Treated their people like animals on the old sailing ships. The only thing that kept the crew from cutting their throats was the fact that there were only two guys on board who knew how to navigate. The captain and the first mate."

Maria said, "My father was a first mate."

Blake smiled at her. "I'm sure he was a good one, honey, not like those guys. They were always in line for a command of their own, so they were completely loyal. The crew was usually illiterate, so the captain and the first mate would make a big deal out of navigation, make it seem as complicated as possible, try to convince the crew they couldn't possibly understand it. They knew they'd have to get the first mate in bed with them to pull off a mutiny, and there wasn't much chance of that."

"So how did they make it seem so complicated?" Kelly asked.

"It became a ritual of survival," Blake said. "Every day at noon the captain and the first mate would show up on deck in full view of the crew, and shoot the sun with a mysterious-looking device called a sextant while the cabin boy swung an hourglass in circles at the end of a string, their equivalent of a stopwatch. It evolved into a black art, something the crew couldn't hope to master."

He closed the weighty book and threw it on the table with disgust.

"Well, if you know how to do latitude," Kelly said, "can't you use the same technique to figure out longitude?"

"That's a whole different animal," Blake said, picking up the *Nautical Almanac.* "That's why Columbus missed the Indies by about 8,000 miles." He skimmed the orange-colored book, then tossed it down. "And if I can't figure out how to do longitude, we may not come any closer to our target."

"I hate to sound stupid," Kelly said, "but why is it so different? What exactly is longitude, anyway?"

"Time," Blake said, rubbing his chin. "Just time."

"I don't get it."

"Picture the earth as a peeled orange," Blake said, "with the vertical lines of the segments representing lines of longitude."

"Okay."

"And if the orange revolved around the sun once every twenty-four hours, that's just a measurement of time, isn't it?"

"I guess so."

"So it follows that time can be converted into longitude, doesn't it?"

"How?"

"Think about it. If the earth makes a full revolution of 360 degrees in a twenty-four-hour period, you can just as easily say there are twenty-four hours to a circle as you can say there are 360 degrees to a circle. Right?"

"Yeah?"

"And if you divide 360 degrees by twenty-four hours, it would follow that fifteen degrees of longitude equals one hour of time, right?"

"You've lost me."

Blake grabbed a pencil and piece of paper and started scribbling furiously. It was coming back to him now. "And if that were true, then one minute of time equals fifteen minutes of arc. And conversely, one minute of arc equals four seconds of time."

"I knew you'd figure it out," Kelly said.

Blake tossed his pencil on the table. "Just knowing that doesn't do us any good."

"Why not?"

"Because the earth is moving."

"Now I really don't get it."

Blake leaned across the table with a pad and pencil, making calculations and thinking out loud. "If the earth spins 360 degrees in a twenty-four-hour period, and each degree of longitude is equal to sixty nautical miles, then the earth is turning at the rate of 21,600 nautical miles at the equator, which is . . . nine hundred miles per hour."

"So the earth is moving. So what?"

"So, if you want to get an accurate line of position, you've got to take a sight on something that isn't moving, something that's constant, like the sun."

"Because?"

"Because if the earth were moving away from the sun at a speed of nine hundred miles per hour, then four seconds of time would make a difference of one mile in your line of position."

"So you're saying a slight error in time would make a huge difference in position," Kelly said. "There must be a way to adjust for it, the effect of the earth moving."

"There is. It's called a chronometer," Blake said, remembering the smashed navigation equipment. "Something we ain't got." He puffed out his cheeks. "And without an accurate chronometer, taking a sight at the sun isn't going to buy us much."

Blake leaned across the chart table and rubbed his eyes, fighting the feeling of hopelessness. Without a chronometer, they were no better off than the earliest sailing ships, as far as the ability to navigate was concerned. The chief was right.

He felt a small hand on his. He opened his eyes and saw Maria standing in front of him. She pushed the sleeve of his khaki shirt back, exposing his digital watch.

"You can use this," she said. "My father showed me."

"I know, honey. I've already thought of that. A quartz watch might be accurate enough, but we'd have to know Greenwich

Mean Time. And without a radio, there's no way to know that.''

"You could figure it out," Maria said. "You are very smart."

Blake smiled at her and cupped her face in his hand. "And you're very sweet, but I don't see how.''

He stared at the Timex strapped to his wrist, at the buttons emerging from the case. The watch contained a function for two separate time zones. He kept one on California time and the other on local time, wherever he happened to be. It also had a stopwatch. A regular watch wouldn't do it, but with the accuracy of a quartz watch, and especially one with a built-in stopwatch, he had something that could pass for a chronometer.

The old Timex had taken its share of hard knocks, but he'd always been careful about keeping accurate time. He was sure it wasn't off by more than thirty seconds. And if four seconds of time equaled one nautical mile, he knew he could get them to within seven miles or so of their destination, accurate enough to bring them to a point somewhere within the sight of land.

He could make it work if he had a way to set one of the time zones on Greenwich Mean Time. If he'd had a radio, he could just set it on the WWV time signal from Fort Collins, Colorado. He'd heard it before, fooling around with his Zenith Trans-Oceanic. It was the sound of a ticking clock that gave Greenwich Mean Time in five-minute intervals, reachable anywhere in the world on several frequencies. But without a radio how could he possibly know what time it was in Greenwich, England? Maria and Kelly were looking at him hopefully, expectantly.

He told himself there was no problem that couldn't be solved if he would just think it through. He went back to the concept of the earth as a peeled orange, 360 degrees around, with the vertical lines of the segments as meridians of longitude. It stood to reason that one of those lines, or meridians, had to be the starting point, circling the globe north to south at zero degrees, then fanning out 180 degrees in both directions, east and west. The prime meridian ran through Greenwich, England, by international agreement, therefore the longitude in Greenwich had to be zero degrees. He knew what their last reported position was, ninety degrees west longitude. So, if fifteen degrees of longitude was equal to one hour of time, it was obvious that ninety degrees of longitude was equal to six hours of time. Therefore, the time in Greenwich was six hours different.

But six hours in which direction? Six hours more, or six hours less? Think! Blake was now talking to himself, ignoring the stares of Kelly and Maria.

"If the sun rises in the east," he said, "and you are in the west, then the Greenwich day starts before your day, therefore, time in west longitude is earlier than Greenwich time. So it follows that—"

"It is a little poem," Maria said. She sang it out in a tinkling voice. "When longitude is east, Greenwich time is least. When longitude is west, Greenwich time is best." She grinned at Blake. "My father taught it to me."

"That's it!" Blake said. It was called Greenwich *best* time when you added time to your local time and Greenwich *least* time when you subtracted from local time. He remembered now. When you added time it was called *zone plus six,* or whatever the number of hours you were adding.

A feeling of exhilaration swept over him. He shouted, "Yes," went down on one knee, and jerked his fist back in a victorious gesture as though he had just slam-dunked the winning two points. In one fluid motion, he came to his feet, picked Maria up by the waist, spun her around, and kissed her on the cheek. She giggled and withdrew into her chin.

Dana Kelly stared at him openmouthed from behind the ship's wheel, then laughed. "Cheer up, Lieutenant."

Blake looked at her and grinned, feeling his face flush with a mixture of embarrassment and excitement. "I think we might just have a shot at this."

Setting the California time zone on his watch to Greenwich Mean Time, he brought the walnut case containing the sextant *El Callado* had left for him over to the table and opened it. The musty smell of the velvet lining rose to greet him. It was a beautiful instrument, a German-made Plath, considered to be the best in the world. It must have belonged to the captain, Blake thought, probably one of his most treasured possessions, a relic of the past, beautifully preserved. Carefully removing it from its case, he smiled at Maria and nodded toward the door. "Come on, pal. Let's go shoot some sun lines."

Kelly manned the helm as Blake and Maria stood out on the bridge wing, alternately holding the stopwatch and shooting the sun. When they were finished, Blake returned and started flipping through the *Nautical Almanac* and the Sight Reduction Tables, looking up the Greenwich Hour Angle, finding the latitude column, looking up the Local Hour Angle, going to the declination column, finding the azimuth, correcting the LHA. He leaned over the chart table and began making calculations, plotting his line of position. Maria stood beside him, handing him calipers, pointing excitedly, chattering in Spanish, catching herself, speaking in English to correct him.

After a few minutes, he turned to Kelly, and said, "I think we've got it."

"You're amazing," Kelly said.

Blake put his hand on Maria's thin shoulder. *"We're* amazing. I couldn't have done it without her."

Maria looked up at him, beaming.

"Your course is two-six-eight degrees," Blake said.

"Two-six-eight, aye, sir," Kelly said, turning the wheel to port.

For the next four hours, the *Latin Star* cut smoothly through the placid waters, seemingly indifferent to her mortal wound. Blake estimated their speed at seven or eight knots, better than he'd expected. He'd checked with the chief for a status report every hour, then every half hour, then every fifteen minutes as the water level got deeper in the engine room. He and Maria kept taking sun sights every half hour and rechecking his calculations. He was certain he was on the right course. They'd been closer to the island than he'd thought. Just a shade over fifty-one miles. At a speed of eight knots, they could make it in just over six hours. He stepped out on the bridge wing and saw a long string of seaweed drifting by, a good sign that some kind of land was near. The sharks were still with them, he noted. If his figures were right, they couldn't be more than twenty miles from the island. He kept sweeping the sky with binoculars, hoping to spot a bird. Glancing at his watch, he picked up the sound-powered phone to the engine room.

After two rings, Kozlewski picked it up. "Yo."

"How does it look, Chief?"

"Not good, water's rising like a bitch, washing up against number one boiler. It's making fearful noises. I'm about ready to send everybody out of here."

"Do it. Get them out of there now if you think—"

A muffled roaring sound came through the earpiece, then the sound of the explosion enveloped the ship as it seemed to lift up out of the water. Blake rocked back on his heels, gripping the telephone cord to keep from falling, nearly pulling the phone free. A sickening vibration rolled up through the super-structure, into the bones in his feet. Dropping the phone, he caught Kelly and Maria, who went flying drunkenly. He lurched toward the bulkhead and grabbed for the handset swinging crazily.

"Chief. Chief!"

A great silence settled over the ship. Blake jammed the earpiece against his head, straining to hear over the thud of his heart hammering in his ears. The only sound was a dead and distant whisper, like the haunting roar of an abandoned seashell.

Chapter Nineteen

Jorge Cordoba sat alone in the corner of the bedroom and stared numbly across the room at Nita's body. He shifted in the white wicker chair and looked at his hands. It had been easy, shockingly easy, to kill. His eyes shifted from the palms of his hands back to the bed where she lay, his fingers curling into fists. She looked small and thin under the sheet. He had cleaned her up and laid her out nicely, covered her so that he couldn't see her face. But he could still see the disbelieving mask that stared at him in her last few moments of life.

The air conditioner started with a bump, stirring the air in the room. Jorge rubbed his face in his hands and forced himself to get control. Nita's death was an unfortunate incident, but he couldn't let it deter him from what he had to do. He pulled the cracked window shade back a fraction and squinted out into the bright light. The tropical sun was high overhead. The bored-looking Peruvian corporal was still leaning against the tree, rifle crooked in his arm, watching the door of the bungalow.

He glanced at his watch and felt his stomach do a little dip. The watch was one of his most prized possessions, a Patek Philippe, a gift from his *padrino*, his beloved godfather, on his twenty-first birthday. Jorge did the calculation to focus his mind. It would have been exactly three months and twelve days after his parents had been butchered. The gold watch sickened him now, but he needed it a while longer. He steeled himself to look at it again. It was almost noon. He wondered when Colonel Suarez would release him.

He pulled on his coat and walked around the bungalow to clear his mind. A narrow hallway connected the bedroom with the living room, with a small bath in between. There was a tiny kitchenette off the living room. He wandered from room to room, forcing himself to focus on details, seeing it for the first time. The cheap wicker chairs and tables, the white enamel chipped away, the cushions stained and dirty; the hemp rugs, faded and worn; the rust-stained water closet and sink; the filmy refrigerator that whirred and clanked; the greasy stove, the cockroaches that scurried out of sight; the pervasive smell of mildew. It was all so cheap and profaned, just what his life had become.

He wandered into the bathroom and looked at his face in the mirror. He bent closer and looked at his eyes. The white membranes were streaked with red. He straightened himself and studied the cloudy reflection. The quicksilver had faded from the mirror's back in patches large enough to give his face a dark, haunted look. Overnight he had aged ten years. There were shadows under his eyes. His hair was matted. There was the stubble of a black beard against a ruddy, splotched complexion. The dark blue pin-striped suit he'd chosen with such care three days ago now hung on him like a sack.

Jorge splashed cold water on his face and walked into the living room. He sat down on the wicker couch and absently took his last cigarette out of the box. He looked at it impassively. It was a custom-made Sherman, brown, with a gold tip. He lit it and leaned back, drawing the smoke deep into his lungs. He'd spent the past four hours working his way through the emotions that had wracked his body since Enrique Lopez had spilled his guts. First denial and disbelief, then shock, then grief, then rage, and now hatred. He inhaled another long drag and blew the smoke out slowly, stoically watching the thin stream. Hatred was the purest kind of emotion, Jorge thought, like love, but in reverse. It could work against you unless it was carefully controlled. Left unrestrained, the hatred would wash up inside him and choke him. For now, he could feel it working beneath the surface, guiding him. It would emerge when he needed it most.

His first thought was to kill his godfather. He had the advantage. Don Gallardo didn't know he was aware of his treachery. And he knew he could do it now; killing Nita had been surprisingly easy. But he also knew he'd never get close enough to him with a weapon. There were metal detectors and pat downs even for him.

But even if he could get to him, Jorge thought, he wanted more than just death for the great betrayer. He took another deep drag and forced himself to think it through. He would have only one shot; once he tipped his hand, his life would be worthless. It was important to understand fully what he wanted and plan for it without emotion, just like any other business objective. He wanted Don Gallardo's death, to be sure, but he wanted more than that. One life for his parents' lives and the loss of his personal honor was not enough. Only with the death of everything Don Gallardo stood for could he hope to find redemption. He had to find a way, one bold initiative that would bring it all down and redeem his honor in the process. *There might be a way,* he thought.

He had been the architect of the financial plan, had advised his godfather that the size and scope of the first bullion purchase should be such that it would impress the confederation, show them that Don Gallardo was serious. The aggressive 1.3-billion-dollar purchase had been financed with a series of short-term loans secured by Don Gallardo's real-estate holdings in Uruguay and Argentina, some 950 million dollars' worth. Don Gallardo had appealed to the confederation members to put up the balance of the cash, 350 million, as a way to get them used to the idea of working together. It would be like a mutual fund, Don Gallardo had said, each member of the confederation

would own shares in the total bullion stockpile in proportion
to their contribution.

Many of the members had balked at putting up such huge
sums of unsecured cash on one man's word, but had gone
along because of Don Gallardo's standing. The money had
been wheedled out of them fifty or seventy-five million at a
time, and had been literally crated and carted down to the docks
and loaded aboard the *Latin Star,* just like any other cargo. It
had been good-faith money, a test of the procedure Don Gallardo had said would bring the *yanquis* to their knees.

But many were still suspicious, skeptical, especially the Gaza
brothers, who headed the vicious Brazilian cartel in São Paulo.
It would be too much of a coincidence for the first shipment
to vanish, just like that, along with the senior financial executive
of Don Gallardo's organization. With the loss of the ship the
confederation would dissolve in a hotbed of bickering and tribal
warfare over the perception that they had been duped. Even
the magnetic personality of Don Gallardo wouldn't keep the
more radical among them from killing him without too much
thought, just as a warning to others who might think about
ways to rip them off.

And with Don Gallardo's death would come the default
of the industrial and real-estate holdings they had pledged as
collateral for the 1.3-billion-dollar loan. With no one around
to fend them off, their creditors would converge like hawks in
a field of mice, gobbling up the choice real-estate holdings and
selling them off to recover their cash. And with the forfeiture
of his property, and the closure of Campanilla, and the disap-
pearance of his chief of finance, his organization would come
tumbling down.

Yes, Jorge thought, *the best way to bring it all down is to
make sure that the ship is never found.* He knew now what he
had to do.

He retrieved his wallet from his coat and flipped to the
telephone numbers in the back. He dialed Admiral Cuartas's
office in Bogotá. After sparring with an overly protective secretary, he mentioned Don Gallardo's name and got through.

"Admiral Cuartas here."

"Admiral, this is Jorge Cordoba. Thank you for taking my call."

"I understood Don Gallardo was on the line."

"I apologize for the confusion. I'm Don Gallardo's godson, calling on his behalf."

"What is it you want?"

"Good news, Admiral. The freighter we talked to you about has been found safe and sound. We have a crew on its way now to recover it. Don Gallardo asked me to call you and let you know that no assistance from the Navy would be required."

"It's a little late for that. The frigate is already on its way," Admiral Cuartas said. "The captain has orders to lend assistance to the American destroyer first, and then to locate the freighter."

"I'm sure the captain of the frigate will be glad to hear that he has only one ship to worry about," Jorge said. "The freighter is under control."

"That may be," Admiral Cuartas said in a controlled voice. "However, the captain of the destroyer has people aboard the freighter. He's going to want to see them recovered."

"We've already arranged to take them off. They'll be reunited with their ship in Buenaventura."

"I can't entrust that to civilians."

"Admiral, I give you my assurance that dedicated professionals will do the job."

"The American captain will require more than that. I will have to assure him personally that his people are safe and accounted for." Jorge heard the distant whisper of static while the admiral paused. "Do I have Don Gallardo's word on this?"

"Admiral, do you know anyone who keeps his promises more than Don Gallardo?"

There was a long pause. "I hope for his sake that he keeps this one." Admiral Cuartas hung up without saying good-bye.

Jorge hung up the phone and dialed his office. Elena picked it up on the first ring.

"Señor Cordoba's office."

"Elena, it's me."

"Where in the world have you been? This place is going crazy. Everybody is calling for you. Your desk is covered with messages."

"Never mind that now. There's something I'd like you to do for me."

"What?"

"Take a letter to Don Gallardo."

"A letter—"

"Ready? 'My Dear Godfather. Attached is our cash-flow summary for the current month and a projection for the next twelve months. As you can see, we will have a significant shortfall from operations due in part to the impending closure of our processing lab at Campanilla, Peru, and the interception and confiscation last month of the shipment en route from Suriname to the Netherlands. Paragraph. As we discussed, I must strongly advise against your suggestion to utilize the confederation's cash for a short-term loan to get us through this difficult period. It is imperative that we establish trust with the members of the confederation with this, our first buy. If we are unable to replace the cash in a timely manner, we run the risk of jeopardizing all that we have worked for. With deepest respect, Jorge Cordoba, acting chief of finance.' Got that?"

"Sure."

"Read it back to me."

Elena read it back in an excited voice.

"Good. I want you to backdate it ten days. Then I want you to put a cover sheet on it. No message. Sign it, 'A friend of the confederation.' Got it?"

"Yes, I've got it. I'll have it ready in ten minutes. Do I send it to Don Gallardo? Where is the attachment?"

Jorge looked in his black book. "Don't send it to Don Gallardo. There is no attachment. I want you to wait four hours and fax it to this number. The country code is 55."

"That's Brazil, isn't it? Who do I send it to? Whose name shall I put on it?"

Jorge gave her the city code for São Paulo and the rest of the number. "No name. Just send it to that number. Don't use our fax machine. Go out to a public machine. After you send it, destroy the original and don't keep any copies."

"You're the boss. When are you coming home?"

"There's one more thing I want you to do. You know the safe in my office?"

"Yes."

"The combination is under my desk mat. There's fifty or sixty thousand dollars in American notes in the petty-cash box. It's unaccountable. I want you to take it."

"Take it and do what?"

"Keep it. You're underpaid. I'm declaring it a cash bonus for you."

Elena gasped. "I can't do that."

"Take it. That's an order."

"Have you gone crazy? When are you coming home?"

Jorge paused and rubbed his eyes. For a brief moment he was sorry he hadn't gotten to know her better. "Take care of yourself."

"You sound strange. Is everything okay?"

"It's going to be."

Jorge heard the hollow thumping of a rifle butt on the door and hung up the phone. He stubbed out his cigarette and twisted the dead bolt.

"Yes?"

The sweating Peruvian corporal leered into the darkened room. There was a black gap where his left front tooth should have been. Jorge could smell him instantly. "My captain says you can go now," he said in peasant Spanish.

Jorge walked back inside for his wallet and the corporal stepped inside the door. "You are alone?"

"Why do you ask?"

"I heard talking."

"That was just me on the phone. There is no one else here."

"I think I should look around."

Jorge opened his wallet and thumbed out five crisp American

hundred-dollar bills. He folded them and slipped the silky bills into the shirt pocket of the corporal's fatigues. "I think you have better things to do with your time." He gently pushed the soldier back out the door, turned, and locked it. He left the corporal standing on the step, peering after him, fingers probing into his shirt pocket, and headed for the Command Center.

Halfway to the concrete-block building, he glanced over his shoulder and saw the corporal climbing into a Humvee that had pulled up, bristling with the rifles of the last squad of soldiers. The Humvee roared out of the compound gate and headed in a northerly direction, back to the base at Punta Arenas. When it was out of sight, Jorge threw the key to the bungalow into a thatch of coca bushes growing wild on the perimeter of the compound, and started on a trot for the Command Center.

He walked through the splintered doorframe and looked around. The floor was littered with radio logs, shell casings, the carcasses of several shot-up radio sets, upended furniture. At first glance the building appeared to be deserted.

"Real nice friends you got there," he heard a voice say from the rear of the building.

He looked back in the far corner and saw a dark figure wearing a cowboy hat slumped in a chair smoking a cigarette, his black cowboy boots perched on a table. He could see from the glow of the cigarette it was the American pilot, Michael Gaines.

"Where are the others?" Jorge said.

"Took 'em."

"Why didn't they take you?"

"Played possum," Gaines said, looking up from under his black Stetson hat with a grin. "Slipped away and hid out back in the jungle."

"Are the helicopters okay?"

"Crazy bastards shot the tail rotor off one. The other one's okay."

"You're sure?"

"It looks okay." Gaines inhaled a drag from his cigarette and blew it out in a long stream. "What we could do, if you could help me get that Blackhawk started, we could take it and get the hell out of here before they come back.''

"Are any of these radios still working?"

"Looks like they missed a couple."

"Can you operate these?"

"I reckon."

"See if you can find one that's working and contact our spotter plane."

"Why?"

"We still need to get aboard that ship."

"Just you and me?" Gaines said. "Not likely."

"It's worth a bonus to me."

"What did you have in mind?"

"Something in the neighborhood of five hundred thousand dollars."

Gaines grunted and nodded. "Nice neighborhood, but I don't much like the idea of a one-way trip. What if that freighter ain't there for us to land on? A half mil wouldn't do me much good."

"All right," Jorge said. "I don't have time to quibble. What do you say we make it an even million. I can have it transferred to any bank you say."

Gaines looked at him for a long minute. "For that kind of money, I might be willing to take a risk." He pulled a paper and pencil from his flight jacket and began scribbling. "Here's the name of a bank in Killeen, Texas. It's a joint account. If I don't come back, my old lady will be covered. It's tough to buy insurance in my line of work."

Jorge picked up a phone to see if it was still working and dialed a number in New York. After two disconnects, he got through. He let the speaker verify who it was to Gaines, then read an authorizing code into the phone and ordered a one-million-dollar wire transfer to the ABA number of the bank Gaines had given him, followed by the pilot's name and account number. The transfer was to be delayed for twenty-four hours, but irrevocable after that. He hung up the phone. "It's done."

"Let's go, Pancho," Gaines said, coming to his feet.

"From here on out, it's Mister Cordoba," Jorge said, standing up. He crushed Gaines's cigarette out with the scuffed toe of his shoe. "Get on that radio and find the exact location of the ship. I'll be back in a minute."

"Yes, sir."

Jorge walked quickly across the tarmac toward a flimsy-looking building at the opposite end of the runway, partially obscured by thick vegetation. It was a monstrous-looking production, he thought, half a city block long, thrown together with corrugated sheet-metal siding and a roof of broken clay tile, with vents every ten feet. Grimy windows, some broken, most cracked, canted out at five-foot intervals along the sides. The building was intended to be loosely constructed, designed to keep out the rain and still allow the chemical fumes that seeped from every pore to escape. It lay on the edge of thousands of acres of coca plants, under a cluster of overhanging trees. The trees were brown from the fumes drifting up through the roof.

He walked up the dirt path that led to the door and glanced at the lush dark green leaf of the plants that edged up to the building, growing in wild profusion. Jorge paused to look at a coca bush growing on the edge of the footpath. He had never seen one up close before. He plucked a leaf from it and stood there looking at its tiny green veins, marveling at its power. The little leaf contained only one-half of one percent of the drug, but it was the stuff of dreams, Jorge thought, the source of great wealth and great power and great aspirations. He twirled it between his fingers and started to throw it away, then astonished himself by putting it in his mouth and chewing it. The mildly bitter taste flooded his mouth. He swallowed and felt an immediate sense of well-being. He plucked another and put it in his mouth, embarrassed to be standing there in the noonday sun, chewing coca leaves like a peasant.

This was how it all began, he thought, glancing around. The humble leaves had been chewed by the Indians for centuries before the Europeans got involved. It had been his own ancestors who had exploited the coca leaf first. Suddenly feeling

ashamed of his heritage, he spit the leaves out into the dust
and glanced around self-consciously.

He walked up to the lab building. The door was standing
ajar. He pushed it open and walked slowly inside. The acrid
stench of chemicals made his eyes water. *No Fumar* signs were
posted conspicuously around. Rows of stainless-steel tanks for
macerating coca leaves stood on both sides of the building, the
waves of chemicals shimmering above them in the noonday
heat. He grimaced at the chemical smell and glanced around
at the vats. He had only a rudimentary knowledge of how the
stuff was made. He knew the peasants picked the leaves by
hand and carted them to a lab like this, where they were soaked
in a mixture of chemicals to begin the process of extraction.
Maceration, it was called. *A real* olla-podrida, Jorge thought,
a rotten stew.

He would need a gun when he boarded the ship. *Everyone
working here would have been armed,* he thought. Glancing
around, he emptied a row of cabinets along the wall and found
nothing. Walking over to a metal shop desk, he pulled the center
drawer open and pawed through a sheaf of papers. Feeling
something cool and metallic, he reached under the stack and
retrieved a pistol, a nine-millimeter Smith & Wesson semiautomatic with molded nylon grips. He ejected the clip. Fourteen
shots in the magazine, one in the chamber. Cocking it, he
snapped the safety on and stuck it in his belt. Above the writing
surface was a warren of cubbyholes. Pawing around through
the upper shelves, he found a package of cigarettes and a book
of matches. Walking around behind a bale of coca leaves, he
spotted a large vat of kerosene.

He stood looking around at the filthy business he had sold
his soul for and wondered if his parents were watching him now,
could see him begin the process of avenging their humiliating
deaths. Fighting down a lump in his throat, he lit the cigarette
and took a deep drag that made the tip glow. Carefully folding
the matchbook around it, leaving two inches of the cigarette
exposed, he laid the homemade fuse on a stack of paper soaked
in kerosene. Estimating it would take about ten minutes for the

cigarette to burn its way down to the matches, he quickly walked out the door and headed back to the Command Center.

Michael Gaines was lifting the headphones off and walking toward the map table when Jorge walked in. Gaines bent over the table, studying the grease-pencil marks showing the location of the ship.

"Where is it?" Jorge asked.

Gaines pointed to a spot on the map west of the grease mark. "I make it about here. The pilot of the spotter plane is coming in. Low on fuel. I diverted him to Lima. Last sighting was about an hour ago. The ship was under way, heading west—"

"West? Why would it be heading west?"

"Beats hell out of me," Gaines said.

"There's nothing in that direction," Jorge said. "If they wanted to reach land, why wouldn't they steam toward the coast?"

Gaines shrugged. "I don't know."

"Let me look at that map." Jorge turned the light volume up behind the map and scanned the blue surface. "What's this?" he asked, pointing to a speck on the chart.

"Some kind of land, I reckon," Gaines said. "Probably just an atoll. A little island, made out of coral. There's millions of them in the Pacific. They only plot the ones that stick up far enough to hang up a ship."

Hang up a ship. The words jolted Jorge. Why would they be moving away from the coast toward something that could hang up a ship? If the American officer had been good enough to survive the storm, why wouldn't he just head for the coast? Why would he be heading west? There was nothing out there but that tiny sliver of coral that could . . . He rocked back on his heels. "I'll be damned."

"What?"

"That's it," Jorge said. "There's only one reason he'd be heading west. The ship was damaged in the storm, and he's trying to save it. He's heading for the nearest land. He's going to try to run it aground."

"Sounds reasonable to me," Gaines said.

Jorge rubbed his face in his hands. He had badly underestimated the young American officer. If he was successful in beaching the freighter, the ship would be confiscated by the Colombian Navy and it would be only a matter of time before Don Gallardo had it back. He had seen how successfully he had manipulated Admiral Cuartas. He had to stop it before it got there.

"What's the range on the Blackhawks?"

"These here have been outfitted with ESSS."

"Speak English!"

"External Stores Support System, it means they got extra fuel tanks, 230 gallons apiece."

"Can we make it out there?"

Gaines looked at the chart. "They're going away from us. It'll be tight. Depends on whether we can catch them before they get too far out."

"Let's go," Jorge said.

"Sure you know what you're doing?" Gaines said. "We only got enough fuel for a one-way trip, barely that. If there's nothing out there for us to land on, we're in a lot of trouble."

"Then we'll have to get there while there's still something to land on, won't we?" Jorge said.

"Then what are we yammering for," Gaines said. "Let's do it."

They walked up to the helicopters. Jorge watched Gaines check the extra fuel tanks mounted on the stub wings on each side of the fuselage and give the external systems a quick check.

"You're going to have to play crew chief on this one," Gaines said. "Stand out in front while I go through the start procedure. If you see the beginning of any fires, anything that looks funny, wave me the hell out of there."

Jorge took a position in front of the helicopter and watched Gaines climb into the right seat and strap himself in. The pilot scanned the flight-control panels and pressed the start buttons. The turboshaft engines spun with a high-pitched whine and caught.

Bracing himself against the downdraft from the four spinning rotors, Jorge checked the engines and fuselage for fires, then scrambled into the copilot's left seat and watched the American go through the cockpit check. "How do you fly this thing?"

"Nothing to it," Gaines said. "This here on the left is called the collective. It's just the engine power control. The stick between my legs is called the cyclic, among other things. It's the pitch and directional controls. That's basically it. Like the foot-feed and steering wheel on a car." Gaines glanced around the cockpit and nodded approvingly. "Nice ships, these Black-hawks. Got an autostabilization system that ties to the flight-control system. So smooth it don't even need a vibration-sup-pression system like most other birds."

"Skip the technobabble. What about those?" Jorge said, pointing down to the foot pedals.

"Don't use them much. They're handy for hovering and such, but we don't really need them."

"Can you fly it from here?"

"Either seat, it don't matter." Gaines looked at him. "What did you have in mind?"

"Nothing," Jorge said. He looked at his watch impatiently. "How long does it take to warm up?"

"Not long," Gaines said. "Good engines, these 701s." He scanned the warning-enunciator lights on the cockpit instrumen-tation panel. One by one the lights turned green.

Jorge watched him intently. It was nothing like the single-engine Cessna he'd learned to fly in, but it didn't look difficult. When the engines had warmed up, Gaines released the parking brake, pushed the cyclic forward, pulled up slightly on the collective to apply power, and taxied forward to an open spot on the runway. Glancing both ways, he pulled up gently on the power control and pitched the stick forward. The heavy Blackhawk lifted off in a swirl of dust and leaves.

Jorge looked down on the shrinking compound, struck by how smooth the Blackhawk rode. Out of the corner of his eye, he saw a flash of fire. Gaines saw it at the same time. He banked the helicopter for a closer look. In the far corner of the compound, the fire was licking through the cracked tile roof of the processing lab. Gaines applied more power and the Blackhawk gained elevation as the lab building lifted up in a violent explosion that rocked the helicopter.

"Think we ought to turn back?" Gaines shouted into Jorge's ear.

Jorge looked down on the spreading fire that was beginning to sweep the compound. A southerly breeze was pushing it toward the row of bungalows where Nita's body lay. He looked at his watch. His homemade fuse had taken less than fifteen minutes to ignite. Unbuckling the crocodile strap of the Patek Philippe his godfather had given him, he gripped the gold buckle between his thumb and forefinger and held it out the door at arm's length, as though he was dropping a dirty sock down a laundry chute. Straining against his shoulder harness with the wind and smoke stinging his eyes, he released it and watched the custom-made timepiece flutter down into the blazing compound like a bird with a broken wing.

"It's too late to turn back now."

Chapter Twenty

Blake knelt down over Frank Kozlewski's body and gently lifted the chief's head out of the water. The old man's face was slack, his eyes lifeless. A pink stain seeped into the water from a wound around his neck. A piece of shrapnel from the exploding boiler must have severed an artery, Blake thought.

He prayed that the chief had been killed instantly by the explosion. The thought that his old friend had bled to death down here alone was more than he could bear. He dragged the chief's body over to the engine-room console and propped him up in a pointless attempt to keep his head out of the water. He looked at the rubbery face for a minute and smoothed the few strands of gray hair out of the old man's eyes.

"You were right, old friend," Blake said in a whisper. The tightness in his throat threatened to choke him. "We should have abandoned this hell ship. I'm sorry."

He straightened himself and sloshed around the engine room, looking for Robertson and Tobin. The shoring was holding. The pumps were still running. He spotted the crumpled forms, half-floating in the swirling water like bags of refuse, and turned them over. Both dead of burns and asphyxiation.

He heard the number two boiler groan ominously. It was situated far enough from the number one boiler to withstand the blast, but it was making agonizing, tearing sounds. He knew it was only a matter of time before it went, too. He waded over and stood in front of it, hoping it would choose that moment to explode. It was pointless to go on. His marriage was over. His career was finished. If by some miracle he should survive, he knew he would be facing a general court-martial for the loss of almost the entire boarding party. He stood there for a minute, gazing into the boiler, mesmerized by the yellow-and-blue flame that danced tenuously through the viewing port.

The labored sound of the turbines, struggling to push the water-laden ship forward, pulled him back. He could feel the tug of the sea, dragging her down. He thought about Kelly and Maria alone on the bridge. He backed away and stepped up to the engine-room console. He looked down on the chief's body for an instant. They had all died trying to save the ship. He would damn well get them to the island or die trying, too. Sick with grief and frustration, he wrenched the throttle valve open with such force that it twisted off in his hands, jamming the throttle in the full-ahead position. It was just as well, he thought, glancing at the brittle valve in his hand. When the water got high enough, there would be no returning to the engine room.

He climbed the ladder into the brightness of the afternoon sun. A few black specks floated and dived gracefully against the western sky. Land birds. At least his navigation had been right. Before the explosion the birds would have been a joyous sight. But the ship was wallowing ahead at three or four knots now. At that speed, the chances of reaching the island before she went down were slim.

If he had been alone, he would have taken his chances, but he owed it to Kelly and Maria to try to build a raft out of something. Something that would float without getting water-logged. He thought about the fifty-five-gallon drums in the number three hold. If he could get the hatch cover off, he could carefully empty a few out, reseal them, hoist them up to the main deck, and lash them together. That would keep them afloat indefinitely. If they could survive the exposure to the elements and the sharks long enough, they might have a chance.

He walked across the weather deck to the number three cargo hold, unlocked the pontoon hatch cover, and rolled it back. The humid, rusty smell rose to greet him. He descended the ladder into the hold, half-expecting to find Sergeant Rivero's body swinging by its ankles. He looked around cautiously. The closer they got to land, the bigger the danger that *El Callado* would emerge. He shuddered in the tomblike air, remembering the cargo in the number three hold: sixty tons of chemicals, thirty tons of cocaine, 350 million dollars in cash. People were coming to kill them for it.

Sliding down the ladder to the second level, he flicked on his light and blinked at the reflection thrown back from the shiny cans of ether. The pleasant sweet scent seemed to have a calming effect on him. Tenderly, he felt the wound in his arm where the chief had accidentally shot him and flexed his muscle. It was sore as hell, but it had healed more quickly than he'd thought. He knew that fasting could do that; that's why animals refused food when they were injured. He flashed his light up the tower of black fifty-five-gallon drums of acetone. It wouldn't be easy to lift the steel drums out of the hold with a bad arm, but he thought he could do it, assuming he could find a way to empty them out without blowing himself up or anesthetizing himself in the process.

Something made him stop and listen, a faint shuttling sound in the distance. The acoustics in the open hold were such that he couldn't tell if it was coming from deep down inside the cargo hold or from outside. He paused and strained to hear. It was the pounding of air, the unmistakable sound of a helicopter rotor drumming through the sky. Blake sprang for the ladder. As his head reached the weather deck, he could tell by the growl of the blades that it was a four-rotor helicopter. His heart leapt. The good old *Carlyle* had come through. He climbed out of the cargo hold and squinted into the sun. It was too far and too high for him to see. Pulse racing, he ran to the bridge for his binoculars.

He took the steps to the bridge two at a time and burst into the empty pilothouse. The ship's wheel was locked on course. Kelly and Maria were standing on the bridge wing, pointing excitedly toward the eastern sky.

"There," Maria said, pointing. "Can't you see it?"

"No," Kelly said, squinting into the brightness with her hands cupped around her eyes.

"I wish I had her eyesight," Blake said, adjusting the binoculars.

"That's two of us," Kelly said, squinting. "Can you make it out?"

"Not yet," Blake said. "But it sounds like a Seahawk."

"I don't think I care what it is," Kelly said. "Just as long as it takes us off this thing."

"Strange," Blake said, adjusting the focus. He could see its face now, a light green grasshopper, hovering in the air. "Looks more like a Blackhawk." He fine-tuned the focus on the binoculars and saw the light green fuselage. "That is definitely a Blackhawk," he said. "I don't get it. What would an Army helicopter be doing way the hell out here?"

"Maybe it's an interservice search and rescue team," Kelly said.

Blake studied the wavering form, the afternoon sun beating down on the back of his neck. The helicopter turned slightly in the direction of the ship and the fuselage came into view.

"Shit!" Blake said.

"What is it?"

"It's a Blackhawk, all right, but it's not one of ours."

"How can you tell? Doesn't it have markings?"

"It's got a big blue star on the fuselage."

"A star? Isn't that what the Army has?"

"Not like that. It's solid blue, like a corporate logo."

"What does it mean?" Kelly asked.

Blake let out a long breath. "It means the owners have come for their ship."

"*Pistoleros,*" Maria said in a whisper.

"Oh, God," Kelly said. She put her arm around Maria. "What are we going to do?"

"We can't let them land," Blake said. "Once they get aboard, we've had it." He unholstered his pistol and checked the chamber. It was still cocked from the boarding. He snapped the safety off. "I don't know how much good we can do with this popgun against a Blackhawk helicopter, but it's all we've got."

"Do you think it's armed?"

"I can't tell, but we've got to assume it is," Blake said. "Probably a pair of M60 machine guns mounted port and starboard. But even if it isn't, the people on it will be." He squinted and sighted down the Beretta, trying to line up the white dot on the front sight with the cockpit, his vision blurred by heat vapors.

"Look!" Maria said, pointing beyond the bow of the ship.

Blake and Kelly turned and squinted at a brown-and-pink lump coming into view on the western horizon.

"You did it!" Kelly said. "You got us to land. I knew you could do it."

"That's the good news," Blake said, turning back to the helicopter.

"What's the bad news?"

"The bad news is that our silent friend doesn't need us anymore," Blake said. "You still have your gun?"

"Sure," Kelly said, putting her hand on her pocket.

"You two go belowdecks and take cover. But keep an eye out for that lunatic. With land in sight, and his bosses here, he'll be emerging any minute now. I'll stay here and see if I can discourage them a little."

"Just you and a handgun?" Kelly said. "Against a helicopter with machine guns? That's crazy."

"I doubt if they'll return the fire," Blake said. "They know the ship is loaded with ether. If I can hold them off long enough to get the ship beached, we can slip down the Jacob's ladder, make a run for it."

"Two guns are better than one," Kelly said. "I'll stay with you."

"No," Blake said. "They might be crazy enough to strafe the bridge. We can't endanger Maria. Hop to it and get below." He took a practice sight at the small green spot coming into view, shaking his head at the ludicrous situation.

Kelly and Maria hung back, hesitating, staring at the helicopter. It turned slowly, exposing the solid blue star on the fuselage, and Maria said something in Spanish. Blake turned and saw her pointing at the helicopter, trembling.

"*La estrella azul,*" Maria said in a shrill voice. "*La mano de muerte.*"

He glanced at Kelly. "What's she saying?"

" 'The blue star. The hand of death,' " Kelly said.

"Ask her what she means."

"She sees the blue star on the fuselage," Kelly said.

"What does that have to do with the hand of death?"

Maria said something in Spanish.

"She said that *El Callado* had a blue star tattooed on the back of his hand," Kelly said. "Everyone called it the hand of death."

Blake's mind flashed on something Doc Jones had mentioned during his update on the bodies. The corpse that had grabbed Alvarez by the ankle had a blue star tattooed on the back of its hand. The corpse from the vault. The corpse that had disappeared . . . Something was gnawing at him, but he couldn't make the connection. He glanced up at the helicopter. "Get below. Now. That's an order."

"Okay, okay. We're going," Kelly said. "But I still think this is nuts."

Kelly and Maria scrambled down the starboard ladder to the deck below. Blake squinted down the barrel of the Beretta, trying to line up the shimmering helicopter in his sights, waiting for it to come into range. Minutes ticked by. The helicopter grew larger in his sights. He heard the sound of footsteps coming up the port ladder to the bridge. He glanced between the approaching helicopter and the door of the pilothouse, his guts churning. Sweat beaded up on his forehead, trickled into his eyes. He heard the latch turn and spun on the door, his pistol aimed in a two-handed grip.

A giant of a man wearing the blue chambray shirt and denim pants of an ordinary seaman stepped into the pilothouse. Square-jawed and expressionless, he stood facing Blake, staring at him with yellowed eyes, a rifle held at waist level. The mass of him blocked out all light from the door. He pointed the rifle at Blake and motioned toward the engine-order telegraph.

Blake tensed, aimed his pistol at the hulking figure. The carbine looked like a toy in his hands. Hands that had pulled him back from the brink of death. He glanced at the rifle. It was Sergeant Rivero's M-16. The man's finger seemed barely to fit inside the trigger guard. They stared at each other for what seemed a full minute.

"So," Blake said with a dry mouth, heart hammering in his chest. "The silent one."

The yellow eyes flashed. He understood. And he didn't like the name. He nodded again toward the engine-order telegraph, this time with more urgency.

"What is it?" Blake said. "You want me to stop the ship?"

One quick nod, a jerk of the massive head.

"That wouldn't be a great idea," Blake said, swallowing hard. "The ship is sinking."

The man nodded toward the helicopter, now more visible in the eastern sky, and jerked his head violently toward the engine-order telegraph.

"You want me to stop it so they can land? Is that it?"

Another nod.

"That wouldn't really be in my best interest," Blake said.

The giant's face turned dark. He seemed to sense that there was more to stopping the ship than pulling the telegraph handle to "All Stop." He needed Blake to do something, but he didn't seem to know what. He jerked the rifle up and aimed it at Blake, the frustration evident on his lined face.

"Uh-uh," Blake said, tensing his grip on the Beretta. He stared back. "I've got one, too. And you don't look real comfortable with yours." Blake wondered if he even knew how to shoot it. He didn't want to kill this giant beast if he didn't have to. "Just put it down, friend."

The man stared at him for a long minute. The rifle seemed to sag. Blake almost felt sorry for him for a minute. He relaxed his stance enough to blink. In that instant, something flew at him with blinding speed. He instinctively brought his arms up to protect his face. The M-16 caught him across his raised forearms and knocked him back against the bulkhead. A mass of flesh covered him in an instant, twisting the Beretta out of his hand, knocking him sprawling across the deck. He felt the wind go out of him as the giant fell on him, straddled him with his massive weight and circled his neck with steellike fingers. The smell of him was overpowering, the acrid stench of a wild animal. Blake's fingers dug into biceps that felt like his own thighs, tried to break the grip. Staring into a face contorted with rage, he struggled with everything he had, but nothing was moving. He felt himself drifting away. A darkness came over him. He felt a sense of peace.

The dark shadows that enveloped him grew lighter. He felt the grip around his throat loosen. He opened his eyes and saw a demonic figure, face blackened with camouflage makeup, pull the giant's massive head back by the hair with one hand and plunge a combat knife hilt-deep into his right temple, the tip of the blade emerging from his left. The square face went slack, eyes wide, mouth open. Sergeant Rivero rode him like a horse, holding the ponderous head back with one hand, twisting the knife handle with the other, grinding *El Callado*'s brains into mush. The mound of flesh went limp and collapsed on Blake, smothering him with his weight.

Sergeant Rivero pulled the Ka-Bar combat knife out of *El Callado*'s skull with a scrape of steel against bone that sounded like a chicken being cut up. He rolled the massive corpse off Blake and wiped the knife on the front of the blue chambray shirt, leaving a trail of bloody brain tissue. He rocked back on his heels, breathing hard, and looked at Blake.

Blake sat up, rubbing his throat, gasping for air. He tried to speak, but nothing came out. He stared at the features beneath the nightmarish face paint. He should have figured it out before now, but even if he had, it wouldn't have prepared him for the apparition that sat before him.

"I thought you were dead," he finally managed to rasp out.

Rivero gave him a condescending look. "Did you think I could be defeated by garbage like this?"

Blake glanced at the blue star tattooed on the back of the corpse's hand and nodded. "The big guy in the vault. The one who grabbed Alvarez by the ankle—"

Rivero snorted with contempt. "That was the great *El Callado,* the silent one," he said, nodding at the pile of flesh sprawled in the corner. "I had heard of this 'legend' for years. When he attacked me in the vault I suspected it was him. When you shared with me what you had read in the log, I knew." Rivero wiped the blade against the leg of his fatigues and stood up. "He was hard to kill," he said, looking down on the corpse. "I thought I had done it until he grabbed that stupid seaman by the ankle." His eyes grew dark. "I should have sunk a knife in him then, but that idiot corpsman pronounced him dead. I thought he was until his 'body' disappeared." Rivero slipped the combat knife into his ankle sheath and snapped it. "That's when I went underground to hunt him down. He was as cunning as a rat and even harder to kill, as you just saw."

Blake looked out at the helicopter hovering against the bluish sky. "That must be the Ramirez cartel, if he wanted to surrender the ship to them," he said. "Looks like you were wrong about who owned it."

"Perhaps," Sergeant Rivero said, picking up his rifle.

Blake sat for a minute to clear his head. The rotors of the helicopter grew louder. He rolled over and picked up the Beretta that was lying on the deck and came to his feet. If it was the Ramirez cartel, this would be payback time for Sergeant Rivero, he thought, remembering the look in Rivero's eyes when he described the murder of his family. Blake glanced at the carnage behind him again and looked out the window at the Blackhawk.

He shook his head, almost feeling sorry for the first guy to scramble out the door of the helicopter.

Sergeant Rivero ejected the banana clip from the M-16 and examined it, then shoved it back in place with a click. He took a practice aim out the window, checked the sights, and made some adjustments. Satisfied, he turned toward Blake and leveled the rifle at him.

"Put the gun down, Lieutenant."

Blake turned, smiling. The look on Rivero's face said he wasn't kidding. He felt something tear in his guts. "What the hell do you think you're doing?"

The Colombian marine's face shifted into a strange, almost apologetic, look. "They need to land soon," Sergeant Rivero said. "They've come a long way, and their fuel is low."

At that instant, Blake saw Kelly's radio backpack by the door. He felt his whole body stiffen, staring at the radio, then back to Rivero's blackened face. He looked at the helicopter. It wasn't the Ramirez cartel; it was the Gallardo cartel, and Rivero had been guiding them in on Kelly's radio. That's why he'd gone underground. He stared at the Colombian marine in amazement, shaking his head, astonished that he'd missed all the signals.

"The gun, please, Lieutenant," Rivero said. "We don't want any shooting with all this ether aboard. This is a very important shipment."

Blake stared at the marine, his blood pounding at his temples. He leveled his Beretta at Rivero. If this was the end of the line, he would take this treacherous bastard down with him. "I can't see any real good reason why I should do that."

"I have the *señorita* and the *chica* safely secured belowdecks. If you put it down now, you have my word that they will not be harmed. If you kill me, the others will not be so kind," Rivero said, nodding at the approaching helicopter.

Blake tried not to show the alarm in his eyes. Kelly and Maria hadn't been gone that long. Did he have them, or was he bluffing? "I don't believe you."

"You have no choice but to believe me. The gun, please. On the deck."

Blake stared at Rivero for a long minute. Whether he had them or not, it wouldn't take these thugs long to round them up after he was dead. He couldn't bear the thought of Kelly and Maria falling into their hands. Rivero was right. He had no choice. "All right," he said finally. "What happens to me doesn't matter, but I want your word that you'll protect Kelly and the girl from those people," he said, nodding at the Blackhawk.

Rivero nodded. "I regret that I can do nothing for you, *Teniente*. You are a casualty of war, but I will not allow women and children to be killed."

"Fair enough." Blake laid the automatic on the deck in front of him and raised his hands. He looked at Rivero and shook his head. "Why are you doing this?"

"You couldn't hope to understand, *Teniente*," Rivero said. "The rich never understand the poor. Kick it over here, please."

"If you think I'm rich, you've been misinformed," Blake said. He shoved the pistol across the deck with his foot.

"It's your rich, arrogant country that doesn't understand," Rivero said. "Coming down here, meddling in things you can't begin to comprehend."

"I don't know what you're talking about."

"No, of course you don't," Rivero said. "If you had grown up among the *campesinos*, as I did, you might."

"Campesinos?" Blake said. "What the hell are you—"

"Peasants, Lieutenant. You don't even know they exist. Your people have everything. Mine have nothing, only the coca leaf. The rich never understand that when the poor have only one thing to sell, it cannot be so easily taken away." Rivero reached down and picked up the Beretta slowly with his left hand, never taking his eyes off Blake. He flung it through the open door of the pilothouse, over the side. It went spiraling into the sea without making a ripple. The distant drone of helicopter rotors grew louder. Rivero nodded to the engine-order telegraph. "Heave to."

"Are you crazy?" Blake said. "This ship is sinking. The only chance we've got is to beach it on that atoll."

"Your shoring job was excellent, with my help," Rivero said. "The ship will stay afloat. Heave to just long enough for them to land. It won't take long."

"So it was you all along," Blake said. "You stole the radio. You killed Sparks and Alvarez."

Rivero nodded, his face impassive.

"And that's how they found us," Blake said, nodding to the radio, "once their search planes got into range."

"You're stalling," Rivero said, glancing at the helicopter. "Heave to. Now."

"What about the *Carlyle?*" Blake asked, moving closer to the engine-order telegraph. "Did you do that, too?"

"You give me too much credit, Lieutenant. I suspect you have your own mismanagement to thank for that. No, I came aboard innocently enough. But when I saw the importance of the shipment I knew what I had to do."

"Why did you kill Sparks? He couldn't have done you any harm."

"He was a loathsome American pig. I've seen his type in every seaport in South America. A drunk, lusting after little girls."

"And Alvarez. Why?"

"I had to send a message to stay away from the money. The Gallardo organization has important work to do. Only if they are successful will the peasants have food and the Ramirez butchers be driven from the face of the earth."

"If you'd sent any more messages, we wouldn't have had enough people to get under way."

"I came to that conclusion after your tirade in the engine room. I tried to help you after that, but you came close to exhausting my patience with your foul mouth."

"That was you who pulled me back?" Blake said, incredulous.

"I kept you alive to do what you had to do. I kept you all

alive, even that stupid *hembra*. If I hadn't tripped her, she would have walked right into *El Callado*'s arms.''

Blake stared at him, torn by equal parts of gratitude and hatred.

Rivero saw the look on Blake's face and snorted. ''Did you wonder why *El Callado* did not bother you while you were getting the ship under way? Did you think it was his self-interest, perhaps?'' His eyes flashed from the hellish makeup. ''It is because he was running for his life.'' He glanced out at the helicopter, lower now, beginning its descent. ''Heave to. They're almost here.''

''If they land, they'll kill us all,'' Blake said, glancing aft.

''Yes, I'm sure they will,'' Sergeant Rivero said. ''So it makes little difference to me whether I kill you first. Heave to, I said.''

''You're not hearing me,'' Blake said. ''They'll kill you, too.''

''I don't think so,'' Rivero said. ''Not when they find out I'm the one who has been guiding them in. Heave to, Lieutenant. I won't ask you again.''

''Go ahead,'' Blake said, waving at the engine-order telegraph. ''It won't do you any good. The throttle valve in the engine room is jammed open.''

''I'm not such a fool as you think I am, Lieutenant.'' Rivero motioned with the M-16. ''Do it.''

Blake moved slowly to the engine-order telegraph under the cautious eye of Sergeant Rivero, intent on dragging it out as long as he could. Looking past Rivero, he saw Kelly ease quietly through the port door of the pilothouse holding the snub-nosed .38 caliber revolver with both hands, pointing it at Sergeant Rivero's back. He didn't know how long she'd been standing outside, listening, but she'd obviously heard enough. He tried not to react, tried not to give away her position. Kelly motioned Maria behind her and took a shooter's stance.

''Drop it,'' Kelly said.

Rivero froze but held the rifle on Blake, watching his eyes.

"Do it now," Kelly said. "I owe you one for that trip down the ladder, but I'll still blow your head off."

Blake tried not to look in her direction, but Rivero caught his line of sight. Quick as a ferret, the Colombian spun around, leading with the butt of the M-16. The butt plate caught Kelly under the chin with a sickening crunch. The revolver went flying across the pilothouse. Rivero spun back around in the same movement and tried to cover Blake, but it was too late.

Blake went into him headfirst, driving him back. Rivero gasped and doubled over with a whoosh of air. His rifle went clattering to the deck and slid into the corner of the pilothouse. Rivero backed up into the opposite corner with a wild look in his eyes, sucking air like a cornered animal. His hand went down to his right ankle and unsheathed the Ka-Bar combat knife. Blake stared at it. The edge glistened under a light coat of oil, dark stains along the blood groove. He glanced at *El Callado*'s scrambled brains leaking out onto the deck and felt a chill go through him. The two men circled, feinting, looking for an opening. Maria stood paralyzed, the heels of her hands pressed against her temples, staring back and forth between Kelly's unconscious body in the corner and Blake dodging Rivero's lightninglike slashes. Blake saw the Colombian lower his head slightly and knew he was driving in for a gut shot. Twisting to the side, he grabbed Rivero by the wrist and chopped the knife out of his hand. It went skittering across the deck and came to rest by the engine-order telegraph. Blake grabbed Rivero by the collar with his left hand and swung for his head with his right. The solid crack of knuckles against jawbone startled Blake, sent Rivero crumpling into the corner where his M-16 lay. Blake lunged for the rifle, too late. Rivero had the muzzle against his chest by the time he got there.

Rivero came to his feet, shaking off the effects of the blow. Blake backed off with the M-16 in his chest, shaking the pain out of his fingers. He looked at Kelly, crumpled in the corner with blood gushing from her mouth and chin.

"You lousy bastard."

"I didn't want to kill you, *Teniente*," Rivero said, breathing hard. "I admired the way you handled the ship through the storm, how you managed to get us here, but you're becoming too much trouble to keep alive." Sergeant Rivero hesitated for a moment, then raised the rifle and pointed it at Blake's head. "Just know that you died for a good cause."

Maria came out of her trance. Scooping up Kelly's revolver, she aimed it with both hands, squinted her eyes, and pulled the trigger with both fingers. The sound of the two shots was almost simultaneous, the revolver a split second first.

Blake dropped back against the bulkhead with a stunned expression, a deep red stain spreading through the left side of his khaki shirt. Rivero grimaced and slumped to his knees, the rifle clattering to the deck. He clutched the open wound in his right shoulder, then ripped the shirt of his fatigues open and gazed at the river of blood pulsing out. He tried to pinch the wound under his right arm closed, but the blood kept gushing.

Maria stood staring at the revolver with wide eyes, her fingers turning red from the grip. She looked at Blake and screamed. She spun on Rivero and said something in Spanish, the smoking pistol still locked in her outstretched arms, pointed at him.

Rivero looked past her at the Blackhawk beginning its descent. Scooping up the M-16 in his left hand, he ran out on the port bridge wing, trailing blood, signaling with the rifle. Maria aimed the pistol at him through the door of the pilothouse. Blake tried to say, "No," and it came out as a moan. She dropped the pistol and flung herself across Blake's chest and began to cry with loud choking sobs. Rivero came back inside and picked up the pistol. He stood looking down on them for a minute as if deciding whether to use it. Turning, he walked out on the bridge wing, threw the pistol over the side, and quickly disappeared down the ladder.

Jorge Cordoba squinted into the western sun and looked down on the narrow wake of the freighter. Even to his untrained eye, he could see that the ship was in trouble. It appeared to be barely moving, slow and ponderous, riding low in the water, struggling toward the dark lump of land now visible on the western horizon. His guess had been right. They were trying to run the ship aground in order to save it. He had to find a way to stop it before it got there.

"Got to take her in pretty quick," Michael Gaines shouted in Jorge's ear. "We're running on fumes." He pointed to the fuel-indicator warning lights flashing red.

Jorge glanced at the warning lights, then down to the freighter. A lone figure appeared on deck with a rifle.

Jorge climbed into the jump seat behind the pilot, slid the door open and positioned himself behind the starboard machine gun. A belt of cartridges fed into it from a green ammunition box mounted on the side. He gripped the handles and swiveled it around. "How do you work this thing?"

"Just release the safety, and let her rip," Gaines said, banking for a better shot. "Hey, wait a minute, that guy looks like a military type, maybe a marine. That might be our contact."

Jorge elevated the handle and sighted down the barrel. He positioned the ramp sight on the figure in fatigues and lined it up with the inner circle on the after sight. The figure stood there, lifting his rifle.

"Hold it, he's signaling with his—"

Jorge squeezed the trigger and a stream of 7.62-millimeter rounds ripped across the weather deck in a diagonal pattern. The figure exploded from shoulder to waist in a cloud of wood splinters, cloth fragments, and blood.

"Jesus Christ," Gaines said, "what did you do that for? He was trying to signal us. You trying to start a war?"

"Circle again," Jorge said. "I want to see if there's anyone else aboard."

"Crazy bastard," Gaines said. He turned in his seat and shouted over his shoulder, "We got enough fuel for about one more pass, then we're going in. When these crates run out of gas, they got all the aerodynamics of a grand piano." He banked the helicopter to the left and circled the ship in a tight radius.

Jorge clenched the machine gun and scanned the superstructure of the ship and the open hatch over the number three cargo hold for any other sign of movement. The ship appeared to be deserted. He motioned for Gaines to land.

"Take it in nice and slow. Hover over the landing pad and be ready to take off again. Don't set it down until I tell you to."

Gaines approached the wallowing freighter slowly from the stern and hovered over the fantail, the rotors whipping the sea around them. Jorge sat with the machine gun pointed at the superstructure of the ship, poised for any movement. The engine coughed and caught again.

"We got to land," Gaines said. "We ain't got nothing left."

Seeing no sign of life, Jorge motioned for Gaines to land. The Blackhawk settled down on the fantail with a heavy sigh.

Gaines pulled the parking brake on and looked over his shoulder at Jorge. "I don't much like the way you do business, mister."

"Leave it running," Jorge said.

"What for? It ain't going to run much longer. Dry as a boiled possum." Gaines throttled the big helicopter down to a slow idle and pulled off his helmet.

"I'm going up to the pilothouse," Jorge said. "Cover me with the machine gun."

"Who are these folks?" Gaines asked. "I like to know who I'm fighting."

"A Navy boarding party."

"Whose Navy?"

"Yours."

"Mine? You saying that's a US marine you cut down?"

"I don't know, and I don't care," Jorge said.

Gaines turned and looked at him over his shoulder. "Well, you son of a bitch. You put one over on old Michael Gaines, didn't you?" He turned back around. "This is the end of the line for me, Pancho. I've done a lot of things in my time, but I don't fight against my own people."

"You have a curious code of ethics," Jorge said. He pulled the pistol from his waistband, snapped the safety off, and pressed the muzzle against the back of the pilot's head. "Get out."

Gaines left the helicopter running and stepped out onto the weather deck. He turned and faced Jorge with his hands raised haphazardly. "It don't have to be like this."

"Turn around."

Gaines turned and faced the superstructure of the ship.

"You're either with me or against me," Jorge said. "Which is it?"

Gaines shook his head. "I can't be with you on this one."

Jorge raised the pistol and pointed it at the base of the pilot's skull. "Very noble of you," he said, and squeezed the trigger. Michael Gaines fell forward on the teak deck and lay still, little pink tufts of brain matter stuck to his face. Stepping around Gaines's body, Jorge walked quickly toward the superstructure.

Blake felt the warm wetness of tears on his face and a trembling form over him, shaking him.

"Don't die, you bastard, don't you dare die."

He opened his eyes a crack and saw two shadowy forms above him.

"You can't die now." A hand was shaking him. "Look, there's land, we've made it."

He pushed the form away with his right arm and heard Maria cry out. He tried to move and felt an excruciating pain in his left side. Kelly gasped and rocked back on her heels.

He opened his eyes and looked at them. Maria snuffled and wiped her eyes on the back of her hand. Kelly stared at him openmouthed. The dried blood on her chin made her mouth look off center.

"Help me up," Blake said. His voice sounded distant to him, the faraway sound of a voice in fog.

"Lie still, you've been shot," Kelly said.

Blake forced himself into a sitting position, clutching the red stain on his left side. He pulled the tear in his shirt open wider. He put his hand in the red mush and probed, grimacing.

"Are you okay?" Kelly said.

"I think he missed the rib," Blake said. He felt high from the natural anesthetic his body was producing. He looked at Maria and made an abortive attempt at a smile. "You saved my bacon, little one."

"You've lost so much blood," Kelly said.

"Where's Rivero?" Blake asked.

"I don't know," Kelly said. "He was gone when I came to. I crawled over to you and heard shooting on deck. It sounded like a machine gun."

"Where's the helicopter?"

Kelly stood up and looked aft. "On the fantail. The motor's running, but I don't see anyone in it."

Blake heard the sound of footsteps coming up the starboard ladder to the bridge. He made a motion to Maria with his trigger finger.

"The *sargento,* he took it," Maria whispered.

A tall Latin man about Blake's age wearing a wrinkled dark blue business suit appeared on the starboard bridge wing and peered into the pilothouse. He had an automatic pistol in his hand. Stepping in cautiously, he stopped abruptly and leveled it at Blake.

"Who are you?"

Blake grimaced and pushed himself slowly up with his back against the bulkhead. He came to his feet clutching his side and blinked the darkness out of his eyes. "Lieutenant junior grade Daniel F. Blake, USN," he said. "Who are you?"

The man smiled. "One courteous introduction deserves another. I am Jorge Luis Cordoba. Forgive me if I do not shake hands."

Blake pulled his blood-soaked right hand away from the wound in his side and looked at it. He shoved it back against the bloody mess. "No apology necessary."

Jorge looked at him and nodded his head. "So you are the brave young American officer who saved the ship."

Blake cocked his head and looked at the man. "Am I supposed to know you?"

"No, *compañero,* but I know you," Jorge said. He smiled. "Too bad. It was all for nothing." He looked around. "How do you stop this thing?"

"I wouldn't," Blake said. "The ship is sinking. We're trying to beach it on that atoll." He glanced out at the pink-and-brown strip of land coming into view.

"I thought as much," the man said, following Blake's line of sight.

"I didn't think we'd get this far," Blake said. "By rights, it shouldn't still be afloat. But it's beginning to look like we just might make it."

The man stared at the atoll for a second, then looked back at Blake. "How do you stop it?"

"Look, friend, whoever you are," Blake said, "maybe I'm not making myself clear. This ship is sinking."

"Cordoba, Jorge Cordoba. Please call me by name. I do not wish to die among strangers."

"Now why would you want to do that?" Blake asked.

The man stared vacantly at the engine-order telegraph. *"Pundonor."* He said the word absently, softly.

Blake glanced at Kelly, looking for a translation.

"Point of honor," Kelly said. She gave Blake a palms-up shrug.

The man glanced up and smiled at the confusion on their faces. "Something you *Norte Americanos* wouldn't understand, *Teniente.*"

"There seems to be a lot lately I don't understand," Blake said.

The man seemed to come back from a faraway place. "Now, how do you stop the ship?" He reached for the engine-order telegraph and Kelly stepped forward. He turned and leveled his automatic at her. "I have no compunction about killing you all, even the *chica.* We're all going to die anyway."

Blake stared at him. In spite of his disheveled appearance, Cordoba had an aristocratic air about him. But he was clearly insane. "There's no need to shoot anyone," Blake said. "If you're so hot to die, just pull that lever straight up and we'll all go down together.'' Slumping against the bulkhead, he squinted his eyes and tried to look vulnerable. It wasn't difficult, Blake thought, afraid he might pass out from the pain in his side.

Cordoba looked at Blake curiously and fumbled with the telegraph handle, cocking his head to read the indicators on the side. Through slitted eyes, Blake saw the opening and knew he wouldn't get another. Pushing himself away from the bulkhead, he grabbed the man's right wrist with his left hand and tried to shake the gun loose. He drew back and swung for his head with his right, catching Cordoba behind his left ear with a resounding crack of flesh on bone. The man went down on one knee, shaking his head. Blake pried the gun loose from his fingers and staggered back to the far corner. He slumped down between the two bulkheads and let himself slide down on deck. He grimaced and shook his head violently. Kelly started for him, and he waved her away. His left side was on fire. His right hand throbbed. He shifted the automatic to his right hand and could barely grip it. He looked at his hand. The knuckle of his middle finger was pushed back. He was sure he'd broken it. He hadn't hit this many guys in one day since his intramural boxing days at Kings Point.

''Now just settle down, my friend, and let's get this ship beached.'' He pointed the gun at Cordoba.

''Kelly, are we still on course?''

''Yes, sir,'' Kelly said. ''Collision course dead ahead.''

''What's our ETA?''

''Thirty minutes, maybe, if we can stay afloat that long.''

Cordoba rubbed his face in his hands and shook his head. Blake could see him peering through spread fingers at the base of the engine-order telegraph. Maria edged closer, staring at him curiously.

Blake suddenly realized what the man was staring at. ''Get back,'' he said, motioning to Maria with the gun.

Cordoba stayed on one knee, rubbing his face a few more seconds to clear his head, then lunged for Sergeant Rivero's combat knife butted up against the base of the telegraph. Picking it up, he swept Maria up in front of him with his left arm and held the knife to her throat.

Blake jerked his hand up, tried to get off a shot in the scuffle, but his hand was so swollen he was afraid he'd hit Maria.

Maria shrieked in a high keening sound and Jorge pulled her closer, the razor-sharp blade almost touching her throat. "Shut up, damn you, shut up."

He backed away from the telegraph stand, the combat knife at her throat. Maria backed up in step with him. "Now, get over here and stop this thing."

"You can't stop it from here," Blake said. "The controls are jammed in the engine room."

"That's not what you said before. You're lying!"

"No, I swear I'm not," Blake said, struggling to his feet. "Don't hurt her."

Jorge smirked. "Your word as an officer and a gentleman, no doubt. Throw the gun over here."

"No," Blake said. "I can't give you the gun, but I promise not to shoot if you don't hurt her."

"Then throw it away," Jorge said. "Throw it over the side, or I swear to you I'll kill her." He moved the blade closer. "I have nothing to lose."

"Okay, okay. Just don't hurt her." It was easy to make a bad decision under fire, Blake thought, and he felt instantly that he was making one. He snapped the safety on and tossed the gun spinning out the open door. He heard a slight plunk, like a fish breaking the surface.

"Take me to the engine room," Jorge said.

"You can't go there," Blake said. "It's flooded. The controls are jammed."

"Liar! Take me there, or I'll kill her."

"He's telling you the truth," Kelly said. "Please don't hurt her."

He studied their faces for a long minute. "Then turn away from the island, head back out to sea."

Blake turned and looked out the bridge window. The atoll

now loomed ahead, looking more like a small island. "We're too close to land, there's not enough turning radius."

Jorge looked at them again, another long minute. "Then you don't leave me any choice," he said. He backed away and headed for the open door to the starboard bridge wing. Maria backed up with him in unison, her eyes wide.

"What are you doing?" Blake said, stepping forward.

"Don't try to follow me."

Blake followed them out on the bridge wing and watched the man in the rumpled business suit descend quickly to the weather deck, pulling Maria stumbling with him. Blake started down the ladder. The man looked over his shoulder and gathered Maria in tightly to him with the knife still at her throat. He turned and walked quickly in the direction of the idling helicopter.

"No!" Blake shouted. He ran down the ladder to the weather deck and nearly stumbled over the shredded body of Sergeant Rivero. He glanced around for Rivero's M-16 and saw it lying in the shade of the superstructure, twisted out of shape. He stepped around the body and started toward them, holding his left side.

Jorge turned around. "Stay back, damn you, stay back!"

"Please, for God's sake, let her go," Kelly said, running up behind Blake.

Jorge turned and dragged Maria toward the helicopter with Blake maintaining a ten-foot distance. Jorge stepped over the body of Michael Gaines and turned at the starboard door of the helicopter.

"I told you to stay back. I'll kill her!"

Blake backed up a conciliatory step, and Jorge slid backwards into the helicopter, pulling Maria in from behind. Blake could see two thin red lines on her throat where the blade had touched her. Jorge slid the door of the Blackhawk closed and locked it. Blake started toward the helicopter, and Jorge pointed the knife at the side of Maria's neck. Blake stepped back. Strapping himself into the pilot's seat, Jorge looked awkwardly around and seemed to be studying the controls, as if trying to remember. He laid the knife down and grasped one control with his left hand and another with his right. The engines whined and the rotors spun. The heavy Blackhawk tilted clumsily to the right, then lifted up with a shudder.

"Oh, dear God," Kelly said. "Stop him, stop him. He's going to kill her."

"He's going to kill us all," Blake said. He could see in the man's eyes that he was quite insane.

The Blackhawk lifted off and hovered awkwardly over the fantail. Blake stood with his hand on his wound, staring at Maria's face, white and terror-stricken, looking down on him from the port window. Feeling a flash of pain in his side that almost sent him to his knees, he pressed down on the wound to stem the pain and felt the outline of Laurie's little blood-soaked picture in his torn pocket. Glancing up, Maria's tiny face became the face of his daughter. He took a flying run and leapt for the helicopter as it lifted off the fantail.

He looped his right arm through the stub wing support on the port side and heard Kelly's scream fading in the background as the Blackhawk lifted up and away, weaving erratically. Looking down, he saw the *Latin Star* shrinking like a toy boat and broke into the cold nausea of instant regret. The Blackhawk dipped, then climbed, then dipped again. Blinded by the pain in his side, he managed to bring his left arm up enough to give the window a single blow with his fist. Maria jerked and stared at him with a dumbfounded look. Grimacing, he motioned for her to unlock the door. She frantically searched for the lock, while Jorge fumbled with the controls, seemingly oblivious to everything else.

The Blackhawk gained altitude, its engines coughing and sputtering. Blake estimated that they were a hundred feet above the water now. Maria found the door latch and unlocked it, sliding the door open. Jorge glanced at them, but couldn't react, his hands full of controls. Blake pulled her out the door as Jorge pushed forward on the stick between his legs, sending the sputtering helicopter higher. They fell like sky divers, screaming through the air toward the calm surface of the ocean, the world a spiral of blue and green.

Blake lost sight of Maria, tried to position himself to go in feetfirst. A green swell rose up to meet him as he plunged through the shiny surface and descended a dozen feet into the inky depths, water roaring in his ears. Black water swirled around him as he struggled upward, his lungs pounding inside his chest, the salt water in his wound excruciating. The water felt incredibly warm as he broke the surface, spitting and gasping. He shook the salt water from his eyes and glanced around for Maria. A gentle swell lifted him up and he could see her fifty yards away, floating in her life jacket, her head lolling. He filled his lungs and plunged forward, knifing through the thick water with long strokes with his right arm, short paddling strokes with his left, ignoring the pain that wracked his side.

He reached Maria and saw that she was unconscious. Diving from that distance in a life jacket would do it. Tilting her head back to keep her mouth out of the water, he looked up, trying to spot the helicopter. The Blackhawk was still climbing, a tiny, coughing green speck against the eastern sky. He looked at the ship. It was listing to starboard now and seemed to be barely moving. Kelly was standing on the fantail, staring, frozen.

"Jump!" His voice sounded weak, floating over the water, deadened against the swells. He heard the helicopter's engines cough, quit and start again.

He cupped his hands. "Jump!"

Kelly stood there, staring in their direction.

Blake waved his right arm frantically. He looked up at the stuttering helicopter and knew he wouldn't have enough time.

He pushed himself up out of the water and shouted again. "Kelly! Jump, goddamn it. Jump!"

Kelly cupped her hands around her eyes and squinted in his direction. She raised her hand and pointed at something nearby. Blake twisted around and saw dark glossy dorsal fins circling fifty yards off. He thought about the blood from the open wound in his side. He looked up at the dark form hovering over the ship. He pointed, and screamed, "Jump!"

Kelly looked up and Blake could see her make the decision.

She ran to the weather rail, slipped her life jacket off, threw it over the side, and dived in after it. She came to the surface, looped her arm through one shoulder strap, and started to swim toward Blake.

Blake watched Kelly's long, clean strokes moving toward him, pulling for her. He looked up at the Blackhawk. It seemed to be unmoving, hung suspended in the sky, but she was still dangerously close to the ship. *Hurry, Kelly, hurry.* The engines stuttered, then fired and spun at full throttle. The Blackhawk tilted forward and came down in a wavering line, headed straight for the *Latin Star.*

Blake frantically waved her toward him, watching the helicopter descend. When they were a hundred yards apart, the Blackhawk flew into the open number three cargo hold, sheared the rotors off, and drove into thirty-six tons of ether. An orange ball rose up out of the hold, followed by a deafening blast that shattered the air.

Shards of sizzling steel spiraled crazily upward through the dense black smoke where they hung suspended in the air, then tumbled into the sea, sending up wisps of steam.

"Dive," Blake shouted. "Go deep!" He slipped Maria out of her life jacket and pulled her down. Kelly followed him from where she was. The water around them was shot with tons of hissing shrapnel as they dived. Twelve feet beneath the surface, the second blast came. Twenty-four tons of dimethyl ketone went through a chemical transformation, releasing energy. The effect was like a nuclear depth charge.

Blake broke through the surface, sputtering and gasping, in time to see the *Latin Star* lift up out of the water and break in half like a rotten log. He looked at Maria and couldn't tell if she was dead or alive. Treading water, he managed to get his life jacket back on her frail body and glanced around for Kelly.

He spotted her floating on her back a hundred yards away. Swimming to her, he lifted her head up and saw that her ears and nose were bleeding. Glancing around for her life jacket, he slipped it around her shoulders, buckled it, and towed her away from the burning hulk, back to where Maria was floating.

He felt heat on his neck and looked back toward the ship. A burning oil slick was spreading toward them. He pulled Maria closer and hooked the shoulder straps of the two life jackets together. He needed a rope, something to tow them with. Taking off his belt, he looped it between the two shoulder straps and started towing them toward the island, swimming with one arm.

The sharks had apparently decided it was a rough neighborhood and quit, but about ten minutes into the swim, Blake knew he was in trouble. His shoulders began to ache and his arms felt like lead. He wondered if he could make it. He had to. It would be ludicrous to drown a mile from shore after all they'd been through. The dull ache in his shoulders spread to his arms and legs. He forced himself to think of other things, to blot out the pain in his body, and stroked grimly on, narrowing the gap.

He felt something tear into his leg, a razor sharp coral formation beneath the surface, and knew he was close. Fifty feet farther, his knees felt something spongy. He crawled up on the sandy shore, got to his feet, and pulled Kelly and Maria up on the beach with him. He turned and looked toward the sea, shivering in the tropical sun. The bow half of the *Latin Star* was gone, only the stern half remained, floating upended with the red and white stars of the ensign flag snapping in the breeze. He watched a trail of flame lick its way up the ensign staff and consume the flag as the stern of the *Latin Star* slid slowly beneath the waves. He looked down at the coral sand beneath his feet. Land. A heavy darkness fell over him. He twisted on the sand and went down into blackness.

Chapter
Twenty-One

"Wake up, Lieutenant," Daniel Blake heard a distant voice say. He opened his eyes and stared up at the white ceiling he'd seen every morning for the last eight days. It still felt strange. He stretched, shaking the stupor out of his brain. He couldn't seem to get enough sleep lately.

"What is it this time, Nurse Ratched? Another sleeping pill?"

"Watch your mouth, Sweetie, or it'll be another enema." The tall, redheaded nurse grinned. "You have a visitor."

"Who might that be?" The only visitor he'd had so far was his mother, who'd brought him the fresh picture of Laurie on his nightstand. He hadn't seen his three-year-old daughter yet. Kids that young weren't allowed.

"You don't know?"

Blake could tell by the look on her face that the visitor was female. It was the voyeuristic look all women got when they thought they saw a match. It wouldn't be Vicki. She hadn't even called. He hadn't expected her to. He scooted up.

The nurse came around to the side of Blake's bed and stood

grinning down on him, plumping his pillow, primly efficient. "She looks capable of introducing herself."

The nurse slipped out, and the door closed behind her. Blake stared at the door. It opened part way and Dana Kelly's face appeared. "Hi!" She walked in and stood there beaming at him, resplendent in tailored dress blues. Blake had never seen her dressed up before. She looked radiant. His sleepy eyes took her in. Short auburn hair in a soft wave, brown eyes aglow, golden skin scrubbed to a healthy sheen. Even with the fading purple bruise on her chin, he thought she looked perfect, a debutante in uniform.

His eyes melted into a smile. He was surprised at how much he'd missed her. "Well, if it isn't Petty Officer third . . ." he looked at her sleeve and raised his eyebrows, "excuse me, Petty Officer *second* class Dana Kelly." He grinned. "Congratulations."

Kelly shrugged. "Thanks."

She came closer to the bed and the soft look in her eyes shifted to one of concern. "How do you feel?"

"I'm fine, really."

"What's taking them so long to release you?"

Blake glanced down at his taped rib cage. "I was wrong about the rib," he said. "He didn't miss."

"Yeah, I heard it was a miracle you didn't puncture your lung with all that jumping around." She let out a relieved sigh and looked around and nodded. "Anyway, you're home now. How does it feel to be back in San Diego?"

"I haven't seen much of it yet, but it feels good to be here," Blake said. "I can't wait to get out of here."

"Be thankful it's a military hospital," Kelly said. "I belonged to an HMO once. They'd have you out of here in one day, dead or dying."

He smiled. "When did you get out?"

"Yesterday. The nurses surprised me with this." She nodded to her new stripe. "They had it all sewn on and pressed and everything."

"Yesterday? Why didn't you come to see me?"

Kelly shrugged. "I didn't know whether I should. You being an officer, and all."

Blake snorted. "That's ridiculous." He looked at her, and his face softened into a smile. "You look great. How do you feel?"

"Fine. A little hearing loss in my right ear still, but it's coming back."

"I'm glad," Blake said. The volume on the television surged. He glanced up at the standard hospital set bracketed to the wall. An image flickered across the screen of an aerial view of a bomb blast. A camera was slowly panning the remains of what had once been a luxurious estate in South America.

"What's happening in the outside world?" Kelly asked.

"Some drug biggie got it in Colombia," Blake said. "Some guy named Guy-ar-do. Wiped out his whole family. I've been following it."

"Why? I thought that sort of thing happened all the time down there."

"Not on this level. There's a big flap. According to CNN, the Colombian Navy may have had something to do with it. Some collusion with some bad guys in Brazil, or somewhere. Loaned them a bomb, or something. Strange bedfellows."

"I wonder if it had anything to do with that ship," Kelly said, "and that nut who wanted to sink it so bad?"

"Who knows?" Blake said.

"The sailors that picked us up on that Colombian frigate didn't seem like the type. Great bunch of guys. When I told them what you did to save the ship and to save Maria, they were thunderstruck. You weren't awake to see it, but they treated you like a god on that ship. Wounded American officer risks his life to save little Colombian girl, and all that. Word got up to their captain and he talked to your captain. I hear old Hammer just grunted. It was Commander Mayfield who wrote up the recommendation. Made the captain sign it."

"What recommendation?"

"You didn't know? You're up for the Navy Commendation Medal."

"You must be joking," Blake said.

"No, I'm not. You're a hero. They're saying that you single-handedly broke the back of the biggest drug cartel in South America."

Blake shook his head. "Politics as usual. It must be funding time in Congress."

"Meaning?"

"Meaning they need something they can point to, to get more money to fight the drug war."

"They're retiring the *Carlyle*. Too much damage. She was overdue anyway," Kelly said. "I hear you're going to be the next operations officer of the *Duncan,* that Perry-class guided-missile frigate. I guess that means a promotion for you too, huh? Full lieutenant. Word is that puts you on the path to command. I know you'll have your own ship someday."

"A general court-martial would be more appropriate."

"Now, why would you say a thing like that?"

"It's obvious, isn't it? I lost seven people out of a nine-person boarding party. You and I were the only ones to come back."

"Don't be so hard on yourself," Kelly said, "You were given an impossible job to do, and you did it. You saved my neck, that's for sure. And don't forget about Maria. You brought her back, too." She got a distant look. "I wonder how she's doing?"

"She's with her aunt in Buenos Aires, recuperating nicely," Blake said. "I just got a letter from her."

"From Maria?"

"No, from her aunt. Maria has told her all about me. About you, too. Says she wants to come here and live, go to school next year."

"That's great," Kelly said.

"Her aunt's all for it. She's quite elderly. But it won't happen," Blake said. "She wants to talk to Mrs. Blake before she'll permit it."

"She's a proper Argentine lady. Wants to be sure you're

married. That's reasonable,'' Kelly said. She looked at Blake hesitantly. ''No word from the missus, I guess?''

Blake shook his head. ''I didn't expect any. It's over.''

''Well, you could always get married again,'' Kelly said. ''But I guess that's not likely to happen. Once burned, twice shy, and all that.''

Blake shrugged and tossed the letter on the nightstand. ''I suppose. What's next for you?''

Kelly shook her head. ''The Navy's great, but life at sea is something else again. It's tougher than I ever imagined. There are too many things you can't control. I satisfied myself that I could do it, but it's no place for me. I'll leave keeping the sea-lanes free to the people who love it, like you. As soon as my enlistment's up in three months, it's back to San Jose State for me.''

''Why not go to San Diego State?''

Kelly looked at him the way she did that day on the bridge wing. ''Why should I?''

Blake shrugged. ''It's a good school.''

''So I've heard.'' Kelly waited.

Blake straightened the sheet across his lap. There was an awkward silence.

Kelly shrugged. ''Well, I just came to say good-bye. I guess this is the point where we go back to our own worlds. You to the world of officers and gentlemen, and me to the world of radiopukes.'' She stuck out her hand bravely. ''Have a good life, Lieutenant. I don't suppose I'll ever see you again.''

Blake took her hand. It felt warm and firm. He released it and felt the soft pad of her fingertips drag against his.

''Well, so long.'' Kelly walked to the door. She stood facing it for a long minute with her hand on the latch.

''I think someday the whole world's going to know who you are,'' she said. She looked over her shoulder at Blake and flashed a plucky smile. ''I'm glad I got to know you first.''

Kelly turned and faced the door again. She opened it and started to walk out.

"I'm getting out of here on Saturday," Blake said. "You going to be around?"

Kelly turned and looked at him. "Why should I be?"

"There's someone I'd like you to meet," Blake said.

"Oh, Jesus." Kelly rolled her eyes and looked up at the ceiling. She let out a long breath and stood staring at the door for a minute, then turned to face Blake. "Why is it that everybody feels compelled to fix up every single person in the world? Look, Lieutenant, I don't need any favors. You don't need to be fixing me up with any—"

"Why don't you shut up and listen once in a while?"

Kelly let out a long sigh. "Okay, I'm listening. What's his name? Joe Dweeb, boilerman third?"

"It's not a him," Blake said.

"You want me to meet a girl?" Kelly asked.

"You'll like her," Blake said, nodding to the picture on his nightstand. "Her name is Laurie."